Lynne Francis grew up in Yorkshire but studied, lived and worked in London for many years. She draws inspiration for her novels from a fascination with family history, landscapes and the countryside.

She has written two historical trilogies, the first set in her home county of Yorkshire, the second in and around Margate in east Kent, following the discovery of previously unknown family links to the area. Her latest sagas are set a little further along the east Kent coast, where she now lives. Lynne's exploration of her new surroundings provided the historical background for the novels, as well as allowing her to indulge another key interest: checking out the local teashops and judging the cake.

THE RELUCTANT BRIDE

LYNNE FRANCIS

PIATKUS

PIATKUS

First published in Great Britain in paperback in 2024 by Piatkus

1 3 5 7 9 10 8 6 4 2

A CIP catalogue record for this book is available from the British Library.

ISBN 978-0-349-43371-4

Typeset in Caslon by M Rules

Printed and bound in Great Britain by Clays Ltd, Elcograf S.p.A.

Papers used by Piatkus are from well-managed forests
and other responsible sources.

Piatkus
An imprint of
Little, Brown Book Group
Carmelite House
50 Victoria Embankment
London EC4Y 0DZ

An Hachette UK Company
www.hachette.co.uk

www.littlebrown.co.uk

THOMAS

PART ONE

SEPTEMBER — DECEMBER 1822

CHAPTER ONE

Thomas was weary. His anger from earlier in the day had dissipated, leaving the dull throb of a headache and an unsettled feeling in his chest. The words he'd hurled at Bartholomew Banks still echoed in his head. 'You killed my aunt, drove my father to drink and destroyed my family. I'll make you pay for what you've done, see if I don't.'

He'd waylaid the man on his way to church, his wife Eustacia on his arm, their two young children following with their nursemaid. Bartholomew had stopped and Thomas had drawn himself up to his full height, although at fifteen he was puny and on the small side. Bartholomew, elegant in his dark frock coat, towered over him. His wife appeared alarmed, Thomas noticed, but Bartholomew laughed. Laughed at him, after everything he had done to ruin the Marsh family. Rage boiled up in Thomas's chest. He wished he'd thought to bring a knife – he could have plunged it into the scoundrel. He was ready to fly at him, pummel him with his fists instead, but he was seized and his arms pinioned by the Banks coachman, who had just delivered the family to church.

Bartholomew had leaned in close. He maintained a pleasant expression but he hissed at Thomas, 'If you haven't left Castle Bay by sunset tonight, what's left of your family will be weeping over the body they find washed up on the beach tomorrow morning.'

Then he ushered his family up the path to the great arched doorway of the church, greeting fellow worshippers as they passed. New arrivals cast curious glances at Thomas as he struggled, gripped in

3

the firm embrace of the burly coachman, who had taken the precaution of clamping a gloved hand over his captive's mouth.

Once the studded wooden door had creaked shut, the man released him.

'You heard what he said. He means it. Get yourself out of this place or it will be the worse for you.' The coachman aimed a cuff at Thomas, but he ducked and ran off up the path past the church, through the graveyard, then out onto the track that threaded through the village.

For whatever reason, Bartholomew chose not to worship in his local church in Hawksdown, but the one a mile or so up the road in Kingsdown. It stood on a hill, commanding a view of the sea responsible for the deaths of so many of the men now buried in the churchyard. It had taken Thomas a while to track down Bartholomew Banks to this place, and to the Sunday routine that had created the rare opportunity to accost him. Bartholomew spent most of his time within the walls and grounds of Hawksdown Castle, a place you couldn't enter without a very good reason for being there. His having ordered the murder of Meg Marsh, Thomas's aunt, and prompting Samuel Marsh, Thomas's father, to drown himself in drink and guilt, wouldn't have been considered a good enough reason.

Thomas stopped in his rapid progress along the track. He'd meant to mention the baby – the one Meg had been carrying when she was taken, the one Bartholomew had fathered. Samuel had let slip Meg's condition to Bartholomew, and this had caused the whole sorry saga to unfold. Samuel could never forgive himself for having put his sister and her unborn child in harm's way. Eliza, Thomas's mother, had mourned the loss of the baby as if it was her own – which indeed they had intended it should appear to be, to spare Meg the shame. That baby would have been at least seven years old now. Thomas had particularly wanted Eustacia Banks to know about the child. Now it was too late – he'd missed his chance. And he needed to get away: Bartholomew Banks, the son of the

Lord Warden, had the men and the means at his disposal to carry out his threat to have him killed.

It was nearly an hour's walk back to Thomas's home in Prospect Street, Castle Bay but, half running and half walking, he made the journey in considerably less time. He found his mother in the room that served as a bedroom and living room for the three remaining members of the Marsh family. His aunt Meg had vanished eight years earlier, presumed murdered on the orders of Bartholomew Banks, an event that was swiftly followed by the death of Thomas's grandmother, Meg's mother, brought on by despair. After that, Thomas's parents had fallen on hard times. Eliza couldn't manage the family bakery on her own, Samuel had sunk into drink and, one by one, the rooms in the house were rented out to make ends meet.

Prospect Street led to the seafront, where inns and bawdy houses alternated, both frequented by sailors who flooded into town while their ships were at anchor in the sheltered waters of the Downs, just offshore. The tenants they attracted were not the sort that Eliza wanted her son to associate with, so she had kept him at the Charity School for as long as she could. But once he had turned twelve, after four years of schooling, Thomas was found a job at the boatyard.

His learning was of little use to him in his new employment. When he wasn't sweeping up, he was endlessly fetching and carrying nails, hammers, brushes and pots of pitch, from one end of the yard to the other, in answer to a boatbuilder's summons of 'Thomas! Here. Now!' Small for his age – no doubt due to the restricted diet forced on him by his family's poverty – he'd proved adept at squeezing into awkward spaces to caulk seams or hammer in nails.

It wasn't long before he'd persuaded the men to show him the right way to saw a plank, or sand an oar so that the precision of the blade helped propel a boat through the water. It would have made sense for the boatyard owner to take Thomas on as an apprentice, but he had refused.

'There's no doubting your work, lad,' he said, 'but I remember your father only too well. Couldn't stay away from the drink, couldn't get himself to work on time and couldn't be trusted to be sober when he was here. How do I know you won't be the same, just when I've invested in your training? It's not a risk I'm prepared to take.'

Thomas's protests that he wasn't like his father – that he had no intention of drinking and needed a trade to help provide for the family – fell on deaf ears. As the months, and then the years went by and other boys began their training, Thomas remained at everyone's beck and call. His resentment grew.

Now, although he hadn't made a conscious decision to leave his work, he had no alternative. Bartholomew Banks wouldn't hesitate to carry out his threat so he must depart from his home and from the town. As he stepped through the front door of the house in Prospect Street and mounted the stairs, his heart was thudding. Not from his hurried return, but in apprehension at what he must say to his mother.

His parents could get by on the rent that came in, he reasoned, even if most of it went straight out to one of the nearby inns to satisfy Samuel's insatiable thirst. He knew, though, as he put his hand on the doorknob of their room, that reason had very little to do with it. His mother would be very upset.

CHAPTER TWO

Thomas closed his eyes briefly at the memory of his hurried announcement. His mother had alternately wept and raged and he had shouted back, saying things about his father he now regretted, even though they were true. His final words before he'd slammed out of the door had been 'The name Marsh is as good as cursed. Even if I could stay, I could never make anything of myself here.' Then he'd left, with nothing but the clothes on his back. Tears started to his eyes as he remembered. His time in Castle Bay was over, at least while Bartholomew Banks remained at Hawksdown Castle.

He'd followed the route to the Dover turnpike, wrapped up in his thoughts, noticing nothing and nobody, without a clear plan in his head. Then, as the last few cottages fell away behind him, he turned on a whim to follow a track inland, away from the sea he'd known all his life. There were no dwellings here, just hedges at either side of the track and more hedges beyond them, carving the gentle rolling landscape into a patchwork of green and brown.

As Thomas's agitation eased, new thoughts surfaced to trouble him. Where was he going? Where would he sleep that night? What would he do? He pushed them away as best he could. It soothed him to trudge along, placing one foot in front of the other, his mind a blank. A windmill sat above him on a small incline, its sails turning smoothly in a wind from which the hedgerows shielded Thomas. He didn't contemplate stopping – he wasn't yet far enough from home and it stood all alone, with no habitation in sight other than the mill house. He walked on.

Bartholomew Banks would be at his table now, with his wife and his family, no doubt full of piety after his morning in church, and intent on a good dinner. Thomas's stomach rumbled. His breakfast had been meagre, and a long time past. He had only a few coins in his pocket – not that there was anywhere to spend them. He passed a stand of trees. Then, all at once, a church revealed itself, its wall replacing the hedgerow along the track.

Thomas rested for a moment, leaning on the wall. There was a village beyond the church, a scattering of houses between the track and the distant turnpike. It was peaceful in the afternoon sun, a village green set around with cottages. Hunger made him want to advance, but he hesitated. He had never left the Castle Bay area before. He knew the close-packed streets that ran down to the seafront like the back of his hand. He could travel barely five paces without someone passing – a fisherman, a sailor ashore, maybe one of the smugglers who frequented the Fountain Inn at the bottom of Prospect Street. Here, no one stirred. The good folk had no doubt been to church and were now, like Bartholomew Banks, behind closed doors with their families. This was not a place to knock and ask to be spared a piece of bread. Thomas thought they would most likely set a dog on him.

A pump stood a little distance from the church, on a patch of grass marking a fork in the track through the village. Thomas went over to it and pumped a little water to splash on his face, before turning his head and holding his open mouth under the flow to quench his thirst. Then, fearing the squealing of the pump handle might have disturbed the nearby residents, he set out once more. He chose the fork veering away from the village and felt his confidence grow as he walked. Every step took him further away from Bartholomew Banks and deeper into the countryside. He felt invisible there.

As the afternoon drew on, he told himself he would stop in the next place and find food and shelter for the night, before seeing where his feet took him the next day. The hedges towered above him and the track went on and on, taking a curve here and there, but with no end in sight. When the hedges occasionally fell away, it became clear there were no features in the landscape – not a church steeple, the roofs of a village or a glimpse of the sea. Just endless, rolling fields, greens turning to yellows with the first hint of autumn. Thomas hadn't seen a soul along the track and he began to feel anxious.

At length, he realised he was approaching habitation. A pair of cottages appeared at the edge of the track, then a couple more, before he found himself at a junction. He hesitated, unsure which way to turn, then carried straight on. He feared the road dipping away to the left would carry him back in the direction of Castle Bay. After a few paces, he judged himself to be in the centre of the village and, after a few paces more, he saw a cottage, set back and low down from the track, with a sign hanging at the gate. It read, 'The Wheatsheaf. Beer House'.

Nothing could be further from the inns of Castle Bay, Thomas thought, busy at all hours. The Wheatsheaf appeared to be someone's house, the front room no doubt converted to a bar for the sale of ale. Perhaps it was all that this hamlet required. The front door was firmly closed and there was no sign that it was open for business.

Thomas considered walking on but the loud rumbling of his stomach decided him. He'd be sleeping the night in a hedgerow with nothing in his belly if he didn't at least make some enquiries. He opened the gate, went down the narrow path and rapped on the door. After a minute or two, a woman opened it. She looked him up and down without speaking.

'I'm a stranger to these parts,' Thomas said, 'just passing through and wondering where I might find food and lodging for the night.'

The woman frowned. 'I can serve you ale,' she said, opening the door wider and standing back.

'I don't drink.' Thomas was apologetic. 'But I'd gladly buy some food if you have any to spare? Some bread and cheese, maybe?'

The woman pursed her lips, thinking, then beckoned him in. The door opened directly into what had once been a front parlour but was now made over for the consumption of beer. Dark wooden stools were set around the edge of the scuffed wooden floorboards, a few small rickety tables before them. At the back of the room, in front of another door, a bar had been built – a crude affair with shelves housing glasses and tankards.

'Shall I light the fire?' The woman indicated a small grate, swept clean and with logs piled ready for use.

'No, no.' Thomas, conscious of how little he had to spend, was keen not to put her to too much trouble. The room was cool, but it was welcome after his walk.

'I'll see what I can find,' the woman said, making ready to leave by the door that Thomas guessed led to the kitchen.

'Just something small,' he said, anxious, thrusting his hand into his pocket to check the number of coins there. His stomach rumbled loudly.

The woman smiled, immediately appearing several years younger. 'Take a seat,' she said, gesturing to the empty room, and went through the door behind the bar.

Thomas went to look out of the window. The Wheatsheaf sat low and the garden around it was overgrown. Did she run the place by herself? Could he offer to lend a hand and earn himself a little money to take him further? Then he remembered his long-held vow, broken already, to stay away from inns.

The door squeaked open and Thomas turned back. The woman entered, carrying a plate, a hunk of bread clearly visible. She set the plate on the table – it held a slice of pie, a piece of cheese and a mound of red-brown pickle.

'There. I hope that will do. And I brought you a glass of my home-made dandelion and burdock – my husband swears by it after a long day in the fields. Restorative, he says. You look as though you might be in need.'

As he fell on the food and drink, the landlady watched him from behind the bar, hands on her hips, a print apron over her skirt. He'd cleared the plate in no time and she smiled.

'Where have you walked from, to have such an appetite?' she asked.

Thomas was guarded. He didn't want to go into the reasons for his journey, so he evaded the question, saying, 'Breakfast was a long time ago.'

In truth, so much had happened that day, he could barely remember the breakfast he referred to.

'You're looking for a place to stay, you said?' The landlady had turned away and was polishing glasses. The sleeves of her blouse were rolled up and her arms were still brown from the summer sun. 'We don't let rooms here, I'm afraid. The house is already too full with family.'

'Is there anything else hereabouts?' Now that Thomas had rested a while, he found himself reluctant to travel further that day. The thought of asking for the fire to be lit after all, and another glass of the landlady's home-made drink, was very tempting. Then he remembered how low his funds were.

'Or do you know of any work to be had?'

The landlady came over and took his empty plate and glass. 'You might ask at the mill. The miller was in here the other day, saying he'd lost his mill boy and didn't know how he'd get another, there being so few young folk around here.'

'The mill?' Did she mean the one he'd passed some miles back? He had no fancy for tramping all the way back there.

'Yes, it's about half a mile from the village.' Seeing his puzzlement, the landlady added, 'I'm guessing you didn't arrive here that way. Go left out of the door, past the big house, then turn off and follow the track down into the dip. When you rise out on the other side, beyond the wood, you'll be able to see it.'

He could make himself useful around the mill, Thomas thought, even though he had no experience of such work. He got to his feet, and settled the bill, which was less than he'd expected. Then he

11

thanked the woman, earning another smile, and went back outside. He shivered – in the short time he'd been inside the temperature had dropped and the weather had changed. The sun had vanished and light clouds had given way to dark ones. Thomas turned up his jacket collar and set out. He hoped that the miller would look kindly on him.

CHAPTER THREE

'Left, then past the big house,' he said to himself, as he exited the beer-house gate. It occurred to him that he didn't even know the name of the place he found himself in. He saw a substantial wall a little way ahead on the right, which must belong to the big house the landlady had mentioned. He realised he didn't know her name, either. He wished he'd thought to ask – it might have been useful for his forthcoming conversation with the miller.

The house behind the wall was, indeed, the biggest he had seen so far in the village. A kind of manor house, Thomas decided, having little knowledge of such things. He glanced in at the gate as he went by and what he saw brought him to a sudden halt. The huge wooden doors to a brick building at the side of the house stood open and a great upright wheel turned within, powered by a donkey that walked inside it.

A girl of about his own age was uttering words of encouragement to the beast, which turned every few minutes within the wheel and began walking the other way. Thomas stared. He struggled to make out what the donkey was doing – he could hear a creaking, and a splash in the wheelhouse each time the animal turned around within the wheel.

The girl had noticed his presence. She was rather well-dressed for her role, Thomas thought. Her loose dark hair flowed down over the shoulders of a white lace dress, although it was grubby around the hem from the dust in the yard. She broke off talking to the beast to throw Thomas a glance and he took the opportunity to call out, 'Could you tell me where I am, please?'

'Marston,' the girl replied, over her shoulder. 'This is Marston Grange, my home,' she added, and gave Thomas a look that made him blush. She had guessed, correctly, that he'd thought her a farm-hand. He nodded his thanks and hurried on, paying little heed to the few houses that remained before the road offered a right turn. It dipped down, as the landlady had said it would, running alongside a wood, before climbing steeply, then bearing right. The windmill rose high beside one of the hedges along the lane ahead of him, the white sails stationary, the dark weatherboarding echoing the colour of the bruised clouds. As he drew closer, he saw the shabby paint and the gaps in the sails and his heart sank. Would there be money enough to employ him? If not, a glance at the sky told him he'd have to beg for shelter. It was that, or a rainy night spent sleeping in a ditch, or in the wood he had just passed – not something that a town-bred boy like Thomas had contemplated before.

He'd be unlikely to find the miller anywhere other than in his house on a Sunday, Thomas decided. He opened the gate and approached the building set beside the mill. Chickens scratched in the yard and a dog began to bark before he'd even knocked at the door. A lot hung on his words, Thomas knew, and he hadn't prepared any.

The door was opened by a whiskery gentleman, somewhat red in the face. A glimpse of the table in the simple room behind him told Thomas he'd disturbed the miller at his dinner.

'I'm sorry to trouble you, sir,' Thomas began, 'but the woman at the beer house in the village told me you might need help at the mill.'

He looked hopefully at the man who, to his surprise, let out a shout of laughter.

'Village, eh? How grand we've become. So, Mercy sent you? Well, come in, lad. You'd best tell me what you know about milling.'

Thomas feared his ignorance would be apparent immediately, but he stepped in anyway and was at once introduced to the miller's wife and his three children. They regarded Thomas with wide eyes.

14

'Fetch the boy a plate,' the miller, who'd introduced himself as Adam Hopkins, instructed his wife. 'He looks half starved.'

Thomas protested that he'd eaten only recently, at the beer house, but Mr Hopkins would hear none of it.

'I'm sure you'll find room for a slice of this beef and a potato or two,' he said comfortably, adding them to Thomas's plate. 'Now, you'd better tell me where you come from and what you know.'

So Thomas told him that he was from Castle Bay, seeking work having left his employment at the boatyard. He found himself confessing, between mouthfuls of the miller's wife's delicious cooking, that he'd never worked in a mill.

'I learn fast, though,' he said. 'And I have some skill in carpentry. I'm sure I can make myself useful.'

The miller regarded him shrewdly. 'Would I be right in thinking that you've left in a hurry so you don't have a character from the boatyard? Nothing to tell me how trustworthy you are and how hard you work?'

Thomas grew hot. He shook his head, and stared down at his plate. His blush surely implied guilt.

The miller pressed him further. 'Would there be something that's driven you away from Castle Bay? A bit of trouble, perhaps?'

Thomas swallowed hard. Surely word of his banishment by Bartholomew Banks hadn't spread beyond the town. Then he told himself not to be foolish – the miller had just made a lucky guess.

'There's been some trouble between my family and someone important in the town,' he said, reluctant to reveal too much. 'I spoke out of turn today and was warned off, told to leave the area.' He shrugged. 'So here I am. Ready and willing to do a hard day's work if you'll give me a try. If not, I'll move on. But I would be very grateful if you could find me somewhere to lay my head before I do.'

He held his breath, waiting for the miller's response. Again, the man surprised him by laughing.

'I'll give you a trial,' he said. 'I can't deny I'm in a need of a boy, the last one having upped and left. And it'll be a while yet before these three can help me in the business.' He smiled at his children, who gave every appearance of having solemnly followed every word.

'You can bed down in the barn tonight, but be ready for an early start tomorrow. In the meantime, try a slice of Mrs Hopkins's apple pie and tell me about yourself. I'm not asking for your secrets – you're welcome to keep those.'

By the time Thomas, yawning, followed the miller across the starlit yard to the barn, he'd told the man rather more about himself than he'd cared to, but he'd wanted to convince him of his honesty and make clear he'd left Castle Bay for family reasons, not for thieving. He thought he'd have trouble sleeping, never having spent a night on a bed of empty grain sacks before, with just a rough blanket for warmth and the constant scratching and squeaking of vermin for company. But, weary from the emotions and exertions of the day, he'd fallen asleep almost at once. When the miller came to shake him awake in the pitch dark of the early morning, he found it hard to place himself.

CHAPTER FOUR

'Up you get. Time to see what you're made of.' The miller's voice had broken into his dreams.

Thomas, struggling to open his eyes and leave sleep behind, saw an unfamiliar figure standing before him, dressed in a white smock. He blinked hard.

'Put your head under the pump in the yard,' the miller said. 'And make use of the privy there, too. Then come to the house for some breakfast before we start work.'

The icy gush from the pump had the desired effect on Thomas. By the time he'd shaken the water out of his hair he was much more alert, although not particularly hungry. It seemed odd to think about eating in what felt like the middle of the night, but he did his best to force down a few mouthfuls of bread.

'Let's get on with it,' Mr Hopkins said, waiting for Thomas by the door. He pushed his chair back from the table, thanked Mrs Hopkins and followed the miller across the yard. The mill loomed above Thomas as he climbed the wooden stairs to the entrance. Inside, all was in darkness but the miller was busy lighting candles inside lanterns set around the walls. The gloom receded, revealing a collection of cogs, wheels and wooden shafts that rose upwards, then vanished beyond the perimeter of light. Thomas began to sneeze.

'Aye, it gets you that way at first,' the miller said cheerfully. 'It's the dust from the milling. You'll get used to it. Now, I'll give you a quick look around, so you can see how it all works, before we make a start for the day.

'The grain sacks are delivered underneath us.' Mr Hopkins stamped on the wooden floor to illustrate his point. 'They're hoisted up to the dust floor, just beneath the cap.' As he spoke, he mounted a ladder that led up through the floor to the room above. He carried on speaking as he went and Thomas hurried to follow his feet as they vanished through the opening. They climbed another ladder immediately, passing two sets of huge stone wheels as they did so. Thomas took them to be the millstones, set horizontally on top of each other.

Each floor was narrower than the last, and circular but with faceted edges, matching the exterior. By the time they reached the top, the space was all but filled with the largest wooden wheel Thomas had ever seen. The miller couldn't stand upright, his head held at an awkward angle to avoid bumping it on the roof.

'The cap is above us,' he said. 'The fantail catches the wind and turns the cap so that the sweeps have the best of it. The sweeps turn this wheel,' he patted its wooden surface, 'which drives a shaft that turns the millstones below us to grind the grain.'

He began to descend the ladders again. 'The grain sacks are emptied into these hoppers here . . .' The miller was talking rapidly as he went, pointing out the mill workings on the way. He told Thomas to look through one of the windows as they passed and he did, becoming transfixed so that he missed every word that came after. The window was draped with cobwebs festooned with dust but, despite that, it gave a view out over the countryside to the east, where the sun was rising: a golden globe among trails of pink clouds as the pale blue of the heavens revealed itself. Thomas knew that the sea lay in that direction and he felt a sudden pang of loss for his home. He had never spent a night away from it before and the strangeness of his situation threatened to overwhelm him. All his years by the coast told him that such a sky promised a brisk wind so, reluctantly, he tore his eyes away from the view and hurried down the ladder after Mr Hopkins.

'As you can see, there's more than enough work to keep one

person fully occupied,' the miller was saying, as he re-joined him. 'And with the whole building and almost everything in it made of wood, needing constant repair, your skills will be very useful to me.' He beamed at Thomas, who swallowed hard, then sneezed several times in succession. He could only hope that what appeared to him as a jumble of machinery would start to make sense as the day – and, perhaps, the weeks if he could prove himself – unfolded.

The miller went towards one of the two doors that led out onto the platform surrounding that floor. 'I'm going to release the brake wheel,' he called back, 'and set the sweeps going. Then I'll show you the rest.' Thomas had managed to work out that the sweeps were the sails but most of the other terms the miller had used seemed unfathomable.

Mr Hopkins had been gone barely a minute before Thomas felt the building shudder as the sails began to move. Creaks and more shuddering followed as the shafts within began to turn, powered by each sweep of the sails. He poked his head out of the door to take a look but ducked quickly back in as he saw one of the sweeps descending towards him.

He heard the miller's voice from behind him. He had come back in through the other door. 'Watch out, Thomas! The sweeps can take your head off. Never step out without checking to see which side they're turning.'

Thomas felt foolish. He could see the power of the sweeps as they passed the door. Would he ever understand how it all worked? But, he told himself, as long as he watched and asked questions, just as he had in the boatyard, it would all become clear.

By the end of the day, Thomas was exhausted. Partly from intermittent bouts of sneezing, partly from concentrating hard on everything he was told, and also from the gruelling physical nature of the work. He had spent most of the day loading the sack hoist, which pulled the sacks of grain up through the building, before he moved up through the flights to empty them into the hopper.

How long, he wondered, would it be before he was considered safe to leave in charge of everything in the mill?

The miller's wife had brought food to them during the day. Thomas, busy checking the levels of grain in the hopper while the miller supervised the mill wheels below, could barely remember taking a break to eat. It had been a hasty affair, bread and cheese eaten standing up. The miller insisted all crumbs were brushed out of the door and onto the ground a floor below.

'Mice,' he said briefly, without elaborating.

That evening, as they sat at the table to eat a meal together, Thomas discovered that Mrs Hopkins used some of the flour to bake bread, which was delivered around the Marston area twice a week.

'That'll be a job for you, Thomas,' the miller said, spearing a potato on his fork. 'You'll enjoy getting out into the fresh air and meeting our customers. You know Mercy, at the Wheatsheaf, of course, then there's Marston Grange, the poorhouse and one or two cottages in between.'

Thomas nodded, a grin slowly spreading from ear to ear. Mr Hopkins appeared to be telling him he'd passed the test. He had a job at the mill, and not only that: since Marston Grange was a customer, he'd have the chance to see the strange girl who lived there again. He found the idea rather appealing.

CHAPTER FIVE

Mr Hopkins was as good as his word. On Friday of that week, Thomas set out from the mill with a large wicker basket, the bread within covered by a linen cloth. As he walked the lane that would take him to Marston, he remembered the bakery back home in Castle Bay, in happier days when his aunt Meg was there. He would come down to the kitchen in the morning, to find it filled with the sweet aroma of the currant buns and biscuits she had already baked to stock the shop that day. If he was lucky, he would get one warm from the oven for his breakfast, and maybe another – broken or misshapen – to take to school with him. All that had changed when Meg had vanished. After that, there were very few happy times in the Marsh household.

Lost in his reminiscences, he found himself at the gate of Marston Grange. He hesitated, wondering whether to go elsewhere first, then thought better of it. The Grange should have first pick of the loaves, he thought. He let himself in and was standing before the donkey wheel, watching the mournful beast plod on its endless journey, before he thought to find the kitchen. It would be around the back of the house, he decided, and he'd just set off to skirt the building when the girl suddenly appeared before him. Her hair was loosely caught up on top of her head and she was wearing what appeared to be a man's jacket over the top of the lace dress he had seen her in before.

'You found employment at the mill, I see,' she said, looking at the basket he clutched.

'I'm delivering to your kitchen,' Thomas said unnecessarily. 'And elsewhere,' he added, feeling foolish.

He looked down at his feet, then glanced up again. She was blocking his way but didn't speak.

'I'm Thomas,' he offered.

'And do you have another name?' she asked.

'Marsh,' he replied.

She appeared surprised. 'So you're from round here, then,' she said. 'I thought you were a stranger.'

Thomas frowned. 'I'm a stranger to Marston, but I suppose I haven't come far from home.'

The girl waited, but he didn't offer any more information.

'Marsh is a local name,' she said. 'The Marsh family once owned this house – they'd been here for generations.'

It was Thomas's turn to be surprised. He gazed at the Grange in astonishment. 'I don't think they can be relatives of ours,' he said. 'I've never heard anyone speak of this place.' He cast his eyes over the house again. It was double-fronted, with a warm red brick façade two storeys high and attics in the peg-tiled roof. Numerous multi-paned windows suggested a great many rooms. He shook his head. 'No, I think we've always been in Castle Bay.' Then he bit his lip. He'd given away more than he'd intended.

He made to step around her, to reach the kitchens. A thought struck him. 'Wait, are you a Marsh, too?'

She laughed and shook her head, so that the loose pins tumbled free from her hair, sending the dark, lustrous locks flying around her shoulders. 'My father is a Cavendish. I'm Isabella Cavendish, although I prefer Isabel.'

Thomas sensed he should be impressed by the name, but it meant nothing to him. 'It's been good to see you again, Miss Cavendish,' he said, suddenly formal. 'But I have a lot of loaves to deliver for Mr Hopkins so I must get on my way or he'll think me a time-waster.'

He was glad to escape her – she'd fixed him with such a look that he'd found it hard to break free from her gaze. Her eyes were the most unusual colour – grey, or maybe blue. They seemed to reflect the colour of the sky as the clouds shifted across it.

When he came back round the house a minute or so later, after making the delivery – the cook was brisk in her dealings and kept him on the kitchen doorstep – there was no sign of Isabel. She had vanished, presumably into the house. As he closed the gate behind him, he thought he saw a movement at the long window over the front door, which he supposed must give onto the staircase. Was she watching him? The idea disturbed him. He'd wanted to see her again but the encounter had left him unsettled. And he wished he hadn't let slip that he came from Castle Bay.

His unease didn't last long. His next delivery was to the Wheatsheaf, where Mercy greeted him warmly.

'I heard Adam had taken you on. He'll be delighted to have a lad like you to help him. And I'm pleased I had a part to play in it, by telling you of his need. Now, what have you got for me today? Emily Hopkins makes bread like no other – I've asked her for the recipe but she won't give it to me. Her bread has a firmer crust and moister crumb than anything I can achieve.'

Thomas, although happy to see Mercy again and keen to thank her for recommending the mill to him, saw it would be hard to make his escape. He began to worry that Mr Hopkins would think he had run off with the loaves. He managed to get away ten minutes later, after downing a glass of dandelion and burdock, for which Mercy refused payment.

Next, he turned into the gate of the most austere building in the hamlet. Mr Hopkins had told him it was a poorhouse for the needy of the parish.

'They work there, mostly spinning and weaving,' the miller had said. 'You don't see them around Marston. They're allowed out once a week, on a Sunday, to walk over to the church in the next village. They won't get as much as a sniff of the bread. It's for the master, there, not for the likes of them.'

No one was keen to engage Thomas in conversation at the

poorhouse, but the occupants of the remaining cottages were eager to talk as he delivered their loaves. Thomas arrived back at the mill out of breath, red in the face and apologetic.

'I'm sorry, Mr Hopkins. I truly haven't been wasting time. Everyone wanted to talk.'

The miller spluttered with laughter at Thomas's pained expression. 'You'd better get used to it. There's little enough happens around here. A visit from the new lad at the mill will give them something to gossip about until you call again next week.'

As Thomas prepared to return the empty basket to Mrs Hopkins, the miller gave him a shrewd look. 'Did you happen across Miss Isabel at the Grange?'

Thomas nodded, aware of a flush of colour rising from the neck of his shirt.

'She's an odd one,' the miller said. 'Lacking a mother's influence and running wild, by all accounts. She must be barely sixteen, but her father has plans for her. Marriage to landed gentry – maybe even a lord – from what I hear.'

Mr Hopkins turned away, intent on loading sacks of flour onto his cart, and Thomas set off across the yard to return the basket. His uneasy feeling about Isabel had faded, to be replaced by curiosity. Perhaps he would have a chance to learn more about her on his next delivery round.

CHAPTER SIX

Thomas had little time to think further on Isabel – as soon as he had returned from his deliveries he was thrown back into mill life. He was only too conscious of how much he had to learn, not just about the mill workings, but also about how to stay safe as he moved around the building. Each heavy sack of grain had to be securely attached to the chain before the rope pulley was used to hoist it through to the top. And it was only too easy to slip on the narrow rungs of the ladders connecting the floors if he tried to climb or descend too hastily. The millstones themselves needed great respect: Thomas shuddered at the thought of the damage they could do to incautious fingers.

Yet, despite all this, he found the days absorbing and the time passed quickly. Mr Hopkins involved him in everything, making his days very different from those he had spent at the boatyard. He was also welcomed into their family, at least after work when he ate with them. Thomas had to try hard not to appear too ravenous in front of the children, Ruth, Benjamin and baby Anthony, because the miller and his wife were particular about manners. However, Mrs Hopkins had noticed that Thomas appeared half starved from the moment he had stepped through the door. She didn't remark on it, but always added something extra to his plate. Thomas had never eaten so well in his life. Every meal featured a delicious pie, savoury or sweet, that Mrs Hopkins had made. Both the miller and his wife were rosy-cheeked and round, and the three children were made in the same mould.

The miller's wife was nearly always to be found in the kitchen, an apron over her skirt and her sleeves rolled up to reveal strong forearms as she kneaded dough or rolled pastry, the children generally at play around her feet. Within the month, Thomas noticed he not only needed to let out his belt by a notch but his trousers were now too short. He was forced to conclude the good food had made him grow.

As the evenings grew chillier, Thomas found it harder and harder to leave the warmth and light of the kitchen, after he had eaten, to go to his cold, makeshift bed in the barn. Many a night he could see his breath in the moonlight and he always slept fully clothed, desperate to trap every bit of warmth next to his body.

It was one evening in early December, after he'd been at the mill for nearly three months, that Mrs Hopkins put a parcel wrapped in brown paper and tied with string on the table in front of him. 'I had to go to Dover today to buy boots for Benjamin – his feet have grown so fast. While I was there, I got you a few things.'

Thomas, surprised but eager, tore into the package while the children looked on. He shook out a pair of brown corduroy breeches and a wool jacket, along with two rough linen shirts.

'You've outgrown the clothes you arrived in,' Mrs Hopkins added, as she busied herself putting food on the table. 'I hope I was correct on the size.'

Thomas began to stutter out his thanks. The clothes weren't new, but they were in good condition and they would keep him warm at work. Mrs Hopkins waved away his thanks, bustling around the table and encouraging him to stand up so she could hold the garments against him.

'They'll do very well,' she said, satisfied. 'And with a bit of room for growth. Mr Hopkins will take a little from your wages each week to pay for them.'

She moved back to the range to take a pie out of the oven – the aroma reached Thomas's nostrils and almost immediately his stomach gurgled loudly. The children giggled and Thomas went red.

Mrs Hopkins ignored them as she placed the pie in the centre of the table, steam escaping from the golden-brown crust.

'You can't carry on sleeping in that draughty barn. You'll catch a chill and then where will we be? You'll be no use to Mr Hopkins if you can't work.'

She set a stack of plates on the table, then began to cut into the pie.

'The last boy lived in Marston so he had no need of a bed here. The house is full, with barely enough space for all of us, but there's a storeroom beside the stable that might do. I've discussed it with Mr Hopkins and you're to give him a hand to clear it out. It's small, but you don't need much more than a place to lay your head at night, and I think you'll be warm enough in there.'

Mr Hopkins had been sitting by the fire, pulling on a pipe, while his wife talked. He might be in charge in the mill, Thomas thought, but it was clear that Mrs Hopkins was the driving force in the house, although she liked to give her husband the credit. He supposed it must be the same in households throughout the land. He was reminded of his own mother and her attempts to manage his father at home in Castle Bay. He rarely allowed his thoughts to stray that way, shutting the door on that part of his life, but he was all at once engulfed by a wave of homesickness, which brought tears to his eyes.

He tried to conquer his emotion to stammer his thanks but Mrs Hopkins noticed and gave his shoulder a squeeze as she set dishes of swede and potatoes on the table.

'You'll be setting me off,' she said. 'It's nothing, and no more than I would expect if my three should end up having to rely on the kindness of strangers. But, look, you missed something.' She pulled another pair of trousers from the package, which had fallen to the floor. 'You needed something to wear to church. We can see how you look in them tomorrow.'

She set aside the pile of clothes on the dresser and Thomas mumbled his thanks once more, thinking, even as he did so, that he would feel proud to look smarter in front of Isabel at the service in the morning, even though she never gave any sign of noticing him when she and her father walked past the Hopkinses' pew on the way out.

Thomas didn't understand what had befallen him with regard to Isabel. He knew why he looked forward to his visits to Marston Grange: he craved an encounter with her. And yet so often he was left frustrated and disappointed. He didn't know how to talk to her – he became tongue-tied and flushed with embarrassment, even when she engaged him in longed-for conversation. She would lose interest very quickly and return to the house, or go to the donkey wheel to talk to the animal. Thomas would return to the mill, head full of puzzlement, vowing to pay no heed to her next time, only to find himself returning to their conversation time and again, wondering how he could have done better. By the time Sunday came around, he was eager for a chance to catch glimpses of her again, even though she never spoke to him. Somehow, that was easier to bear.

CHAPTER SEVEN

Every Sunday, whatever the weather, the miller and his family walked to church in the next village, Marston being too small to have a church of its own. The walk took well over half an hour, due to the short legs of the children, during which time the gig kept by Richard Cavendish invariably passed them. Mr Hopkins always doffed his hat but Mr Cavendish, who drove himself, never acknowledged him. Isabel, swaddled in blankets to keep out the chill, kept her eyes fixed ahead and gave no sign of having noticed them, either.

It was the same when they arrived at church. Isabel and her father would be already seated in their pew at the front and neither looked around as the congregation settled into their seats behind them. There was always a muted hum of conversation until the minister turned from the altar to signal the service was about to start, but Thomas never noticed a word pass between Isabel and her father. After the service, they were the first to leave, glancing neither left nor right as they passed along the central aisle.

The church, an austere grey stone building, was very plain on the inside, with windows that Thomas thought small for a building of that size. The whitewashed walls were sparsely adorned with memorial plaques and the dark wood rafters found an echo in the dark wood pews, which differed only in being highly polished. Thomas had studied the interior, such as it was, in great detail, for his mind always wandered during the service. His thoughts inevitably strayed to Isabel, to wonder what was going through her mind while she sat so quietly. It was fortunate that gazing at her back allowed him to keep his eyes fixed forwards, so that he appeared attentive. He also did his best to stand up and sit down at the appropriate moments, to murmur the correct responses during the prayers and to find the hymns in good time. Mrs Hopkins would not have approved if she had known how much his mind was on Isabel rather than on the Lord's work.

She'd commented on the father and daughter on more than one occasion, clearly thinking Mr Cavendish might take more care to instruct his daughter about her appearance.

'It's only too apparent a mother's influence is lacking in that house,' she'd remarked to Mr Hopkins as they walked back from church. 'The girl either has no suitable clothes or her father doesn't think to tell her to wear them to church. They're the wealthiest folk in Marston yet she looks as though she's dressed from the ragbag.'

Thomas, of course, never reported such conversations to Isabel. She'd surprised him one day by asking when he had time to himself and he could only reply, 'Sunday,' when he was free after church and the family dinner.

'A shame,' Isabel had said to him. 'I could have shown you the badger's den in the woods and, in the spring, the trees where the hawks nest.' She shrugged. 'But on a Sunday my father is usually at home all day.'

'Perhaps you can show me next spring,' Thomas suggested, 'in the evening, once it stays light for longer.'

As a child, Thomas had roamed freely in Castle Bay and his mother had paid scant regard to his whereabouts. Even when he was older, he'd preferred to be out of the one room they were reduced to living in, although, in any case, his work had kept him away for long hours. Here in Marston, a pattern had already been established. He spent the day in the mill, followed by evenings in the family kitchen. Thomas knew he couldn't break from that without causing comment and questions. Something told him Mrs Hopkins wouldn't approve of him meeting Isabel Cavendish other than when he made his bread deliveries, but he couldn't put his finger on why.

He began to wonder how to make some free time for himself away from the family, to prepare the ground for the new year. He had set up his sleeping quarters in the storeroom but Mrs Hopkins was right – there was barely room to do more than lie down to sleep at night and he always stayed with the family until it was time for bed. He'd discovered he could make himself useful teaching Ruth and Benjamin, the older children, some basic arithmetic, as well as helping with their letters.

Thomas puzzled over how he might be away from the family without causing comment. He'd thought of pretending to visit the Wheatsheaf, but that would be too easily discovered as a lie. The miller or Mrs Hopkins might mention it to Mercy, and her surprise would expose his untruth. In any case, Thomas had a suspicion that, if he said where he was going, Mr Hopkins would offer to accompany him.

He thought of saying he was going fishing, or rabbiting, to contribute to the family's dinner table, but that would mean poaching on Cavendish land and no doubt drawing down all sorts of trouble on his head. He was no nearer to solving the problem by Christmastime, when he was making his final visit to deliver fresh bread around Marston. Mrs Hopkins had made mince pies, too, which Thomas had been instructed to deliver as a small gift to whoever he dealt with on his round.

Isabel was waiting to waylay Thomas in the yard, despite the threat of snow on the brisk wind.

'Your basket looks particularly full today,' she remarked, peering into it. She spied the mince pies nestling on top. 'Are some of these for us? How lovely!'

She'd seized one and bitten into it before Thomas could explain. He put the basket down on the ground behind him before she could make another raid on it, and blew on his cramped fingers to warm them.

'I have news,' Isabel said, through a mouthful of crumbs. 'I'm to go to Ramsgate in the new year, to learn how to be a young lady.'

Her hands now free of the mince pie, she pushed each one into the opposite sleeve of her father's jacket, to warm them, unaware of Thomas's reaction. He felt as though he'd been delivered a body blow.

'So, we can't make our trip to the woods in spring?' was all he managed to blurt out.

'I don't think so,' Isabel said. 'I expect I will still be away. But be happy for me. There will be parties and outings and music lessons.' She frowned. 'I'm not sure I shall like the lessons but I'm curious about the aunt I have never met, and my cousins.'

The heavy sky released the first flakes of snow and Isabel shivered. 'I must go in,' she said, turning away.

'Won't I see you again before you leave?' Thomas had to stop himself reaching out to grasp her arm.

'In church at Christmas, perhaps,' Isabel said. 'I may still be here in the new year – I'm not sure yet.'

The snow began to swirl about them more thickly and Thomas picked up the basket and hurried to the kitchen, his mind in a whirl. He concentrated on making his rounds as fast as he could, for he'd come out bareheaded and his ears were half frozen, his hair full of snow. In his confusion over Isabel's news, he found half of the mince pies remained in the basket so he had to retrace his steps to deliver them where he'd previously forgotten to do so.

One was left and he ate it as he carried the empty basket back to the mill, past the wood. He glanced at the trees, their bare branches now coated in snow, and thought bitterly of how quickly life could change. There would be no eagerly anticipated visit here in the spring with Isabel. How long, he wondered, would it be before he had the chance to speak to her again?

ISABEL

PART ONE

SEPTEMBER 1822 — MAY 1823

CHAPTER ONE

Isabel had seen the boy several times since that first Sunday. She thought of him as 'the boy' even after she had learned his name – Thomas – and his age. He was a few months younger than she was, fifteen as opposed to her just-turned sixteen. And he was working at the mill on the lane that led to the Dover turnpike.

She'd been surprised to see a stranger at the gate that Sunday. No one came to Marston unless business or family brought them there. The hamlet dreamed time away much as it had for the past hundred years, and as it would for the next hundred, Isabel feared, unless she discovered a way to leave.

In the summer, strangers came to work on the land and to drink in the beer house when the day was done. They were older men for the most part, weather-beaten, wiry and used to a life on the road. More recently, there had been younger navy men among them, no longer needed now the war was over. They struggled to find work, moving from place to place, bitter and hard-drinking, according to her father, who had warned her not to speak to them. But it was autumn now, and the boy had seemed anxious and somehow out of place. His clothes were rough enough to suggest he was a casual labourer, but he didn't belong to the countryside, Isabel decided. First, he'd started when a flock of rooks took flight, uttering their harsh caws. His reaction to the donkey wheel had confirmed her opinion. Surely they weren't such an unusual sight on farms hereabouts. The one at Marston Grange had been in use since long before she was born, drawing full buckets from the well and returning the empty ones, an arduous process when done by hand. The water wasn't only destined for the house – her father ran a small brewery on the site and sold the ale on the virtues of the pure water used for brewing.

Isabel felt sorry for the donkey. It plodded in the wheel for hour after hour, day after day, until it grew too old and weary and another beast was found to replace it. She'd had to argue with her father to allow her to keep the retired animals in a paddock, to give them some sort of decent life in their final days. Mr Cavendish had eventually granted her wish, telling her she was as stubborn as the donkeys. She inherited that aspect of her character from him, she was sure. Her mother, a tall and elegant raven-haired beauty, was a shadowy figure in Isabel's life, barely remembered. She used to see her at the end of the day when the nursemaid took her in to say goodnight. Mrs Cavendish would pat her head or brush her daughter's cheek with her lips, leaving a lingering trace of perfume. The scent of musk roses, Isabel realised, later in life, when she bent to smell a deep crimson bloom in the garden and was instantly drawn back to her childhood.

One day, the nursemaid had stopped taking her downstairs to say goodnight. Isabel asked about her mama and was told she was away, in London. After a while, she'd stopped asking, then stopped wondering. When she was too old to need a nursemaid, she'd joined her father in the panelled dining room in the early evening while he ate his dinner. She'd sat on a hard wooden chair, her feet dangling a good distance from the floor, staring at a portrait on the wall opposite while her father talked about the tasks that needed to be done on the land, or the problems with the latest brew of ale. The painting was of her mother, and Isabel wondered whether it was this image that she remembered, rather than the woman herself. She'd certainly faced it often enough at the huge dining table that never received any guests. She could summon the image at will: a striking dark-haired, dark-eyed woman, dressed in a revealing white lace gown, a collar of pearls at her throat, amethyst droplets sparkling in her ears. She was painted against a dark background, the portrait held in an ornate gilded frame.

For a long time, she'd believed her mother must have died and her father was too distressed to talk of it. As she grew older, she'd begun to suspect her mother had left, returning to her native France now that the war with Napoleon was over. Isabel struggled to imagine the woman in the painting being happy in such a quiet place as Marston. She belonged to a more glamorous world, not one that involved nightly discussions of the price of grain or the laziness of workers.

Yet she didn't question her father. And there was no one else she could ask. The nursemaid was long gone and although Cook had been there as long as Isabel could remember, she hadn't known her mother. Cook had a name – Mrs Bridger – but Mr Cavendish either couldn't remember it or couldn't be bothered to use it. Isabel didn't use it either, but for different reasons. She used the title almost as a term of endearment: Cook was as close to a mother as she was ever likely to have.

Despite searching, she'd found nothing that could belong to her mother in her father's bedroom. She'd searched more than once, taking care to do it when he'd left to go out into the fields or down to the brew house, thinking she must surely have missed something. She'd found one thing in the end, bundled up in the bottom of a cupboard in one of the unused bedrooms in the Grange. When Isabel shook it out, she saw it was the white lace dress her mother had worn to have her portrait painted. She'd wasted no time in trying it on, once she'd inspected it carefully to make sure no spiders had set up home among its folds. She was only ten years old at the time and she knew, even without a looking glass, that she appeared ridiculous – a little girl in her mother's clothes. But the dress was all she had to connect them so she bided her time, trying it on every now and then. Finally, when she was fifteen, it fitted her. At least, it barely trailed on the floor, but it was still too large in the bodice. Undaunted, Isabel found a piece of ribbon to wrap around the seam and pull it in more tightly. Then she wore it whenever the mood took her – but only when her father was out of the house. Since he was mostly gone from breakfast until darkness fell, he hadn't yet caught her. She wasn't sure what his reaction would be. She'd been wearing it the day the boy appeared, while she was talking to the donkey as she so often did. She had little other company.

The boy had piqued her interest. Her father wouldn't countenance her getting to know him, of course, but unless he kept his vague promise to send her to stay with a distant relative, what else was she to do? Strangers of her own age were a rarity in Marston and Isabel was hungry for something to relieve the monotony of her days. Through her childhood she'd had no one to play with, her father considering the few local children beneath her station in life. Now that she was so nearly grown-up, she didn't see why she shouldn't choose her own company. A shy boy, with a sensitive face and handsome features, would suit her very well.

Chapter Two

The next time she saw the boy, he'd come to deliver bread baked by the miller's wife. She'd seen him from the upstairs window, loitering in the yard as if unsure where to go. She'd snatched up an old jacket of her father's, with no thought of her appearance, and hurried down the stairs to waylay him in the yard. On that occasion, she'd learned his name and told him hers. She'd also discovered that he was from Castle Bay, but didn't want her to know it, which was intriguing.

After that, she began to ask Cook casually when she was expecting a bread delivery and she took care to be on watch for his arrival. With each visit, she discovered a little more about him. He was around her age and had had some schooling – which caused her a pang of envy, for her father had been neglectful in that respect. He always appeared glad to see her, offering a smile, but he seemed unable to hold her gaze with his golden-brown eyes, looking away with a flush of embarrassment. He never stayed long, indicating the full basket he carried, and saying, 'I must get on with my rounds.'

Isabel thought of telling him he should make the Grange his last stop, so they could talk more, but she guessed he was following orders from the miller. The Grange was the most important place in Marston and, therefore, had to have first choice of the loaves.

As October turned to November and the weather grew colder, he was even less inclined to tarry, stamping his feet and blowing on his fingers as she tried to detain him with another question, or tell him of something she had seen: the badgers' den just inside the wood between the Grange and the mill, the great hawk that had peered down at her from the treetops while she watched it. His clothes were too meagre for the weather, she realised, but at least he had filled out since she had first seen him. He had benefited from Mrs Hopkins's cooking, no doubt, despite the hard work at the mill. He told her a bit about it, the constant running up and down the ladders, the handling of the sacks of grain and flour, the noise of the machinery and the grinding of the mill wheels.

'I should like to come and see for myself,' Isabel declared. 'Perhaps you could ask Mr Hopkins.'

He seemed worried then, and mumbled something before vanishing to the kitchen. She knew he wouldn't ask. If she wanted to go she would have to manage it herself. She was impatient: time was passing and her life seemed to hang on these brief and all-too-infrequent meetings, with no other diversions in her days. He was in church on a Sunday, but there was no chance to speak there. The Cavendishes always arrived early and were seated at the front before the rest of the congregation appeared, and they always left first. Her father wouldn't have it any other way, seeing it as befitting his status. She didn't feel able to turn around during the service but she was sure she could feel his eyes boring into her back throughout.

One Sunday in December, at the dinner table after the service, her father said, 'You need new clothes, Isabel. It's been brought to my attention that the things you have are unbecoming to a young woman of your age and standing.'

Isabel gazed down at her plate, but gripped the edge of the table to disguise her rage. Who had been gossiping about her? Was it Cook? Or Mercy, at the inn? Before she could ask the question, her father spoke again.

'I've arranged with your aunt Sophia Crawford in Ramsgate that you will spend some time with her. She will take you to visit her seamstress and she will also arrange some tuition for you – music, painting and the like. Occupations more becoming to a young lady than running wild in the woods and fields.'

Isabel could barely speak for astonishment. She welcomed the idea of new clothes, for her dresses from girlhood were barely respectable. But lessons in music and art, to make her fit for the drawing room, held little appeal. And who was Aunt Sophia? She wasn't sure she had ever met her.

'How long will I be away, Father?' she asked.

Mr Cavendish shrugged. 'Six months, perhaps longer. However long it takes to make a young lady of you.'

He saw Isabel's frown and added, 'You will enjoy it, I'm sure. I've heard Ramsgate described as being very like Brighton, these days. Promenades along the seafront, carriage outings, dancing ...' He seemed to run out of ideas.

'And Aunt Sophia? Who is she?' Isabel asked.

'My sister,' her father said, then stood up from the table to indicate that the conversation was over.

No sooner had her father spoken of his intention to send her to his sister than the plan seemed to move on apace. He'd told her more at the table on Christmas Day, after they had attended the service at St Augustine's. The minister had delivered the same sermon he had given the previous Christmas, and the one before that, as far as Isabel could remember. The congregation behind them sang enthusiastically, but Isabel retained the same composure she always kept when in church. It was the only way she could get through the service without screaming – at the minister, for his predictability; at her father, for his coldness towards her; at herself, in impatience to be gone from Marston.

As she walked out, she noticed for the first time that the church had been decorated with fresh green boughs, bringing the sharp scent of pine into the chill air of the building. And candles burned on every windowsill, lifting the gloom of the day outside. She almost smiled at Thomas as she passed the end of the miller's pew.

He had such an eager look on his face, as though he was desperate to speak to her. She remembered, though, that her father had said she must always conduct herself with dignity at church so she made her way out, expressionless.

CHAPTER THREE

At dinner, Isabel had been gazing around the dark-panelled dining room, thinking it would have been improved by some festive greenery, when her father remarked, 'I have arranged with my sister that you will join her in Ramsgate next week. She will send a carriage for you. Pack anything you think you may need, but I have let her know you will require at least one complete set of new clothes.'

He was carving the roast goose as he spoke, and barely glanced at her as he handed her two slices of meat on a plate.

Isabel, with so many questions filling her head, hardly knew where to begin. 'Father, please tell me more about your sister. Where does she live? Does she have a family? What will I do there?'

Her father, having added several slices of meat to his own plate, was now helping himself to potatoes and a liberal quantity of gravy. 'I dare say your time will be filled with dressmaker's appointments, or whatever it is you ladies do.'

He began to eat his dinner with great concentration and Isabel waited, hoping he would answer more than just her last question.

He waved his knife at her. 'Cook has spent a great deal of time preparing this food. Eat up now, before it gets cold.'

Having created a small amount of space on his plate, he added another slice of meat. Isabel, her appetite replaced by excitement at the news, took a potato and a small spoonful of swede. She began to eat slowly, watching her father.

He wiped his mouth and raised his glass to his lips. 'My sister is, in reality, my half-sister. That is to say, we have different mothers.' He frowned. 'We aren't close, not having grown up together. In fact, I can't remember the last time I saw her. She has two daughters, I believe, or perhaps they are sons.' He shrugged. 'And she has a preposterous address. The Plains of Waterloo. You can find out the rest for yourself when you're there.'

Satisfied he had done his duty, he turned to his plate again. Isabel was content to mull over his answers while she tried to do justice to her dinner. It was clear her father knew very little of his relative, and cared even less, although he was happy to deliver his only daughter into her hands. She wondered why, but set the thought aside. Delicious anticipation of what might await her saw her through the plum pudding. She decided she would pack a bag that very night, to ensure she was prepared the minute the carriage arrived.

At least there would be family members there to keep her company. And the Plains of Waterloo sounded as though it had a military connection. Was Aunt Sophia's husband a military man? Isabel's imagination was her solace and companion over the next few days as she waited with great impatience for the arrival of the carriage.

It appeared at Marston Grange early in the morning four days after Christmas. Isabel travelled unaccompanied all the way to Ramsgate, a cold journey, despite the rug the coachman had given her, of at least three hours. Within an hour of setting off, they travelled through Castle Bay and she thought fleetingly of Thomas. This was his home town. They passed the castle she supposed the place to be named after – a squat, curved building with an imposing entrance and a flag snapping in the wind on the battlements. She turned, craning her neck for a last glimpse as they rattled onwards.

Isabel had never seen the sea – or not at close quarters. On the high lane out of Marston, which she had often walked along on a summer's day, you could catch a glimpse of blue in the distance, the white cliffs sparkling in the sun. The carriage was running beside it now. Today, the wind had churned it into a seething mass of brown, crested with dirty white foam. All the fishing boats were pulled in close to shore and Isabel turned her gaze on the houses they were passing. She realised many were, in fact, inns and taverns, their names painted on the brickwork or on wooden signs that swung and rattled in the wind. There were a few people about – not all of them muffled against the cold, she was surprised to note. Women leaned out of the windows or against the doorways of some of the inns, laughing as they called to each other or to men passing by. As the buildings fell away behind them, she glanced out to sea once more and this time noticed how many ships waited out there at anchor, some in the far distance.

The carriage jolted along for some miles, with the sea on one side and flat, open countryside on the other, just the occasional church spire showing here and there. Despite the discomfort, Isabel fell into a doze, exhausted by the excitement that had robbed her of sleep over the nights since her father had told her of the arrangements. She woke with a start as she began to slide forward in her seat and realised the carriage was descending a hill. She was stiff and cold – the rug had slipped off during her awkward nap. She caught a glimpse, once more, of churning brown waves at the bottom of the hill but it was the buildings that made her sit upright and gasp out loud.

They were passing flat-fronted terraces of graceful proportions, at least three storeys high, with row upon row of chimneys on their roofs. Some had pillars around the front door, holding up wrought-iron balconies. Even on a grey day, the white-painted buildings seemed to shine.

Onwards they went, until they reached a harbour, and the carriage began to climb. Here was the scene of a great deal of building work, the roadway churned into a morass of mud by the carts delivering supplies. The sounds of hammering, sawing and shouting filtered through the window. Isabel found it hard to believe there was so much life here, barely twenty miles from the countryside where she had dreamed away the last sixteen years.

The carriage came to a halt before a house that was also in a terrace, although not as grand as the ones they had passed earlier. Nevertheless, it had wide steps leading up to the front door, adjacent to which an oriel window jutted out over the floor below. The coachman had already climbed down from his seat and was holding open the carriage door for her, so she had to step down, although the house door remained firmly closed. Clutching her small valise, she went up the steps and raised the brass knocker, letting it fall.

After what felt like a very long time, but was probably less than a minute, the door swung open. A young girl stood there, in a dark dress, a cap and an apron. Before either she or Isabel could speak, a lady swept up behind her.

'Isabella!' she cried. 'Come in, do. You must be exhausted after your journey. Kitty, take her shawls and bag. Have you a trunk?'

When Isabel, mute, shook her head, she gestured to her to follow and opened the door leading to the room with the oriel window. Isabel saw at once that it gave a view down to the sea, even though the house didn't face in that direction.

She supposed the lady to be Aunt Sophia, although she could hardly be more unlike her brother, Isabel's father. He was tall, slightly stooped, wiry and weather-beaten from all the time he spent outdoors. Aunt Sophia was pale and plump, and wearing an apricot-coloured dress in a draped fabric, which served only to enhance both aspects of her appearance. She had auburn hair and wore an abundance of jewellery that clanked and sparkled as she moved. 'Sit here, by the fire,' she said, patting a chair, then taking the one opposite. 'Now, let me have a good look at you.'

Her gaze swept Isabel from head to toe. Then she frowned. 'Indeed, your father was right,' she murmured. 'There's a great deal of work to be done to turn you into a lady.'

CHAPTER FOUR

Before Isabel could gather her thoughts to respond to her aunt's remark, the drawing-room door opened and two young ladies entered, walking across the room to stand behind their mother. Isabel judged them to be around her own age. One was pale and fair, while the other had hair more red than auburn. Neither was tall and both wore dresses in what Isabel considered to be unflattering shades of pink, highly unsuitable for the winter weather and muddy roads outside the window. They stared at Isabel, wide-eyed. Determined not to be intimidated, she stared back.

'My daughters,' Aunt Sophia said. 'Rebecca,' she indicated the red-headed girl, 'and Amelia. They are similar in age to you, Isabella – seventeen and fifteen. I wonder that your father never thought for you to make our acquaintance before now. It's clear we could have been of service to you.' She pursed her lips and shook her head, then said, 'We will have much to do. But first we must settle you in. Amelia, show your cousin to her room and then ask Cook to find her something to eat and drink. She will be hungry after her journey, but no doubt she will want to change out of her travelling clothes first.'

Isabel looked down at her dark skirt and linen blouse, given to her by Mercy who had said she couldn't go to Ramsgate in her old clothes. She had worn two woollen shawls over the top for warmth, and been glad of them in the carriage. The only other clothes she had brought were nightdresses and some undergarments, since her father had told her one of the main reasons for her visit was to acquire new clothes.

As Amelia led her upstairs, Isabel realised the house was not as large as she had first thought. The rooms were smaller than those at Marston Grange and the staircase ran up one side of the house, not centrally. The lack of oak panelling undoubtedly made the place feel lighter and airier, as did the pale colours on the walls. There was much to take in – not least the discovery that she was to share a room with Amelia. Isabel was taken aback. An only child, she had always had her own room. How would she manage with someone else sleeping in a bed so close to her own, watching her as she dressed and undressed?

Amelia was watching her now. 'Is it true that your mother ran off to France with a duke?' she asked.

Isabel sat down abruptly on the nearest bed. 'I – I don't know,' she stammered, caught by surprise. 'I barely remember her. And my father never speaks of her.'

The thought that her mother had gone to France had taken root in her mind a long time previously, but her involvement with another man, and what sounded suspiciously like a scandal, was unwelcome.

Amelia, seeming rather pleased at the reaction her words had elicited, said, 'I'll leave you to change now. That's your bed,' she pointed to the one Isabel wasn't sitting on, 'and I've made some space in here for your clothes.' She pulled open a drawer in the chest by the window. 'Come and join us in the drawing room.'

'I have nothing to change into,' Isabel confessed.

'Haven't you?' Amelia, astonished, looked her up and down just as Aunt Sophia had. 'Well, I expect you'd at least like to wash your hands and face.' She showed her the mahogany cupboard that served as a stand for the china jug and bowl, patterned with trailing ivy leaves in green and gold, the matching chamber pot stored away beneath.

She withdrew and Isabel did what was expected of her, thankful for the few moments alone. She hesitated before returning the chamber pot to the cupboard, uncertain where to find the privy and unsure whether or not a servant would attend to it. It was the first time she had been away from home, and she found it hard not knowing what she should do.

This feeling was repeated many times in the weeks to come, when barely a day was to pass without at least one situation that found her uncertain how to proceed. No other day quite matched all the surprises of her first day in Ramsgate, though.

Amelia introduced her to below-stairs: the cook, Mrs Potter's, domain, where she ruled over a scullery maid and a house maid. Isabel discovered it wasn't acceptable to sit at the kitchen table in what was the only truly warm room in the house, as it had been at Marston Grange. Instead, Amelia explained, she must summon the maid, using the bells located throughout the house. Today she was served a bowl of broth with bread and butter in the dining room at the back of the house. A fire burned in the grate and Isabel sat with her back to it, gazing out of the window, which looked over a yard and onto the backs of another row of houses behind. All the style had been lavished on the front façades, while the backs were plain, the blank windows revealing little of what went on inside. She had little time to contemplate this further: as she spooned up the last of her broth, Aunt Sophia bustled in and sat down facing her.

'Now, my dear, I have made a plan. We will visit the dressmaker tomorrow. In the meantime, you must borrow something from Rebecca to wear, for you cannot go out in the streets of Ramsgate looking like this.' Aunt Sophia shuddered and the maid, who had come in to remove Isabel's bowl, ducked her head to hide a smirk.

'I fear you are taller than Rebecca.' Aunt Sophia frowned. 'I only hope I can prevail upon Mrs Symonds to make you something with the greatest possible haste. We will have to manage until then.'

CHAPTER FIVE

Isabel was taken aback when, barely two hours later, as darkness fell in the late afternoon, Aunt Sophia told her, 'I've instructed Kitty to prepare a bath for you. As we are to visit the dressmaker I think it would be . . .' she hesitated '. . . advisable.'

Rebecca, sitting by the window and working on a piece of needlework, sniggered. Her mother shot her a look.

'Your hair needs washing, my dear,' her aunt continued. 'Then you can try on something of Rebecca's to see what will fit.'

Rebecca's amusement vanished, to be replaced by a scowl.

Isabel was embarrassed to be singled out in this way. Baths were a rare occurrence at Marston Grange and hair washing took place when she remembered. It had been very cold over Christmas and, although the idea of bathing before her visit had occurred to her, she had rejected it. It meant disturbing the kitchen routine, for that was the only place warm enough to bathe, where the water wouldn't cool on its way up through the house.

She soon discovered bathing was a different and more pleasurable matter in the Crawford household. The bath was set in front of the fire in her aunt's bedroom, due to a lack of space in Isabel and Amelia's room. Kitty had already filled it with hot water, the curtains were drawn and only one lamp was lit. Still, Isabel felt shy divesting herself of her clothing in front of her aunt and the maid.

Aunt Sophia, seeming to divine her feelings, said to Kitty, 'Would you go to Rebecca's room and bring me one or two of her dresses? Whichever you think would be most suitable for Miss Isabella to wear.'

Kitty, evidently pleased at being entrusted with this task, hurried away. Isabel was quick to undress in her absence, while her aunt busied herself at her dressing table. Isabel realised, too late, that her reflection was revealed in the looking glass. By then, though, she had sunk into the bath and was enjoying it so much that she hardly cared. Her aunt handed her a block of soap, scented with lavender, and Isabel obediently began to wash herself.

Kitty returned, laying dresses on the bed and earning a murmur of approbation from Aunt Sophia. Then the maid began to wash Isabel's hair briskly, massaging her scalp rather hard but taking care, when rinsing, not to pour water into her eyes.

With the water cooling in the bath, she held out a towel and waited. Isabel, unused to so much female attention, pushed herself up and out of the bath, keeping her back to the maid.

More humiliation was to come. Her undergarments were greeted with horror by her aunt, who declared that drawers, chemises and petticoats must be added to the list of items to be procured for Isabel. She was heard to mutter darkly that she would need to apply to her brother for more money. Then, seeing Isabel now attired in one of Rebecca's muslin dresses, her damp hair held up by combs, she brightened.

'My dear, you will do very well. Very well indeed. Look at yourself in the glass.' She propelled her towards the dressing table, where Isabel was confronted by an image of a tall, slender girl in a lilac dress, which revealed far too much of her neck and shoulders. She made a move to tug at the neckline but her aunt, standing behind her, stayed her hand.

'You have been hiding behind layers of clothing for too long, Isabella. If you are to find a husband, you must learn the art of displaying yourself to advantage. You must hold your head high, like so.' She tilted Isabel's chin upwards. 'Just look at those collarbones.

How they will suit a well-placed necklace, the sparkle of precious gems.'

She frowned. 'The dress is too short, of course, but it must do for now. You will have to keep to the house until the dressmaker can oblige us. The colour suits you rather better than it does Rebecca. As does the style.' She sighed. 'Thank you, Kitty. We will go downstairs now.'

As they entered the drawing room, Isabel was still preoccupied with her aunt's words: 'If you are to find a husband.' Her father hadn't mentioned such a thing – she would have remembered if he had. Surely her visit to her aunt was to improve her wardrobe and make her into a lady.

She flopped into a chair, frowning, then noticed Rebecca and Amelia staring again. 'What?' she asked crossly.

Rebecca didn't reply, glancing at her mother instead, while Amelia said, 'How different you look.'

Keen to change the focus of the conversation, Isabel asked whether Mr Crawford would join them at dinner. She rather hoped that would be soon. The meal would have been eaten at Marston Grange by now and, despite the broth, she was hungry.

'Good heavens, no.' Aunt Sophia laughed. 'He spends winters in London and we girls are all very comfortable here, aren't we?' She turned to her daughters for confirmation, and they nodded. 'He'll come to see us in March, by paddle steamer, once the weather is better. We like our little household as it is, with just ourselves to please. And, of course, the rents are so reasonable here in the winter. We couldn't afford this place in the summer.' The last bit was said almost to herself and she lapsed into thought until the clock on the mantelpiece struck six and roused her.

'Time for dinner, girls,' she said, and they filed through into the dining room.

Here was another revelation for Isabel. The fare at Marston

Grange had been organised to suit her father, she now realised. Heavy dinners of meat pies or roast fowl, with potatoes and little else other than gravy. Here, Aunt Sophia preferred Mrs Potter to serve dishes that were light on roast meats, but always with a choice of two or three desserts. Her aunt and her cousins always partook of them all.

CHAPTER SIX

Isabel feared that pondering the strangeness of everything she had experienced that day, along with sharing a bedroom with Amelia, would cause her a restless night. The Crawfords, however, kept later hours than she was used to, and by the time she was in bed she craved sleep so much that she was awake for barely a minute after her head touched the pillow.

She awoke to a faint lifting of the light in the room and, for a moment or two, she couldn't work out where she was. The curtained window was in the wrong place, her head was surely where her feet should be, and she was surprised to hear someone else breathing in the room. Then it all came flooding back to her and she lay quietly, thinking over the events of the previous day. Her aunt, even on such a short acquaintance, was nothing like Isabel's father. Isabel resolved to learn more of the family background, and of her own mother, whom Amelia had referred to in such a startling fashion. The portrait at Marston Grange had, in a strange way, kept her in daily contact with the idea of her mother. Now that she was away from home for the first time, it struck her that her mother was still alive somewhere, over the sea. And she had never tried to contact her daughter after she'd left.

Amelia stirred in her bed and Isabel thought she was waking but, instead, she turned onto her other side. She was friendlier than Rebecca, Isabel decided, although both girls seemed puzzled by her. Had she led a life so very different from theirs?

It was still quiet in the house but she was sure it was past her normal time to rise. She thought she would wait a little longer then go downstairs to see whether anyone was awake. Barely five more minutes passed, as Isabel fidgeted under the covers, before she could bear it no longer. She jumped out of bed, throwing her shawl around her shoulders, then opened the door and peered out onto the landing. All of the bedroom doors were firmly shut, but faint noises from below suggested someone was about.

Isabel ran lightly down the stairs, peeping into the drawing room and dining room, which were empty, the fires lit. She hesitated, then carried on down to the basement. She suspected what was acceptable at home would be frowned upon here. As she reached the last step on the stairs she came face to face with Kitty, who was carrying a tray bearing a steaming pot and several cups and saucers. Kitty gave a start and the china on the tray rattled.

'Oh, miss, you gave me a fright. What are you doing down here?' She didn't wait for an answer but said, 'I was just bringing up your morning chocolate. I'm not late, am I?'

'Morning chocolate?' Isabel was confused. 'I'm sorry if I startled you. I didn't know the time . . .' She trailed off, as Kitty was staring at her.

'It's nine o'clock, miss. Mrs Crawford likes her chocolate served at nine and breakfast at ten.'

'Thank you,' Isabel said. Nine o'clock! She would have been up and dressed long before this at home. As for breakfast at ten – that was two hours later than she was used to.

Kitty was shifting her weight from foot to foot and Isabel realised she was holding her up. She apologised, then hurried ahead of the maid up to her room, where she perched awkwardly in bed and waited. Kitty came in, set the tray on the chest of drawers and opened the curtains.

'Good morning, Miss Amelia,' she said. 'Miss Isabella,' and she nodded at her. Then she poured a cup of chocolate for each of the girls and took away the tray.

Amelia yawned. 'Did you sleep well?' she asked.

'Thank you, yes.' Isabel tasted her chocolate. It was rich and creamy and seemed an odd way to start the day.

'Mmm! I love this, don't you?' Amelia said, sipping greedily. Without waiting for an answer, she said, 'You have the dressmaker today. Are you excited? It's my favourite thing. I so love to have a new dress.' She seemed wistful. 'But I usually get Rebecca's when she has outgrown them.'

'I'm sure she'll stop growing soon. Then you'll be able to have dresses made just for you,' Isabel said, although she really couldn't have cared less. It seemed odd to be having such a conversation. Her clothing came to her in irregular ways, usually when a female of her acquaintance, such as Mercy or Cook, realised she had outgrown everything. Then they would either provide her with a dress of their own, or prevail upon her father to let them buy some cloth so they could make her one.

'What do we do now?' Isabel asked. She had finished her chocolate and was impatient. At home she would have been out in the yard encouraging the donkey in his work, or talking to Cook in the kitchen, or taking a walk over the fields if the weather was suitable. She would have liked to go out and wander around Ramsgate but had a feeling that wouldn't be allowed.

'We'll get up when Kitty brings the water for washing, then have breakfast. Rebecca and I have lessons after that.' Amelia didn't look very happy at the idea.

'Lessons?' Isabel asked.

'Yes, we study art and music. It's my morning for the pianoforte.' Amelia sighed. 'I forgot to practise yesterday. I will get a scolding. Do you play?'

Isabel shook her head.

Amelia was surprised. 'I dare say Mama will arrange for you to have lessons. It's expected of all young ladies.'

Kitty knocked and came in bearing a jug of water, then took away the empty chocolate cups.

'Do you want to wash first?' Amelia asked.

Isabel, mindful of the bath she had had the night before, shook her head. It seemed, however, that washing consisted only of face and hands, before Amelia exchanged her nightdress for a cotton dress with a high neck and long sleeves.

'What's that?' Isabel asked, pointing rather rudely at the dress and wondering why she wasn't attired as she had been the day before.

'Morning dress,' Amelia said. 'It's what we wear when we are at home, when no social calls are expected. Before we go out,' she added helpfully, seeing Isabel's puzzlement. 'You don't have one?'

Isabel shook her head. At Marston Grange, she dressed for warmth as soon as she got up. She never dressed for anyone else. She got out of bed and, unable to find her travelling clothes from the day before, she put on Rebecca's loaned dress, splashed her face with water and threw the shawl around her shoulders. It seemed her aunt was right – the dressmaker would be kept very busy.

CHAPTER SEVEN

Aunt Sophia and Rebecca were already in the dining room by the time Isabel and Amelia descended the stairs. Like Amelia, they were dressed informally, and Isabel felt conspicuous in Rebecca's revealing gown. She sat down and, seeing that her aunt and cousin had already finished, she helped herself from the dishes set out on the crisp white tablecloth: bread rolls, curls of butter and jewel-coloured preserves. Breakfast at Marston Grange was a heartier affair, probably because her father preferred something substantial before he went out into the fields.

Kitty came in and offered her more chocolate but she declined and settled for tea, unlike her aunt and cousins. Aunt Sophia dabbed at her mouth with a napkin, then pushed back her chair.

'We have the dressmaker at eleven thirty, Isabella. I've asked Mrs Potter to send a boy out for the carriage, to be here by eleven fifteen. Amelia, your lesson starts in half an hour. Rebecca, yours too. I've asked Mrs Windsor to keep an eye on you both while I'm out. Isabella, make sure you are ready in good time.'

As far as Isabel was aware, she was quite ready but she nodded at her aunt and then asked, as soon as the door closed behind her, 'Who is Mrs Windsor?'

'The art tutor,' Amelia replied. 'I think I had better go and practise before Mr Brooke arrives. He's very strict.' She got up and left the table and a few minutes later Isabel heard the pianoforte being played in the sitting room. Isabel supposed she must be performing exercises, for there was no noticeable tune.

There was a silence at the table and Isabel knew Rebecca was scrutinising her.

She spoke abruptly. 'Don't imagine you can turn yourself into a lady with a nice gown or two. It's going to take a lot more than that to make anything of you.' With that, she pushed back her chair and marched out of the room.

Stung, Isabel sat on, rolling breadcrumbs on the tablecloth until Kitty came in to clear the table. Seeing Isabel still seated, she began to back out. 'Please, don't mind me.' Isabel gestured to Kitty to continue. She got up and stared into the fire, then sighed deeply.

'I hope you enjoy your trip to the dressmaker, miss,' Kitty said. 'I hear she's the best in the town.'

'Thank you, Kitty.' Isabel gave her a smile as she left the room. Such a fuss about the dressmaker. Everyone in the house, from her aunt to the servants, seemed to view this as quite the most exciting outing. Did so little of interest happen in their lives?

At least, as Isabel discovered, the carriage ride afforded the chance for another glimpse of the town, still trapped under gloomy skies. They took the road down towards the harbour, then back up past the rows of splendid houses before turning into the narrow streets and coming to a halt behind a discreet shop façade, with a cobbler and a greengrocer as its neighbours.

Isabel stood on the pavement while her aunt spoke briefly to the coachman. Then they entered through a door that led directly into a room housing a large wooden counter with rows of narrow drawers beneath and shelves behind, stacked with rolls and folded lengths of fabric. Isabel felt a faint stirring of interest at the sight.

A woman with glossy brown hair and a striking figure was writing in a ledger on the counter as they entered. 'Mrs Crawford. And this must be Miss Cavendish. I'm delighted to see you both.' She gave them a warm smile.

59

'Isabella, this is Mrs Symonds,' Aunt Sophia said. 'The cleverest dressmaker in town. She can make any woman look spectacular.'

Isabel was just thinking that Mrs Symonds hadn't done her aunt any favours when she heard her say, 'One day I hope to persuade you to let me make you a dress, Mrs Crawford.'

'My dressmaker in London is so particular, Mrs Symonds. If word should get back to her that I had used someone else . . .' Aunt Sophia threw up her hands in horror.

Mrs Symonds laughed. 'Well, it will be a pleasure to make something for your niece. She has the perfect figure for today's fashions — tall and elegant. And I've just received a delivery of some of the latest fabrics, from London and France, so you will have plenty of choice.'

She ushered Isabel and her aunt into the back room, which was clearly where she worked. A hanger displayed a finished dress while another was laid over a small table. A folding screen stood in a corner, away from the window, where a young girl sat stitching a lace trim to the puffed sleeves of another gown.

'This is my daughter, Grace,' the dressmaker said. 'She has nimble fingers and very neat stitches. She does a good deal of the fine work, to save my eyes. Now, Miss Cavendish, if you'd like to step behind the screen, I'll take some measurements and we can make a start.'

Two hours later, Isabel had a headache but her aunt professed herself delighted. Mrs Symonds said that, due to it being the quietest time of the year for her, she could make one dress immediately and the rest of the order over the following two weeks. Aunt Sophia had ordered three dresses for visiting, two dresses for use at home, and one evening dress. She had hesitated over the latter but decided that, since so few people were in town, it was unlikely Isabel would need more than one.

'We will be very busy by April,' the dressmaker warned, 'so if you decide you need another let me know as soon as you can.'

She had declared that stronger colours were now fashionable in

London, suggesting a shade or two darker than the usual pastels for the day dresses, which were to be made in lavender, green and primrose muslin. The evening dress was in a blue-grey French silk, with both Aunt Sophia and Mrs Symonds exclaiming how well the shade enhanced the colour of Isabel's eyes.

The other two dresses were in sprigged muslins in different colours. By then Isabel was thoroughly bored and stood gazing out of the window while her aunt and the dressmaker held the fabrics up against her and debated over the best choice. She dropped her eyes to catch Grace looking at her, amused. The girl gave her a shy smile and bent to her work again. She was very like her mother, Isabel thought, with the same dark eyes, but her hair was mid-brown. It was too soon to tell whether she would be as striking as Mrs Symonds.

'How is Mr Symonds?' her aunt asked, as the dressmaker wrote up their account.

'Very well, thank you. All the building work here is keeping him so busy that I hardly see him. He's called here and there by his father to advise on the stone, then has to travel to buy it. Since we moved from Margate, Grace and I are left very much to our own devices.' She looked across at her daughter and smiled. 'I'll let you know as soon as the first dress is finished. We will do a final fitting and I can use that to guide me when making the others.'

The carriage was waiting outside and Isabel sank gratefully into her seat. She had no idea that standing up could prove so tiring.

'We still have shoes to buy,' her aunt said thoughtfully, looking at the cobbler's shop as the carriage moved away. 'And a chemise or two, and petticoats. But there's no need to trouble Mrs Symonds with those.' Seeing Isabel's expression, she laughed. 'And there's no need to do anything else today. I will write to your father and keep him apprised of the account.' Mrs Crawford sat back in her seat opposite Isabel and smiled with satisfaction at what they had achieved.

CHAPTER EIGHT

Aunt Sophia insisted that Isabel should be confined to the house until she was well enough attired to be seen in public.

'You must make a good first impression,' she stated firmly. 'Don't imagine that, since it is the quiet season here, you can go about unnoticed. The quieter it is, the more people will seize upon anything to gossip about. I know you will attract much attention. I want it to be for the right reasons.'

Isabel had little idea what she was talking about. It irked her to be kept indoors, especially as the gloomy, damp weather had given way to bright sunshine, although accompanied by brisk winds.

Two days after the visit to the dressmaker, Aunt Sophia and her daughters stepped out for an afternoon walk. Isabel watched them enviously from the oriel window, and laughed as she saw them clutch their bonnets with one hand and attempt to hold down their flapping skirts with the other as they felt the full force of the wind. Flopping disconsolately onto a chair by the fire, she picked up a journal Rebecca had discarded there. She flipped through pages filled with fashion plates, then sighed and set it aside. It held little interest for her.

The doorbell jangled and she heard Kitty's footsteps in the hall. She supposed her aunt and cousins had returned early, beaten back by the gale. It was the kind of weather that exhilarated her back in Marston. She would have been striding out across the fields, relishing the icy sting on her cheeks even as she struggled to keep her hair secured by its pins.

Kitty knocked on the door and came in. 'Please, miss, it's the dressmaker, Mrs Symonds. Will you see her, since Mrs Crawford isn't here?'

'Of course.' Isabel leaped to her feet, delighted by the diversion. Mrs Symonds divested herself of her bonnet, handing it to Kitty, then came into the drawing room bearing a long box.

'Good afternoon, Miss Cavendish. I'm sorry not to find your aunt at home but, since this is for you . . .' she held out the box '. . . I hope it might be convenient for you to try it on. It would mean I could get on with making the rest of the dresses, once I'm assured of the fit. I'm sure you are impatient to see them.'

'Oh, indeed I am,' Isabel said. She didn't add, 'But only because I'm eager to escape the confines of the house.'

She took the box and rested it on the sofa, raising the lid to reveal the green dress, neatly folded into a nest of tissue paper. She lifted it free and surprised herself by exclaiming, 'Why, it's beautiful.'

Indeed it was. The colour was that of the sea glimpsed from Marston on a summer's day, she decided: pale green with a hint of blue. The draped fabric fell from the bodice, its seam bound with a satin ribbon, the binding repeated on the narrow cuffs of the puffed sleeves.

'If you could try it on, then I can see what adjustments need to be made.' Mrs Symonds was looking at her expectantly.

Isabel seized the dress and took it to the door.

'You don't want to call your maid?' The dressmaker appeared mildly surprised.

'No. Should I?' Isabel stopped, her hand on the door knob. 'I know well enough how to dress myself.'

Mrs Symonds smiled. 'I can see you are a capable young lady.'

Isabel, puzzled, hurried upstairs.

She returned a few minutes later, delighted at what she had seen in the glass in her aunt's bedroom.

'I'll keep it on,' she declared. 'Thank you so much.'

The dressmaker shook her head. 'I can see one or two little

alterations I need to make,' she said. She turned Isabel to face her, then frowned as she surveyed the garment. 'A little lift on the shoulders, I feel. And an adjustment to the hem.'

Isabel was crushed. 'I can't leave the house until I have something suitable to wear.'

'Then you shall have it first thing tomorrow morning,' Mrs Symonds promised. 'Grace will deliver it to you. And I will make a start on a morning dress.'

Isabel sighed and, dejected, began to make her way back up the stairs just as her aunt and cousins came in through the front door.

'Isabella!' Aunt Sophia exclaimed. 'How lovely you look. Is Mrs Symonds here?' She was divesting herself of her bonnet and pelisse as she spoke, handing them to Kitty. She moved through to the drawing room to speak to the dressmaker and Isabel began to mount the stairs again.

'You look beautiful,' Amelia said.

Isabel turned to thank her and saw Rebecca's expression. She was glaring at her and muttered something that sounded like 'Ridiculous fuss,' before following her mother.

When Isabel came back downstairs to return the dress to Mrs Symonds, Rebecca was playing the piano loudly, making conversation difficult. The dressmaker expertly folded the dress back into the box and replaced the lid. 'It will be with you tomorrow,' she said.

Isabel watched from the window as she walked away down the street towards the sea. She felt a pang of envy. Mrs Symonds was free to come and go as she pleased, and was held in high esteem by the ladies of Ramsgate. Yet it was considered a far finer thing to be a prisoner here, as she was, in a comfortable house with servants and a pianoforte.

Aunt Sophia was at her side. 'Once you have your dress, we will be able to go out and order all the other things you need. Shoes, bonnets, petticoats . . .' She clapped her hands and beamed. 'I declare, it is quite as much fun as shopping for myself.'

CHAPTER NINE

The following days tested Isabel's patience for, as her aunt had suggested, they consisted of visits to the cobbler, the milliner and further trips to Mrs Symonds. Grace had been prevailed upon to make the necessary chemises and petticoats so Isabel now had the green dress and a pair of boots in the softest leather, as well as a bonnet in cream-coloured linen, chosen to be suitable to wear with all three of her day dresses. Aunt Sophia had also insisted on several pairs of gloves, both long and short, and Kitty was now instructed to massage oils and creams nightly into Isabel's hands.

'You have the hands of a servant girl,' Aunt Sophia had declared, in front of Kitty, who had pursed her lips and all but pinched Isabel's skin as she massaged.

All of that was a small price to pay, Isabel supposed, for being able to walk out in Ramsgate at last. The good weather had held and she had finally been able to see for herself the great stretch of coastline, the towering cliffs, and the teeming life of the harbour. She had delighted in these walks, marvelling at how different the town was from the countryside she was used to. She was less pleased by their destinations. Every afternoon involved a visit, mostly to take tea and endure polite conversation, while mothers and their daughters appraised Isabel. She found it exceedingly dull, but had adopted the practice of speaking as little as possible, smiling sweetly and concentrating hard on the clock on the mantelpiece as its hands crept round the face in fulfilment of an hour's duty. This was far preferable, though, to receiving visitors at the house in the

Plains of Waterloo. This was always a consequence of paying a visit elsewhere, and consisted of more polite conversation with very little of interest to discuss since they had all met so recently.

After a fortnight of this, Isabel was delighted to hear that an evening entertainment was to be arranged in honour of Sir Charles Coates, who was making an unexpected visit to the town. Isabel was curious to know who he was and why he was coming to Ramsgate in February. She had learned enough over the past few weeks to realise that no one of any importance arrived in Ramsgate much before May.

'I believe he's here on the King's business. To make arrangements for a sea journey from the harbour, or something of that nature.' Aunt Sophia wasn't greatly interested in the detail. 'What's more important is that his son will be with him, along with all manner of other young men – the sons of the families you have met, who will be making the journey from London.' She clapped her hands in excitement. 'How fortunate that your dresses are ready. It's the perfect opportunity for you to make an impression, my dear. Your father has done nothing about putting you in society and this will be your very first formal appearance.'

Rebecca was scowling and Isabel felt some sympathy. Her aunt should have been concentrating on her own daughter's prospects, rather than her niece's. But there was little time to consider this further. Her aunt had already discovered that Isabel had never learned to dance and had spoken of arranging lessons with a dancing master. Now she flew into a flurry of anxiety, insisting Isabel must learn before the evening of the entertainment.

'We will have to teach you ourselves,' she decided. 'There simply isn't time to arrange lessons. Rebecca can play the piano and you can dance with Amelia.'

'But the invitation says "An evening's entertainment", Mama,' Rebecca protested. 'Surely there won't be dancing, too.'

'With so few families here at present, I wouldn't be at all surprised if there was informal dancing after supper.' Aunt Sophia was not to be deterred and so, as winter weather had returned, bringing snow flurries on an icy wind from the north, the afternoons were spent in dance practice.

This proved to be less straightforward than Aunt Sophia had anticipated. Since it was important that Isabel learn the steps, Amelia had to play the part of the man. She was not only shorter than her cousin, but found it hard to adjust to her new role in the dance, leading to several collisions. Rebecca kept dissolving into laughter at the piano, until her mother lost patience.

'Amelia, take your sister's place at the piano. Rebecca, let us see whether you are any better suited to this.'

Rebecca gripped Isabel's hand, a mulish expression on her face, but she made a better job of it and, after half an hour, Isabel declared herself proficient enough to stop. In fact, she was uncomfortably warm, the fire in the sitting room having been banked up against the chill outside. Rebecca, too, was rather red in the face, her curls clinging damply to her forehead. Amelia, who had stumbled her way through the musical accompaniment, was only too pleased to close the lid on the keys.

'We will try this again tomorrow afternoon,' Aunt Sophia said. 'Rebecca, you must practise the piano in the morning, for I feel sure Mrs Tremaine will invite you to play during the entertainment.'

The flush colouring Rebecca's cheeks intensified and Isabel thought she caught Amelia looking at her sister. That night, as they made ready for bed, she asked Amelia whether Rebecca was thought of as a particularly good musician.

'Not really,' Amelia confided, as she climbed into bed, 'but Mama would like her to make a match with Giles Tremaine, the son of the house where the entertainment will be held. I expect he will be there. And I know Rebecca likes him very much.'

With that, Amelia turned on her side and was asleep in seconds. Isabel lay on her back, staring at the dark ceiling, and wondered what lay in store.

CHAPTER TEN

On a chilly evening at the end of February, Isabel and the Crawfords assembled in the hall, as Kitty handed them their wraps. Isabel cast a judgemental eye over her companions and found Aunt Sophia overdressed, as usual, Amelia sweetly pretty and Rebecca trying too hard. Her colour was high and she was wearing a feather confection in her hair that forced her to hold her head at an uncomfortable angle.

Aunt Sophia beamed. 'What a marvellous treat to have such an occasion before the season has even begun. I can hear the carriage – do be careful of your gowns. The ground is wet outside.'

Her warning was aimed at Isabel, unused to managing fine clothing. Impatient by nature, she found it hard not to attempt to stride out, but her dress didn't allow it. She tiptoed cautiously to the carriage, trying to avoid splashing her dress. She felt awkward, dressed in her finery, and hoped she could fade into the background. On arrival at Mrs Tremaine's residence, a grand, pillared house overlooking the sea, they had to join a queue to leave their outer garments before they could enter the ballroom where the entertainment would take place. Shrugging off her wrap in preparation to hand it over, she managed to drop a glove, unnoticed. She had just shuffled forward a few steps in the throng, gazing around the entrance hall at the high ceiling, the ornate plasterwork and the sweep of the staircase up to the first floor, when a voice murmured in her ear, 'Excuse me, I believe you may have lost this?'

She turned to find herself face to face with a young man a little taller than herself. He had dark curly hair and deep brown eyes, which were clearly appraising her. He was holding out the glove she didn't know she had dropped.

A smile lifted the corners of his mouth as he said, 'I don't believe I've had the pleasure of your acquaintance?'

Aunt Sophia turned her head sharply and said, 'This is Miss Isabella Cavendish. And you are?'

But there was a sudden movement forward and Isabella found herself beside her aunt, who took a firm grip on her arm.

'You mustn't strike up a conversation with young men in that way,' she hissed in her ear. 'You must wait to be introduced.'

Isabel glanced over her shoulder but the young man was nowhere to be seen.

Their wraps safely stowed away, the guests were invited to sit down on gilt-backed chairs, laid out in rows in the ballroom. Isabel was sure they would be monstrously uncomfortable.

And so it proved, as they sat through one rendition after another, performed by every young woman staying in the town and keen to show off her prowess. There was singing with a piano accompanist, piano playing with no singing, and piano playing with vocal accompaniment by the pianist. Isabel had to stifle a yawn on more than one occasion but Aunt Sophia smiled throughout and clapped enthusiastically, particularly before and after Rebecca took her turn at the piano. Isabel was mesmerised by the way the feathers in her cousin's hair trembled and shook in time to the music. She would have liked to see whether she could spot the young man she had encountered earlier but all the men were clustered at the back, standing behind the chairs, and she couldn't look at them without craning her neck and earning a reprimand from her aunt.

After what felt like an interminable hour, Mrs Tremaine rose from her seat in the front row and turned to the assembled company. 'I know you will join me in thanking all the young ladies who have entertained us so delightfully, and in welcoming our honoured guest, Sir Charles Coates. We hope his business in the town has been conducted to his satisfaction and that we can, perhaps, entice him to return in the summer.'

Isabel at last felt able to look to the back of the room, for the ladies had all turned in their chairs and were clapping vigorously. A group of men dressed in cream trousers and brocade waistcoats in a variety of shades, topped by sober-coloured jackets, lounged against the wall, although they stood a little straighter when they saw all eyes upon them. Standing in front of them was an older man, whom Isabel took to be Sir Charles. At his side stood the young man who had addressed her earlier. Her heart skipped a beat as she saw his gaze fixed upon her, and her colour rose.

Their hostess was speaking again. 'Supper is served in the dining room. Afterwards, I do hope you will stay to enjoy some dancing.'

Sir Charles stepped forward and took Mrs Tremaine's arm and she led the way through a set of double doors at the side of the room, as a swell of chatter rose from the audience.

'How fortunate you have been practising your steps, Isabella,' her aunt said, as they rose to their feet. 'There are many young men here and I feel sure you will be in demand. Now, we must go and congratulate Rebecca.'

Once more, Isabel found herself in her aunt's firm grip as they made their way into the dining room, where a long table draped in a white cloth was laden with plates of roast fowl, lobsters, dishes of shellfish, raised pies, bowls heaped with potatoes and vegetables. A separate table to the side bore jellies, pineapple, oranges, sweet cakes and biscuits, while at yet another table, Mrs Tremaine's servants were dispensing punch. Isabel hoped to catch sight of the young man, but he was nowhere to be seen. Had he left already? she wondered, surprised at herself for caring so much.

Isabel had been looking forward to supper throughout the recital, but now found her appetite had fled. A feeling of dread, rising from the pit of her stomach, had replaced it. Dancing had been entertaining enough in the privacy of the drawing room, with her aunt and cousins for company. To undertake such a thing for the first time in front of so many people, with a complete stranger as a partner, was a different matter entirely.

Chapter Eleven

Once those inclined to take advantage of the fine supper provided by Mrs Tremaine had eaten their fill, the guests began to drift back into the ballroom, where the chairs had been cleared to the edges of the room to make ready for the dancing.

Aunt Sophia immediately took charge of four chairs in a prominent position and seated her party, Rebecca and Amelia to her right, Isabel to the left.

'Sit up straight and smile,' she hissed in Isabel's ear, as the young men sauntered past. Isabel studied their faces but there was still no sign of the handsome young man who had spoken to her. One young gentleman, however, detached himself from the group and approached to address Aunt Sophia.

'Giles!' she exclaimed. 'I'm delighted to see you again. You remember Rebecca, of course.' She turned to smile at her eldest. 'I told her I felt sure you would come down for your mama's party.'

The young man made a bow as he said, 'Mrs Crawford, the Misses Crawford. But I don't believe I've had the pleasure of this young lady's acquaintance.' He fixed his gaze on Isabel.

'Miss Isabella Cavendish, a country cousin. Giles Tremaine.' Her aunt was keen to turn Giles's attention back to her own daughters, Isabel thought. Was he the one Amelia had spoken of as Rebecca's hoped-for intended?

Giles, however, was regarding Isabel with undisguised admiration. She flushed, but returned his gaze, taking the chance to give him a frank appraisal. His blond hair flopped and curled untidily over his collar, which bulged with the effort of restraining the folds of flesh at his neck. His waistcoat button was struggling, too, appearing to be in imminent danger of bursting open. Giles Tremaine had the appearance of a man who enjoyed partaking of the finer things in life. He reminded Isabel of one of the fat pink pigs in her father's fields, and she had to bite her lip to restrain the urge to giggle.

'I hope I might engage you for the first dance, Miss Cavendish.'

To her horror, he was holding out his hand to her. Isabel heard her aunt's sharp intake of breath and saw her put a hand on Rebecca's arm, before she said, 'Isabella would be honoured, I'm sure.'

Isabel sat as if frozen. The small band of musicians had begun to play and couples were already taking to the floor. Giles's expectant expression had changed to a frown and Aunt Sophia turned to glare at her.

'I ... I'm really not feeling well,' she said. 'I hope you will excuse me.'

'Nonsense!' her aunt said firmly. 'It will do you good to take a turn around the dance floor. Helps the digestion.'

A reluctant Isabel was forced to rise to her feet and allow herself to be led to join the other couples already in position. She endured an agony of embarrassment as she struggled to remember the steps she had practised only the day before. She trembled with nerves and one mistake led to another as Giles did his best to guide her. She registered the expressions on the faces of her aunt and cousins as the dance brought them within reach. Amelia was giggling, and Rebecca's lips were pursed, her brows drawn together in a frown. Aunt Sophia was looking at her lap, as though she couldn't bear to watch.

Giles gallantly escorted her back to her chair. 'I expect you don't have much opportunity to dance in the country,' he said kindly.

Isabel gave him a weak smile. Her legs were shaky and she let out a shuddering sigh of relief that her ordeal was over. Giles had moved on to ask Rebecca to partner him for the next dance. Her cousin shot her a look of triumph as she took to the floor, but Isabel couldn't help but notice that each time the couple passed by, Giles sought her out to smile at her.

'Excuse me,' Isabel murmured to her aunt. 'I'm finding it rather warm. I think I'll take the air.'

Her aunt nodded, distracted by her delight in seeing Rebecca dance with Giles. Isabel kept her head down and made her way back to the dining room, where she had noticed two sets of double doors leading out onto the balconies that were such a feature of the front of the property.

Little knots of mostly older people, uninterested in the dancing, were gathered in the room. Isabel noticed Sir Charles conversing with their hostess as she turned the brass knob on one of the doors and stepped out. The wind struck her immediately and she struggled to close the door behind her. It took less than half a minute for her to begin to shiver – the wind off the sea was really very chilly. She would need to find somewhere else to take refuge from the party.

As she turned to go back inside, the door opened and a figure stepped out. Isabel's heart skipped a beat as she recognised the young man who had picked up her glove.

'You're not dancing?' he asked.

'I'm a terrible dancer,' Isabel confessed. 'I've just trampled all over Giles Tremaine's toes and now I'm hiding to avoid inflicting pain on anyone else.'

The young man gave a snort of laughter. 'A young woman who isn't bound by social convention. How very refreshing.'

Isabel had no idea what he was talking about but she was keen to detain him, so she said, 'You aren't dancing, either?'

'No, I was staying by my father's side, tasked by his doctor to make sure he doesn't drink too much red wine or port.' Seeing Isabel's questioning look, he added, 'He suffers from gout, and his temper during an attack is quite frightful.'

'Then I am guessing you must be Sir Charles Coates's son?' Isabel hazarded, having seen them standing together earlier.

'I do apologise – how rude of me not to introduce myself. Yes, I'm Daniel Coates, the youngest son.' Daniel swept her a bow. 'And you are Isabella Cavendish, who looks as though she might freeze to death any minute now. Shall we go back inside?'

Isabel's teeth were chattering, but she was reluctant to return to the dance floor, even if there was the prospect of dancing with Daniel Coates. Especially if there was the prospect of dancing with him, she thought in horror. She wouldn't like to disgrace herself with such a partner.

'Don't worry,' Daniel said, his hand on the balcony door. 'I won't force you to return to the ballroom. I know somewhere we can talk in private. I have a fancy to learn more about you, Isabella Cavendish.'

CHAPTER TWELVE

Daniel ushered her back into the dining room, the cold draught that accompanied them earning startled glances from the company there. They soon returned to their conversations, although Isabel was sure she could feel Sir Charles Coates's eyes upon them as Daniel guided her into the corridor between the two rooms, before taking a sharp right.

'Where are we going?' Isabel was both intrigued and alarmed.

'I spent many summers here when I was a child, as Giles Tremaine's playmate. I know the house like the back of my hand.'

Daniel opened a door and stepped aside with a flourish to invite Isabel inside. It was a small room, lit by lamps, the walls lined from floor to ceiling with books. The only visible wall, over the fireplace where a fire burned low in the grate, was painted a deep red. Daniel picked up the tongs in the brass coal bucket on the hearth and added fuel to the fire.

'Why don't you sit here?' he said, pointing to one of a pair of leather armchairs that faced each other in front of the fire.

Isabel sat down, crossing her arms and hugging them.

Daniel frowned and quickly removed his jacket, handing it to her. 'There, put that around your shoulders. I'm quite warm.'

Isabel snuggled into the warmth of the jacket. It gave her a little thrill that it had so recently been wrapped around Daniel Coates, a young man she was finding more than intriguing. But he was speaking again and she needed to concentrate on what he was saying.

'So, Isabella Cavendish, why have I never seen you before?'

'Please, call me Isabel. Only my aunt chooses to call me Isabella,' Isabel replied, before answering his question. 'This is my first visit to Ramsgate – and my first evening invitation.'

'But I don't believe I have seen you in London,' Daniel persisted. 'I'm sure I would have remembered.'

'London!' Isabel burst out laughing. 'I've never been there. Ramsgate is the furthest I've travelled. I live in the countryside a few miles from here, with my father.'

'That's a great shame,' Daniel said. 'You would like it in London, I'm sure.'

'Not if there is too much dancing,' Isabel said. She was still smarting from the humiliation of her first attempt.

'And what do you do in the country?' Daniel asked. 'Do you paint? Ride?' He seemed at a loss for what else to suggest.

'Neither of those.' Isabel made a wry face. 'Nor do I play the pianoforte or do fine needlework. I walk in the fields, read, help on the farm.' She shrugged. 'My father has sent me to stay with his sister to learn how to be a young lady.'

Daniel's lips twitched. 'I can see you have a great deal to learn, and not only about dancing.' Seeing Isabel's expression, he added hastily, 'I've never met a young woman such as you – I wouldn't have you anything other than you are.'

He hesitated, then asked, 'And your mother? She didn't see fit to provide you with the accomplishments your father believes you lack?'

'She left when I was small.' Keen to discourage this line of questioning, Isabel said, 'But tell me about yourself. You are here with your father and you said you are the youngest son. Where is the rest of your family?'

'Mama is in our London house with my sisters,' Daniel replied. 'I accompany my father on visits such as these. My eldest brother, Edward, is in Dorset with his wife, at our country estate. My other brother, James, is in London.'

Isabel began to wish she had made more of her own background. She'd stopped short of telling Daniel about her father's brewery and the donkey wheel, but could she have described Marston Grange as their family seat? On balance, she thought not.

'Will you stay long in Ramsgate?' she asked. It would make social engagements a great deal more tolerable if he would be there.

Daniel shrugged. 'That will depend on my father.'

There was a silence while they gazed into the fire. Isabel had a great many questions she longed to ask him, not least whether he had a sweetheart in London, but she couldn't think how to begin. She became aware of the distant sound of clapping, as the clock on the mantelpiece struck twelve.

'I have a feeling the dancing will be at an end,' she said, jumping to her feet. 'My aunt will be looking for me.'

Even as she spoke, Isabel had a premonition that her absence would not have been well received by Aunt Sophia. She hurriedly removed Daniel's jacket from her shoulders and handed it back to him.

'Thank you,' she said. 'I'm perfectly warm now.'

At that moment, the library door swung open, to reveal Rebecca and Amelia framed in the doorway.

'There you are, Isabella!' Rebecca's eyebrows had almost vanished into the curls framing her forehead.

Isabel, although conscious of trouble ahead, was seized with an urge to laugh but managed to say, 'Have you been looking for me? Daniel was just showing me the library.'

She couldn't help but notice that Daniel, putting his jacket back on, was the focus of her cousins' gaze.

'Rebecca and Amelia Crawford, my cousins,' Isabel said, performing the introductions. 'And this is Daniel Coates, Sir Charles's son.'

'Mr Coates.' Rebecca gave him a brief nod. 'Isabella, come with us.'

Isabel followed her cousins to the door. With two strides, Daniel caught her up.

'I very much hope to see you again, Isabel Cavendish,' he whispered in her ear. She could still feel his breath on her neck, the nearness of his lips, as she followed her cousins down the panelled corridor and into the ballroom.

The musicians were packing away their instruments as the three girls entered the room. Aunt Sophia was in conversation with another lady, but broke off and came over as soon as she saw Isabel. 'Where have you been?' she demanded.

Rebecca answered before Isabel could speak. 'She was in the library, alone with the boy who picked up her glove.'

'That was Daniel Coates, Sir Charles Coates's son,' Isabel said hastily. She hoped the name would impress her aunt enough to divert some of the storm she could see building. 'He used to play here as a child with Giles Tremaine, and was keen to show me around.'

'It is most unseemly to spend time alone with a young man, unchaperoned.' Aunt Sophia was tight-lipped. 'Have you no sense, Isabella? If anyone other than Rebecca or Amelia had witnessed this your reputation would be in tatters.' She glanced around the room. 'We should leave at once.'

She ushered all three girls before her, making a perfunctory farewell to their hostess as they passed. Rebecca protested that she wished to speak to Giles before they left but Aunt Sophia would have none of it.

They donned their wraps on the front step as their carriage pulled forward from all the others lined up in the street. Aunt Sophia all but pushed her daughters and Isabel into it.

'Was a woman ever so afflicted?' she exclaimed, as the horses picked up their pace and the crowds outside the house fell away behind them. 'If only Mr Crawford was here. He would know what to do. Isabella, it seems you lack even a modicum of understanding of how to behave in public. I can only hope you are not disgraced before the season has even begun.'

She fell back into her seat and clutched at the pearls round her neck, while Isabel adopted a mulish expression. She longed to turn in her seat and try to catch a last glimpse of the crowd – and, perhaps, Daniel.

CHAPTER THIRTEEN

Kitty had stayed up to welcome the party back to the house. She helped them with their wraps and gloves, trying to stifle a yawn.

'Did you have an enjoyable evening?' she asked, earning a short answer from Aunt Sophia.

'Some of us enjoyed themselves rather too much,' she said, glaring at Isabel. 'Kitty, we will have our chocolate at the usual hour tomorrow. Several gentlemen are in town and I expect we will have callers.'

Isabel was puzzled by her words. As she and Amelia undressed and readied themselves for bed, donning nightgowns and taking turns in front of the glass to comb out their hair, she asked her cousin, 'What did your mother mean by gentlemen callers being expected in the morning?'

Amelia yawned. 'After an entertainment, especially one with dancing, it's customary for young men to come and pay respects to families with young ladies who may have caught their eye. Mama is expecting Giles Tremaine will pay a visit. I imagine Rebecca is hoping for the same.'

Amelia fell asleep the moment her head touched the pillow, but Isabel lay awake staring at the ceiling. She had wondered how she could see Daniel again. Now it seemed an opportunity had presented itself. Surely he would come to call in the morning. Hearing a distant clock strike twice, she realised such a visit couldn't be many hours away and squeezed her eyes shut in an attempt to force sleep. It felt like only moments later that she opened them with a start, as Kitty drew back the curtains.

'Good morning, Miss Isabel, Miss Amelia.' She deposited a cup of chocolate on Isabel's nightstand with a lack of ceremony, so that the liquid slopped over the edge. Isabel yawned and would happily have fallen back to sleep when the memory of what the day held in store returned to her. Gentlemen visitors. She sat up in bed, hugging her knees to her chest, and thought back to the night before: Daniel's jacket around her shoulders, how handsome he appeared in the firelight, the way his eyes held hers when he spoke.

'What are you smiling at?' Amelia was sitting up, too, and greedily sipping her chocolate. She was still sleepy, her hair tumbling round her shoulders. Isabel had a sudden realisation that she was going to be much prettier than her older sister.

'I was thinking about last night.' Isabel smiled even more widely.

'You're going to be in trouble, you know.' Amelia tipped her cup to encourage the last drops of chocolate into her mouth. 'Mama will have a lot to say. There'll probably be a scandal, like the one with your mother.'

Isabel's smile vanished abruptly. She supposed she must accept a scolding from Aunt Sophia, but she didn't like Amelia's reference to her mother.

'Your chocolate is getting cold. If you don't want it, can I have it?' Amelia was already climbing out of bed.

'No.' Isabel scowled and raised the cup to her lips. The thick sweet liquid nearly caused her to gag, but Amelia had annoyed her and she wasn't going to be nice to her. Her annoyance only increased at breakfast when Aunt Sophia chose to give Isabel a dressing-down in front of her daughters.

'I didn't realise I was expected to instruct you in the most basic behaviour expected by polite society,' she said, once she had drunk her chocolate and eaten a large piece of Madeira cake. 'I barely know where to begin,' she added, dabbing her lips with her napkin. 'The first thing to remember is you must never, ever be alone with a young man to whom you are not related. You must be formally introduced to each other, and if you wish to spend time in each other's company, you need a chaperone. If your behaviour last night has been noticed, you are ruined.'

Aunt Sophia had worked herself into quite a state. She stood up abruptly, pushing back her chair with such vehemence that it rocked and threatened to topple.

'Now, go and get dressed, all of you. We need to be prepared for visitors.'

Rebecca gave Isabel a look of triumph and swept out after her mother.

In the room she shared with Amelia, Isabel pulled her dresses off their hangers and laid them on the bed. Should she wear the yellow, green or lavender? She held them up against her, gazing at her reflection in the glass. Definitely lavender – she was tired and the other two colours made her appear even paler. She pinched her cheeks hard and checked her appearance again. A definite improvement. Rebecca had some rouge and, in a fit of generosity, she had allowed Isabel to use a hint of it the previous evening, but it was unlikely she would be so forthcoming today.

All at once, Isabel longed for the freedom of home. The thought of having to dress up for a morning of polite conversation in the drawing room when she could be striding out over the fields was almost too much to bear. She had barely thought of Thomas in days but an image of him sprang to mind, loitering shyly in the courtyard hoping to speak to her. Back in Marston, no one had suggested that it was wrong for them to speak to each other alone – she would have laughed at them if they had.

Kitty ran between the bedrooms, finding lost ribbons and helping Rebecca and Amelia with their hair. Isabel rejected her offer. 'I can do it myself,' she said, twisting her dark curls on top of her head and jabbing a tortoiseshell comb into them to hold them in place.

The sound of the jangling front-door bell sent Kitty hurrying down the stairs.

'I wonder who it is.' Amelia was already out on the landing, peering over the banister.

Isabel had gleaned enough to know that Amelia was unlikely to receive gentleman callers while she had an unmarried sister only a little older than herself, but she appeared genuinely excited.

'We must hurry,' she urged Isabel. 'Rebecca and Mama are downstairs already.'

Isabel trailed after her. A glance outside at the glorious sunshine only strengthened her desire to be free of all this nonsense. Amelia entered the room first and, as Isabel followed her, the gentleman sitting on the sofa leaped to his feet.

'Miss Cavendish. I am delighted to find you at home. I most especially wished to see you this morning.' It was Giles Tremaine, beaming.

Isabel stared at him. Where else did he expect her to be? He was pasty-faced, with pouchy eyes – the result of a late night, perhaps. She took in the thunderous expression on Aunt Sophia's face, and the pure rage on Rebecca's. She considered – it was tempting to encourage Giles, just for the satisfaction of annoying Rebecca. But what of Daniel? She couldn't risk jeopardising a chance to get to know him better. Would he visit them that morning, too?

CHAPTER FOURTEEN

Isabel seated herself as far as possible from Giles, who was still beaming at her.

'I trust you enjoyed the evening?'

The wretched man was directly addressing her. She remembered her manners just in time. It had been his mother's party, after all.

'It was most pleasant. We all enjoyed it.' Isabel tried to include her aunt and cousins in the conversation. 'You have a beautiful house. Quite perfect for the occasion.'

'I still feel honoured that you chose me to be your first-ever dance partner.' Giles was leaning forward, directing all of his attention to Isabel.

She frowned. Where had he come by such an idea? As she remembered it, her aunt had forced her to partner him. And who had told him she had never danced before? Was it Rebecca or her aunt? She glanced at her aunt to see her reaction but looked quickly away when she saw her pinched lips and barely suppressed look of displeasure.

Giles pressed on: 'I shall ask Mother to arrange a ball, so that we will have the chance to dance together once more.'

Isabel could bear it no longer: the man was a fool. She blurted out, 'Is Sir Charles still with you? And his son?'

Giles was so delighted to have her full attention that he failed to register the import of her words, although Aunt Sophia gave her a sharp look.

'He returned to London directly after breakfast, saying his business was successfully concluded.'

'And his son?' Isabel prompted.

Giles seemed mildly surprised. 'Daniel? I didn't know you knew him. He's gone with his father.'

A crushing wave of disappointment swept over Isabel. She was fortunate that Aunt Sophia took control and directed Giles's attention to the piece of needlework Rebecca was working on. She had no wish to speak another word to the man and gave monosyllabic answers to his further attempts to draw her into the conversation. She feared, though, that her frostiness only served to enchant him further. When he took his leave at the end of an hour that felt several times longer, he grasped her hand warmly and bent to kiss it as she recoiled.

'You must all pay a visit to us before I return to London. Perhaps tomorrow? I will mention it to Mother, along with my idea for a ball.'

He was wreathed in smiles as Kitty showed him out. Silence reigned in the drawing room until the front door had closed behind him and he was safely away.

'Isabella, your manners require serious improvement.' Aunt Sophia glared at her.

'But ...' Isabel was about to make a hasty reply then collected herself. 'I'm sorry, Aunt. I don't wish to encourage him, because I know Rebecca likes him. I'm thinking only of her.'

She wanted to add that she found Giles repulsive but held back. Surely her aunt would appreciate her apparent concern for her cousin.

Aunt Sophia, though, had a speculative gleam in her eye.

'Your father is keen for you to marry well, Isabella. You could hardly do better than Giles Tremaine. The family is by far the wealthiest in town.'

Isabel was shocked by her aunt's words and, judging by Rebecca's face, they had found no favour with her daughter, either. How could her aunt seek to further Isabel's interests against those of Rebecca?

Her aunt was already making plans. 'We will visit tomorrow,

whether or not Mrs Tremaine sends an invitation. Giles has invited us, and we can use the excuse of thanking her for her hospitality. You are extremely fortunate, Isabella. Giles's words suggest that your indiscretion has either gone unnoticed or been overlooked.'

Rebecca got to her feet, her cheeks bright red. Clutching a handkerchief, she ran from the room, banging the door behind her.

'I'm not going,' Isabel stated. 'I have absolutely no interest in Giles Tremaine. I can't bear him,' she all but shouted, getting to her feet, too. She left the room, close to tears as a result of her disappointment at hearing of Daniel's departure.

She flung herself onto her bed and raged at the stupidity of it all. Her aunt thought Giles a great catch, when Daniel came from a far wealthier family. And yet she wasn't allowed to have anything to do with him because they hadn't been formally introduced. Tears of rage sprang to her eyes and she cried herself into an exhausted sleep. After some time, she woke with a start, her flushed, damp face buried in the pillow, her hair in disarray and her gown dreadfully creased.

Kitty came into the room, her knock having woken Isabel. 'A letter for you, miss.'

She held out a folded piece of paper and took in the state of Isabel's dress with some dismay. 'Shall I help you change, miss?'

Isabel got to her feet and broke the seal on the letter as Kitty undid the gown, allowing it to fall to the floor. She unfolded the paper and, standing there in her chemise, began to read.

'Put this on, miss, before you get cold.' Kitty was holding out her day dress and, with a sigh, Isabel put aside the letter and allowed herself to be dressed again. She had already all but memorised the few words on the page.

My dear Isabel,

I hope I may address you as such, rather than Miss Cavendish? I feel we already know one another so well, yet even so I long to see you again. Alas, I must return to London with my father so I send you

these words in great haste. I will return and, when I do, you will be
the first person I seek out.
  Yours respectfully,
  Daniel Coates

It was bittersweet – an expression of admiration, at the very least, but with no firm prospect of another meeting. Just the tantalising promise of something to come, on a date as yet unknown.

'Did my aunt see this arrive?' Isabel was seized with worry as to what she would say. She would surely demand to know what the letter contained.

'No, miss. She was supervising Miss Amelia's piano practice. I don't think she heard the doorbell.'

'I see.' A look passed between Isabel and Kitty. 'Thank you, Kitty. I would be grateful if you didn't mention it to her. And if anything else should arrive, if you could bring it straight to me?'

Kitty bobbed her head and left the room. Isabel read the letter once more and slid it beneath her mattress. Perhaps it would be as well to encourage Giles Tremaine in his wish to hold a ball, in the hope that his good friend Daniel Coates would be invited, too.

CHAPTER FIFTEEN

By breakfast time the following day, Aunt Sophia had managed to persuade Rebecca and Isabel to pay a visit to the Tremaines'. Isabel, her spirits restored by Daniel's note, was happy to encourage Giles in his plan to hold a ball, as long as she could find a way to persuade him to pay court to Rebecca instead of to herself. She convinced herself he wouldn't stay long in Ramsgate and was bound to return to London soon. It would give her time to plan how to be rid of his attentions.

Rebecca's decision to visit was, perhaps, due to a desire to fight back and win Giles for herself. By the time they assembled in the hall, she was looking particularly well, dressed in one of her more restrained gowns, her hair very prettily curled. This was not her own inclination, however. Isabel had taken Kitty into her confidence and asked her to make sure Miss Rebecca did not go out in one of her more garish dresses, or wear elaborate feathers in her hair. Isabel hoped this would help to turn Giles's attention back to her cousin. Complicity in this plan had earned Kitty a scolding from Rebecca, who was angry at being told that her favourite dress wasn't in a fit state to wear, due to the washerwoman having been delayed that week.

Rebecca, unaware that Isabel was working on her behalf, was still angry with her cousin, as well as her mother, and it was fortunate that the carriage ride to the Tremaine residence was short, for conversation was sparse. Mrs Crawford had intended they should walk there, but it was a foggy morning and she quickly decided that the moisture would ruin their carefully arranged hair.

As they stood on the broad marble steps leading up to the house, Isabel gazed out to sea and tried to marshal her reserves, ready to face another onslaught by Giles. Little could be seen of the water, enveloped as it was in a swirling, coiling mass of grey. It was as though the clouds had come down on their heads, muffling all sound and draining the Crawfords of their colour. She shivered and hoped the Tremaines were at home, for her aunt had sent the carriage away.

At last, the door swung open and they were admitted. A maid directed them to a sitting room at the back of the house, where a fire crackled in the grate and double doors led out into a courtyard. Isabel perched on a chair and began to remove her gloves, until Aunt Sophia frowned at her. They sat in silence, the loud ticking of the clock on the mantel the only sound in the room, although Isabel could discern doors banging and scurrying footsteps elsewhere in the house. She became more and more uncomfortable as time passed. She feared their unexpected arrival had found the household still in disarray.

She was about to suggest they should leave, when the door opened and Mrs Tremaine entered, her maid standing back and waiting by the door.

'What a delightful surprise.' Mrs Tremaine addressed Aunt Sophia. She was in a dark blue silk gown, unusual when fashion still favoured pale colours, but it complemented her silvery grey hair. She was striking, and elegant, Isabel thought.

Aunt Sophia failed to register the edge in their hostess's voice. 'It was very kind of Giles to invite us,' she said.

Mrs Tremaine's eyebrows rose a little.

'We would, of course, have visited in any case to thank you for your hospitality and the most delightful entertainment when Sir Charles Coates was with you. It quite lifted all our spirits, when the days are so dark and spring seems such a long way off.'

'And thank you for inviting me to play the pianoforte, Mrs Tremaine,' Rebecca spoke up. 'It was a most successful evening.

Giles – Mr Tremaine – mentioned yesterday he hoped to persuade you to hold a ball before too long.'

Mrs Tremaine seated herself carefully on the remaining chair, crossing her ankles. 'So, Giles paid you a visit yesterday,' she said thoughtfully. Her eyes rested on each of them in turn. Isabel was sure her penetrating gaze lingered longest on her.

'I'm afraid Giles has returned to town,' Mrs Tremaine continued. 'He didn't mention a ball, but since you have, I do believe it could be entertaining.' Her eyes rested on Isabel again. 'In May, perhaps, when the visitors return. I will start to put the plans in place. Now, refreshments, I think.' She nodded to the maid by the door, who departed swiftly.

'Miss Cavendish, I understand this is your first visit to Ramsgate?'

Isabel wasn't sure that she liked being singled out for attention. But she did her best to answer Mrs Tremaine's queries about Marston, and the reasons behind her stay with her aunt.

'She has been little out in society,' her aunt interjected. 'Her father felt the influence of her cousins would be useful.'

Mrs Tremaine subjected Isabel to her cool regard once more. 'Indeed, I am sure it will be most beneficial. Rebecca is an accomplished young woman and Isabella would do well to emulate her. I know your father, of course.'

Her abrupt address caught Isabel by surprise.

'You do?'

'Yes. I knew him well when I was young, your mother, too. You are very like her.'

Isabel felt her colour rise and she was grateful that the maid entered at that moment, bearing a tray heavy with cups and two silver pots of chocolate. The subject of her mother didn't arise again after the interruption and the remainder of the allotted hour passed in small-talk, until their carriage was announced. As they filed out, offering thanks to their hostess, Isabel couldn't prevent herself exclaiming, 'I am sure you must have the most beautiful house in Ramsgate, Mrs Tremaine.'

They were standing in the entrance hall, which had its own fireplace, although it did little to warm the splendid space. It was bright despite the gloom outside, due to the glass cupola that shed light all the way from the roof over the great curve of the staircase, which was lined with gilt-framed paintings.

'Thank you, Miss Cavendish.' Mrs Tremaine regarded her with frank blue eyes.

She was a great deal more handsome than her son, Isabel thought. Perhaps he took after his father.

'I gather you enjoyed spending time in the library when you were here. Are you a great reader?'

Isabel barely knew how to respond. She glanced around quickly to make sure her aunt hadn't overheard, but she was busy admiring a rather splendid Chinese vase on a table near the door.

'I . . . yes, I love to read,' Isabel managed to stutter in the end.

'Then you must return and borrow some books. I would be most happy to see you, even if Giles isn't at home.'

'I'm sorry we missed him,' Isabel murmured, thinking it the polite thing to say but hoping it wouldn't lead Mrs Tremaine to believe her to be interested in her son.

Fog still shrouded the carriage on their journey home, and although the Crawfords chattered on, discussing every detail of their visit, Isabel sat in silence. Her lack of understanding of how to conduct herself in society weighed heavily on her and she felt as though her brain, too, was filled with fog. Had Rebecca and Amelia been taught such things at their mother's knee? Back in Marston, she had never been concerned with refined manners. She had no one to ask what she should make of Mrs Tremaine's puzzling remarks, or to confide in about Daniel. Not for the first time, she felt distress at her mother's desertion of her.

Chapter Sixteen

Having given some thought to her situation, Isabel decided she must learn some of the skills apparently so necessary for young women in polite society. She feared that if she was to have any hope of furthering her relationship with Daniel she would need to be accomplished in art, music and needlework, despite his words: 'I wouldn't have you anything other than you are,' he had said in the library. She remembered every detail of their conversation, just the two of them together. It had felt so natural, yet it was apparently entirely wrong. She would have to learn how to be the young lady everyone would have her become, if she wasn't to forfeit her chance of seeing him again.

She reached that conclusion as she lay in bed the morning after the visit to the Tremaines'. It didn't bring her any satisfaction – in fact, she was filled with gloom while she waited for Kitty to bring their morning chocolate. How could she hope to learn these things in such a short time, when Rebecca and Amelia had been instructed in them since they were children? After all, her recent attempts to master dancing had ended in disaster. A blush rose to her cheeks at the memory of how many times she had stood on Giles Tremaine's toes, or collided with him as she had attempted to execute a perfectly straightforward part of the dance.

She would start with needlework, she decided. Surely that would prove easy enough to learn. And she would ask Aunt Sophia to arrange lessons with the dancing master. As there was to be a ball in just a few weeks' time, she would need to be better prepared, not least because there was a chance Daniel would be there. The thought made her smile with pleasure and Kitty caught her expression as she came into the room.

'Goodness, Miss Isabel, you look happy this morning. You can't have seen the weather outside.' She set down the tray and drew back the curtains to reveal windowpanes awash with rain, and a sky so gloomy it was hard to believe day had dawned.

'And on the day the washerwoman is with us, too,' Kitty said, and sighed as she set down Isabel's cup of chocolate. Isabel remembered how wet wash days meant the kitchen at Marston Grange would be filled with damp sheets and clothes, to the great irritation of Cook. She felt as though she had left that life behind far longer than just eight weeks ago.

Isabel broached the subject of increasing her accomplishments at the breakfast table.

'I'm delighted to hear it,' Aunt Sophia said. 'I do believe there will be time for you to learn how to acquit yourself well on the dance floor, before the Tremaines' ball. But there are plenty of young women accomplished enough on the pianoforte,' here she smiled fondly at Rebecca, 'to spare you being called upon to perform.' She was struck by a thought. 'Perhaps, though, you can sing?'

Isabel considered. She sang in church and had no difficulty holding a tune, but singing solo would be another matter entirely.

'Rebecca can play for you after breakfast,' her aunt declared. 'Then we will start you on a piece of embroidery, since the weather is against us today. Embroidery is a fine pursuit for young ladies, to keep the hands and mind engaged.'

And so began the first of many days in which Isabel endeavoured to better herself in accordance with Aunt Sophia's guidance. She visited the dancing master three times a week in his chilly front room in Albion Place, just around the corner from the Plains of Waterloo. A fire burned in the grate at one end, next to the piano, and Isabel was always grateful when the dance took her and Monsieur Lavigne past the feeble warmth it emitted.

Early March brought bitter winds and snow, which kept everyone indoors for hours on end. Her short journey around the corner in the company of her aunt, both of them slipping and sliding on the icy cobbles, was Isabel's only chance to breathe fresh air.

Monsieur Lavigne, a dapper man always impeccably dressed in cream trousers and a cut-away jacket, spoke fractured English, although during her fourth lesson Isabel heard him address his wife, the pianist, in undertones that gave her pause. Instead of 'A leetle – 'ow you say? – queecker, *s'il vous plait*,' she was sure she heard him say, 'Play it quicker, for Heaven's sake.'

As the weeks went by, she showed definite signs of improvement and Monsieur Lavigne was encouraging, declaring her his most able pupil. He addressed himself to Aunt Sophia, who sat muffled in her cloak with a blanket over her legs throughout the lesson.

'Your niece, Mademoiselle Eezabel, she 'as, 'ow you say?, a lightness of the foot.'

Isabel was gratified, although she rather doubted she would be able to remember all the steps to all the dances without Monsieur Lavigne issuing constant reminders and counting the beats. 'To ze left, one, two, three, turn. To ze right, feet together, dip, forward, one, two, three.' His commentaries ran through her dreams.

Aunt Sophia had been delighted with his praise and congratulated Isabel as they fought their way home through a gale that flapped their cloaks and all but whipped away her words.

'I do believe you will be a success on the dance floor, Isabel. I foresee great triumphs. Your father will be pleased.'

Needlework, however, proved to be a different matter. Isabel had imagined herself embroidering the sort of things she had seen Amelia working on – posies of flowers on cream silk, destined to be turned into the many cases and coverings considered necessary to store gloves, nightdresses and all manner of personal effects. Alas, smooth, even satin stitch seemed beyond her, becoming jagged and irregular as she sewed. Her French knots were misshapen and hung lopsided from the fabric, yet she seemed perfectly able to create all manner of knots of the wrong kind in her thread almost every time she made a stitch.

Aunt Sophia gazed on her supposedly finished piece of work for quite some time before suggesting that perhaps she had been too ambitious. 'A sampler might be just the thing,' she declared. 'It will allow you to practise all the stitches before embarking on something such as this. We will make a start on one tomorrow. It's where children begin, after all.'

Isabel, mustering all her self-control to avoid flinging the wretched piece of work on the fire, caught sight of Rebecca's face before she quickly bent her head to her own, quite perfect, needle-point cushion cover. Her cousin appeared gleeful at Isabel's failure. It had been much the same when Isabel had attempted to sing to Rebecca's piano accompaniment. She went along well enough until the need for a pure high note presented itself, at which point her voice cracked and she went off key for the remainder of the song.

Aunt Sophia had winced and Isabel was convinced she saw a tear roll down Rebecca's cheek, although the smile lurking at the corner of her lips suggested mirth had provoked it.

Isabel comforted herself with the thought that at least she had shown prowess in dancing. After all, that would be the most important skill to exhibit when she next saw Daniel.

CHAPTER SEVENTEEN

A note was waiting beside Isabel's plate at breakfast the next morning. She was surprised, and cast an enquiring glance at Kitty, then realised it wasn't in Daniel's hand. The script was very handsome: bold strokes on heavy cream paper, sealed with blood-red sealing wax. Her aunt alternated between gazing at the note and Isabel with undisguised impatience. Isabel took her time, drinking tea and buttering her bread, before taking a few bites.

'For goodness' sake,' her aunt burst out, unable to contain herself a moment longer. 'Don't you wish to know who has written to you?'

Isabel dabbed her mouth with her napkin and tried not to smile. She longed to suggest that Aunt Sophia's wish to know outweighed her own, but that would be impertinent.

'I think it is the Tremaine seal.' Her aunt had clearly examined the note before Isabel came into the room.

Any curiosity Isabel had felt drained away at once. What if it was a note from Giles Tremaine? Some time had passed since they had seen him. Had he returned to Ramsgate? Three pairs of eyes were fixed on her as she broke the seal and unfolded the paper.

Dear Isabel,

I would be delighted if you would join me this afternoon, for tea and to peruse the library. I am sure you are feeling the lack of a good book in this weather.

*I will send my carriage for you at three. Please assure your aunt
you will have no need of a chaperone.*
    Arabella Tremaine

Isabel raised her eyes from the note to find herself still the centre
of attention.

'Well?' her aunt demanded.

'It's from Mrs Tremaine. She has invited me to visit this afternoon, to borrow a book.'

Aunt Sophia clapped her hands in delight. 'How wonderful.
Although I can't imagine why she didn't write to me.' She turned
to her daughters. 'Girls, don't wear the same gown you wore on
your last visit.'

'The invitation is just for me, Aunt,' Isabel said. 'Mrs Tremaine
says she will send her carriage and I will have no need of a chaperone.'

'Let me see.' Her aunt held out her hand for the note, read it with
an ever-growing frown, then laid it down.

'Well, really.' She was momentarily lost for words, then two
spots of colour appeared on her cheeks. 'I do believe she means to
insult us.'

Isabel bit her lip. She had a great wish to go not only to visit the
Tremaines' library, for she realised all at once how much she had
missed reading, but also to have a change from the company of her
aunt and cousins. But would her aunt take offence and forbid it?

A few painful minutes passed while her aunt's lips worked as
though she was having an argument with herself before she sighed
and said, 'You must write a short note to thank Mrs Tremaine and
accept her hospitality. Mrs Potter can send the boy to deliver it. I suppose it is in our interests to stay on good terms with the Tremaines.'

She left the room then, swiftly followed by Rebecca and Amelia,
leaving Isabel to finish her breakfast alone while contemplating the
afternoon to come.

*

The carriage arrived promptly and Isabel stepped into it, attired in her primrose-coloured muslin, even though it felt too summery for the winter weather. She waved to the Crawfords, who had assembled, grim-faced, to see her off. Then she settled back into her seat, unable to suppress a smile of satisfaction. She was looking forward to an afternoon in the company of Mrs Tremaine and, although she had no wish to know anything about how Giles was spending his time in town, perhaps she could discover news of Daniel.

She almost skipped up the steps to the Tremaines' front door, which swung open before she could knock.

'Come in, Miss Cavendish. The mistress is waiting in the library.' The maid led the way along the corridor. Isabel was glad she had worn her velvet spencer, a new addition to her wardrobe, but the fire in the library was banked up and she could feel the heat the moment she stepped into the room. A table was laid for tea between the two chairs and Mrs Tremaine was standing at the window.

'We will have tea now,' Mrs Tremaine said to the maid, who nodded and shut the door behind her.

'You look well, my dear. How have you been passing the dreary days of winter? I do find the gloom oppresses the spirits so.' Mrs Tremaine sat down and gestured to Isabel to take the other chair.

'I have been taking dancing lessons and trying to become a needlewoman.' Isabel made a wry face. 'I've had more success in one than the other.'

Mrs Tremaine laughed. 'I do hope you found the dancing more amenable. The ball is only a few weeks away.'

Isabel nodded. 'I did. But without Monsieur Lavigne at my shoulder, telling me what to do, I fear I will make an exhibition of myself again.'

Mrs Tremaine smiled. 'Have no fear. The young men will be dazzled by you, whatever you do. As for needlework, you will have little use for that here. I have no daughters, only sons, so it has never fallen on me to impart what little knowledge of the subject I have.'

She seemed sad for a moment, Isabel thought, although her countenance lifted as she said, 'But you are exactly as I would have any daughter of mine to be. Your company has already brightened my afternoon and I hope this will be the first of many visits.'

The door opened to admit the maid with the hot water to make the tea. The performance of the ritual by Mrs Tremaine gave Isabel a minute or two to consider her flattering words. Would her own mother have been anything like Mrs Tremaine? How could she know, when she had so few memories of her?

Mrs Tremaine handed Isabel a cup and encouraged her to eat something. 'I always like to eat around now. In fact, when no one else is here I'm inclined to over-indulge and then forgo dinner, which makes me most unpopular with the cook.'

Isabel sipped her tea and nibbled a sandwich. Having resolved not to speak of Giles, she realised mentioning him was the easiest way to introduce the subject of Daniel.

'Has Mr Tremaine – Mr Giles Tremaine, that is – been home recently?' she asked.

Mrs Tremaine gave her a sharp look. 'My dear Isabella, don't expect me to believe you have any interest in my son. He's a well-meaning boy, I dare say, but not for the likes of you.'

Isabel didn't know how to interpret that: did Mrs Tremaine mean she wasn't good enough for Giles, or was this a comment on him? Her hostess had moved on, however.

'I suspect you are rather more interested in the whereabouts of Daniel Coates?' Mrs Tremaine regarded Isabel with one eyebrow raised.

Isabel sensed the blush rising to her cheeks. She opened her mouth to speak but couldn't conjure the right words.

Mrs Tremaine carried on: 'Daniel is trailing around after his father, as usual, but he will be here for the ball. I impressed upon Sir Charles that I would be very offended if he failed to return to Ramsgate. I feel sure he can tell the King that there are matters here still needing his attention before the royal sea voyage.'

Isabel's heart was racing and she struggled to do more than sip her tea as Mrs Tremaine talked.

'Now I've set your mind at rest, I hope. If you have finished your tea, do take a look at the books. Choose as many as you like – but wait. Why not take just one? Then you can return all the sooner and give me the pleasure of your company again.'

Isabel spent the remainder of her visit browsing the shelves, while Mrs Tremaine pulled out a volume here and there to recommend, then changed her mind. As dusk began to fall, the maid came in to light the candles and clear away the tea things. Isabel realised it was time to go.

She took Sir Walter Scott's novel, *The Bride of Lammermoor*, and departed in the carriage with some reluctance. It had been, she decided, by far the most pleasant afternoon of her stay in Ramsgate.

CHAPTER EIGHTEEN

To Aunt Sophia's chagrin, each week Isabel received an invitation to visit Mrs Tremaine to return her book, choose another and to drink tea.

'There's a perfectly good subscription library in the town,' her aunt said crossly. 'If I'd known you had need of books, I could have arranged a ticket for you.'

She spoke of books as though reading was not a proper accomplishment for a young lady. Isabel didn't share her aunt's belief that Mrs Tremaine was lonely and used the excuse of books to have her company. Her hostess clearly enjoyed their afternoons closeted in the library, where the fire was becoming less of a necessity as the weather inclined towards bursts of spring sunshine.

She also didn't reveal the confidences that came her way. Mrs Tremaine had let slip – on purpose, Isabel thought, on reflection – that Rebecca was wasting her time hoping to make a match with Giles Tremaine.

'I know it is more your aunt's doing than Rebecca's. After all, she's a dutiful and accomplished young lady and should, by rights, make a perfectly acceptable match. But not with Giles, or any other young gentleman of good breeding.'

Here was another baffling example of polite society, Isabel thought. She could tell from Mrs Tremaine's expression that she was expecting Isabel to question her, so she obliged.

'But why, Mrs Tremaine?' Her hostess had asked her to call her

Arabella, but she hadn't been able to break the habit of the more formal address.

'Well, your aunt may be unaware of this, my dear, so you are sworn to secrecy.' Mrs Tremaine regarded Isabel with a solemn expression.

Isabel, unsure whether she wished to hear what was coming next, nodded.

'Her husband, Hugh Crawford, has in town a mistress, whom he keeps openly and in some style. It is why he chooses to have his wife and daughters stay in Ramsgate throughout the year.'

All at once, Isabel felt very sorry for her aunt. Presumably all the other ladies in town, who came and went freely between London and Ramsgate, must be aware of this. It certainly explained why her uncle hadn't visited his family yet.

'I've shocked you,' Mrs Tremaine said. 'Your aunt isn't alone in her predicament, however.' She directed a glance full of meaning towards Isabel. 'I don't choose to be here,' she continued, 'although I have a choice of properties where I can spend my time. And I make sure I can run my household as I wish. In return, Mr Tremaine has to meet the bills and agree to be discreet if he wants me to maintain the illusion of our happy marriage.' A shadow crossed her face and Isabel guessed at deep hurt, not completely buried. 'I'm afraid I've given you a glimpse into a world that isn't as perfect as you had hoped. Don't despair – there are men who can't be bothered with lying and dissembling.' She sighed. 'Now, a piece of advice about Daniel Coates.'

Isabel feared what she was about to hear.

'He's a fine young man,' Mrs Tremaine continued. 'I would certainly encourage you to have a dalliance with him. But don't lose your heart to him. Sir Charles has plans for him – ambitious plans.'

She changed the subject to discuss Isabel's thoughts on the book she had brought back with her and the moment passed.

Isabel was disappointed in her expectation of seeing Mrs Tremaine the following week. She had thought a great deal about their conversation and had many questions – about Sir Charles's plans for Daniel, as well as about the complicated marriages of the Tremaines and the Crawfords. She hoped she might glean some information about her mother and father's relationship, too, since Mrs Tremaine had mentioned knowing them. But the note she received on the morning of her regular visit dashed her hopes. It sat beside her breakfast plate, addressed in Mrs Tremaine's instantly recognisable hand, and earning glares from Aunt Sophia, who had come to resent their friendship.

Isabel opened it to read:

My dear Isabel,

I'm sorry to break our arrangement today, but the date of the ball is fast approaching and I find myself caught up in the preparations with a great many decisions to make.

I hope we can continue our afternoons in the library, once the day has passed. I am sure we will have a great deal to discuss!

Arabella Tremaine

Isabel laid the note beside her plate and stared glumly into her cup.

Her aunt, who had been watching her closely, said brightly, 'Will you be going to Mrs Tremaine's as usual, this afternoon?'

'No,' Isabel said flatly. 'Not today.' Seeing her aunt was waiting for her to impart more information, she added, with an effort, 'She has too many arrangements to make for the ball.'

The mention of the highlight of the social calendar, now just a few days away, sent Aunt Sophia into a flutter.

'Girls, you must try on your dresses today. If there are repairs to be made, Kitty must be employed to do them. There may be ribbons and gloves to be bought, too.' The last was said with a look at Amelia, who seemed unable to keep such things for more than one outing.

Isabel saw her aunt had brightened considerably at the thought of a shopping trip. The mention of the dresses reminded her, with a jolt, that she had already worn the only dress she owned that was suitable for the ball on the previous visit to the Tremaines', when dancing had taken place.

'Aunt,' she said, with some urgency, 'I wonder whether I should have a new gown. I have already worn the only suitable one just a few weeks ago. I don't believe I can wear the same one again.'

Her aunt shook her head. 'There is no time to make something new, Isabella. Mrs Symonds made it very plain that she would be far too busy once May arrived. You will have to wear what you have. Besides,' here she frowned, 'I would need to apply to your father for more money.'

Isabel experienced mounting panic. How could she appear before Daniel for the second time, dressed just as she had been before? Tears started to her eyes, out of disappointment over the cancellation of her afternoon plans and frustration at the lack of another suitable dress.

As they rose to leave the table, Rebecca turned to Isabel and said, 'I have a dress you can wear.'

Isabel stared at her in surprise. Rebecca had verged on hostile for weeks now. Her astonishment gave way to suspicion. What could she mean?

'It doesn't fit me,' her cousin continued, 'but I think it will fit you, although it will be too short, of course. I do believe it can be made longer with a trim – Kitty will know how. Come to my room and try it on.'

And she linked arms with the bemused Isabel and drew her away, up the stairs.

CHAPTER NINETEEN

Isabel had never ventured into Rebecca's room – her cousin always kept the door firmly closed. Now she saw that it was simply furnished, much like Isabel and Amelia's room, with a rug covering the floorboards beside the bed, which had a pale blue coverlet. A china jug and bowl patterned with forget-me-nots sat on the marble top of the mahogany washstand. If you craned your neck at the window, you could catch a glimpse of the sea.

It was the quantity of dresses that caught Isabel's eye when Rebecca opened the clothes press. She had at least twice as many as Isabel possessed, folded neatly onto the shelves.

'Try this one,' Rebecca said, shaking out a dress of pale rose-coloured silk and thrusting it into Isabel's hands.

She hesitated, unsure whether she should go to her room to try it on, but Rebecca was already divesting herself of her day dress, so Isabel turned her back and followed suit.

Rebecca's gown was a little large on Isabel's slim figure, and too short. Kitty came in just as Rebecca was struggling with the fastening on the gown she intended to wear for the ball: peach silk, with too many frills and fancy details for Isabel's taste, although her cousin was preening in front of the full-length looking glass she had in her room.

Kitty quickly dealt with the fastening, nodding as though in agreement when Rebecca said, 'It looks well, don't you think?'

The maid turned her attention to Isabel, who caught her raised eyebrows and wry expression, suggesting her nod had been a polite one.

'I can lift the shoulders for you.' Kitty demonstrated and instantly the gown hung in a more flattering fashion. 'But I can't do anything about the length. You'll have to take it to Mrs Symonds to see what fabric trims she has. I'm sure she'll be able to help you.'

She helped the cousins change back into their day dresses, then went off to see Amelia, Isabel's borrowed dress hanging over her arm.

'It's very kind of you to let me take your dress, Rebecca. You are sure you don't mind it being altered?' Isabel felt awkward now they were alone again. Was Rebecca expecting payment, perhaps?

Rebecca grabbed her arm and hissed in her face, 'In return, I expect you to stay away from Giles Tremaine all evening. Don't dance with him, don't even talk to him. Do you understand?'

Isabel, fearful Rebecca's fingers would leave bruises on her arm, attempted to disengage herself. How could she explain that she would like nothing better? Whether or not Giles would be prepared to leave her alone was another matter. She hadn't shared Mrs Tremaine's words – that she didn't consider Rebecca suitable for her son. Her cousin would have to discover that for herself.

'You have my word,' she said.

'You can go now,' Rebecca said, giving her a little shove towards the door.

Shaken, Isabel went in search of Kitty, to find out when she might take the altered dress to Mrs Symonds. If Rebecca hadn't attacked her in such a way, she might have suggested that the maid persuade Rebecca to wear a different dress to the ball, one in a colour and style more becoming. Her cousin's words had made her think again. For all she cared, Rebecca might as well continue to make a fool of herself at the Tremaines'.

The following afternoon, Isabel presented herself at Mrs Symonds's shop, Kitty having made her alterations to the rose-coloured dress overnight. Her aunt had gone in search of ribbons and gloves for Amelia, who had mislaid her full-length satin ones.

Isabel found the shop in a more disordered state than on previous visits. Bales of fabric, some half unfolded, were scattered across the counter, and lengths of trimmings were gathered up in unruly bundles.

Mrs Symonds beckoned her through to the workroom at the back. 'I'm not sure whether we will be able to help you, Miss Cavendish,' she said.

Isabel noticed her face was flushed and her hair escaping from its pins.

'We have a great many orders to complete before the ball. I did warn your aunt previously ...' She tailed off.

Dresses hung around the walls in various stages of completion. No wonder Mrs Symonds seemed so harried, Isabel thought. Grace, though, sat in her usual spot in the window, sewing steadily.

'It shouldn't be too great a task, Mrs Symonds, as I said in the note I sent over this morning. My maid has made alterations – the dress just needs to be made longer.' Isabel hoped she sounded firm but feared she had adopted a wheedling tone.

'Hmm. Sometimes adjustments take more time than you think, Miss Cavendish.'

Isabel registered the note of reproof in Mrs Symonds's voice. 'Perhaps if I try on the dress. Then you could tell me your thoughts.' She had tried to sound conciliatory.

Mrs Symonds let out a gusty sigh but nodded, so Isabel slipped quickly behind the screen in the corner, emerging shortly after in the rose-coloured dress.

'Ah, it's the one I made for Miss Rebecca.' Mrs Symonds brightened at the sight of it. She stepped back and scrutinised the dress. 'The colour suits you well, Miss Cavendish. I do believe we could use some of the lace we have just received from France. A layer to extend the hem, and another slightly above it to disguise the seam. Grace, could you fetch it?'

Grace obediently laid down her work and went into the shop, returning to find her mother already on her knees, pins to hand.

'Now, a length around the hem.' Mrs Symonds pinned it expertly in place. 'And then another, just above it, like so.'

She stood up and turned Isabel to face the glass. 'It conceals the ankles, while discreetly revealing them, too.'

She was pleased with the effect, Isabel could tell, and she was caught off guard when the dressmaker said, 'Do you have a beau, Miss Cavendish? Is there someone at the ball who would appreciate a glimpse of a dainty ankle?'

She was teasing, and Isabel went scarlet.

Mrs Symonds laughed. 'Don't worry, Miss Cavendish. Grace and I are very discreet. We hear a great many things and never repeat a word. Now, I think you will look quite lovely in this dress.' She bent closer to whisper, 'A great deal better than Rebecca Crawford did,' just as the doorbell jangled to announce a visitor.

As Mrs Crawford entered the room, the dressmaker said loudly, 'Grace can stitch on the lace for you. It will be ready in time, don't worry.'

'All successfully resolved?' Aunt Sophia asked. 'Good, then I think we need keep Mrs Symonds no longer. I can see she has a great deal to do. The carriage is outside, Isabella.'

Isabel changed quickly, smiled at Grace, who was now stitching away in the window again, thanked Mrs Symonds and hurried out to join her aunt in the carriage. She was surrounded by rather more packages than the purchase of ribbons and a pair of gloves suggested. Isabel was reminded of what Mrs Tremaine had said about Mr Crawford's mistress, kept with no expense spared. He must be a very wealthy man to afford to keep his wife and daughters in style, too, she thought.

Chapter Twenty

The town became noticeably busier in the week leading up to the ball. The weather was much improved, the sun sparkling on a calm sea, with temperatures lifting so that it felt more like high summer than early May. Promenading became a favourite pastime of the afternoons, eagerly awaited by Isabel and her cousins. Each day they walked from the Plains of Waterloo to just beyond the Tremaines' house, which was set a little way back from the seafront in the terrace of similar grand homes, before Mrs Crawford would announce a return home.

'Too much sun is bad for the complexion,' she said, even though they all carried parasols.

Isabel gazed with longing at the Tremaines' house. She imagined it to be a seething mass of activity behind that impenetrable white façade. She would have loved to call on Mrs Tremaine but without an invitation she could not. Above all, though, she wanted to know whether Daniel had arrived. And even if he had, would he be staying there, as before? She stared at the front door, hoping it would open and he would step out. The very thought made her giddy.

Isabel wasn't the only one to experience a build-up of nervous excitement. With each day that passed, and as more regular visitors returned to the town, the feverish anticipation grew.

'Oh, look, the Wilmslows,' (or the Deverells, the Fortescues or the Barrowbys) 'are in town,' became the daily cry from one or other of the Crawfords, as they spotted a carriage belonging to a family they knew, or glimpsed the new arrivals promenading.

The day before the ball, Isabel's curiosity as to her uncle was satisfied. She and her aunt had arrived back from the dressmaker's, Isabel's trimmed ball gown packed carefully in a box, when both became aware of a deep male voice emanating from the drawing room. It was accompanied by peals of laughter from Amelia and Rebecca.

Aunt Sophia stiffened for a moment, then exclaimed, 'Hugh!' and hurried through to join her family. Isabel loitered in the hallway, taking time over untying the ribbons of her bonnet. Then, feeling a little awkward, she followed her aunt.

Hugh Crawford's presence filled the drawing room. He had taken up a chair in front of the fireplace, his legs stretched across the rug. Isabel had the impression of a tall, broad man, with sandy whiskers, who seemed too big for all the dainty furniture. He didn't get up when Isabel came in, perhaps because his daughters were perched on each arm of his chair, but his gaze swept her from top to toe.

'Now, who do we have here? Isabella Cavendish, if I'm not mistaken.'

Isabel flushed. Her aunt was hovering behind her husband's chair, looking flustered, while her cousins appeared to resent her intrusion.

'Uncle Hugh,' she said. 'I'm delighted to meet you. Have you come to join us for the ball?'

'Ball?' Mr Crawford raised an eyebrow. 'No one mentioned a ball.'

'Oh, Hugh, I told you in my letters,' Aunt Sophia said, before anyone else could speak. 'At the Tremaines' house, tomorrow evening.'

'I hadn't planned to stay.' Her husband appeared to be deliberating. 'But why not? It might be fun.'

His daughters began to talk over each other, while Isabel murmured a polite excuse, which no one seemed to hear, before withdrawing to her room. The Crawfords needed time together as

111

a family, she reasoned, and for a while she was happy, looking at her ball gown, holding it up against her and turning from side to side so it swished.

Then she sat down on the bed and began to think about her own family, such as it was. She had heard nothing from her father since she left, even though she knew her aunt wrote to him regularly, usually when there were bills to be paid. Her aunt sometimes said, 'Your father sends his regards,' as she laid down a letter at the breakfast table. But there had been no letter for her, although, of course, she hadn't written to him, either. She resolved to do so, as soon as the ball was over. Then she would have more to tell him, she supposed, although she doubted he would be interested.

Had her father and mother met at a ball? It was hard to imagine her father dressed up and enjoying such an occasion with the woman in the portrait in their dining room, but he had been young once, of course. She would ask him, in her letter, and perhaps it was time to mention returning home for a visit. After all, she would soon have been away for five months.

Amelia came into the room, disturbing her reverie. 'Ooh, is this your dress? How lovely it looks. Just imagine, at this time tomorrow, we will be starting to get ready. I can't wait to see everyone dressed up and dancing.'

Isabel managed to raise a smile, but for the life of her she couldn't work out why her spirits seemed to have taken a downturn. Was it something to do with Hugh Crawford returning to complete the family? Or was it because she had been thinking about her own home?

Amelia had been despatched to take her back to the drawing room, so Isabel had no time for further reflection. Rebecca played the piano for her father, while Amelia sang. Isabel, thankfully, wasn't pressed to do anything and the rest of the afternoon passed swiftly.

Dinner that evening was a jolly affair. Isabel noticed that Hugh Crawford devoted most of his attention to his daughters – not unusual, she supposed, since he had been absent for some time. Her aunt appeared pensive, and she saw her watching as her husband repeatedly poured liberal amounts of wine into his glass. But she laughed and smiled when spoken to and seemed happy enough to have him home. Even so, Isabel couldn't help but think of Mrs Tremaine's words about Hugh Crawford keeping a mistress.

That night, Amelia fell asleep as quickly as usual, but Isabel lay awake for a while, the anticipation of seeing Daniel at the ball keeping her from sleep. As she was beginning to drift off, the sound of raised voices from below pulled her back into consciousness. Her uncle's voice carried – she thought she heard him say loudly, 'It's out of the question,' and then her aunt's quieter, indistinct reply. She wondered whether to go and listen on the landing, but didn't want to risk disturbing Amelia. She heard further fragments – 'The bills are too high', 'I can't afford this', 'Why did you agree to it?' – in her uncle's carrying tones, before a door slammed and all was quiet.

Isabel strained her ears for anything further, but silence had descended. Eventually, her eyelids began to droop and, the next thing she knew, Kitty was in the room.

'Wake up, Miss Isabel, Miss Amelia. The sun is shining – and it's the day of the ball, at last.'

CHAPTER TWENTY-ONE

There was no sign of Hugh Crawford at the breakfast table that morning, or of Aunt Sophia. If they had breakfasted, Kitty had already cleared their places. Perhaps they were just late to the table, Isabel thought. Then a memory of the raised voices she had heard the previous night returned to her. Had Mr Crawford left the house after the argument, and if so, had he come home? Or had he gone back to London?

Amelia, full of excitement about the ball, was chattering to Rebecca. Neither of them appeared perturbed. Isabel concluded she must have been the only one to hear the disagreement. She thought it best to say nothing about it and concentrated instead on eating while listening to her cousins.

'Who will you dance with first, Rebecca? Will it be Giles?'

'I can't ask him, you silly goose.' Rebecca was exasperated. 'I have to wait for him to ask me. I suppose it doesn't matter who I dance with first, as long as I dance with him at least once during the evening.' She shot Isabel a look as she spoke. 'And you know that if I dance with him more than twice, it will cause gossip. Now, who are *you* going to dance with?'

Amelia went bright red and protested that she was more than happy to sit and watch everyone else. Rebecca, however, continued to torment her, reeling off a string of names, each one earning an emphatic 'No!' until, laughing, Amelia put her hands over her ears. 'Stop! Stop!' she pleaded.

Keen to divert her sister, Amelia turned to Isabel. 'And who will you dance with?'

'I don't know. I hardly know anyone here. I will have to wait and see.'

'We can only hope your partners have the foresight to wear their sturdiest boots.' Rebecca stood up, smiling sweetly, and left the room.

'Don't take any notice of her,' Amelia said. 'Mama told us how well you dance now.' She stood up, too. 'I wonder where Mama is this morning?'

Isabel made a noncommittal reply, then suggested to Amelia she might continue to work on the box she was decorating with shells, begun the previous day but abandoned when her father arrived. The hours until it was time to ready themselves for the ball would pass very slowly unless they found something to amuse themselves.

Amelia had just laid the last shell in place on the lid of her box, while Isabel sat on the window seat, turning the pages of her novel without taking in a word, when her aunt came into the room. 'We'll take an early walk,' she said. Isabel thought she appeared pale and red-eyed, but Amelia seemed not to notice and hurried upstairs to change.

'Is everything all right, Aunt?' she ventured.

'Yes. Why shouldn't it be?' The sharpness of her tone precluded further questioning, so Isabel followed Amelia up the stairs. If something had happened, her aunt wasn't prepared to speak about it.

When they were all gathered in the hall, Rebecca too, Amelia asked, 'Will Papa be joining us?'

'No, he had to return to town on business.' Aunt Sophia, her back to them, was busy with her gloves and parasol.

'Oh, what a shame. He'll miss the ball.' Amelia didn't seem unduly put out and Isabel thought Rebecca seemed relieved. Perhaps she would have felt constrained by her father's presence.

They weren't the only ones to promenade earlier than usual. They were greeted by several of their acquaintances, and whenever they stopped to talk, the conversation invariably revolved around the ball.

Isabel, feeling she could play no part in the gossip about which young men had been seen around the town, confined herself to gazing out to sea and earned her aunt's displeasure in doing so.

'For goodness' sake, Isabel, try to at least look interested,' she said, after one group had moved out of earshot. 'Eligible young men have sisters and mothers, you know. You don't wish them to speak badly of you when their opinion is sought, do you?'

Isabel, taken aback, shook her head. Her aunt had set her train of thought in a new direction, though. If Daniel had come to town, would he be with his father or his mother? He had mentioned sisters. Would they be there, too? In a few hours, though, she would find out.

Once they had returned home, it was time to begin slow preparations for the ball, starting with a light meal, which Aunt Sophia insisted upon, although their stomachs were all a-flutter with excitement.

'You will have no chance to eat again until late this evening, when supper is served. After three or four dances, you'll wish you'd eaten when you had the chance.'

Despite their protests, Rebecca, Amelia and Isabel managed to eat some cold chicken, sweet pastries and fruit. Aunt Sophia sat implacably at the table, watching each mouthful pass their lips. She appeared to have little appetite herself, Isabel noticed, merely picking at a pastry and some fruit.

Then they all retreated to their bedrooms, where Kitty had laid out their dresses, along with ribbons, gloves and dancing shoes. Isabel and Amelia put on wrappers and waited for Kitty to finish dressing Aunt Sophia's and Rebecca's hair. It was too soon to consider putting on her dress, Isabel knew, or it would be horribly creased by the time they arrived at the ball. But those final hours before the event, which had been anticipated for so long, were very hard to bear.

116

Finally, Isabel was seated before the glass, Kitty expertly twisting her hair up, piling it on top of her head and pinning it into place, while Amelia watched. Aunt Sophia came into the room, reflected in the glass in all her glory. She wore a dress of gold-coloured silk, its sleeves puffed and trimmed with ruched ribbons that also formed a double layer above the hem.

Isabel opened her mouth to formulate an appropriate compliment on her aunt's appearance, but Aunt Sophia took her by surprise. She thrust a small velvet box into Isabel's hands. 'Your father wanted you to have these for this evening,' she said. 'For your first proper ball.'

Isabel lifted the tiny clasp and opened the box. A pair of amethyst earrings, the droplets hanging from gold wires, nestled on the midnight blue velvet within. She recognised them at once – the earrings her mother was wearing in the portrait that hung at Marston Grange.

'He sent these?' she asked, raising her eyes to meet those of her aunt, reflected in the glass.

Isabel's suddenly swam with tears, which threatened to spill onto her cheeks.

'They'll look lovely with your dress, miss.' Kitty took one from the box and held it to Isabel's ear. Her vision cleared enough for her to recognise a startling resemblance to her mother in the portrait.

Chapter Twenty-Two

There was quite a crush of guests waiting to enter the Tremaines' house – far more than on the previous occasion. Isabel was grateful for the mild weather, since they were outside for a good fifteen minutes before it was their turn to step through the great front door, hand over their thick card invitation and leave their wraps and pelisses in a side room that had been repurposed as a cloakroom. Isabel picked up her dance card from a table and joined the throng of ladies making their way into the ballroom, the younger ones chattering in great excitement while their elders fondly looked on.

'Such excitement!' Aunt Sophia exclaimed. 'I can remember to this day how I felt when I attended my first ball.'

She was about to say more, but her daughters weren't listening. They had other things on their minds. Rebecca was standing on tiptoe, trying to see over the heads of the crowd, while Amelia called out in excitement every time she saw people they knew.

'Lily Deverell is wearing such a beautiful gown. And that must be her brother – he's very handsome.'

The only person Isabel wished to see was Daniel Coates. But what if he wasn't there? Isabel couldn't decide whether she felt sick, faint or nervous – perhaps all three.

Aunt Sophia had practical matters in mind. 'We need to find some seats before they are all taken,' she said, forging a way through the crowd. Her daughters and Isabel followed obediently, but it was soon apparent that the seats with the best vantage points had been filled. They were obliged to tuck in along the wall, rather too close to where the musicians had set up.

'We'll be hard-pressed to hear ourselves speak,' Aunt Sophia complained. Isabel didn't mind – they might not be well placed but they had a clear view of the ballroom entrance. Her gaze swept the room. There was no sign of Daniel, or of Mrs Tremaine and her son. Perhaps they were together somewhere else in the house, she thought, and immediately wished she could go in search of them. She knew it was out of the question, though. Her aunt had impressed upon her that she must stay within sight.

Aunt Sophia now began to grumble about the number of guests. 'I can't imagine what Mrs Tremaine was thinking. This isn't one of the Assembly Rooms. It's a modest ballroom within a private house. And yet she has packed it so full I can't see how you will begin to dance.'

She looked to her daughters for affirmation but Rebecca burst out, 'Mama, how am I to fill my dance card when we are so badly placed here?'

Isabel followed her gaze and saw that although groups of young men had begun to circulate, so far they had barely progressed beyond the entrance. They were engaging the nearest young ladies in conversation and she saw several reach for their dance cards, smiling as they filled them in.

For ten or fifteen minutes more, the family had to endure Rebecca's complaints, while her dance card remained empty and her mother refused to countenance moving. Then another group swept into the room, pushing the cluster around the entrance further onto the dance floor. Isabel saw Giles Tremaine and his mother among them at the same moment as Rebecca let out a gasp. Isabel had to resist the urge to jump to her feet to see whether Daniel might be with their party. Instead, she sat up a little taller and tried not to look as though she was staring.

The Tremaines greeted their guests as they made their way around the room, and Isabel very quickly realised that Daniel wasn't with them. She had been so convinced he would come that she scarcely knew how to cope with the disappointment. Overcome by a wave of misery, she turned her head to concentrate on the musicians, now busily setting up their instruments. So determined was her attempt to hold back tears that she wasn't aware of the Tremaine party's arrival until Mrs Tremaine spoke.

'My dear Mrs Crawford – how lovely to see you all. Isn't this wonderful? There are so many people!' Mrs Tremaine clasped her hands together in delight, forcing Aunt Sophia to agree that, indeed, it was most well attended.

'I do hope you will allow me to borrow your niece?' Mrs Tremaine continued. 'There are some old friends I would particularly like to introduce her to.' She didn't wait for an answer but held out her hand to Isabel who, with a swift glance at her aunt, stood up.

Aunt Sophia was too flustered to do anything other than nod, since she was very taken by the sight of Rebecca and Giles Tremaine in conversation. Isabel saw Rebecca reach for her dance card as Mrs Tremaine put an arm through hers and drew her away.

Isabel was most curious to know who her hostess wished her to meet, but she had to stand patiently by as Mrs Tremaine continued her circuit around the room. Finally, they reached the entrance just as the musicians struck up. Isabel cast a quick glance back into the room, to see a host of gentlemen claim their partners and take to the floor, Rebecca and Giles Tremaine among them.

'I won't keep you long from the dance,' Mrs Tremaine said, leading the way to the dining room. Servants were busy preparing a long table for the supper to be served later, while a few groups of people loitered there. She approached one of the groups, deep in conversation with their backs to them.

'Sir Charles and Lady Coates, do let me introduce Isabel Cavendish. She has become a particularly dear friend of mine over the last few weeks.'

The group turned towards Isabel and she did her best to smile and focus all her attention on Sir Charles and his wife, even as she registered, with shock, that Daniel was one of the party.

They exchanged a few pleasantries and then Mrs Tremaine said, 'But how remiss of me. Isabel, this is Sir Charles's youngest son, Daniel. I am sure he is keen to escape our dull conversation and join the other young people on the dance floor. Daniel, why don't you take Isabel with you? You'll find Giles out there, somewhere.'

And with that, Mrs Tremaine effected the introduction that allowed Daniel to lead Isabel into the ballroom, without any of them giving away the scandalous fact that they were already very well acquainted.

Chapter Twenty-Three

Isabel walked at Daniel's side, hardly able to believe what had just happened. She cast a covert glance at him. He was there, at the ball, after all. And Mrs Tremaine had taken such care to formally introduce them. Now that her wish to see him had come true, she felt too shy to speak.

Doubt assailed her. He had sent her such a warm note after they had first met. Surely he had said that she would be the first person he would seek out. And yet he hadn't come to look for her.

'Have you been long in Ramsgate?' she asked, giving voice to her thoughts.

'We arrived late this afternoon. I've been in attendance on my parents since then.' Daniel stopped and turned to her. 'Would you like to dance?'

Isabel hesitated, remembering the disaster of her previous occasion on this very dance floor, then nodded. She must be brave, and remember everything Monsieur Lavigne had taught her. The dance that had been in progress had just come to an end and couples were parting and seeking out new partners. That gave her a few minutes to prepare before the music began again.

She had imagined this moment many times but now it seemed a strangely intimate action to take Daniel's hand and partner him in a dance when they hadn't exchanged a word in weeks. They had talked so easily and naturally in the library the last time they had seen each other; now they seemed ill at ease. She was about to suggest they find a quiet corner, to converse, but the musicians

122

struck up once more and couples began forming two long lines on the dance floor. She found herself facing Daniel close to the ballroom entrance, a good way from where Aunt Sophia was sitting. It would be a while before they had worked their way up to the top of the line. At least it would delay her aunt's surprise and possible disapproval.

The dancers clapped the lead couple all the way down the aisle and all the way back up again, before it fell to the rest of the couples to perform their part. They stepped forward and back, met each other and turned about, in the time it took for the first couple to peel away and a new couple to lead the dance. It allowed Isabel and Daniel snatches of conversation: 'Are you here with your aunt?', 'And are your sisters with you?', which helped to ease any tension between them.

At the end of the dance, they faced each other, breathless and laughing. All awkwardness had vanished. This was the moment to part company, Isabel knew, and to hope for another dancing partner. But she wanted to spend more time with Daniel, to talk at length as they had done before. Over Daniel's shoulder, she caught a glimpse of Aunt Sophia, eyes fixed upon them. She ought to take Daniel over, and make plain to her aunt that Mrs Tremaine had formally introduced them.

As Isabel hesitated, reluctant to do the right thing, Daniel said, 'Should we dance again? Or is that presumptuous of me? Perhaps your dance card is full.' He didn't wait for an answer but said, a mischievous glint in his eye, 'Or shall we hide in the library once more?'

Isabel couldn't prevent a look of delight spreading across her face. Daniel didn't wait for her answer, but seized her hand and they pushed through the crowd on the dance floor to arrive in the main hall. Isabel glanced back as they left the ballroom to see Aunt Sophia on her feet, before she lost sight of her. They loitered for a moment in the hall, then, when it became clear no one was interested in them, they darted hand in hand down the corridor to the room she now knew so well.

The fire had burned low in the grate and Daniel attended to it, while Isabel sat down in one of the leather chairs. She discarded her dancing shoes, wiggling her toes as she pulled her knees up to hug them, resting her feet on the chair seat. Such an unladylike pose would have earned a shriek of horror from her aunt, but Isabel felt it was perfectly demure. Her dress still covered her legs to the ankles, after all.

'I feel guilty,' Daniel said, although his expression belied his words.

Isabel was apprehensive. What was he going to say?

'Keeping you all to myself,' Daniel continued, 'when no doubt half the young men out there are searching for you on the dance floor.'

'Nonsense!' Isabel laughed.

Daniel was suddenly serious. 'It's true – I will be the envy of them all. I do believe I'm supposed to say how striking you look tonight – that dress, those earrings – but as you can see, I'm not well practised in the art of flattery. At least, only in my father's line of work, with foreign dignitaries and the like.' He made a wry face.

'Then let's not waste time on such things,' Isabel exclaimed. 'Tell me what you have been doing since I last saw you. Have you been accompanying your father as he goes about the King's business?'

'I don't think you would find much to interest you in the way I spend my days, moving around the country with Father. Winter coach journeys are anything but enjoyable – you are either being jolted along rutted roads for hours on end, or the wheels are mired in mud and you have to get out to lessen the burden and allow the horses to pull them free. It's cold and draughty, the inns along the way leave a lot to be desired, and you find yourself longing for the comforts of home.' He cast a sideways glance at Isabel. 'And counting down the days to the ball here, of course.'

Isabel blushed, and was then confounded when he asked her to account for how she had passed the previous weeks. 'I saw a dancing master, and tried to improve myself in other ways.' She sighed.

'But it seems I will never be a skilled needlewoman or entertain a gathering with my prowess at the pianoforte.'

Daniel began to laugh. 'What a fine pair we make. Hiding from the dancing and lacking the skills that are considered so important today. I should introduce you to my father's estate on the Scottish borders. I don't think embroidery and musical accomplishments count for much there, and flattery would bewilder Mrs Musgrave, the housekeeper.

'My grandmother loved it there and refused to come any further south. She used to hold a gathering once a year, to thank all the workers on the estate. There was dancing and supper, but it was nothing like tonight's occasion. I could see you there, Isabel, striding out across the moor, with the hills rising in the background.'

He stopped and their eyes locked. Isabel had never seen a moor and knew next to nothing about the landscape beyond her immediate surroundings, but if Daniel could see her there, that was good enough for her. In the silence, they both became aware that the music had stopped.

'I suppose supper is being served,' Isabel said.

'I'd prefer to stay here all evening,' Daniel said, 'but the truth is, I've barely eaten since breakfast.' He gave Isabel a look of appeal. 'Shall we?'

Isabel was reluctant to leave their place of sanctuary and she wasn't particularly hungry, since Aunt Sophia had insisted she eat earlier, but she knew that if they didn't show their faces, her aunt would doubtless send her cousins to look for them. They couldn't risk being discovered alone again.

'Come on then,' she said, reluctantly slipping her feet back into her dancing shoes. She stood up and held out her hand. 'I'd better introduce you to my aunt.'

CHAPTER TWENTY-FOUR

Isabel quailed before the press of people in the dining room. It was hot, and the smell of hair pomade and overheated bodies, mingled with the aroma of the roast meats laid out in the centre of the table, was almost overwhelming. Mrs Tremaine had laid on an impressive supper – her guests were balancing plates piled high with food as they searched for somewhere to sit.

Daniel took a plate and speared several slices of roast duck, adding potatoes and relishes as they circled the table, while Isabel tried to catch a glimpse of her aunt. It wasn't until they had procured glasses of punch that Isabel spotted her, close to the dessert table. She supposed she should have thought to look there first.

'There you are!' Aunt Sophia exclaimed, as they arrived at her side. 'Wherever have you been, Isabel?' She looked Daniel up and down.

'This is Daniel Coates, Aunt. Mr Coates, this is Mrs Crawford.'

Daniel hastily set aside his plate and glass. 'I'm delighted to meet you, Mrs Crawford. Isabel has spoken so warmly of the hospitality you have extended to her.'

Isabel gave him a sideways glance. She had done no such thing. Then she realised Daniel was simply displaying the tact he must use when he and his father went about the King's business.

It certainly worked on Aunt Sophia, who lost her frosty expression as she set aside her plate and extended her hand for Daniel to kiss.

'I must introduce you to my father,' Daniel said, casting a cursory glance around the room. 'He will be here somewhere with my mother and Mrs Tremaine.'

'She introduced me to the Coates family earlier,' Isabel interjected hastily, keen to reassure her aunt that Daniel's presence was entirely proper. It was hardly necessary – Aunt Sophia appeared enchanted by Daniel, to the extent that Amelia caught Isabel's eye and gave her a small smile. There was no sign of Rebecca, Isabel noticed. Was she keeping company with Giles Tremaine?

She stood patiently by while Aunt Sophia quizzed Daniel, only too well aware that it was in her interest to gain her aunt's approval. She decided she might as well eat a dessert, since she was standing right beside them. As she scooped a spoonful of syllabub onto her plate, a voice boomed over the table.

'There you are!' It was Giles Tremaine. 'I've been looking for you. Would you care for the next dance, Miss Cavendish? After you've eaten your syllabub, of course,' he added, as her hand stilled, then returned the serving spoon to the bowl.

'Sorry, Giles, Miss Cavendish is promised to me for the next.'

Daniel took the plate from her hand and set it down, then gave Giles a broad grin and a small bow before leading Isabel away from the table.

'I've barely managed three mouthfuls of supper,' he lamented. 'Your aunt wouldn't stop talking. But I couldn't bear the thought of Giles having you all to himself.'

They arrived in the ballroom to find an energetic reel already under way, leaving them no chance to exchange anything other than glances as they whirled around. Isabel concentrated hard, imagining Monsieur Lavigne's voice in her ear. She felt sure she had managed a creditable performance, as she and Daniel subsided into breathless laughter as the dance finished.

Daniel was suddenly serious. 'Isabel, my father and I have to leave this evening. Now, I fear.'

Isabel glanced around, following the direction of Daniel's gaze, to see his father standing in the entrance to the ballroom.

'Will you write to me?' she pleaded, wanting to hold on to him and prevent his going.

'Of course,' he said. He held her gaze and the noise of the ballroom fell away – the musicians retuning their instruments, the chatter of the dancers. Isabel wanted to say so many things and her lips parted but she couldn't utter a word. Daniel reached a finger to her lower lip, then his hand brushed her face and he was gone. She turned to watch him – a slender figure threading his way through the crowd to his father's side.

Isabel stood for several minutes on the edge of the dance floor, until a tugging at her arm made her realise Amelia was at her side. She stared blankly at her, still caught up in the moment of Daniel's parting.

'We have to go,' Amelia said urgently.

'Go?' Isabel was confused, thinking this had something to do with Daniel.

'Yes. Mama is waiting for us in the cloakroom.'

'But the ball ...' Isabel gazed around. A new set of dancers had taken to the floor. Then she shrugged. She had no appetite to stay without Daniel. It would suit her to leave, too.

She followed Amelia and they found Aunt Sophia in the cloakroom, ineffectually trying to calm Rebecca, who was in floods of angry tears.

'But you don't understand, Mama,' she wailed, as Isabel and Amelia quickly reclaimed their wraps and pelisses. 'Giles Tremaine is to be married. He's betrothed. I feel like a fool.'

Rebecca alternately raged and wept throughout the short carriage journey home, while Amelia and Isabel remained silent. It seemed the bride-to-be hadn't been at the ball, having stayed in London, so Rebecca couldn't even make herself feel better with spiteful remarks. Aunt Sophia's attempts to placate her fell on deaf ears, while Isabel was reminded of Mrs Tremaine's warning that Rebecca couldn't count on a match with someone such as Giles Tremaine.

At least three of the occupants of the carriage were relieved to spill out of it when they reached the house in the Plains of Waterloo. They stood for a good minute or two in the hallway, divesting themselves of their outerwear before Kitty appeared to help them. She appeared befuddled by their unexpectedly early arrival; Isabel suspected she had been asleep in the kitchen as she waited.

'You are early home, ma'am. I trust all is well?'

Kitty realised the error of her innocent enquiry when Rebecca flung at her, 'No, it most certainly is not,' and flounced into the drawing room.

'Some chocolate, I think, Kitty.' Aunt Sophia, distracted, followed her daughter. Isabel had been hoping to go up to bed, to ponder the events of the evening, but her aunt poked her head back around the door and beckoned Isabel and Amelia to join her.

She waited until Kitty had stoked the dying embers of the fire and added more coal, then left them with a tray of chocolate, before she spoke.

'Now, Rebecca,' she said. 'I hesitate to add to your woes, but your father has left me no option.'

She picked up her cup and Isabel noticed that her hand shook as she raised it to her lips.

'I'm afraid we are unable to remain in this house beyond the end of next week.'

Rebecca and Amelia gasped. Isabel, puzzled, looked from one to another of the family.

'Your father is unwilling to meet the cost of the rental, which has risen considerably to take account of the demand in the summer months. Therefore, we are to move to smaller premises next week.'

Isabel, worried to see her aunt so visibly moved, was unprepared for what followed.

Her aunt turned to her and said, 'You will return home, Isabel. I shall write to your father tomorrow to tell him to expect you.'

As Isabel began to protest, she raised a hand. 'It's no good, my dear. There simply isn't enough space. Rebecca and Amelia will be sharing a room. I hope, however, your father will be happy with what has been achieved. You have a new wardrobe, you can dance and you have been out in company . . .' She tailed off, aware of the expressions of her daughters and niece. It was unwelcome news, indeed.

Isabel had one overriding concern. Daniel had said he would write to her, but he had only her address in the Plains of Waterloo. If he didn't write and include his own address before they had to vacate the house, how could she ever get in touch with him again?

Her mind raced – could she visit Mrs Tremaine, or get a message to her, to ask for Daniel's address? Would that be considered too forward, especially as Mrs Tremaine had warned her off any expectations over Daniel? And Rebecca had made a scene over Giles's engagement as they had left the ball. Isabel felt hot at the memory. She feared Mrs Tremaine would not be well disposed towards the family. Perhaps Kitty could be prevailed upon to check for letters after they had left, then forward them.

Isabel bade goodnight to her aunt and cousins and trailed up to bed, leaving them to discuss their straitened circumstances. She had imagined spending a pleasurable half-hour or so thinking about Daniel and the events of the evening. Now her thoughts were consumed by what this unexpected return home might mean for her future.

Chapter Twenty-Five

Five days later, Isabel waited in the hall for the carriage to draw up outside. She had arrived in Ramsgate with one small valise. Now she had had to acquire a trunk to enable Kitty to pack her new wardrobe.

Aunt Sophia's announcement had propelled the household into a state of upheaval. Rebecca and Amelia had demanded to view the new abode, and Mrs Potter and Kitty had gone too, to discover how they were to go about their duties. Isabel had remained at home, attempting to read a novel as she sat in the window seat, but in re-ality on the lookout for a messenger bearing a letter. The party had returned within the hour, during which time no letter had arrived.

'It's very small,' Amelia said, when Isabel asked how they had liked the house.

'And not well placed,' Rebecca added.

'It is near the seafront,' their mother said placatingly.

'Down a mean little side-street.' Rebecca's opinion was fixed.

Aunt Sophia sighed. 'I don't think Mrs Potter and Kitty were impressed. The kitchen isn't large and the room next to it, which they will have to share, is barely adequate.' She frowned. 'I don't know what your father was thinking of. Although it seems Ramsgate is now so popular in the summer, even the smallest house can command a high rent.'

'The place we stayed in last summer was far superior.' Rebecca was not to be mollified.

The days since the viewing had been filled with packing some items and disposing of others. There was no room for the pianoforte at the new address so it was arranged that it would remain for the use of the new tenants of the house, for a small fee.

'Why can't we go back to London?' Rebecca, now that Giles was lost to her, had taken against Ramsgate. 'We've spent two years here. I think you should ask Father when we are to return.' Her mother's expression not being encouraging, she added, 'My prospects, and Amelia's, are limited here. Surely it is in his interest that we should find good matches.'

Isabel had been forcibly reminded of Mrs Tremaine's words in relation to Hugh Crawford. In her view, it suited him only too well to keep his family out of the way. And now she was to be got out of the way, too, and sent back to her father.

The sound of a horse and carriage drawing up outside the house signified it was time for Isabel to depart. A wave of despair seized her. Daniel still hadn't written. She had asked Kitty whether she could come back to the house to enquire about letters addressed to her, but the maid had shaken her head. 'The new place is on the other side of town, miss. And I'll be too busy trying to get it set to rights to think about calling back here.'

Aunt Sophia, Rebecca and Amelia came through from the drawing room where they had been conversing in subdued tones.

'Send my regards to your father, Isabel. Do tell him to come and visit us, and bring you with him. I've sent him the new address.'

Isabel nodded. 'Goodbye,' she said, trying to include all three of her relatives in her weak smile. 'Thank you for having me to stay.' Unable to find any other words, she began to follow Kitty, who was assisting in loading her trunk onto the carriage, before stopping on the threshold to say, 'I'll write.'

Then Kitty held open the carriage door for her and Isabel placed her foot on the step. As she did so, Kitty slid something from her apron pocket and pressed it into Isabel's hand.

'Came this morning, miss,' she whispered. 'I haven't had a moment to get it to you.'

She stepped back and, in a louder voice, said, 'Safe journey, miss,' then slammed the carriage door.

Isabel sat back in her seat, the folded piece of paper Kitty had given her clutched in her hand. She'd seen the writing only once before, but that was enough to show her it was in Daniel's hand. She remembered her manners in time to wave to the Crawfords, unable to contain a broad smile that must have puzzled them, before the carriage pulled away.

Isabel broke the seal on the letter and flattened the paper on her lap. She was delighted to see several closely packed lines of script but, although she was impatient to read it, she forced herself to gaze out of the window as the carriage passed along the seafront and wound its way through Ramsgate. She didn't know when she would see the streets again, or be in such close proximity to the sea, and she wanted to savour these last few moments. As they passed the Tremaines' house, she wished she had been able to call in to see Mrs Tremaine. But her departure had been so hastily arranged and, in truth, she felt a sense of shame, as though she had been banished to the country. Perhaps she would write to her instead.

With the outskirts of Ramsgate now upon her, Isabel could wait no longer. She sat back in the seat, picked up the letter and began to read.

Winton House,
Berkeley Square,
Mayfair, London

My dear Isabel,

I've scarce had a moment to put pen to paper since I last saw you, and I fear I may have forgotten half the things I wished to share with you. Let me start by saying how sorry I was to witness something of your cousin Rebecca's distress at the ball. I fear Giles must have been the cause – he has recently become betrothed and no doubt shared the news in his customary blunt manner. I can only hope your cousin has recovered her equilibrium.

I do so wish we could have spent more time together that evening. There was much I would have liked to say. I have formed the opinion we have a similar outlook on life but I would have welcomed the chance to find out whether or not I am right. If my father's business hadn't called me away, I would have enjoyed walking with you (and your aunt, of course) along the seafront the following day.

As it is, I despair of finding the time to make another trip to Ramsgate in the coming months. I wonder whether you could prevail upon Mrs Crawford to conduct you, and your cousins, to London instead. With enough warning, I could arrange it so I am free to spend at least a part of a day with you over the course of a week. You might be greatly entertained here – you could have your choice of a visit to the theatre, an entertainment or a ball most nights of the week.

I have included my address above – do write and tell me whether you might come. Or just write anyway and tell me how you are filling your days. If you do not receive a prompt reply, be assured that I am somewhere between London, Bristol, York or Edinburgh, trailing my father as he goes about the King's business.

I must finish now. Would it be presumptuous of me to ask for something to keep close to my heart, to remember you by? A lock of hair, perhaps – I am not well versed in such things.

Your devoted servant,
Daniel Coates

Isabel smiled in delight as she smoothed the folds of the letter on her lap. She could hardly have hoped to hear more promising sentiments. He had asked for a love token! If she had been able, she would have cut a curl from her head there and then.

She picked up the letter and re-read it, frowning when she reached the comment about Rebecca's distress. She hadn't been aware of Daniel and his father when she, Aunt Sophia and Amelia had bundled Rebecca out of the cloakroom and into the carriage.

She felt a rush of shame at what they – and no doubt other guests – must have witnessed. Rebecca had lost all inhibition as she raged and wept. Isabel feared it reflected badly on them all.

She forced herself to leave such memories behind and turned again to Daniel's words. Now she felt fortunate to be leaving Ramsgate, since Daniel could not foresee returning there. A trip to London with the Crawfords would have been out of the question, also. But at least now she had Daniel's address. She could write to him whenever she wished.

CHAPTER TWENTY-SIX

The contemplation of Daniel's letter kept Isabel occupied throughout much of the homeward journey, so that she was surprised to find herself at the gate of Marston Grange. If she had been anticipating a warm welcome on her return, she was disappointed. The donkey began braying at the carriage horse and Cook came out to see what all the noise was about, to find Isabel standing beside her trunk and valise in the courtyard.

'Miss Isabel! Welcome!' Cook was beaming, but Isabel was a little put out.

'Is my father here?' she asked, although she had a good idea of the answer.

'He's somewhere around the farm.' Cook was vague. 'He'll be back for his dinner. Leave the trunk – I'll get one of the men to move it when they come up from the field.'

Isabel went into the house. It was so dark inside – had it always been so? She took in the wooden floor, the panelling and the beams as if she was seeing them for the first time, and thought how light and airy the house in Ramsgate had been in comparison.

She walked into the dining room and gazed up at the portrait of her mother, trying to divine the secrets hidden behind her eyes. She would question her father about their marriage, she decided. It seemed as though everyone knew something of what had happened between them, apart from Isabel. She surely had a right to know.

She took the valise up to her bedroom, put it on the bed and gazed out of the window. She was restless, unsure how to fill the time until her father returned. Perhaps she should take a walk: the fields were fresh and inviting in the sunshine. It was a sight that would have gladdened her heart just a few months ago. Now she looked down at her dress and her shoes. Would they be ruined? She doubted there was anything in her trunk that was more suitable. She tried to remember what she had worn for such a walk previously. With a sinking heart she thought back to the clothes she had worn to travel to Ramsgate in January. The skirt, shirt and the sturdy boots had been disposed of, on her aunt's orders.

Isabel let out a sigh, turned away from the window and went down to the kitchen. Cook was stirring a pot on the stove. A ball of pastry sat on the table, ready to be rolled out. Isabel sat down and Cook turned at the noise of the chair legs scraping on the flagstones.

'Oh, Miss Isabel, you'll spoil your lovely frock. There's flour and goodness knows what on the table.'

Isabel shook her head, impatient. 'I don't care. Tell me what has been happening here while I've been away.'

Cook went back to her stirring. 'I can't rightly say.' She thought, stirring some more. 'The donkey went lame and your father was all for shooting it, but I said you'd never forgive him. He's better now, the donkey, as you can see.'

Isabel smiled. She shouldn't have been surprised. What else had she expected? After all, so little had happened in Marston in all the years she had lived there.

Her eyes alighted on an uncut loaf sitting on the table. 'Have you seen anything of Thomas, the miller's boy?'

Cook turned to look at her. 'He was here this morning, delivering the bread. Why do you ask?'

'No reason.' Isabel began to drum her fingers on the table. How was she going to get through all the hours in the day in Marston?

'I've asked Abraham to take your trunk to your room,' Cook said. 'Why don't you unpack? By the time you're done, your father will be home, I expect.' She carried the pot to the table, ready to start making the pie for dinner. She cast a shrewd eye over Isabel. 'He'll be pleased when he sees you. Your aunt has worked wonders. You're quite the young lady now. I hardly recognised you when I saw you standing out in the yard.'

Isabel, hearing the noise of the trunk as it was bumped up the stairs, stood up. It wasn't lost on her that Cook thought her transformation would please her father more than her presence. She made a sour face as she went up to her room. Presumably he would be happy he had got his money's worth, she thought.

She opened the trunk and began to lay out the dresses on the bed. When would she wear any of them again? There was little point in dressing for dinner, since her father usually came to the table in what he'd worn in the fields. She felt a piercing sense of loss for her life in Ramsgate. How long would she have to stay here, buried in Marston? Or would her father have plans to send her to London, perhaps? She stood a chance of seeing Daniel there. Her heart lifted at the thought. She resolved to ask the question that very evening.

Mr Cavendish was at the table as the clock struck five, as always. He looked up as Isabel entered the dining room and gave an approving nod.

'Your aunt has done well, very well.' He sliced into the golden crust of the pie, releasing a cloud of steam. 'She had enough money from me, mind, so I would have been disappointed if it had been otherwise.'

'Thank you, Father. I feel sure I learned a great deal in Ramsgate.' Isabel glanced up at the portrait of her mother, watching over her. 'And thank you for sending my mother's earrings. I wore them to my first ball.'

Her father grunted, and added a few more potatoes to his plate.

Isabel served herself a slice of pie. Now was the moment, she decided, glancing up at the portrait again to give herself courage.

'Father, won't you tell me more of my mother? Why did she leave? And why did she never write to me?'

Mr Cavendish carried on eating as though he hadn't heard her. Isabel waited a few moments and tried again. 'Cousin Amelia mentioned something about a duke? And France?' she ventured.

Her father flung down his knife and fork with a clatter. 'Did she, now? If I'd known my sister was making free with tittle-tattle I would have chosen to send you elsewhere.'

Isabel quailed before his thunderous expression and meekly began to eat. She feared his wrath too much to press further for answers.

'She did write to you.' Her father spoke abruptly. 'Each year, on your birthday. I destroyed the letters unopened. I didn't want your young mind poisoned, your thoughts tainted by someone of such low morals.' He all but spat out the last words, and sloshed some ale into his glass from the jug on the table.

Isabel, scarcely able to believe her ears, bit her lip and clenched her fists beneath the table. To think her mother had written to her many times and she had never known! And she was alive somewhere, over the sea perhaps, wondering why her daughter had never replied. She glanced up at the portrait, trying to glean something of the woman from her expression. Her father caught the movement.

'You're wondering why I keep her likeness here? It's a reminder,' he said. 'A reminder of how beautiful she was, and how weak I was. I'll not make such a mistake again. And nor will you. Marrying for love is a fool's game.'

He picked up his knife and fork and began shovelling food into his mouth as though he was starving. Isabel watched him clean his plate, as the truth of what lay ahead began to dawn on her. She had chafed at the restrictions in her aunt's house, but now she longed for her life there. Was this to be her future? Long, empty days with nothing to do but roam the countryside, followed by evenings at the table with an embittered father, who had so little to say to his daughter?

139

Isabel's appetite had all but fled, but she tried to do justice to the food on her plate. Cook would be disappointed if she didn't. And Cook was the only sympathetic presence in a house that otherwise felt devoid of love. She could cling to the one tiny spark of light in what otherwise appeared to be a bleak wasteland stretching before her. Daniel had written her a letter – she had several passages off by heart – and now that she had his address she could write back. She just had to find the means to do so without her father coming to know of it.

THOMAS

PART TWO

MAY — AUGUST 1823

CHAPTER EIGHT

Thomas, sitting at the dinner table one bright evening in early summer and concentrating on the meat pie on his plate, heard Mr Hopkins remark to his wife, 'I saw Mercy when I was out delivering the flour sacks today. She said the Cavendish girl is home again.'

Thomas, who had just crammed a large piece of pie into his mouth, almost choked. Mrs Hopkins frowned at him before turning to her husband. 'You just chanced on Mercy, did you? Or did you happen to find yourself in the Wheatsheaf, glass in hand?'

Thomas listened warily, expecting the sort of argument that would have erupted back home in Castle Bay even though the miller's wife was smiling.

'It's been a warm day,' Mr Hopkins said comfortably, 'and it's thirsty work unloading those sacks of flour.'

'And has Miss Cavendish been transformed into a fine young lady?' Mrs Hopkins enquired.

'Mercy hasn't seen her yet, but she came back with a trunk full of new clothes by all accounts.'

Mrs Hopkins glanced at Thomas, who had recovered from his shock at the news. 'You'll see her soon enough,' she said, reading his mind. 'But don't go getting ideas into your head.'

Mr Hopkins nodded. 'You're of an age now to start thinking about finding yourself a nice girl to settle down with. I married Emily here,' he nodded towards his wife, 'when I was barely seventeen and she was no more than sixteen.' He picked up his knife

143

and fork and began to eat again, his wife making ready to cut him another slice of pie. He chewed thoughtfully, then said, 'It's a shame our Ruth isn't a bit older. I'd be glad to have you as part of our family.'

'Adam!' his wife exclaimed, shocked. Ruth and Benjamin began to giggle and Anthony looked between them before joining in.

Thomas turned bright red and could barely force the rest of his pie past his lips. He had to endure the agony of waiting until the miller had finished his dinner before he could escape out into the yard. Now that the evenings were lighter and warmer, the miller took his pipe out there, while the children played. Mrs Hopkins saw to the dishes and Thomas usually did the drying up, but tonight she sent him out, too, saying she would manage well enough.

Thomas hoped the subject of marriage had been forgotten, but it was still on Mr Hopkins's mind. As he tamped down the tobacco in his pipe he said, 'You're the best worker I've ever had, Thomas, and you fit well into our family. I know Ruth seems but a little scrap of a thing now, for she's only eight years old. It might seem like a big difference but, mark my words, in another eight years' time you'll think differently.'

The pair of them watched Ruth pulling her little brother Anthony around the yard in the wooden cart that had served all three children well. Benjamin came over to show them something he had caught in his cupped hands, crouching down so that Anthony could see. Their three heads were close together and the setting sun caught the red tones in their hair. Thomas tried, and failed, to imagine Ruth as a young woman. Would she look more like her mother or her father? She had the pink-cheeked healthy look of her sandy-haired father, but perhaps her hair would turn brown, like her mother's, when she was older. She had the same calm disposition as her parents. She would be most unlike Isabel Cavendish, he decided.

Once again, it was as though his thoughts had been read. 'Isabel Cavendish isn't for the likes of you, lad.' The miller spoke abruptly.

'Don't go making that mistake. Her mother was a flighty thing. It seems she thought Cavendish had some sort of country estate and got a shock once they were married and he brought her home. She kept taking herself off to London to see her dressmaker, although she had little need for fancy gowns around here. While she was there, she found herself a duke and went off to live with him in France. Cavendish was left to bring up Isabel. I don't think he had any idea what to do with her. I doubt a few months in Ramsgate have made her into a young lady. She was running wild when she left here and I dare say she's inherited more than her mother's looks. She'll be trouble for someone, you mark my words.'

It was an uncharacteristically long speech for the miller, who usually confined himself to the most basic conversation. Thomas gave him a sideways glance before returning his gaze to the yard. He appeared to be watching the children at play but his mind was elsewhere. Could he manage to see Isabel before he was next due to deliver bread at Marston Grange? Would he find her much changed? Would she find him much changed? He'd had a birthday during the time she was away; somehow sixteen felt much older than fifteen. He'd mentioned it casually to the miller, not in expectation of anything since he was used to his parents forgetting the day.

To his surprise, Mr Hopkins seemed put out he hadn't spoken of it earlier. He'd left Thomas to keep watch over the corn grinding between the great millstones, while he went in search of his wife. He seemed pleased with himself when he returned.

Dinner that night had been rabbit stew and dumplings, which Thomas had never eaten in Castle Bay but which Mrs Hopkins had previously served for her husband's birthday. Thomas had exclaimed on that occasion, 'This is the best dinner I've ever eaten!'

'It's a shame you couldn't have thought to let me know earlier about your birthday,' Mrs Hopkins grumbled, as she dished up the stew. 'I could have made you something special.'

'But you have!' Thomas protested. He thought himself the luckiest boy alive.

Mr Hopkins had entrusted him with more and more of the mill work, so that he could go out with the cart to deliver flour or pick up grain. Thomas was enjoying the responsibility and liked being trusted to work on his own. After Isabel had left so suddenly, he had thought about her a great deal and missed seeing her when he made his delivery to Marston Grange. But gradually the memory of her had begun to fade; he no longer thought about her every day. He had been drawn into the warm and happy Hopkins family, finding there the sort of life he had missed since his aunt Meg had disappeared eight years earlier.

'I've a mind to turn a corner of the yard over to vegetables,' the miller said suddenly, making Thomas start. 'Mrs Hopkins has been asking me to do it for long enough. Now that Ruth and Benjamin are a bit older, they can help me of an evening and Anthony can do some watering. Will you give me hand with it?'

Thomas nodded. 'Of course,' he said.

Mrs Hopkins came out to call the three children to bed, and Thomas's thoughts strayed from the peaceful scene around him to Marston Grange. What was Isabel doing now? He imagined her somewhere upstairs in the house, gazing out of a window across the darkening fields, watching an owl swoop on its prey. Could she see the mill from there? Had she thought about him at all? Was she thinking of him now?

CHAPTER NINE

Now that he had heard of Isabel's return, Thomas was impatient to see her again. He had to contain himself, however, until he was due to go out with the bread, two days later. By the time he reached the gate of Marston Grange on delivery day, his heart was racing. He glanced up at the windows, hoping to catch sight of her there, and loitered beside the donkey wheel in case she should step out of the house. There was no sign of her and Thomas's shoulders slumped in dejection as he made his way to the kitchen.

'That's a sorry face, if ever I saw one.' Cook took the loaf from him and set it on the table. 'Miss Isabel, is there anything you can say to cheer up the boy?'

Thomas had failed to register the figure standing by the dresser, back to him as she leafed through Cook's recipe book. He swallowed hard and put a hand on the table to steady himself, for the Isabel who turned around was very different from the girl he had last seen in church on Christmas Day. Gone were the plain linen skirts and blouses and the white lace dress, the man's tweed jacket and serviceable boots. She was wearing a dress the colour of the primroses that had so lately studded the banks along the lane to the mill and her hair no longer flowed over her shoulders but was piled on top of her head.

Thomas attempted to master both his voice and his thoughts to address her. 'I hope you enjoyed your stay in Ramsgate.' He hesitated. 'Are you to be here for long?'

He was more interested in hearing her second answer than her first.

Isabel came over to the table and set down the book. 'I can't find the recipe,' she complained. 'I know you have made it for me before.' She gave Cook a look of appeal. 'Can you remember?'

Cook sighed. 'I think you've muddled me with the cook in Ramsgate. Your father would never eat the sort of dessert you describe. But I will see what I can find.'

Thomas, embarrassed at being ignored, picked up his basket and was about to slip away but Isabel turned to him. 'I'll walk with you. It's a beautiful day and I need an excuse to be outside. Come.' She moved to the door and waited for him to follow.

Thomas hurried after her. He thought he heard Cook chuckle as he closed the door.

'Where shall we go first?' she asked.

'The Wheatsheaf,' he mumbled. He was taken aback to be walking at her side. All their previous encounters had taken place in the yard at Marston Grange. They had gone barely twenty paces along the lane before Isabel stopped, flung her head back and shut her eyes, holding her face up to the sky.

'Ah, that breeze. And the lovely scents of the countryside. How I've missed it.' She set off again, Thomas hurrying after her. 'You asked about Ramsgate ... let me see. I enjoyed it – some of it. But the wind – such a scouring blast off the sea. I missed all of this.' She flung her arms wide and spun around. Thomas noticed the dainty leather slippers she was wearing. They wouldn't last long on the rough lanes and tracks around Marston.

They turned in through the gate of the Wheatsheaf and Isabel ran on ahead of him, to rap on the door before pushing it open.

He heard her call, 'Bread delivery,' as she went inside, and smiled to himself. This high-spirited Isabel was the one he remembered. He followed her, to find her deep in conversation with Mercy, who was exclaiming over her dress and walking around her so she could admire front and back.

Thomas unloaded the loaves onto the bar and watched as the

landlady felt the primrose fabric between her fingers, declaring it the finest she had ever seen.

'You're too grand now for the likes of us.' Mercy shook her head. 'What are your father's plans for you?'

Isabel shrugged. 'I don't know. He hasn't said. But I have some of my own.'

Thomas paid particular attention to her last words, and the smile that crossed her face as she uttered them.

There was no time to ponder her meaning, for Isabel was holding out her hand and saying, 'Where to now?'

She didn't wait for him, but set off out of the door and, with a bemused shake of his head for Mercy's benefit, Thomas followed.

Isabel danced at his side as they made their way along. She waited at each gate while he delivered bread to the poorhouse, and then the cottages, waving at the occupants to acknowledge them. Thomas supposed he would lose her there, for the lane turned and continued to the mill, but she showed no sign of turning back. He glanced down at her fine leather slippers, now smeared with dust, and feared for their thin soles.

They had just begun their descent into the dip of the lane when Isabel stopped and peered into the woods. 'I wonder if the badgers are still there?' she said. For a moment, Thomas thought she meant to plunge in among the trees there and then but she collected herself. 'We'll look another day,' she said, smoothing her dress. He glowed at being included.

'What have you been doing while I was away, Thomas?' she asked. She turned her gaze full on him and he couldn't meet it, looking down at his feet instead.

'Working mostly, I suppose,' was the best he could do.

Isabel nodded, apparently satisfied, and they walked on a little way in silence.

'I find myself needing to send a letter,' she said suddenly, 'but I don't wish to ask my father to do it. Can you think how it might be done?'

149

Thomas at once wished to be of service to her. It would have been easy enough to manage in Castle Bay but he had no idea how it could be done out here in the countryside. 'I could ask Mr Hopkins,' he offered. 'I'm sure he will advise.'

Isabel frowned. 'I'm not sure I trust anyone else to know.' She turned to him again. 'Only you.'

She stopped once more, forcing Thomas to a halt. She held his gaze as she said, 'And now I think of it, I wouldn't like the replies to come to me. Do you think I could have them sent to you?'

Thomas blushed crimson. He wanted to help Isabel more than anything else, but wouldn't the miller and his wife find it strange if he suddenly began to receive letters? They would want to know who was writing to him and what was in them. Theirs wasn't a household for secrets. And Isabel wanted her letter-writing to be kept secret from her father. What did this mean?

'Could you ask Cook?' he ventured. 'Or Mercy, at the Wheatsheaf?'

Isabel shook her head. 'I don't want anyone to know,' she repeated, 'other than you.'

She began to walk on again. 'Promise me you will think about it,' she said.

Thomas, relieved not to be pressed for an immediate answer, nodded vigorously.

Now another dilemma presented itself. As they rose out of the dip in the lane they were drawing closer to the mill. Should he invite Isabel in to take some refreshment? But what would Mrs Hopkins say? He remembered Isabel had once expressed a wish to see inside the building. Would she remember, and request to do so today?

To his relief, when they were within a few paces of the mill, Isabel said, 'I'll go back now. No doubt you have work to do. I enjoyed our walk, Thomas. I hope we can do it again. And you will think about what I asked?'

She didn't wait for an answer but smiled at him before turning

150

away. Thomas watched her go, her dress a bright flash of yellow in the shade cast by the trees. How could he help her? He had no idea, but he knew it was important to try.

CHAPTER TEN

Thomas returned the delivery basket to Mrs Hopkins before he went to find the miller, who was hard at work on an upper floor. Hearing the grinding of the great millstones, Thomas didn't bother to call up to him.

He busied himself stacking empty grain sacks and sweeping up, then set to work to repair one of the sieves used on the meal floor. He didn't cross paths with the miller until Mrs Hopkins summoned them and they sat down on the bench in the yard, where she had placed two plates of bread, cheese, pickles and slices of pork pie. They were hungry and ate in silence until Mr Hopkins, after using his finger to chase up the last crumbs on his plate, sat back with a contented sigh.

'Was that Isabel Cavendish I saw you with in the lane?' he said suddenly.

Caught by surprise with his mouth full, Thomas could only manage a nod.

'I thought as much. I saw you from up there.' The miller indicated the small window in the upper storey of the mill. 'She's a proper young lady now.' He gave Thomas a sideways glance. 'Remember what I said. Don't go getting tangled up with her.' He got to his feet to signify their break was over and Thomas hurriedly stuffed the last of his bread and cheese into his mouth.

Throughout the afternoon, Thomas racked his brains to find a way to help Isabel. At dinner that evening, he asked the miller, in what he hoped was a casual fashion, how he might send a letter.

'I thought I might write to my mother to tell her how I am getting on,' he said. He had no such intention – he was sounding out how to send a letter on Isabel's behalf – but the miller's wife seized on his words.

'Why, how worried she must be! Why ever didn't we think of this before? You must go and visit her. I'll make up some pies for you to take.' She turned to her husband. 'Mr Hopkins, you must give the boy a day off so he can see his mother and tell her how he does.'

Mr Hopkins pulled on his pipe and nodded. 'Aye. The brewery cart makes some deliveries to Castle Bay or thereabouts. You could take a ride next time.'

'A letter would be enough,' Thomas protested. 'My mother would expect no more.' He was in no great rush to show his face in Castle Bay. In fact, he wished to avoid it in case Bartholomew Banks should catch sight of him and remember his threat to have him killed.

But Mrs Hopkins was immovable in her belief that he must make the journey. She was only distracted from her plan when little Anthony fell over and cracked his head on the flagstones, setting up a great wail.

It was the next day before Thomas realised he might have the solution to Isabel's problem. If he could persuade the miller and his wife that it was sensible for him to first send a letter, to supposedly warn his mother about his forthcoming visit, he could enclose the letter Isabel wished to send inside his. He would need to include a coin or two for his mother to make sure it was sent on. He could also suggest to Isabel that her correspondent could reply to the Castle Bay address and his mother could enclose the letter within a reply to him at the mill. There was a regular postal service to and from Castle Bay using the stagecoach, and they could use the brewery driver to get letters there and bring back any replies.

The more he thought about it, the more pleased Thomas became. He could see no disadvantage to the plan, other than a delay in communication caused by having to wait for the brewery to make deliveries to Castle Bay. He could barely wait for his next bread delivery to Marston Grange so he could explain it to Isabel.

It was a particularly warm day when Thomas set out. He was full of excitement as he walked along the lane from the mill, relishing the shade of the trees as he passed the basket of loaves from one hand to the other. By the time he reached Marston Grange he was perspiring, despite the early hour, for the sun beat down relentlessly on the open stretches of road.

Isabel was in the yard. 'There you are,' she said.

She sounded impatient, Thomas thought. She was wearing a blue-green dress that reminded Thomas of the colour of the sea in Castle Bay under summer clouds. The battered straw hat jammed on her head appeared incongruous with her outfit, as did her foot-wear. She'd forsaken her delicate slippers and was wearing sturdy boots.

She showed no inclination to talk or accompany him to the kitchen so Thomas delivered his loaf, gratefully accepting and gulping a glass of cordial from Cook. Then he returned to join Isabel in the yard. She was standing by the donkey wheel, fanning the beast with her straw hat as it plodded ever onwards.

'The Wheatsheaf?' she asked, and Thomas nodded.

'I have a plan,' he announced, as soon as they were out in the lane.

'You do?' Isabel, a little surly until then, was now all smiles.

As they covered the short distance to the Wheatsheaf, he quickly outlined his idea of using his mother to send and receive letters.

'She can send any answers to me and I can pass them to you,' he said. They'd reached the gate of the Wheatsheaf and Isabel stopped, frowning. 'And you think it could work?' she asked.

'It just requires the assistance of a brewery-cart driver.' Thomas was proud of his plan.

Isabel's frown deepened. 'They all work for my father. They mustn't suspect my involvement in this.'

This time, she seemed disinclined to join him, waiting outside while he took the loaves in to Mercy.

'Is that Miss Isabel out there?' Mercy asked, although Thomas knew full well she had seen her at the gate. When he nodded, she smiled. 'Is she going to be your regular companion on your rounds?'

Thomas refused to be drawn. He made for the door, keen to re-join Isabel.

'Don't get ideas in your head,' Mercy said waspishly. 'Her father has her future mapped out, I'll be bound. And you won't feature in it.'

Thomas made a face. Did the whole of Marston want to offer him advice about how ill-suited he was to Isabel? He hurried down the path to where she was waiting.

'Have you any money?'

Her abrupt question caught him by surprise. He patted his pockets, even though he knew they were empty.

'We'll need money. For the postage and beer for the cart driver.'

They were walking through Marston as Thomas completed the deliveries, their conversation interrupted each time he stopped to knock on doors.

'You have none?' Thomas was surprised.

Isabel shook her head. 'My father doesn't give me an allowance. If I want something, I suppose I must ask for it, although I never have. He would want a full account of what I had spent it on.'

By the time they had made the last delivery, to the cottages, Thomas had reached a decision. 'I have a bit of money put aside from my wages,' he said. 'There is no reason for the cart driver to know he is carrying a letter on your behalf. He will think the letters going back and forth are for me alone, for your letters will be sealed inside. So it is only right for me to pay him.'

He pushed away the uneasy thoughts that clamoured for his attention: who was Isabel writing to and why must it be kept a secret? Instead, he congratulated himself that his plan to act as her

155

go-between meant he would have every reason to continue seeing her. And she would surely be grateful for his actions. In some ways, everything had fallen perfectly into place.

CHAPTER ELEVEN

That night, Thomas told Mr and Mrs Hopkins that he would be writing to his mother, to tell her he was happily settled in employment and to see when it might be convenient to visit her.

'She often goes to see her sister,' he said, surprising himself with the smoothness of his untruth. 'I don't want to arrive and find her not there.'

In fact, his letter pointed out the impossibility of a visit, for he knew she would be only too aware of the risks. Instead, he wrote,

I hope this letter finds you well. I'm sorry I haven't written before and I hope my tardiness hasn't caused you any distress.

I have had the good fortune to find myself work with the miller in Marston, a place not too far distant. Mr Hopkins and his wife have been very good to me and I am happy here.

They have suggested I visit you and I have told them that this letter is to arrange it, but we both know that is impossible. Please write back, though. And when you broke the seal, you will have been surprised to find another letter and coins concealed within. The money is to pay for the onward carriage of the letter, on the stagecoach to London.

You may receive a letter in return, addressed to Isabel Cavendish at your address. Do not open it, but enclose it within your reply to me. You can leave your letter at the Crown on Beach Street. Ask the landlord to give it to the brewery wagon driver from Marston when he next makes a delivery there.

The sending and receiving of these letters is to help a friend of mine in Marston, who turned to me when she didn't know who to entrust with their safe delivery. I hope you will feel able to do this for me.

Please let me know how you are in your reply, and send any news.

Your loving son,

Thomas

When he next took the bread to Marston Grange, he told Isabel that his letter was written and asked her to have hers ready for his next visit.

'It's done,' she said. 'Can we despatch it now?'

Thomas hadn't anticipated this. 'I didn't bring mine with me.' He saw a flash of annoyance cross her face and hastened to add, 'But in any case, I must speak with the wagoner and find out when he next plans a journey.'

They were standing in the courtyard of Marston Grange, Isabel scowling and scuffing the ground with the toe of her boot. 'It's been too long already,' she burst out. 'I've been gone from Ramsgate nearly four weeks. And who knows how long I must wait for a response?'

Her words were a blow to Thomas's heart. No matter how he had tried to convince himself otherwise, it was clear Isabel's letter was intended for a special person, someone she greatly missed.

A minute or two passed in silence before he ventured, 'Shall we walk?'

'Not today.' Isabel flounced into the house. She no longer paid attention to her hair, Thomas noted. Today it flowed around her shoulders as it had in the past. She still wore the dresses she had acquired in Ramsgate, but she hadn't treated them well. The hem of the lavender one she was wearing that day was dusty and beginning to come down.

A thought struck him. 'Isabel!' he called after her.

She turned towards him on the doorstep with a sigh.

'Bring me your letter,' he urged. 'I will take it with me now, and set it inside mine. Then it will be complete.'

158

Without a word, she went into the house – he could hear her feet racing up the wooden stairs and down again. She was at his side in less than a minute. She glanced swiftly around, although there was no one to see them, and tucked the letter into the basket among the bread. She nodded at him and went back through the front door.

Thomas continued on his rounds, a frown knitting his brow. Her churlishness had disturbed him. He supposed she found it frustrating to be back in Marston where the pace of life was so much slower than it was in a town. And it was true that it could be at least two weeks, if not a great deal more, before his letter had found its way to Castle Bay, hers was sent on its way, and a reply received and despatched.

He resolved to search out the brewery wagoner as soon as he could, before Isabel's impatience led her to do something rash.

He had not expected the miller to have been working on his behalf and he was surprised by his words when he arrived back with the bread basket. 'I've spoken to Nathaniel,' he said. 'He's making a delivery to Castle Bay today and he'll stop by with the wagon. Make sure you have that letter ready.'

Thomas felt a guilty flush spread across his cheeks. Isabel's letter lay in the bottom of the basket. 'I'll fetch it now,' he said, glancing back just before he entered the house. The miller was examining his new vegetable patch for signs of life and Thomas slipped Isabel's letter into his jacket pocket as he hurried inside. He gave the basket to Mrs Hopkins, then went to his room in the outbuilding and retrieved the letter to his mother from under his mattress. He folded his page around Isabel's, took some coins from those held in a leather pouch, also under his mattress, and went to look for Mr Hopkins, now in the mill.

'I need to seal this,' he said, waving the letter, 'but I haven't the means.'

'No need for that,' Mr Hopkins said comfortably. 'I doubt Nathaniel can read.'

159

'I'm sending my mother a little money,' Thomas said, another blush spreading across his face even though his words were true.

'In that case . . .' The miller began to hunt around on the dusty desk where he did his paperwork. 'I know there is sealing wax somewhere, although I have little use for it.' He scattered papers, muttering to himself, until he found the red stick he was looking for. 'Here you are. You'll need to warm it in a flame. Shall I show you how it's done?'

'No,' Thomas said hastily. He was keen the miller shouldn't see the other letter tucked inside. 'There's no need. I've seen it done often enough. At the boatyard,' he added, seeing the miller's sceptical expression. It was true – one of his jobs at the boatyard in Castle Bay had been to deliver messages and he'd waited and watched while the owner applied his seal before sending him on his way.

Thomas took the tinder box and struck the flint, then lit a stub of candle while the miller carried on with his work. Thomas's hands shook as he placed the coins over the folded flap of the paper, then heated the tip of the wax stick in the flame. He didn't like being devious but the miller seemed oblivious. As the wax softened and threatened to drip, he pressed it over the coins to form a rough disc, holding the money in place. When he was satisfied it was thick enough, he twisted the stick to break the contact.

He eyed the blob of red wax. He had no ring to imprint his seal so, after a moment, he pressed his thumb into the wax. It was warmer than he had expected, but as he lifted his hand away, a perfect thumbprint was left behind. No one, other than his mother, would be tempted to break the seal now, he thought.

Thomas set the letter on the desk and hurried to start his tasks for the afternoon. Not a quarter of an hour later, the miller called down from the grain floor: 'I see Nathaniel coming along the lane. Run out with your letter, Thomas.'

Thomas did as he was bade. It was only as he was handing the sealed paper up to Nathaniel that he realised he had no money to pay him.

'It needs to go to the old baker's shop in Prospect Street, number five. Will that be all right?'

'Aye.' Nathaniel nodded. 'Number five Prospect Street. And if I forget, I can ask the landlord at the inn to tell me what's writ here.' He pointed at the front of the letter.

'There'll be a letter to come back, to pick up from the inn, but not today. Another day,' Thomas said.

Flustered, he realised he was speaking slowly and carefully as though Nathaniel was simple, rather than just unable to read. Already embarrassed, he was forced to add, 'I must run and get some money for you, to pay you for your service. Will you wait?'

Nathaniel shook his head. 'No need,' he said. 'Glad to help. You get Mrs Hopkins to send me round one of her pies when I come back. That's better than any money to me.' He tipped his cap to Thomas, shook the reins and the horses lumbered forward, straining a little on the incline until the wheels picked up momentum.

Thomas watched for a moment or two, feeling some guilt at his deception. He would at least pay Mrs Hopkins for the ingredients of Nathaniel's pie, he thought.

Chapter Twelve

On his next visit to the Grange, Thomas was able to confirm to Isabel that her letter had not only left Marston, but was probably on its way to London, if his mother had done as instructed.

The glumness with which Isabel had greeted him that day was instantly banished from her face. 'It's already gone?' She clasped her hands together and beamed. 'Oh, thank you, Thomas.'

He didn't have to ask her whether she would walk with him, for she was already at the gate. She all but skipped along at his side as they made their way to the Wheatsheaf.

The letter she had sent clearly meant a great deal to her, Thomas realised, with pain. She was talking ceaselessly while they walked – a lot of inconsequential nonsense. It was as though all her pent-up worry about the letter had been replaced by a fountain of joy she was unable to repress.

'Perhaps you could show me the badger sett one day,' he ventured, as they walked past the woods on the way back to the mill, all deliveries made.

'Why not?' Isabel wrinkled her nose. 'Although I think my father has plans for me to go to London.'

Shocked, he would have questioned her further, but Isabel had already turned back.

'Goodbye, Thomas, and thank you again.'

Thomas stood and watched her. She broke into a run as she followed the dip of the road, spreading her arms out at either side, like a child, and he thought he heard her laugh.

He had little time to dwell on Isabel's mention of going to London, for the miller had plans to keep him busy. He had decided that they should make repairs to the mill before the late-summer harvest brought increased demands for their services. He wanted treads replacing on the internal ladders, and some of the exterior weatherboarding needed to be stripped back and painted. Thomas, glad of the break from routine, was able to put to use the carpentry skills he had learned at the boatyard. He was less happy one morning to find the miller leaning a tall ladder up against the mill. 'What's that for?' he asked, although he feared he already knew the answer.

'There's loose slats to be fixed on the sweeps, and rotten ones needing replacing,' the miller said cheerfully.

Thomas wasn't sure he had the necessary head for heights to do such a job, but he gripped the sides of the ladder and began to climb. A trembling began in his legs, and increased the higher he climbed, so he was glad to finally grasp the edge of the sail, which was so much larger then he had imagined now he was up close. He concentrated hard on levering out the rotten slats, throwing them to the ground with a warning to the miller to beware.

One broken slat remained, above the ones he had already tackled. He would have to stand on the top rung of the ladder and cling to the sweep to reach it. He bit his lip and breathed deeply, watching the swifts scooping up the insects over the fields, screaming as they swooped past him. He was just summoning his courage to take the final step when he was distracted by the sound of a wagon rumbling down the lane.

He heard Nathaniel call out 'Whoa,' and the wagon slowed to a halt outside the mill gate.

The miller hailed him and, to Thomas's horror, stepped away from his post at the base of the ladder to go and stand by the wagon. Thomas spread-eagled himself on the sweep and shut his eyes, too terrified even to call out.

He heard the exchange of a few indistinct words, then a

vibration as the miller took hold of the ladder again and the wagon moved off.

'All right up there, Thomas?' the miller called. 'I have your mother's letter for you.'

Impatience overrode Thomas's fear. Would the letter contain a secret one for Isabel? Throwing caution to the winds, he reached up and tugged hard at the broken slat to pull it free. It came away more easily than he had anticipated and for a heart-stopping moment he felt himself falling backwards, before he slammed himself against the sweep, hugging it for dear life.

'Come down now, Thomas,' the miller called.

Thomas's legs had begun to shake again, but he felt around with his foot to gain a toehold on the ladder, making painfully slow progress from one rung to the next. When he finally reached solid ground, he found the miller regarding him with some anxiety.

'You've gone very pale,' he remarked. 'Why didn't you tell me you don't like heights?'

Thomas, who feared he was going to be sick, said weakly, 'I had no way of knowing. I've never climbed so high before.'

'Take your letter.' The miller held it out to Thomas. 'Sit down and read it.' He caught Thomas's glance at the debris on the floor and the work still to be done on the sweeps. 'Leave all this for now.'

Thomas, grateful, went to sit on the bench in the sun. He stared at his mother's writing on the front of the folded paper for a moment or two. He hadn't seen her hand for nine months. An image of her as he'd last seen her came to him – her strained expression as he'd told her what he'd said to Bartholomew Banks, and the warning he'd received in return.

He'd left her alone in the house in Prospect Street, with less than savoury lodgers filling the other rooms, and he'd thought only of saving himself. He hadn't once considered how she was getting by, or whether she had suffered any retribution from Bartholomew Banks. Thomas was filled with guilt – what a terrible son he was. He had never been close to his mother, or his father for that matter, feeling more affinity with his aunt Meg, now long gone. But that was no excuse for his behaviour.

He turned over the letter and broke the seal, registering at once that something else was folded inside it. He glanced up, but the miller was nowhere to be seen, so he slipped the letter for Isabel into his pocket and spread his mother's flat on the bench, smoothing out the creases.

My dear Thomas,

How worried I have been about you! I leave you to imagine how happy I was to receive your letter. Before I go on, though, I must tell you that although I did as you requested and sent the letter you enclosed to London, and am now enclosing the reply, I urge you to be careful. I have to assume this is a correspondence between a young lady of your acquaintance, and a young man: something she wishes to keep secret. I'm not sure why you would wish to involve yourself and fear the outcome, in case it reflects badly upon you.

There – I am done with scolding and free to turn to happier matters. I would like you to convey my most sincere thanks to Mr Hopkins and his wife for taking you in and looking after you. I know you will work hard for them. When I see the sails of the mills on the edge of town, I will think of you, not too far distant.

The past winter found me suffering a great deal with aches and pains but I am improved by the summer weather and haven't felt a twinge since March.

Friends and neighbours have enquired as to your whereabouts but I have been careful to give as little information as possible, other than to say you are working away and I believe you to be well. I am glad, now, to know that both these things are true, but I will say nothing that might reach the ears of Bartholomew Banks. He continues to be a disappointment to his father – I have heard rumours that he is to be forbidden to come within fifteen miles of Castle Bay after involving himself

*in smuggling. On the happy day I know this to be true, I will
send word to you at once. In the meantime, I know we must stay
apart, no matter how much I long for it to be otherwise.*

   Your loving mother,

   Eliza

Thomas re-read the letter then set it aside. He saw how his
impetuous behaviour had affected his mother's life, although she
didn't complain of it. He had removed himself from Bartholomew
Banks's sight and now hardly thought of him, but he hadn't given
enough consideration to how his mother might feel, still living in
Castle Bay. She had made light of her illness but he wished now
that he could visit her to see the truth of it. She hadn't mentioned
his father, he realised, but then neither had he in his letter. Samuel
Marsh rarely entered Thomas's thoughts.

He thought of the money in his leather purse under the mattress – he had saved nearly every penny of his wages after his board
and lodging had been deducted, and he was pleased by the way the
amount had grown. Sometimes, at night, he had indulged himself
by imagining going to Isabel's father and asking for her hand,
telling him proudly of the money he had saved. A blush rose to
his cheeks at the thought. He would be scorned and turned away,
without a doubt. That money should be used to help his mother, he
could see that now. He must find a way to send it to her.

He glanced up at the mill doorway. How long had he spent in
contemplation of this letter? It was time to get back to work, but
first he should hide the reply intended for Isabel. He took both
letters to his room, secreting Isabel's beneath the mattress. As he
did so, he caught sight of the handwriting – the bold slope of the
'I', the flourish on the 'C'. It was a confident hand, he thought.
Someone prosperous, he imagined, and well-educated. It was with
a heavy heart that he made his way back to the yard and climbed
the steps to the mill.

CHAPTER THIRTEEN

'I heard you had a letter from your mother, Thomas.' Mrs Hopkins served him a slice of meat pie, rich with gravy. 'Has she set a date for your visit?'

Thomas, caught unprepared, tried to marshal his thoughts. 'Yes, she has written. She was very pleased to hear from me and I am sorry that I didn't think to write to her before.'

'I should have thought to suggest it.' Mrs Hopkins was adding potatoes to his plate. 'And so have you a date?' She set the heavy china dish on the table and gave him a questioning look.

Thomas bit his lip and poured more gravy over his dinner.

'She hasn't suggested a date. But I will write to her again.' He hoped that would dissuade Mrs Hopkins from pursuing the subject but, instead, she turned to her husband.

'Find out when Nathaniel is to make his next trip to Castle Bay. Thomas can sit alongside him and surprise his mother.'

'She might not be there,' Thomas protested hastily. 'She said she might leave town soon to . . .' He stopped, unable to lie under the scrutiny of five pairs of eyes.

'Let the boy alone,' Mr Hopkins told his wife. 'I dare say he has his reasons. He'll arrange it all in good time, I'm sure. Another letter will do nicely, for now.'

A wave of gratitude towards the miller washed over Thomas. Finally, he felt able to pick up his knife and fork and begin to eat.

'A delicious pie, Mrs Hopkins,' he said. 'Nathaniel requested a pie instead of payment for delivery of my letter. Could I ask you to make him one?' He hoped the question would mollify her.

She'd been looking a little put out since her husband had put a stop to her questions but now she smiled. 'Did he, now?'

'Yes, but please let me pay you. For the ingredients,' he added hastily, for Mrs Hopkins was frowning.

'I won't take payment,' she said. 'As long as you promise to arrange a date to visit your mother. I'll make Nathaniel a pie and you can give it to him when you next deliver the bread.'

Two days later Thomas set off for Marston Grange, a pie balanced on top of the bread and the letter for Isabel in his pocket. He saw her face at an upstairs window as he pushed open the gate, and his heart leaped. By the time he had latched the gate behind him, she was hurrying across the yard. He saw with surprise that she was wearing the white lace dress again, her hair flowing over her shoulders. He was reminded of the first time he had seen her.

'Have you a letter for me?' Her blue-grey eyes were fixed on his.

He set down the basket and slid the letter from his pocket. Mindful of his mother's warning, he took a quick look around to see whether they were observed.

Isabel seized the letter. Before he realised what was happening, she stood on tiptoe and kissed his cheek. 'Oh, Thomas, I can't thank you enough.' She whirled around in a flurry of lace and ran into the house, leaving Thomas rooted to the spot.

Conscious of the blush suffusing his cheeks, he picked up the basket and took it into the kitchen.

'Is it hot out there? Or have you by chance just seen Miss Isabel?' Cook regarded him with raised brows.

Turning even redder, if that was possible, Thomas mumbled something and set the loaf on the table. Without a word, Cook poured him a glass of cordial. He drank it gratefully. His throat felt parched after the encounter with Isabel.

He remembered the pie. 'Could I leave this here for Nathaniel, the brewery wagoner? I don't know where to find him.'

Cook nodded. 'He'll be along later. And very glad of one of Mrs Hopkins's pies.' She set it on a blue and white china plate on the dresser. 'It'll be safe here for now.'

'Tell him it's from me,' Thomas said. 'For carrying my letter to Castle Bay.'

Cook, taking his empty glass, sent him a look of enquiry.

'It was a letter to my mother.' Thomas, only too conscious of the other letter contained inside it, a letter Isabel wished to keep secret from the household, could feel his colour rising again.

Cook nodded, but something in her expression made Thomas wonder. Had Isabel mentioned the letter to her? She would surely have advised against sending it, if she had. Did she suspect?

He said goodbye to Cook and left, telling himself he was im- agining things. Even so, he felt uneasy by the time he returned to the mill, his round completed. He would tell Isabel he couldn't convey any more letters for her, he decided. It was too much of a risk. If her father discovered what she had done, and learned of Thomas's role as go-between, he would no doubt speak to the miller and demand he was punished. Mr Hopkins would have no choice but to let him go. Thomas couldn't begin to contemplate what he would do then.

The miller was busy in his vegetable patch when Thomas walked into the yard. Mr Hopkins had his back to him as he weeded be- tween the rows of carrots. It was something he did more and more by day, leaving Thomas to the daily business of the mill.

'Mr Cavendish was here while you were gone,' the miller said.

Thomas nearly dropped the basket in shock. Had his fears al- ready been realised?

'We haven't seen him in a while. He came to let me know he'll be away for a month with his daughter and to ask whether I might check up on the brewery in his absence.'

The miller eased himself upright, rubbing his back, and turned to face Thomas. 'I said I'd be more than happy, given that I can leave the mill in your capable hands.' He frowned. 'Are you all right? You've gone quite pale.'

Thomas swallowed.

'Go and get yourself a drink in the kitchen. I hope you're not about to fall ill after the promise I've just made.'

Thomas found his voice. 'It's nothing. When will they be leaving?'

'Tomorrow, Mr Cavendish said.'

The miller's words dashed Thomas's hopes of seeing Isabel before she left.

ISABEL

PART TWO

MAY — AUGUST 1823

CHAPTER TWENTY-SEVEN

Until Isabel returned to the quiet routine of life in Marston, she hadn't realised how swiftly each day had passed in Ramsgate, with dancing lessons and gossip, appointments for dress fittings, and promenades. She had dismissed so much of it as tedious but now she sorely missed it all – even Rebecca and Amelia's chatter. Most of all, though, she longed for the afternoons spent in Mrs Tremaine's library, and the delicious feeling she had there of somehow being close to Daniel.

Thinking of Daniel brought a sense of loss that was hard to bear. As she paced the floor of her bedroom at Marston Grange, or wandered through the fields, she racked her brains as to how to get in touch with him. Would he wonder why he hadn't heard from her? Would he write to the address in the Plains of Waterloo and take offence when he heard nothing in response? Would he think to contact Mrs Tremaine to enquire as to her whereabouts?

She longed to send him a letter but was at a loss as to how to do so. It couldn't be despatched from Marston Grange without her father hearing of it. She considered asking Mercy, or Cook, but could she be sure of their discretion? It would put Cook, in particular, in a difficult position.

It didn't take too long before she alighted on Thomas as her best hope. The boy came to the house regularly while he was delivering bread around Marston. Before she'd left for Ramsgate, he'd been a distraction from the monotony of her days and she'd found it tolerably amusing to talk to him, recognising how his infatuation with her grew by the week.

Now, when he arrived in the courtyard, he looked for her with such a hopeful expression that she was almost overwhelmed by irritation. But she fought it down because, as raw and unsophisticated as he was, she realised he was her best chance of getting a letter to Daniel. His visits became the high point of her week, but not for the reasons he had begun to believe. She could see it written across his face – his eagerness, the way his eyes fixed hungrily on her, his nervous deference that wouldn't allow him to speak his feelings.

If she had still been in Ramsgate, she could have been enjoying the balls of the summer season, watching how the young men reacted to her presence: a welcome new addition to the social scene. She would have become skilled in dealing with the likes of Giles Tremaine, she felt sure, delighting in tormenting and teasing as she had seen other young women do.

Instead, she had to make do with Thomas, the only other young person for miles around. It was too easy to have him in her thrall – she was quite sure he went back to the mill after their encounters and thought of little other than her. She would play along, just to get him to somehow arrange for a letter to be sent to Daniel.

And how easily it was done! At first, she had thought he would refuse. Clearly worried about getting into trouble with her father, he had put up obstacles. She'd become impatient, then regretted it afterwards. She couldn't afford to lose her one hope. He'd returned to her, though, having thought about it, and with a plan, to his credit. She'd almost felt sorry for him, seeing how keen he was to be of service.

None of it moved fast enough, of course. She couldn't bear to think of how long had passed before a letter was finally despatched. It wasn't even direct – Thomas had explained that the letter must be sent first to his mother, which worried her. Could the woman be trusted to treat it with the urgency it deserved?

Isabel was cast into despair in case Daniel thought her incon-
stant, and it took Cook little time to divine the reason for her
mistress's moods.

'I do believe you have left a young gentleman behind in
Ramsgate,' she remarked one day, as Isabel sat at the kitchen table,
helping to shell peas and sighing at regular intervals.

Isabel thought of denying it but instead burst out, 'Yes, but not
in Ramsgate. He is in London and will wonder what has become
of me.' In relief at being able to speak of Daniel at last, the words
tumbled from her mouth. 'He is tall and slim, and has the darkest of
eyes and curly hair. He is well born – his father works for the King.'

'That's as may be,' Cook said, 'but your father has plans for you.
A good match, with land involved.' She shot Isabel a look. 'So don't
go filling your head with ideas about this young man.'

Isabel scowled. Daniel was a fine young man. Surely no father
could object to him. She considered speaking to her father that
night, but caution held her back. She would wait until she had heard
from Daniel. She felt sure he was true, but she hoped her letter –
in which she had told him how much she missed him, and how
impatiently she longed to be in his presence again – would bring a
swift response. As he had requested, she had enclosed a lock of her
hair, a silky curl cut from the nape of her neck, where she knew it
wouldn't be noticed.

'It's no good looking like that, Miss Isabel,' Cook continued.
'When your father makes up his mind, there's little anyone can do
to change it, as you well know.'

Isabel had succeeded in changing her father's mind in the past.
She had persuaded him to treat his donkeys better. She could surely
dissuade him from whatever match he had planned. His recent
words came back to her: 'Marrying for love is a fool's game.' Perhaps
it wouldn't be so easy after all.

Daniel's reply reached her sooner than she had dared think
possible. Thomas handed it to her, that foolish expression on his
face as he did so. He must have seen the name on the letter he had

sent for her, and known she was writing to a man. But he hadn't mentioned it, and he'd done her bidding just the same.

She was so happy to recognise Daniel's hand on the letter Thomas gave to her that she forgot her irritation and, on impulse, kissed his cheek. He would have to make do with the imprint of her lips and forgo her company: she wouldn't be walking with him that day. Instead, she took the letter straight up to her room.

She sat on the bed with it set on the quilt before her, all at once nervous about the words she might find within. Then she turned it over, pausing to press her lips to the seal where she imagined Daniel's hand had last touched it, before cracking the wax and unfolding the paper.

My dear Isabel,

How happy I was to receive your letter, but how distressed to hear of your sudden and enforced departure from Ramsgate. I feel indignant on your behalf at such treatment. It is clear that Mr Crawford does not respect his family; indeed, he dishonours his wife by his behaviour in London, where he does little to disguise how he lives.

But enough of that – imagine my delight to read the sentiments you expressed, and to discover how well they match my own. We must, dear Isabel, find a way to be together very soon, for I cannot bear this separation. I confess the delay in hearing from you caused me much pain, but now I feel chastened to think how much you have had to endure, closeted away from the society you had only just begun to enjoy. I take some comfort from the memory that you once told me how much you loved the countryside, but I fear you must long for company other than that of your father.

Do you think he might be prevailed upon to bring you up to town? I will have to remain here for much of the summer and it would lighten the burden of my work to know that you were close by, and that we would be able to see each other once again.

Please write to tell me of your plans. I will cling to the hope they

176

may bring me joy. In the meantime, I keep your lock of hair safe
within my watch case, worn close to my heart in my waistcoat pocket.
    Yours, with my utmost affection,
    Daniel Coates

Isabel read, and re-read, Daniel's words, then stood and went to the window, gazing out over the fields. The corn was turning golden – she thought the harvest would be early that year. But she wouldn't be there to see it. She would speak to her father that very evening and tell him about Daniel. She would try to remember every detail about his father, Sir Charles Coates. Surely the name alone would be enough to impress. She would ask whether they might make the trip to London that she longed for, and there she could effect an introduction. How could her father fail to be pleased?

Chapter Twenty-Eight

Isabel spent much of the rest of the day pacing the house in nervous agitation. She asked Cook whether she would prepare a pie for dinner, knowing it to be her father's favourite. Cook regarded her with suspicion. 'Dinner is planned, Miss Isabel. One of the men brought in a fine rabbit from the snares and I'm making a stew.'

'Could you turn it into a pie instead?' Isabel pleaded.

'I'm already making a pie – a cherry pie,' Cook said firmly. 'The cherries are nearly over so I must make the most of them while I can. We can't have two pies,' she added.

Isabel thought her father wouldn't complain if they did, but Cook had an obstinate set to her mouth so she gave up trying to persuade her and went out into the yard. 'Will you miss me when I go to London?' she asked the donkey. The beast plodded on in the wheel, paying her no heed.

Isabel sighed. How was she to fill the hours until dinner was on the table? Then she remembered the dresses she would need to take to town with her. She supposed she must check to see whether they needed laundering or repair, although with no maid to attend to such things she wasn't sure how it would be done. She had almost given up wearing them by day in Marston, although she made a point of changing for dinner. It wouldn't do to let her father see her in the white lace dress. As she climbed the stairs to her room she was reminded of the shoes she had ruined so thoughtlessly on the rough roads. She would need to ask her father to buy new pairs as soon as they arrived in London.

She spread the dresses on her bed and got through the rest of the afternoon by making a practical examination of the garments, which soon gave way to daydreaming about the occasions when she might wear them once more, in the company of Daniel and his father. Perhaps when taking a promenade in one of London's parks, or going to the theatre as Daniel had suggested. In the end, when she heard the boom of her father's voice in the hall, she had quickly to divest herself of the white lace dress and don the lavender one, hurriedly pinning up her hair and adding her mother's earrings as a final touch.

Seated at the dinner table, she waited impatiently until her father had finished his stew, mopping the plate clean with bread. Isabel had barely touched a mouthful of hers, her stomach was so knotted with excitement and apprehension.

'Father,' she began, as he sat back with a sigh of contentment, 'there's something I want to tell you.'

'There's something I wish to tell you, Isabel,' her father interrupted. 'We're going to London in the morning. So make ready – I plan to leave as early as possible.'

Isabel could summon no words. How had her father divined her wishes?

'There's someone I wish you to meet,' Mr Cavendish continued. He sat back, while Cook removed the plates and dishes and returned bearing the cherry pie.

'I have arranged a most suitable match for you. A widowed gentleman with a fine spread of land in Sussex. He has no children and is looking for a bride. I hear excellent things of his prospects. I hope to have it all settled within the month – I cannot leave the farm and brewery for longer than that at this time of the year.'

He cut himself a large wedge of pie, oblivious to the despairing look Isabel cast towards Cook, who was standing by with a jug of cream and an unreadable expression on her face.

Isabel found her voice at last and burst out, 'But, Father, I have a young man already. In London. I was going to tell you this evening.

I have just today received a letter from him. He has asked me to visit.'

Her father had stopped, his spoon halfway to his mouth. Then, with an expression of irritation, he indicated to Cook that she should put the cream jug on the table. He poured a generous quantity onto his pie and continued to eat, as Isabel's words dwindled to nothing.

'Father,' she began again.

Mr Cavendish scraped up the last few crumbs from his plate and set down his spoon with some force. 'Now, listen to me, Isabel. I know best. Lord Oliver Marchant has a generous property in Sussex as well as a residence in London. You will have a carriage and servants, all the dresses you will require and an array of jewellery, too, I have no doubt. Without a fortune, you are very lucky indeed that Lord Marchant has wealth and land enough not to care about a dowry. He requires an heir and you have many years ahead of you to provide him with one. Let me hear no more nonsense about fine young men. Land and property are everything, Isabel, and you will have reason to thank me many times over in the future. We will leave at dawn.'

Mr Cavendish stood up and left the room before Isabel could utter another word. She sat on at the table, her plate before her, her thoughts skittering this way and that. She raised her eyes to her mother's portrait and sent up a silent appeal. What was she to do? How could her father have done this to her? He must hate me, she thought.

She would run away, she decided, even as tears began to course down her cheeks. She would pack her small valise and leave at dead of night. There wouldn't be many hours before dawn broke but she could put distance between herself and Marston, especially if she went across country. When her father realised she was missing, he would search along the route to the turnpike. But where would she go? To Ramsgate, perhaps, to the Crawfords'. No: Aunt Sophia would feel duty bound to tell her father and that would never do. To the Tremaines', then, or London. Unless ...

At that moment, Cook came in to clear the table.

'Miss Isabel!' she exclaimed.

Isabel turned her tear-stained face towards her. 'Did you know?' she demanded.

'I knew something of it,' Cook admitted, 'but not the whole story. It's why you were sent to Ramsgate, of course. Your father needed to present you as an accomplished and desirable young woman.'

'You speak of it as though I am one of his animals, groomed to be presented for sale at the market.'

Cook gave Isabel a sharp look. 'In some ways, that's as it is. You have little say if those are your father's wishes. At least it sounds as though your husband-to-be is well-to-do and you will have every luxury and convenience. No doubt you will be able to lead a separate life if you wish – you in the town while he remains in the country, or the other way around. I'm sure you will make it work to suit you.'

What did Cook know of such things? Isabel thought. She was making every effort to cast the whole enterprise in a favourable light, but she wasn't the one faced with the prospect of marrying a hideous man she had never met.

A thought struck Isabel. 'Do you know how old this man is? This widower, Lord Marchant?'

Cook busied herself picking up cutlery from the table. 'I believe he is a mature gentleman,' she said at last.

'Mature?' Isabel was at once alert to her phrasing.

'In his forties, perhaps.' Cook picked up the pie plate. 'Or fifty, maybe.'

'Fifty!' Isabel all but screeched. Older than her father! Surely he couldn't force her into such a match.

'I may be wrong,' Cook said hastily. 'You can find out for yourself in London. I am sure you could reason with your father if you find him unacceptable.' She kept her face turned away as she spoke.

'Or perhaps Lord Marchant won't like me,' Isabel said darkly. She had already reached a decision. She wouldn't run away. Instead

181

she would go with her father to London. It would take her closer to Daniel. She would find him there, somehow, and explain her predicament. He would help her, she felt sure. And in the meantime, she would do everything in her power to make herself as disagreeable as possible to Lord Marchant.

CHAPTER TWENTY-NINE

Isabel barely slept that night, kept awake by her troubled thoughts, finally falling into a deep sleep just before dawn. It seemed barely a few minutes later that she was shaken awake, groggy and disoriented, by Cook.

'Time to get up, Miss Isabel.' Cook half pulled her from the bed and propelled her to the washstand, splashing her face with water. Isabel gasped in shock.

A frown furrowed Cook's brow as she hurried Isabel into her dress, wrapping a cloak around her shoulders. 'There's a chill in the air this morning,' she said. 'Your father is at the table if you wish to join him. I'll send a man up to collect the trunk.'

Isabel had no wish to sit with her father, thinking to wait in the yard, but Cook was right. It was a cool morning, under grey skies, and felt more like January than July. Reluctantly, she joined her father in the dining room.

'Good morning, Isabel. We leave very soon, but you have time for breakfast.' Her father waved his hand over the dishes on the table. 'The cherry pie is just as good this morning as it was last night.'

He was in a cheerful mood, Isabel saw, and if he remembered her objections of the previous evening, he chose to ignore them. She poured herself a cup of the strong coffee he favoured in the mornings and waited silently until, replete, he pushed his chair from the table.

'Make haste,' he said, as if she was the one keeping him waiting.

Then he strode from the room and she heard him issuing orders in the yard. Cook came in and pressed a package into Isabel's hands.

'Take this for the journey,' she said. Her eyes filled with tears and she glanced up at the portrait on the wall. 'If only your mother was here,' she said. 'Remember, your father is trying to do the best for you.' Then she embraced Isabel and hurried from the room.

Would Mrs Cavendish's presence have made any difference? It was impossible to know, but Isabel couldn't help thinking she was being punished for her mother's misdemeanours. There was no point in dwelling on it, she decided, as she went out to the carriage. She must use her own wits to escape her situation.

First, though, there was a journey of many hours to endure in her father's company. He had hired a carriage and coachman for the journey, which surprised her. Mr Cavendish was usually keen to avoid unnecessary expense. It was, at least, noticeably more comfortable than their own carriage, for which Isabel was grateful. They passed the mill on the way to the turnpike and Isabel noticed that the sails were turning, despite the early hour. Presumably Thomas was at work. She wondered whether she would ever see him again. She feared it would be some time before she returned to Marston. The thought occurred to her rather late and as the horses drew the carriage out of the dip in the lane she turned and craned her head for a last glimpse of the place. She saw a few cottages straggling around the road and a rear view of Marston Grange and the fields of the estate. This was lost to sight as they approached the turnpike and turned towards Dover, grey sky and grey sea meeting on the horizon.

The weather improved a little after they had passed through the streets and turned inland. Gloomy skies gave way to broken cloud as the carriage made slow progress up the long hill out of Dover. Isabel, fearing for the horses, asked why they hadn't taken the stage coach from the town.

'I can't abide being closeted in a small space for hours on end with strangers. And if we are to make the right impression in

London, we'll need a carriage. Although the cost of hiring this, along with the toll charges, is a drain on my purse I could well do without.'

Mr Cavendish took some papers from his bag and began to study them, which Isabel took as a sign he wished no further conversation. An hour into their journey, she could no longer resist opening the package Cook had handed to her. It contained ham, bread and cheese; Isabel nibbled on bread and ham but her father refused it.

'We'll have to stop and rest the horses soon. I'll take refreshment at the inn.'

By the time they left the inn, the clouds had cleared to reveal vivid blue sky. The carriage interior became unbearably hot and stuffy, but letting down the windows allowed clouds of choking dust to enter, thrown up from the road by the wheels. Isabel was grateful when they stopped once more at an inn, not an hour further along the route. The coachman and Mr Cavendish conferred, with raised voices, while Isabel found a patch of shade in the coach yard.

'We have to rest the horses again, due to the heat.' Mr Cavendish was clearly not happy. 'And the coachman says he can't risk pushing them to do the journey in a day, so we will have to spend the night somewhere along the road.'

Mr Cavendish stomped into the inn and Isabel followed, glad to escape the heat for the cool interior. It was hardly surprising that the horses were suffering, she thought, gratefully accepting the cordial her father had purchased for her. His temper seemed to improve after he had drunk his ale and he was asleep and snoring within five minutes of their journey recommencing.

And so the day wore on, with frequent stops that Isabel welcomed and her father chafed at. Finally, at five o'clock, with the horses looking fit to collapse in their traces, he grudgingly accepted the coachman's advice and engaged rooms for himself and Isabel at an inn.

'We are close by Greenwich,' her father grumbled. 'Our journey's end isn't far beyond that. We are certainly close enough to the city for the inn to command high prices.'

They were standing in the square hallway, as Isabel's trunk and other bags were unloaded from the carriage so the exhausted horses could be led to the stable. Isabel, too, was worn out – her eyes gritty with dust, which had also lodged in her throat and the folds of her dress. Her body ached from every jolt of the journey and she was eager to reach the peace of her room. Instead, it seemed they were caught up in a crush of travellers, as one stage coach had just arrived and another was set to depart.

'We must wait in the parlour, it seems,' her father said, having consulted the man at the desk. 'The rooms need to be made ready after the departing guests.' He was offended by the delay, Isabel could tell, although she suspected his attempts to haggle over the room price had not endeared him to the landlord.

The parlour was quiet, at least, but Isabel was perturbed to find a fire blazing in the hearth. 'Surely this is unnecessary,' she said, seating herself as far from it as possible.

'There's a clear sky,' her father said. 'I dare say it will be cool this evening.'

Isabel couldn't conceive of ever feeling cool again. Her cheeks were flushed with the heat of the journey and she longed for nothing more than to plunge her face into some cold water and wash away the grime. Within half an hour, her wish was granted and a maid showed her to a room tucked into the eaves of the inn, overlooking the coach yard.

It was stifling, and Isabel wasted no time in flinging open the window, only to discover the room quickly filling with the aroma of horse manure from the yard below. She made a hasty toilet, splashing her face and looking with some dismay at the colour of the water in the bowl. Then, having changed her dress, she felt able to face the hubbub once more.

CHAPTER THIRTY

Isabel knocked at the door of her father's room and found him before the looking glass, attempting to knot his cravat. 'Wretched thing!' he exclaimed, tearing at it with his fingers. He was out of practice, rarely having cause to dress for dinner.

'Can I help?' she ventured. She'd never knotted a cravat but had seen them worn often enough by the gentry in Ramsgate.

Her father shook his head impatiently, but after another failed attempt he turned towards her with a sigh. Isabel tied a deft knot, earning her a nod of approval after Mr Cavendish had checked his appearance in the mirror. 'Very good, Isabel. Another accomplishment to please a husband.'

The novelty of staying the night in a coaching inn had kept all thoughts of the reason for their journey from Isabel's mind. Now the unpleasant reminder dashed her spirits.

'Dinner,' her father said, opening the door. 'Let us hope the quality of what is on offer matches the prices.'

Isabel trailed down the stairs after her father. A pie liberally doused in gravy would suit him, she thought, despite the heat. She hoped for lighter fare for herself.

Thankfully, their table in the dining room was closer to the door than the fire and Isabel was grateful for the breeze that wafted through. The tables were all but full, and once she had made her choice from the menu, she sat back and observed the other occupants of the room. It was then she made a startling discovery. Sitting at a table on the far side of the room, close to an open window, was Sir Charles Coates. And the figure facing him, with his back to her, could only be Daniel. Isabel gasped, causing her father to look up from his menu.

'Is all well?' he enquired. 'Now, shall I have the beef and oyster pie, or the pigeon?'

Isabel, heart beating rapidly, couldn't contain herself. 'I've just seen someone I know. From Ramsgate,' she said. How could she attract Daniel's attention? And could she engineer an introduction between Sir Charles and her father?

Her father grunted, disinterested, and returned to frowning over the menu.

'It's Sir Charles Coates. He travels on the King's business.' Isabel was determined to impress. 'Although he lives in London, so I'm not sure why he is here.'

'Hmm.' Her father was looking for the waiter, so he could place their order.

'I think you should meet him,' Isabel said. 'I could introduce you?'

'No need to disturb a man at his dinner.' Her father, having made his choice of pie, settled back in his chair.

'As they leave, then,' Isabel said. She peered across the room, trying to see the stage of dining they had reached.

'Don't stare, Isabel,' her father said. 'Remember your manners.'

Isabel saw the waiter approaching Sir Charles's table, bearing two plates, and relaxed a little. Her father would eat quickly, she knew. Perhaps they would finish their dinner at a similar time. She shifted impatiently, unable to settle until their orders arrived. As predicted, her father despatched his pie in record time. Isabel was glad that Daniel and his father were not close enough to witness his lack of finesse as he did so. Filled with nervous apprehension over how to manage an introduction, she could barely do justice to her cold chicken.

Her father insisted on a pudding and she had to sit on in an agony of anxiety, although it appeared Sir Charles was of the same mind. At last, as the waiter cleared their plates, she saw Sir Charles rise and Daniel follow suit. Surely he would see her as he left the room. Yet it became apparent that he was intent on following his father and had no curiosity about anyone else. Father and son were close to the door when Isabel reached a decision.

'Sir Charles!' she called, half rising and raising her napkin in his direction.

'Isabel!' Her father spoke sharply.

Sir Charles hesitated, having heard his name above the babble of conversation but unsure of the direction of the call. With a lurch of her heart, Isabel saw that Daniel had spotted her. He stopped dead and quickly spoke in his father's ear.

Sir Charles, having located them, strode over to their table.

'Miss Cavendish. How delightful to see you again. I must apologise for not recognising you, seeing you here so unexpectedly.'

Isabel was on her feet. 'Please do not apologise, Sir Charles. It has been several weeks, after all, and a coaching inn is hardly where you might expect to see me. May I introduce my father, Mr William Cavendish.'

Isabel felt sure everyone must hear the thud of her heart. Yet she felt she had acquitted herself well enough when making the introductions. Her father was on his feet now, shaking Sir Charles's hand, which gave Isabel the chance to cast a covert glance at Daniel.

His eyes were fixed on her, as though he was scarcely able to believe what he was seeing. How she longed to make everyone else disappear so that she and Daniel could talk and catch up on each other's news. Her eyes slid involuntarily to his waistcoat pocket, wondering whether his watch and her lock of hair were safely lodged there.

'And this is my son, Daniel,' Sir Charles was saying. 'We were due to leave London this morning, but our departure was delayed and we find ourselves forced to spend the night here.'

'How fortuitous,' Isabel said. 'Otherwise we might have missed each other completely.'

Sir Charles appeared bemused by her words, as if trying to decide whether they knew one another quite as well as her words implied, but he recovered himself. 'Have you finished your dinner?' he asked. 'Perhaps you would care to join us for brandy. It's a little early to turn in, but I feel the need to escape the noise in this room.'

Isabel turned a look of appeal on her father, fearing he would refuse, but it seemed he had decided Sir Charles might be a useful man to know. Within five minutes they were all settled in the parlour, where brandy was served to the men and Madeira to Isabel.

Sir Charles addressed her father. 'What brings you to London, Mr Cavendish?'

Isabel, who had just raised her glass to take a sip, almost dropped it at her father's reply. 'We are meeting the gentleman my daughter is to marry, sir. Otherwise I could never leave the business of my estate at such a busy time of year.'

Isabel shot Daniel an anguished look, then demurely lowered her eyes. She wasn't sure he had caught the import of her father's words.

'Ah, an engagement, Miss Cavendish. May I offer you my congratulations?' Sir Charles, smiling, was oblivious to the effect his words had on his son. 'And who is the lucky gentleman?'

'Lord Oliver Marchant,' Mr Cavendish replied, with a good deal of self-importance.

Sir Charles frowned and turned to his son. 'Do I know that name?'

'I believe you do,' Daniel replied faintly. 'The older gentleman who owns Heathfield Manor in Sussex. We visited him last year about ... about some monies owing to His Majesty.'

Sir Charles's frown deepened. 'Ah, yes, I remember.' He turned to Isabel. 'Have you met him, Miss Cavendish?'

Isabel could only shake her head, too frightened to speak and reveal her emotions.

'Well, well, I dare say you will make an admirable match for a widower with no children.' Sir Charles sounded unconvinced. He swallowed his brandy swiftly and stood up. 'We start out early. You must excuse us.'

Isabel felt as though he had passed judgement on her and her father based on what he had just heard. Her heart sank.

'Perhaps you might call on us when you return to London?' she blurted out. 'Father, what is our address there?' She addressed her father, but fixed her eyes on Daniel, hoping he might understand her intention.

'Twenty-six Mount Street,' Mr Cavendish said. 'You would be very welcome.' He seemed oblivious to the meaning behind the slight nod Sir Charles gave him.

Daniel reached for Isabel's hand and clasped it as they left. 'It was delightful to see you, Miss Cavendish. I hope it won't be too long before our paths cross again.'

'I look forward to it,' Isabel said, with as much decorum as she could muster. 'We plan to be in town for a month.'

Daniel inclined his head and then they were gone. Isabel subsided into her chair. Had he understood the hint she had given him and would he find a way to call in to see her? Or had he believed her ready and willing to marry the despicable Lord Marchant?

CHAPTER THIRTY-ONE

The discovery that Sir Charles had claimed the drinks bill inclined Mr Cavendish to speak favourably of him. Isabel was more interested in knowing what conclusions her father had drawn with regard to Daniel. This, however, proved less easy to ascertain.

'A pleasant enough young man, from what little I learned of him,' her father said. 'Quiet, though. I'm not sure he spoke, did he?' He seemed inclined to be dismissive, and eager to see his bed.

Isabel, despite her weariness, found it hard to sleep. The room was still stuffy and although she kept the window open at first, the noises drifting up from the yard – the rumble of wheels as carriages came and went, muffled calls and greetings, and the echo of horses' hoofs on the cobbles – forced her to get up and close it. Then the bedding became too warm, so she had to fling back the coverlet and rely on the linen sheet.

Was Daniel similarly restless, somewhere close by in the inn? What did he make of the news of Isabel's engagement? Her greatest fear was that he believed her untrue to him, that she had long known of this arrangement with Lord Marchant, and was toying with him. She sat bolt upright at the thought. Surely he knew her better than to suspect such wiles. If only she could get a note to him to explain what had befallen her and to urge him to be in touch with her in London. She couldn't be sure he had understood the few hints she had been able to drop. Or would he send a note to her, demanding an explanation? She suspected he was sharing a room with his father – it would be impossible to do such a thing without arousing Sir Charles's curiosity. Isabel remembered Mrs Tremaine's words yet again, that Daniel's father had ambitious plans for his son. If he confessed to a fondness for Isabel it would not be well received.

Anxiety continued to plague her until she finally drifted into a dream in which her father was marching her into a church, where a man waited at the altar. When he turned, he was an ancient, wizened man and she awoke with a start in a tangle of sheets, convinced she had uttered a shriek. The thin grey light at the window and increased noises from below told her dawn was close. She and her father would not need to be up and away at an early hour, but Isabel knew she would struggle to return to sleep.

Daniel and his father must be somewhere below, she thought, perhaps even now readying themselves for departure in the coach yard. Once that thought had entered her head, Isabel found she could no longer stay in bed, but must get up and peep through the curtains. Ostlers scurried about the yard and coachmen checked their conveyances, but her view of any travellers was solely of the top of their heads. She was about to return to bed, when she spotted them. Daniel and his father stepped into a carriage, the coachman cracked his whip and the horses drew away beneath the arched entrance. She watched for a moment longer before, shivering, she jumped back into bed and pulled the coverlet over her. How long would they be away? Not too long, she hoped, for she must hold off her father's eagerness to have her wed. She would need Daniel's presence in town to help her do this.

The journey to the lodgings her father had taken for them in Mayfair was conducted at a slower pace than Isabel would have preferred. Within an hour of leaving the inn, the roads they travelled were congested with all manner of carts, wagons and coaches, so that at times they were travelling at walking pace. At first, Isabel was fascinated as countryside and market gardens gave way to an ever-increasing number of dwellings.

Progress was particularly slow as they approached the bridge that her father said would take them across the Thames and into the city. Isabel drew back from the window then, perturbed by the crush of people around them. They were poorly dressed and, for the most part, incurious, but one or two glanced in and she thought she read envy and even anger on their countenances. The sight of the river caused her to sit forward once more – she had never seen such an expanse of water that wasn't the sea. The sunlit, sparkling surface was busy with boats and she would have liked to see more, but her view was obscured by the shopfronts of the buildings lining both sides of the bridge.

'I could never have imagined such a place!' Isabel exclaimed.

Her father grunted. 'Can't abide it. I hope we can attend to the business of your marriage without delay. I already wish myself safely back in Marston.'

Isabel, made anxious, sat back again. That was not at all what she wished to hear, but the remainder of their slow journey helped to distract her. Once they were across the river the meaner dwellings began to give way to establishments of the kind familiar to her from the grander roads in Ramsgate: white stucco houses of several storeys on streets with ample room for carriages to pass, some with gardens laid out in the centre of the squares.

The carriage finally drew to a halt outside a house with black railings and a pillared entrance, identical to its neighbours in an elegant road. The coachman opened the door and Isabel alighted, conscious of how crushed her dress must appear after several hours confined to her seat.

'At last,' her father grumbled. 'I can only hope this place turns out to be worth the expense.'

The apartment took up the first floor, laid out so that the drawing room gave a view over a small green space opposite. Isabel longed for a balcony, so they could step outside, but her father assured her that a large park lay nearby, where she could promenade if she wished.

The bedrooms were at the back and Isabel noted that, as in Ramsgate, they lacked any view other than into the backs of the row of houses on a neighbouring square. She was about to embark on unpacking her trunk when, to her surprise, a young girl came in and introduced herself. 'Louisa, your maid, Miss Cavendish.'

Isabel went in search of her father who confirmed that he had indeed engaged a maid, and a cook, for the duration of their stay.

'I won't be with you all the time,' Mr Cavendish said. 'Your maid can act as a chaperone should you need to go out while I'm attending to business.'

Louisa was young, Isabel thought, and hopefully malleable. Could she be the key to helping Isabel meet Daniel without her father's knowledge?

The cook, Esther, had prepared a light repast for them after their journey and once they had eaten, Isabel said, 'Shall we take a walk, Father? I'm eager to get to know our neighbourhood.'

Her hopes of exploring, and perhaps discovering whether Berkeley Square, and Daniel's home there, lay nearby were dashed by her father's reply.

'I suggest you rest, Isabel. And then you must make ready. We are to dine with Lord Marchant this evening and I want you to look your best.'

CHAPTER THIRTY-TWO

Mr Cavendish must have advised Louisa of the plan, for Isabel found a bath had already been prepared for her, and the primrose dress laid out on her bed.

'I don't wish to speak out of turn, Miss Isabel,' Louisa said, as she helped her out of her clothes, 'but you will need to talk to your father about acquiring some more dresses. Your clothes are barely fit for company. These dresses,' she indicated the sea-green one, just removed, and the lavender, flung over the back of a chair, 'are dirty around the hems and there are rips and broken seams. I've sponged this one,' she pointed at the primrose dress, 'and it will do well enough by candlelight, but as to what you will wear on your feet ... It looks as though you've been tramping the fields in your shoes. I've asked Cook to see whether she can find something to restore the leather.'

Isabel, surprised by the scolding she was receiving, began to revise her opinion of Louisa as malleable. She would need to manage her carefully if she hoped to win her round to help her.

'With so much of society out of London for the summer,' Louisa continued, 'most of the dressmakers will have closed. It will be difficult to have anything made in a hurry.'

Isabel lowered herself into the bath with a sigh. 'I don't think Father will wish to spend any money on my wardrobe. He's hoping to have me off his hands as soon as possible.' She slid under the water to wash the dust of the journey out of her hair. When she surfaced again, Louisa was regarding her with a puzzled expression.

'Whatever do you mean, Miss Isabel?'

A feeling of recklessness seized Isabel. Why shouldn't she appeal to her maid's better nature? She was very much alone here in London. Louisa might be her only hope of finding a way out of her predicament.

'I'm to be married off to some widower I've never met. It's my father's doing. He maintains he wants security for me but I wonder whether he means for him, really.' As she spoke, Isabel's thoughts crystallised and she began to see her father's plan with great clarity. Her youth and beauty were to be exchanged for Lord Marchant's wealth and the prestige of tying the Cavendish family to his lordship's land and ancestry. Isabel knew she had no dowry. Was money making its way to her father instead, to help him with his farm and estate? Was she just an instrument of barter for her father?

Louisa helped Isabel from the bath and began to vigorously towel her dry.

'So, you see, I hardly care what I look like when I see Lord Marchant tonight.'

'I suppose your father knows best.' Was Louisa saying what she thought she must say, rather than what she truly believed? She was close to her own age and must have some sympathy for her plight, surely. Perhaps, if she was careful, the maid could be persuaded to help her.

An hour later, as the clock on the mantel struck six with a tinkly chime, Isabel entered the drawing room.

Her father turned from the window. 'Good, good.' He nodded. 'You will do very well.'

Isabel had to admit that Louisa had skill: her hair looked far better than anything Kitty had achieved in Ramsgate. She had threaded a primrose-coloured ribbon through her dark, glossy curls and, with the addition of Isabel's mother's amethyst earrings, Louisa had declared her, 'Very striking, Miss Isabel. Lord

Marchant won't be able to keep his eyes from your face.' She'd rather spoiled the compliment by adding, 'Which is a blessing, since it will keep him from looking at your dress.'

Isabel had burst out laughing, then wondered whether she should have chided her for her impertinence. But she liked Louisa already. She had spent the best part of an hour gazing at her small face with its open expression and snub-nosed countenance as she had dressed her and worked on her hair. Isabel had told her something about her time in Ramsgate, and how she had been forced to leave when her aunt and cousins had moved to smaller premises. She'd held back from mentioning anything about Daniel.

It hadn't taken her long to discover that Louisa, despite her youthful appearance, was a good few years older than she was, and that the cook, Esther, was Louisa's mother. The two of them were employed as a pair whenever the apartment was let out and they were clearly very happy in their domain. Isabel thought she would rather have stayed there, in the kitchen, with Louisa and her mother, than obey her father's wishes that evening.

'The carriage is outside,' Mr Cavendish said. 'Shall we go down?'

He hadn't made a great deal of effort, Isabel noticed. His cravat was askew and she feared the grime of the journey still clung to his shirt. But he wasn't about to be judged. She was.

The carriage took them quite a distance to Gordon Square, where Lord Marchant kept an apartment when he was in town. Isabel had imagined something drab and dark, the barely used home of someone like her father, who had little time for home comforts and soft furnishings. Instead, the panelled walls of the room they were shown into were painted the palest of greens, a thick Oriental rug cushioned the wooden floor and the cream-and-gilt painted furniture was upholstered in striped silk. It was lit by a myriad of candles.

Isabel's look of astonishment must have been obvious to the man who rose from a chair in front of the fire, smiling as he took her hand and greeted her. 'I'm delighted to meet you at last, Miss Cavendish. I've heard a great deal about you from your father. His words have barely done you justice, I have to say.' He drew her towards a couch set a little distance from the fire. 'I sense you are surprised by my surroundings. My late wife, Lady Marchant, enjoyed spending time in London. I indulged her in her taste for decorating. Now, a drink before we dine?'

Lord Marchant turned to Mr Cavendish, offering him a choice from a range of decanters, which gave Isabel a chance to examine him in more detail. He was, she quickly realised, perfectly acceptable as a friend of her father but not as a suitor. He was amiable enough, not particularly tall with grey hair and a pleasant manner. It would be difficult to behave badly towards him, she thought.

It was very apparent, though, that Lord Marchant was enchanted by Isabel. She supposed that he had decided on the fact before they had met, and now that he had seen her, he was resolved. Mindful of her father, she behaved herself over dinner, speaking when she was spoken to and offering thoughtful opinions if asked. From snippets of conversation between the two men, she gleaned that her suspicions were correct: money had changed hands – or was about to – in her father's favour. Mr Cavendish appeared very content as the evening drew to a close.

It was only as they stood to leave that Lord Marchant said, 'Regretfully, I must leave for the country in the morning. There are pressing matters on my estate that require my urgent attention. I am disappointed, for I had been looking forward to getting to know you a good deal better, Miss Cavendish.' He bowed, and bestowed a kiss on her fingertips, then turned to her father.

'Never fear, though. I will return within the fortnight and in the meantime I trust, sir, that you are in agreement that the banns can be published in the church at the corner of the square.'

He turned to Isabel again. 'We can be wed there the week after

I return.' He beamed as he spoke and Isabel fought down a rising tide of mixed emotions. Anger that no one thought her worthy of consulting on the matter. And despair that she had so little time to engineer her escape.

CHAPTER THIRTY-THREE

'A pleasant evening.' Mr Cavendish's frown belied his words. 'Although I do think Lord Marchant could have offered you the courtesy of staying in London to get to know you better.'

Isabel, who was relieved that he was doing no such thing, found herself in the position of defending him.

'He seems like a busy man, Father.' She gazed out of the window as the carriage rattled through the darkened streets. 'I expect he has a good reason to be away.'

'I knew we shouldn't have stayed that night in the coaching inn. Had we been here a day earlier, you could have had more time together.' Then Mr Cavendish's frown lifted. 'Well, we will have little need to spend money on socialising and can stay quietly at home. As befits a bride-to-be.'

Isabel thought it far more likely that a lady about to be wed would spend a great deal of time in society, but she stayed silent. At least she was spared the agony of being squired around town on Lord Marchant's arm. Yet her father's plan did not fill her with joy. It would be dull indeed if she was to be closeted in Mount Street for the next two weeks.

Louisa appeared in the hallway as they entered the apartment. Mr Cavendish announced he would stay up a little longer, sitting by the fire nursing a brandy, Isabel imagined. She had no wish to discuss the prospective wedding, so told Louisa she wished to retire for the night.

'Did you have a pleasant evening, Miss Isabel?' the maid enquired, as she brushed out her hair.

'Pleasant enough, I suppose.' Isabel sighed. 'I think I will have little need of the new wardrobe you proposed. My father wishes us to stay at home and live quietly until Lord Marchant returns in a fortnight. And after that, there will be a wedding.' She shuddered, as the reality of her words struck her.

'And what are you to be married in?' Louisa demanded. She shook her head. 'Do I take it that you have but three weeks to prepare? You will need new dresses to take with you, too. You can hardly begin a new life as the wife of a lord with the few things you have.'

Isabel brightened. She was determined she would have no need of a wedding gown, or any other dresses beyond the ones she had, but the need to pay regular visits to a dressmaker would give her the opportunity to get to know the area, and perhaps to discover where Daniel lived. He was away on his travels, but when he returned she wished to be able to get in touch with him. Had his father said how long they would be away? She thought not, but the knowledge that her wedding would take place in three weeks' time caused her to toss and turn for a good hour before finally falling asleep. It wasn't the prospect of her husband-to-be that kept her awake, however, but contemplation of finding a way to see Daniel again. He was surely the only one who could help her out of her predicament.

At breakfast the next morning, she was quick to broach the subject of the dressmaker.

'Father, I will need a wedding gown. And dresses to wear when I go down to the country with Lord Marchant.'

Her father was taken aback. 'I suppose you will.' He laid down his knife and fork. 'I should have asked my sister to join us. She could advise you on this.'

'There's no need, Father. I will take my maid, Louisa. I feel sure, from what she has said, that she will know of a suitable place to go. I may need some other things, too. New shoes.'

Her father, relieved to have the problem solved for him, picked up his knife and fork and returned to his eggs.

'I will need money, Father,' Isabel pressed.

Mr Cavendish, mouth full, shook his head. 'Get them to send the bills here. You will have the carriage to transport you. I don't see that you will have need of anything else.'

Isabel, although disappointed not to have access to funds of her own, was happy that she had permission to leave the apartment. That was more important to her than the shopping. She turned to her own breakfast and left her father to read the newspaper while he ate.

As it turned out, she enjoyed the experience of visiting the dressmaker. Louisa knew of several establishments in the area with excellent reputations, and they were lucky enough, on their fourth attempt, to alight on one still open in Curzon Street. Madame Dubois, although initially taken aback at being asked to provide a dress for a wedding when surely all of society was out of town, began to embrace the idea with enthusiasm when it was apparent that more than one garment would be required.

'I am sure his lordship will invite his many friends. You must look your best,' she said, as she began to pull bales of silk and lace from the shelves.

Isabel rather thought that Lord Marchant intended it to be a quiet affair, but she held her counsel. After all, it was her intention that the wedding would never take place. Despite herself, she was drawn into the discussion over which lace would work best with the silk that Madame Dubois proposed, before guilt overtook her. It would be wrong to spend a great deal of money on a dress that would never be worn. And she was uncomfortably reminded of the white lace dress that belonged to her mother.

'This,' she said firmly, pointing to a bale of lace they had discounted early in the proceedings. 'This, with pale blue satin, not silk.'

She stood firm against Madame Dubois's attempts to persuade her, and ignored Louisa's raised eyebrows.

'Lord Marchant is so old, I dare say his eyesight is failing and he will barely be able to appreciate it,' she said, by way of closing the discussion.

It was a mean remark, and untrue, but it stopped further argument. Madame Dubois, shocked, quietly put away her best lace, and Louisa hastily changed the subject to discuss the need for at least two day dresses for her mistress, too.

Isabel, feeling these would at least be worn, allowed herself to be cajoled into using Madame Dubois's most expensive fabrics and so, by the time they left, the dressmaker was somewhat mollified.

Louisa insisted they pay a visit to the cobbler further along the same street and, as they walked there, she asked, 'Miss Isabel, why wouldn't you take that beautiful lace for your wedding gown? It isn't too late to go back and say you have changed your mind. For a marriage such as yours, you should have only the very best.'

Isabel stopped dead and glared at her. 'I don't love this man and I don't intend to marry him. I plan to leave before the wedding can take place. There is someone else.'

She walked on, leaving behind a startled Louisa.

The maid scrambled to catch up. 'But, Miss Isabel ...' She attempted to absorb what she had just heard. 'Does your father know?'

'Of course not, and you mustn't tell him.' Isabel gave her a fierce look. She regretted being so outspoken. She had been driven to it by the pressure of making decisions over a wedding gown she would not wear, then having to listen to the excited prattling of Louisa and Madame Dubois.

She knew she was being too familiar with her maid, but time was running out. It was clear that she would need Louisa's help. She would have to find a way of rewarding her for her silence and cooperation. They walked on in silence for a few more steps, Isabel running various possibilities through her head. Then, as they reached the door of the cobbler's shop, she turned to Louisa. 'Where is Berkeley Square?' She couldn't wait for Daniel to pay a visit, she had realised. She needed Louisa's help to get word to him.

CHAPTER THIRTY-FOUR

Louisa waited until they had left the cobbler – and placed an order for two pairs of dainty leather shoes – before she revealed to Isabel that Berkeley Square led off the top end of Mount Street.

Isabel, seated in the carriage, could hardly contain her astonishment. 'You mean it is just around the corner?' she asked.

'Yes, Miss Isabel.' Louisa appeared amused by her mistress's lack of knowledge about London.

'I can walk there from the house?'

'Yes. But not without a chaperone,' Louisa added hastily, seeing the gleam in Isabel's eye. 'Why do you ask?'

'Oh, someone I know lives there,' Isabel said. She hastened to change the subject. 'Where do people go to walk in London?' She was still disappointed that their apartment was not on one of the garden squares she had seen.

'Hyde Park and Green Park are the closest places, Miss Isabel,' Louisa replied. 'Carriage promenades are also popular there.'

'I prefer to walk,' Isabel said firmly. 'Every day.'

'Then we will start tomorrow,' Louisa said.

Isabel was about to suggest they might go there and then, but subsided when she recollected that Louisa no doubt had duties to attend to. She had already taken up half her day with the trip to the dressmaker and she remembered what Louisa had said about the work required to make Isabel's existing dresses fit to wear. Isabel had to content herself with a restless afternoon spent mainly by the window, picking up a book and putting it down again, then looking longingly at the sunny street below. Her father had absented himself on business, but she found herself almost glad to see him when he returned in the late afternoon, although he provided little by way of diversion.

And so Isabel found a routine established for her days. She and Louisa would walk in the park, the carriage depositing them there even though, in Isabel's opinion, they lived too close to make that a necessity. Berkeley Square, even closer, was deemed unsuitable as a destination for a walk, but Louisa took pity on Isabel and suggested she should instruct the coachman to drive them around the local area, by way of diversion.

'That way, there is no danger that the coachman will be suspicious and report back to your father,' Louisa assured her.

Isabel admired her practicality. During their daily walks in the park, she had already taken the opportunity to confide in Louisa about Daniel, releasing a little more information each day. In truth, she had realised there wasn't a great deal to tell her. She and Daniel had met but three times – twice in Mrs Tremaine's house in Ramsgate and once at the coaching inn on the way to London. But the retelling had made it sound like a mysterious and overwhelming attraction, which indeed it was, for her at least. And, she hoped, for Daniel, or how would she escape marriage to Lord Marchant?

Her father had insisted they take the carriage each Sunday to attend the church in Gordon Square, and hear the banns read. Isabel had blushed and squirmed inwardly on hearing her name coupled publicly with that of Lord Marchant. After their first visit, her father had made a point of introducing himself to the minister at the end of the service.

The clergyman had said how delighted he was to meet her, and how much he looked forward to conducting the wedding ceremony. 'Such a great man, Lord Marchant,' he had said to her father, who had nodded and seemed pleased. Isabel had kept her eyes cast down.

Madame Dubois had made the wedding gown within the first

week, summoning Isabel back for a fitting, which had proved all but unnecessary. Isabel had tried to delay, but since the gown was finished, apart from the hem, she realised it was pointless. The money had already been spent.

It was hard not to admire Madame Dubois's skill. At the back, the dress hung in folds from her shoulders. 'So that the congregation have something to admire while you are making your vows,' the dressmaker said. The lace was incorporated into the puff sleeves and two panels that fell from the bodice to sweep along the floor. Isabel, turning this way and that, could hardly not admire herself. The dress now hung in her bedroom in Mount Street: a daily reminder of the event that drew ever closer unless she could find a way to extricate herself.

'Two weeks are all but over,' Isabel said, in some desperation, as she walked with Louisa in the park on yet another warm and sunny morning. She was thankful for the parasol that shielded her from the sun's heat – one of the purchases she had made at Louisa's suggestion.

They were walking by the lake, nodding at acquaintances they had made there: mostly older couples who had chosen to remain in town for the summer. Isabel was, at least, glad of the dresses Madame Dubois had made. They were more fashionable than the ones made in Ramsgate, she felt sure, or perhaps it was that those were a little shabby now, despite Louisa's best efforts.

Isabel turned abruptly to her maid, walking a couple of paces behind her. 'I will send you with a note to Daniel's address. Time is running out. I need him to be aware of the urgency of the situation, and my feelings about it. I can't bear him to believe I wish to go through with this wedding. He must have been shocked to hear of it at the coaching inn.'

Panic seized Isabel as the import of her words hit home. Daniel must surely be back by now. She had been patient since she had seen him at the coaching inn, hoping he had understood her invitation to call. But now it was clear she would be married within the next

208

week if she could find no means of escape. Louisa, conscious that Isabel's agitation was drawing curious looks, drew her mistress to a bench overlooking the lake.

Isabel had no sooner sat down than she burst out, 'If I can find no other way out, then I swear I will drown myself here.'

'I will take your note for you.' Louisa bit her lip, clenching and unclenching her hands in her lap. 'But I will be in a great deal of trouble if your father should find out. I will deliver it tonight, under cover of darkness. You must write it this afternoon. Choose your words well.'

Isabel rewrote her note to Daniel several times, in the end deciding to keep it brief.

My dear Daniel,
   Since our chance encounter at the coaching inn, I have wished many times that there had been an opportunity for me to explain my father's words. The wedding to which he referred is being forced upon me and I fear there is little time to prevent it. Daniel, if you have returned to London, I beg you, please send me a note. I have asked my maid to ensure any such communication reaches me in secret. I am in despair and long to speak to you,
   Your Isabel

The note was now safely lodged with Louisa, who had promised to deliver it that very evening. Isabel felt calmer, having done what she could to ensure Daniel understood her situation. Now she could only hope that his business was complete and he had returned to London.

Her father was in a good mood at the dinner table. Isabel, who now understood that his absences during the day took him to some club, assumed he had won at cards. She didn't have to wait long to discover his good humour had an entirely different cause.

'I heard from Lord Marchant this afternoon,' her father said, deliberating over the cheeses on the table that had followed dessert.

Heart beating at twice its normal rate, Isabel waited.

'He is in town, but asked us to excuse him this evening, to recover from the journey. He will call here in the morning.'

Her father beamed. 'Is that not exciting, Isabel? Your wedding can take place after Sunday, when the final banns have been read.'

Isabel could not find the words to respond. How many days might still remain to her before Lord Marchant would expect to claim her as his bride?

CHAPTER THIRTY-FIVE

The knowledge of what awaited Isabel the following morning meant she did not pass an easy night. Each time she drifted into sleep, she woke with a start, fearing she heard Lord Marchant's voice in the hallway, only to find the room shrouded in darkness with no sign as yet of the dawn.

When Louisa came in to rouse her, she was already awake, staring at the ceiling. Apart from uttering the occasional heartfelt sigh, she remained silent as Louisa poured warm water into the bowl for washing. She shrugged when the maid asked her what she would like to wear.

'One of your new dresses?' Louisa ventured.

Isabel cast an involuntary glance at the wedding dress and shuddered. 'I have no wish to make a particular effort for Lord Marchant,' she said. 'Anything will do.'

Despite her mistress's words, Louisa laid out one of the new dresses, a cream-coloured Indian muslin with delicate tucks around the neckline and beading on the cuffs of the short sleeves. 'It will make Mr Cavendish feel better about the expense,' she said. 'And it won't hurt Lord Marchant to see how very lovely you look. You may find an advantage in being able to bend him to your wishes.'

Lord Marchant called on them an hour after breakfast, a meal to which Isabel had failed to do justice. Seeing the effect her appearance in the muslin dress had on Lord Marchant, she had to concede there was some truth in Louisa's words.

'My dear Isabel,' he exclaimed, 'seeing you this morning, a vision before me, has enhanced what is already a beautiful day. I deeply regret the business that has kept me away from you this past fortnight. Yet my visit to Somerset has allowed me to bring you a token of my deepest affection.'

He felt in his waistcoat pocket and pulled out a small jeweller's box. 'This ring belonged to my dear wife. I want you to have it, as an expression of the great hope I have that our love will be as blessed – nay, even more so – as mine and my dear Emily's.'

Lord Marchant's expression changed and, all but overcome with emotion, he gazed at his feet. In so doing, he missed how the polite smile on Isabel's face had frozen into a grimace.

Had she heard him correctly? The man was presenting her with a ring belonging to his dead wife, in honour of the great love they had once had for each other. Surely this exhibited the most appalling lack of sensitivity. She threw a glance at her father, who was smiling and had clearly failed to register anything untoward. She turned her head to look at Louisa, who was maintaining a discreet distance in the background, and caught her raised eyebrows.

Isabel now felt an overwhelming urge to laugh, abruptly replaced by a dawning horror as she heard Lord Marchant's next words.

'I see no reason for us to wait a moment longer than necessary, dearest Isabel. I propose we marry on Monday, the day after the final banns have been read. Then, on Tuesday, we can begin the journey to Somerset. I am longing to show you your new home.'

Isabel bit the inside of her cheek to stop herself from crying out. Then, with an effort, she gathered herself. 'My lord, I am honoured by your gift, and your wish to marry with such speed. But would it not be wise for us to get to know each other a little first?' Seeing the surprise on Lord Marchant's face, and the storm clouds gathering on her father's countenance, she added hastily, 'I would like to learn more of your estate, and what would be expected of me there.'

'Nonsense, Isabel.' Her father's voice brooked no argument.

'Lord Marchant's plan is an excellent one. You will have plenty of time to discover anything you need to know on your journey to Somerset. For my part, I can stay away from Marston no longer.'

Isabel felt herself superfluous during the remainder of Lord Marchant's visit. He addressed himself exclusively to her father, and the discussion was all of the plans for Monday. As he was leaving, he turned to Isabel and said, 'I will call again tomorrow, my dear. We have a few days to get to know each other before the wedding and I hope that will put your mind at rest. Now, pray let me see the ring on your finger.'

Reluctantly, Isabel took up the box from the table where she had placed it, and opened it. A large sapphire, encircled by cut diamonds, sparkled on a bed of blue velvet. Lord Marchant took the ring and slid it onto her finger.

'I knew it!' he exclaimed. 'Your fingers are as slender as my dear Emily's.'

Isabel's skin crawled at the thought of the ring so recently on his dead wife's hand. It was ugly, she thought, and ostentatious. Seeing her father glaring at her again, she did her best to look grateful and held out her hand for the ring to be admired.

Louisa showed out Lord Marchant and Isabel readied herself for a scolding from her father when she heard a new voice in the hallway. It was one she had so longed to hear that she could scarcely believe her ears.

A moment later, Louisa entered the drawing room. 'There's a Mr Daniel Coates here, sir, calling to pay his respects on behalf of his father.'

'Who?' Mr Cavendish didn't recognise the name and seemed ill-disposed to receive another visitor.

'We met them at the coaching inn, Father.' Isabel spoke before he could. 'And I invited them to call, if you remember.' She turned to Louisa. 'Please show him in.'

Her father would not be happy, but she was determined not to miss the opportunity to see Daniel.

A few moments later, Daniel strode into the room, making straight for her father.

'Mr Cavendish, I won't keep you long, sir, I see you have only just bade farewell to another visitor.' The brief glance he cast in Isabel's direction showed he knew exactly who that visitor was. 'My father and I have only recently returned to town, and now he has been called away to our estate in Sussex. He asked me to pay his respects and apologise for not being able to offer you our hospitality.'

Isabel noticed the faintest blush colour Daniel's cheeks and guessed his last words to be an untruth. He had come in response to her note, she felt sure, and she struggled to contain her joy.

'I hoped I might show Miss Cavendish something of London while she is here?' Daniel turned to Isabel and bowed low.

'I'm afraid not, Mr Coates. Isabel is to be married on Monday and such an outing would be improper.'

Mr Cavendish's tone was frosty, but it was lost on Daniel, who could not help exclaiming, 'So soon?' before collecting himself to make another bow, this time directed at Mr Cavendish. 'Then I shall take my leave. May I wish you the very best for your wedding day, and for your future, Miss Cavendish.'

Daniel's words to Isabel caused her to twist the newly acquired ring on her finger in an agony of frustration. He left the room before she could utter a word and she heard a brief murmur of voices in the hall before the door shut behind him.

'Well, thank goodness we are resolved.' Daniel's visit had distracted Mr Cavendish and made him forget his displeasure with Isabel, but now he returned to the subject of the wedding. 'Once the wedding is over on Monday, we can leave this city on Tuesday. I will be glad to be done with the expense.'

Mr Cavendish left the room before Isabel could speak. She imagined he had gone to seek out Esther and Louisa, to tell them their services wouldn't be required after Tuesday, so that he need not pay them a day more than necessary.

Lost in miserable contemplation of what lay ahead, she didn't hear Louisa come back into the room. She started when the maid pressed a folded piece of paper into her hand.

'Mr Coates left this for you, Miss Isabel,' she said, and hurried out again.

Isabel gazed at the handwriting she had come to know so well and felt hope flare in her breast. Would Daniel have a plan to save her? She took the note to her bedroom before her father returned, unable to wait a moment longer to find out.

Chapter Thirty-Six

Daniel's note had, of course, been written before he had come to visit, with a view to leaving it should Isabel not be at home. She scanned it quickly, then re-read it fully to take in his words.

My dear Isabel,

I was struck with guilt on receiving your note, for I had already been back in London a few days. I feared you to be already married and no doubt out of London, at Lord Marchant's estate.

I cannot tell you how it gladdened my heart to discover the marriage has yet to take place, but I was concerned to read of your feelings with regard to it. I am therefore planning to visit you this morning, but will leave this note with your maid should you be out.

Let me assure you of my deepest regard for you. I will help you in whatever way I can.

In haste,
Daniel

He had obviously decided to leave the note anyway, Isabel thought, perhaps because he hadn't been able to speak openly with her in front of her father. There was no plan, but she was heartened by his words.

Should she wait to see whether he wrote again, now he knew the wedding was planned for Monday? The wave of panic that swept over her at the thought of how little time was left decided her. Jumping to her feet, she went in search of paper and ink. Half an hour later, Louisa had been entrusted with the delivery of another missive. Isabel feared her desperation showed in her words, but could that be a bad thing?

My dear Daniel,
    I cannot tell you how wonderful it was to see you today, and so close on the heels of the wretched Lord Marchant. I have already told Louisa I will fling myself into the lake on one of our daily walks, rather than stand at the altar this coming Monday.
    Please, I beg of you, if you would have me preserve my life, find a means to spirit me away as far as possible from this despicable situation. I have no one else to turn to.
    Yours, with the deepest affection,
    Isabel

Louisa insisted that she and Isabel should walk as usual that afternoon, even though Isabel was more inclined to mope indoors.

'I won't be able to deliver your note until this evening, so it will help occupy the hours,' she said firmly. 'And it is a good idea to keep to your usual routine, in any case.'

She refused to be drawn on what she meant by that, but Isabel was glad to take some exercise. During the short carriage journey to the park, Louisa suggested she tell the coachman not to wait, but to proceed home after dropping them.

'Tell him it is but a few steps and you plan to visit a shop on the way home,' she urged in a low voice.

Isabel was surprised, but did as she asked once they had alighted. As soon as the coach had departed, she turned to Louisa. 'So, where are we going after our walk?'

'Nowhere,' Louisa said, and led the way towards the lake. Isabel was unable to persuade her to divulge anything further and, by the time they arrived back in Mount Street an hour or so later, she was decidedly irritated. Her hair was plastered to her brow and rivulets of sweat ran down her back, for the day was warm and sultry. She bit back her irritation, however – Louisa was acting as go-between with Daniel, at some personal risk, and she couldn't afford to upset her.

As Isabel turned into their gate in Mount Street, already eagerly anticipating the coolness of the hallway and stairwell, she heard Louisa address the coachman. He was waiting outside in full sun, in case either of the Cavendishes should have further need of him that day.

'Yes, it's a very hot afternoon,' she heard Louisa say. 'And I'm afraid we had a wasted walk home. Miss Isabel's package wasn't ready, so we must try again before the end of the week.'

Puzzled, Isabel turned at Louisa's words, only to find herself encouraged to go inside the house by her maid's slight shooing motion with her hands.

'What . . .?' Isabel began, as they stepped inside.

'You will see,' Louisa said. Then, leaving Isabel to cool off in the drawing room with the shutters closed against the heat, she vanished into the kitchen to busy herself with the tasks awaiting her there.

Isabel awoke on Thursday, filled with hope. Daniel would have her letter by now. He would come up with a plan, she felt sure. After breakfast, she stationed herself by the window in the drawing room, pretending to read while keeping watch on the street. As the morning wore on, with no word, her optimism faded.

Louisa came into the room shortly before noon, to find Mr Cavendish still there, reading his newspaper. She appeared surprised: he had normally left for his club before then.

'Oh, excuse me, sir,' she said. 'I came to see whether Miss Isabel was ready for her walk. I didn't realise you were still here.'

Mr Cavendish pulled his watch from a waistcoat pocket, consulted it and declared, 'Great heavens, is that the time? Why didn't you tell me, Isabel?' He hastened out of the room, stopping in the doorway to say, 'I will need the carriage but we can go by way of the park to drop you there: I will ask the coachman to return and collect you.'

He addressed his daughter, who nodded, although she saw Louisa smile to herself and shake her head slightly. Isabel shot her a puzzled look, which was met by another almost imperceptible shake of the head. Whatever could Louisa mean?

It was a cloudier day than the previous one, for which she was thankful, but it wasn't until they reached the park that Isabel realised there was a threat of rain. Clouds were massing in the west and a strong breeze had picked up. She considered asking her father to take them straight back but, sensing his impatience, she stepped out of the carriage to stand beside Louisa.

'I think perhaps we should return home at once,' she said to her maid. 'I fear we will get a soaking otherwise.'

'I don't think so,' Louisa said, with confidence, setting off into the park and leaving Isabel to follow.

'Louisa!' Isabel was now thoroughly irritated. 'Look at those clouds. We must go home.' She was struck by a thought that made her demand even more urgent. 'What if Daniel – Mr Coates – should call, in response to my note? I cannot afford to miss him.'

'He won't,' Louisa said, walking on.

'You didn't deliver it?' Isabel panted, trying to keep up with the pace set by her maid.

'I did,' came the reply. They had reached the carriage drive alongside the lake and Louisa appeared intent on reaching the very bench where Isabel had uttered her threat to throw herself into the water.

As they walked on under the lowering clouds, Isabel saw that only one or two carriages remained in the park – carrying the sensible people home, she thought. Whatever had got into Louisa's head? She prepared to follow her to the bench and remonstrate with her there, but had to stand back to allow a carriage to pass. As it did so, she heard the passenger inside rap on the roof to request the coachman to stop. It drew to a halt a few paces beyond her, the door was flung open and Daniel stepped out.

'Miss Cavendish!' he exclaimed. 'Are you here on your own? Where is your maid? And your carriage?' He glanced up at the sky, even darker now. 'I fear you are about to get wet.'

Isabel saw the first drops of rain darken the silk of her gown as she replied, rather crossly, 'My maid is by the lake. I am here at her behest, although I have come to believe she has lost her mind. My father has the carriage in town.'

'Then you must let me conduct you home,' Daniel said.

Louisa appeared around the side of the carriage and Isabel could have sworn she saw the ghost of a smile pass between her and Daniel, before a squally shower drove her to scramble into the carriage. Louisa seated herself beside her, and Daniel, shaking the rain out of his hair, sat opposite.

To Isabel's great surprise, he leaned forward and took both her hands in his. Speaking low and urgently, he said, 'I have not replied to your letter.'

She struggled to comprehend his meaning. Had Daniel, her only hope, forsaken her?

She forced herself to concentrate, for he was still speaking.

'Tomorrow, in the afternoon, my carriage will collect you, alone, from outside Madame Dubois's premises. We will journey to Mrs Tremaine in Ramsgate and throw ourselves on her mercy.'

Daniel sat back, pleased with himself. Isabel, bewildered, looked from him to Louisa and back again.

'I'm sorry, I didn't understand. Did you just say . . .?'

'It is all arranged.' Louisa spoke up. 'You and I will walk in the park tomorrow, as usual, but tell the coachman to return home as we wish to walk back and collect a package – the one that wasn't ready two days ago. You will step into Mr Coates's carriage, while I will delay before returning home to say I lost you somewhere in Curzon Street. Thinking you must be in one of the shops, I searched but failed to find you and had to return alone.'

'You have arranged this between you,' Isabel said, with a sense of wonder. Louisa's behaviour in the park, as well as her reaction to Mr Cavendish taking the carriage, was beginning to make sense.

The carriage drew to a halt outside the house in Mount Street, where the rain still coursed down.

'Tomorrow, three o'clock,' Daniel said, in a low voice, just before the coachman opened the carriage door, umbrella held aloft. Then, more loudly, 'I'm so glad I could be of service, Miss Cavendish.'

CHAPTER THIRTY-SEVEN

Isabel was keen to quiz Louisa about how the plan had been arrived at, but the maid vanished to the kitchen as soon as they were in the house. Her father returned later that afternoon so she had to restrain her curiosity – and hide her excitement. How was she to get through the hours until their walk the following day? And what if it should rain again? There had been no mention of an alternative plan.

Isabel lived through an agony of anxiety – first during dinner, when she had an irrational fear her father might suspect her. Usually uninterested in her day-to-day affairs, he asked her whether all was ready for the wedding.

'You have your wedding dress, I believe?' he asked. 'And some new dresses, too. I certainly have the bill for them. I trust there is nothing else you require?'

Isabel saw her opportunity to reinforce the plan by creating a credible story for the next day. 'There are one or two other requirements, Father. But all is in hand. I hope to collect them tomorrow, after my walk.'

'Good, good.' Mr Cavendish had lost interest and returned to his chop. The rest of their dinner passed in the usual silence until, at the very end, he said, 'You will be happy, I am sure, Isabel. Lord Marchant will make a good husband and one day you will thank me.'

Isabel was startled by this rare sign of awareness in her father. Had he recognised her feelings? For the first time in a long time, she wondered how different things might have been had her mother remained with them. Would she have spoken out on Isabel's behalf?

She knew better than to mention her mother in front of her father. He would refuse to enter into any sort of discussion about her. She was pierced by a bitter longing. Why had her mother abandoned her? What would she think if she knew what Isabel was about to do? She had a sudden certainty that she would approve. After all, her mother had followed her heart and left her father. Had she been forced into that marriage? The thought had never occurred to her before, but suddenly the mismatch made more sense.

Deep in thought, she hadn't realised that her father had left the room and Louisa was hovering by the door, waiting to clear the table.

'Louisa!' Isabel tried to remember everything she had wanted to ask her maid earlier, but Louisa put her finger to her lips.

'I'll clear everything now, Miss Isabel, if I may?'

Isabel saw her father walk past the doorway and on along the hallway. 'Yes, of course. Perhaps I'll have an early night,' she said.

It was far too early to go to her room, but she wasn't sure she could bear to keep her father company. Then it dawned on her that this might be the last time she would see him, or at least for a very long time. She forced herself to go to the drawing room and take up her book, with the pretence of reading until it was an acceptable time to withdraw.

Louisa came to help her to get ready for bed. Isabel observed her in the mirror as she brushed out her hair, and noticed the dark circles under her eyes and the yawn she tried to stifle.

'You look tired, Louisa.'

Louisa simply replied, 'Yes, Miss Isabel,' without attempting to give any reasons.

With a sudden flash of guilt, Isabel thought of how she had expected Louisa to go out late at night, at the end of a long working day, to take her letters to Daniel.

'Louisa, you won't get into trouble for helping me, will you?' The thought had only just occurred to her. Would her father accuse her maid of involvement in the escape plan, once it had become clear that Isabel had vanished?

'I hope not. If the plan works, I don't see that there is anything to tie it to me.'

She spoke bravely, but Isabel thought she caught a hint of unease in her voice.

'I must give you something.' She gazed around the room. 'Take anything you want. All this must stay here.'

Louisa shook her head.

Isabel frowned. 'My father won't know how many dresses I had.'

'But they are finer than anything I own, Miss Isabel. If they were to be found in my possession, I would be accused of stealing.' Louisa was firm.

Isabel bit her lip. Her eyes slid to the wedding dress. She hadn't wanted to wear it for Lord Marchant, but for Daniel? If they were to marry, that is. He hadn't asked her, of course. He'd only offered to help her.

'Do you think . . .?' She stood up and went over to the dress, running her hand over the fabric. 'Would it be possible to take some sort of bag tomorrow?'

'Oh, miss.' Louisa made a face. Then she sighed. 'I suppose I could carry something. Something small,' she added hastily.

A few minutes later, as Isabel slid between the sheets of her bed, she gave a little shiver of glee. It would be a shame to leave all her new things behind. Surely a way could be found to carry some of the dresses with her.

The following morning, when Louisa came to wake her, Isabel said she would wear her other new dress, not the Indian muslin.

'But perhaps we could take the muslin with us, and the wedding dress?' she suggested, as she splashed her face with the water Louisa had brought in.

Louisa gave an emphatic shake of her head. 'Something small, I said, Miss Isabel. Your hairbrush and undergarments, perhaps?'

'But I can't manage for days with just one dress.' Isabel, who had done just that in the not-so-distant past, was horrified at the idea.

'It would require a trunk to pack your dresses properly. I can hardly take that with me to the park,' Louisa pointed out, not unreasonably. She followed the direction of Isabel's gaze, to the wedding dress hanging there. Isabel, who had cared not one jot for it when it was destined for her wedding to Lord Marchant, had now conceived a great fondness for it.

'The fabric is very fine. Would it not be easy to fold up quite small?' she asked.

'Yes, and produce a great many creases,' Louisa said crisply. Then, seeing the tears brimming in Isabel's eyes, she said, 'Oh, great heavens. I will roll it, to ward off creasing, and stow it in a valise. But, Miss Isabel, it is folly to take it, surely.'

Isabel, her head full of romantic notions, could only look at her pleadingly.

'I will see what can be done. I make no promises,' Louisa said. 'Now, you must get through breakfast as best you can, without saying or doing anything to make your father suspicious. I have said nothing to my mother. Only you and I, Mr Coates and his coachman know what is to happen today.'

She helped Isabel into the other new dress, cream cotton with an intricate hand-painted floral design. 'Your mother's earrings would look well with this,' she said, regarding her with her head on one side. 'But I think we should wait until your father has departed for town.' She went over to the window. 'The weather looks set fair. We need not fear a drenching today.'

Chapter Thirty-Eight

Isabel made a poor show of eating her breakfast. She took a roll, and a spoonful of jam, but resorted to mostly crumbling the bread on the plate, since she could get barely a mouthful past her lips. What if her father should change his usual routine and decide to stay at home?

Mr Cavendish frowned as he observed her wasted breakfast. 'Have you lost your appetite, Isabel? You aren't sickening for anything, I trust?'

'No, no,' Isabel hastened to assure him. 'Just excitement – I mean, nerves.'

'Hmm. Well, not long to wait now. In a few more days you will be presiding over your own breakfast table.' Her father rose. 'I'm going into town but will send the carriage back for your use.' He nodded and left the room.

Isabel picked up her cup but had to put it down again. She found she was trembling so much she was in danger of slopping tea on the cloth. With her father safely away, there was nothing to stop Daniel's plan coming to fruition. It proved to be a challenge, though, to occupy herself until it was time to leave for her walk. Louisa cleared away the breakfast things, having failed to persuade her mistress to eat something. Isabel was left to pace around the drawing room, waiting for the return of the carriage. After ten minutes, she picked up a novel and sat in the window seat, but turned the pages on unread words. When the carriage at last drew to a halt outside, she leaped to her feet and hurried in search of Louisa.

She found her in the kitchen, a domain Isabel didn't usually enter. 'The carriage is here,' she blurted out.

Louisa gave Isabel a warning look, throwing a glance in the direction of her mother, Esther. 'It's a little early for our walk, Miss Isabel, and I have work to finish first. I'll come and find you when it's time to go,' she said.

Isabel was about to argue, then thought better of it. Louisa was right – they should arrive at the park at the usual time, so that they would reach their appointed meeting place with Daniel's carriage as planned.

She withdrew from the kitchen and resumed her pacing, until Louisa came to find her.

'It's still a little early, so we will have to take a seat in the park for a while,' she said, as Isabel struggled to tie the ribbons of her bonnet with shaking hands. As they stepped out to the carriage, she saw that Louisa carried a small valise. She passed no comment, but cast covert glances at it, trying to ascertain how much the maid had managed to pack.

The walk in the park was as excruciating as the wait at the apartment in Mount Street. Louisa had to keep reminding Isabel to smile and nod as they passed their park acquaintances. When any of them was disposed to stop and exchange a few words, the maid had to prod her mistress in the back to encourage her to respond.

After one particularly lacklustre performance, Louisa was moved to beg, 'Please try harder! No one must suspect anything.'

After that Isabel, contrite, made more of an effort, with the result that by the time they approached the wrought-iron gates at the exit, she felt wrung out and half ready to abandon the whole enterprise.

What if Daniel's carriage didn't arrive as planned? She didn't think she could bear the disappointment. The thought made her stumble as they passed through the gates, causing Louisa to give her mistress an anxious look.

'Should I take your arm? We don't want anyone to stop and insist on taking you home in their carriage. We are so close now.'

At that, Isabel grasped Louisa's arm and drew herself upright. Not another word was said until they were in Curzon Street.

'Look in the shop windows, Miss Isabel,' Louisa urged, relinquishing her arm. 'Then turn back to me and utter a few words before moving on to the next. I shall look ahead for Mr Coates's carriage.'

Isabel did as she was told, resolutely refusing to turn to see whether she could spot the carriage. By the time she had reached the fifth window she was beginning to wilt, from the heat and from hunger, when Louisa spoke quietly.

'It's here, Miss Isabel. Just beyond Madame Dubois's shop. Take the valise and walk towards it. I will wait until I can see you are safely in the carriage. Then, I will wait a little longer before enquiring after you in the dressmaker's.'

As Isabel reached out to take the valise, Louisa briefly gripped her hand.

'Go swiftly and go well, Miss Isabel. And be happy.'

Then she turned away, leaving Isabel to walk the few yards to the carriage where the coachman, lounging at the back, sprang smartly to his feet as he saw her approach. A couple walking towards her gave her a curious glance, Isabel thought. She didn't recognise them so she ignored them and stepped swiftly into the carriage.

As it pulled away, she turned to look out of the tiny back window, hoping for a glimpse of Louisa, but she had vanished from sight. Isabel sat back in her seat, heart beating fast. For the first time that day, she allowed herself to believe the plan would succeed.

They would be in Berkeley Square within minutes. She pressed her hand to her breast to still the pounding of her heart. She wasn't sure exactly what would happen next but she was happy to put herself in Daniel's hands. He would, she was sure, have made a plan.

Daniel, who had been watching out for them, was seated in the carriage within five minutes of its arrival in Berkeley Square. They set off at once, Isabel shrinking away from the carriage window, fearful of she knew not what.

Once the horses had clopped briskly out of the square she relaxed a little, only to be overwhelmed by thoughts of what she had done. She had been so caught up in the execution of Daniel's plan that she hadn't thought of the consequences, other than feeling relieved to escape marriage to Lord Marchant, of course. Now, alone with Daniel for the first time since Mrs Tremaine's ball, she found herself shy.

'Well, Miss Cavendish, you are unusually quiet.' Daniel, who appeared perfectly relaxed, smiled as he teased her. 'I do hope you aren't having second thoughts?'

Isabel shook her head vehemently. 'I was just thinking about how well everything has worked out,' she said, not entirely truthfully.

'Did you ever doubt it?' Daniel pretended to be hurt. 'My plans always work out, one way or another.'

Isabel managed a tremulous smile. She hadn't thought beyond her desperate wish to escape. But presumably Daniel had.

As if reading her mind, Daniel continued, 'We are going to stop at the Spread Eagle, the coaching inn on the edge of Greenwich, where I saw you with your father. We will have separate rooms,' he added hastily, seeing Isabel's worried expression. 'I will say you are my sister if anyone asks. We can dine there, and rest before making an early start for Ramsgate. I have written to Mrs Tremaine to expect us. I am relying on her advice for what to do next.'

Isabel was reminded of her uncertainty over Daniel's intentions. She had allowed herself to hope that Daniel was saving her from Lord Marchant so they could be together. She struggled to remember the wording of his letters – surely they had implied as much. So what need would he have of Mrs Tremaine's advice?

Chapter Thirty-Nine

Isabel would have questioned Daniel but, overwhelmed with weariness now that the difficult part of the enterprise had been successfully concluded, she wasn't sure she could reason coherently. She gazed out at the streets of London, crowded with people and other carriages, so that they were forced to travel at walking pace as they journeyed eastwards. The heat in the carriage, and her exhaustion, made her eyelids droop and, before long, she fell into an uncomfortable doze. She awoke with a start some time later, to discover the carriage at a standstill in the bustling yard of the Spread Eagle, and Daniel gently shaking her arm.

'Wake up, Isabel, we are here. And remember, you are my sister.' He jumped down and held out his hand to assist her. A little dazed by sleep, and trying to suppress a yawn, she took it and stepped down, then followed him into the inn. The bustle there made her shrink back against the wall. What if they were seen by someone who knew Daniel? She heard him say, in clear, confident tones, 'No, I'm not travelling with my father today, but with my sister. We will need two rooms.'

The woman he was speaking to swept her with a glance but Isabel ignored her and pretended to be studying a map displayed on the wall. She was relieved when a boy was despatched to take their bags to their rooms, while they followed him up the narrow, dark wood staircase and along a landing lined with doors.

'Here you are,' the boy said, opening one and standing back. 'This is yours, miss. Your brother is next door.' He dropped her bag onto the bed and hurried to attend to Daniel, no doubt in search of a tip. Isabel drifted to the window and took in the view. This time, the room looked over the road that took the coaches out into the Kent countryside. Bordered by trees and fields, it was in stark contrast to the London streets she had been looking at just before she fell asleep. Her thoughts ran over what lay far in the distance – her home in Marston, their destination in Ramsgate. What was happening in these places at this very moment? She found it hard to envisage – her life at Marston Grange seemed a lifetime away, even though it was barely three weeks since she'd left. As for Mrs Tremaine's house – would the family be there for the summer? Her heart quailed – she had no wish to see Giles or meet Mr Tremaine, even though it seemed unlikely that news of her flight would reach anyone other than Mrs Tremaine by tomorrow.

She thought of her father's bewilderment at her absence – and his anger as he realised what she had done. He would accuse Louisa of helping her; she hoped they had done enough to make it seem as though she had managed the entire enterprise alone. Her father would surely never think to ask about the wedding dress, but she regretted taking the bag now. If discovered, it would implicate Louisa in the plan.

A knock on the door made her start guiltily.

'It's me,' Daniel called, in a low voice, and she hurried to open it. 'I thought we might go and dine,' he said. He hesitated. 'Unless you wish to change?' he asked.

Isabel, thinking of the wedding dress in her bag, blushed scarlet. 'No, no, I will go down as I am,' she said. 'But first I should tidy myself.'

'Forgive my impatience,' Daniel said. 'I will return in a short while.' He nodded and withdrew.

Isabel splashed water on her face and re-pinned her hair, which had fallen into disarray while she dozed. She should have looked in her bag to see whether Louisa had packed a hairbrush, but shrank from seeing her folly enshrined in the wedding dress. Instead, she paced the room, waiting for Daniel's return.

At his knock, five minutes later, she flung open the door.

'Ah, quite a transformation,' he said gravely.

She laughed and, on impulse, gave him a playful push, which caught him off guard and propelled him into the path of an elderly couple making their way to the dining room.

Daniel apologised profusely, but they were not mollified and gave Isabel a frosty look. She could barely restrain her giggles and, although Daniel did a better job, a giddy mood had set in. When they took up their table in the dining room, they saw the miserable couple nearby, studying their menus by holding them close to the tips of their noses. This set Isabel giggling again, and Daniel seemed only too willing to encourage her. Later, she thought it must have been a reaction to all the pent-up anxiety of that day.

Caught up in their game, they failed to notice they were attracting curious glances, verging on scandalised in some quarters. They were about to vacate their table, having finished their meal, when Isabel noticed a large gentleman bearing down on them, his much smaller wife scurrying behind him. Their almost comical difference in stature would have been sufficient to precipitate another bout of merriment, if Isabel hadn't perceived that the gentleman had his eyes fixed on Daniel.

'Well, Mr Coates, I thought it was you,' he boomed, a few paces from the table. 'Here without your father, I see?' He gave Isabel a hard stare, necessitating a response from Daniel.

'Let me introduce my sister Isabella, Mr Fortescue. And this must be your wife.' Daniel gave a small bow. 'Delighted to meet you.'

Mr Fortescue didn't seem convinced, Isabel thought. He was regarding her closely and she tried to appear unmoved but was grateful when Daniel continued, 'My father is in Sussex. We are travelling to stay with friends in Ramsgate and he will join us there.'

He pushed back his chair and stood up. 'Now, you must excuse us but we have an early start. Mr Fortescue, Mrs Fortescue.' He gave them the smallest nod by way of goodnight and led the way from the dining room, Isabel looking to neither left nor right. Her giddy mood of earlier had deserted her.

'I don't think he believed you,' she murmured, as they climbed the stairs.

'No, he didn't,' Daniel agreed. 'But I *do* have sisters, whom he's never met, and who's to say you aren't one of them?'

They stopped outside her door and, glancing to left and right, he quickly brushed her cheek with his lips.

'Goodnight, dearest Isabel. I will knock for you at dawn.'

She stepped into the room and quickly closed the door, then leaned against it. They'd behaved foolishly at dinner and, she realised now, attracted attention. She couldn't wait to be away from the place – they should never have stopped at such a popular coaching inn. Reasoning that the sooner she slept, the sooner they would be free of it, she divested herself of her dress, barely taking the time to lay it out so it wouldn't appear too creased in the morning, before she fell into bed. There, fully expecting to toss and turn until dawn, she instead fell into a deep sleep until she was roused by a knock on the door at an hour that felt far too early.

CHAPTER FORTY

Isabel and Daniel escaped any further awkward encounters with guests before they departed in their carriage. They were both dazed with sleep and the first hour of the journey passed quietly, Isabel gazing out over a landscape that was also just waking to greet the day. They passed small groups of people, the men in shabby work shirts and loose trousers, the women in worn, sun-faded dresses, walking beside the roadway. Isabel supposed their destinations to be the farms along the route; in one yard, a child scattered corn for the hens; in another, workers were gathering before they went out to the fields.

It was going to be a glorious day. Wisps of mist lingered here and there in hollows and ditches, but the rising sun was burning away any haziness, revealing an overarching clear blue sky. After an hour, Daniel called for the coachman to stop at a small inn. He despatched him in search of refreshments and he returned shortly after with freshly baked bread rolls and small cups of strong coffee.

Isabel and Daniel stood in the yard to make their breakfast.

'I thought it best to get away from the Spread Eagle as quickly as possible,' Daniel said, blowing on his coffee. 'Breakfasting there would have delayed our journey.'

'This is much better,' Isabel agreed. She bent to stroke an old dog that had ambled across the yard to greet them, and broke off a piece of bread for him. 'There,' she said. 'I expect that's the first of many tidbits you'll be given today.'

Daniel finished his roll and drained the last of his coffee, handing the cup back to the coachman along with a few coins.

'Time to be on our way again,' he said to Isabel. 'There are many hours ahead of us.' He took her hand and helped her back into the carriage.

She spent the next hour quizzing Daniel about his family, his sisters in particular, although she felt it unlikely she would be called upon to masquerade as one of them that day.

'There's Lizzie,' Daniel said. 'She's older than me, married with two children. She lives on our Somerset estate, where my younger sister Lucy also lives, with our mother.'

'And how old is Lucy? Is she married?' Isabel asked.

'Lucy is seventeen and, no, she isn't married.' Daniel broke into laughter. 'I doubt anyone will have her. She's the baby of the family and has been allowed to run wild.'

Then I will be Lucy, if called upon, Isabel decided. She rather liked the sound of her.

Daniel had moved on. 'Edward is the eldest, and the steadiest. He has charge of our lands in Dorset, along with a fine manor house.' Daniel seemed rather wistful, Isabel thought. That was explained when he added, 'I've always loved it. We spent a lot of time there when I was young and I have fond memories.

'Then there is James, who is something important to do with law.' Daniel made a dismissive gesture. 'He lives in London.'

'In Berkeley Square?' Isabel was alarmed. James would wonder at Daniel's mysterious departure.

'No, no, near his chambers in Lincoln's Inn.' Daniel didn't seem disposed to talk any further of James, leading Isabel to suppose there must be some coolness between them.

'You have a big family,' she observed, thinking of her own solitary upbringing. 'And a lot of property,' she added.

'There's another I may have mentioned before,' Daniel said. 'It's a wild place on the Scottish borders, all but falling down. It came into the family from my mother's side. I've been there with Father, but

I don't think any of the others have, or will ever want to. It feels a great distance from anywhere, but it's not so very far from Carlisle.'

He lapsed into silence and gazed out of the window. There was a distant glimpse of water on one side, although it wasn't the sea, Isabel thought, for she could see land beyond it. The view from the other window was of undulating hills, clothed in green, in places becoming dry and parched after the heat of the summer. 'The landscape up there is not so different from this,' Daniel said suddenly, continuing their previous conversation. 'Hills, water – yet somehow it could hardly be more different.'

Isabel, who had once struggled to imagine what Ramsgate might be like, having never travelled beyond Marston, kept quiet. Daniel, who was in his early twenties and just a few years older than she was, had seen so much more of the country.

It was time to break the journey again, and to change horses. Isabel was glad to step down and take the air, but less keen to enter the inn. The route they travelled was well-used and, although it wasn't yet midday, others would be stopping there, too. She was reluctant to encounter anyone else who might know Daniel. She thought it unlikely she would see anyone who might know her. Although – what about her father? He hadn't entered her thoughts until now, but what if he had somehow learned of their plan and set off in pursuit? What if, even now, he was close behind them on the road? She shrank back as another carriage clattered into the yard.

'Let us go in,' Daniel said gently. 'We'll stay only a short while. It's dark inside, with many quiet corners. We can hide away.'

He knew the inn well, Isabel thought, having presumably stopped there before on the way to Ramsgate. It was, indeed, dark after the sun-drenched coach yard, and full of nooks and crannies, furnished with dark wooden booths. A good place to hide, she thought, as Daniel went to fetch her a glass of cordial.

She was glad of it, for not only did she fear discovery but vanity made her long for obscurity, too. Her dress was crumpled from travelling and, without Louisa to help her, she feared her hair was a tangled mess. She still hadn't opened her bag to see what it contained – their rushed early start had prevented it, as well as a reluctance to face the folly of the wedding dress.

Daniel returned with the drinks and slid into his seat. 'I can scarcely believe it,' he said. 'I've just seen someone who knows me, although he didn't see me. He's a friend of my father's, and of the family.' He regarded Isabel. 'You can't pretend to be my sister, I'm afraid. We'll just have to stay out of his way.' For the first time during their journey, Isabel thought he seemed troubled.

She racked her brains to find a plausible reason for an unrelated young man and young woman to be travelling together in a private carriage, and could come up with none. It would never do.

'We must leave separately,' she said finally. 'I will go first and wait in the carriage. You must follow five minutes later. Then, if you are seen, no one will suspect you aren't travelling alone.'

Daniel frowned, but nodded in agreement. They sat in silence, each wrapped up in their own thoughts, making their drinks last for the half-hour Daniel thought necessary before the carriage would be ready again. Isabel enquired of a barmaid where she might make herself comfortable before embarking on her journey once more, and was shown to a small closet made available for female travellers. Then, trying to appear as though she was a perfectly respectable young woman travelling alone, she walked out to the carriage. She half expected to be challenged, to hear her father call her name in ringing tones, but she reached it without mishap.

Five minutes later, Daniel tumbled through the door. 'I don't think I was seen, but it was a close thing,' he said. Then he laughed. 'We're behaving for all the world like a pair of runaway lovers when we have nothing to hide,' he said.

Isabel, confused once more by his words, gave a tentative smile and stared out of the window as they rolled away. What were they, then? What was Daniel's intention when they reached Ramsgate? She glanced involuntarily at her bag. She longed to fling that wretched wedding dress from the carriage so that it was caught by the wind and blown back along the roadway, to be trampled into the dust and torn by the wheels of the next carriage and pair that came by.

Chapter Forty-One

Daniel and Isabel passed the rest of the uncomfortable journey by dozing, gazing out of the window, or making conversation, which Isabel found increasingly awkward. Her mind was filled with questions she wanted to ask, but where to start? Why had Daniel agreed to help her? Why was he undertaking this journey, helping her to escape Lord Marchant, if he didn't have intentions himself?

As the carriage grew hotter and more uncomfortable, she wondered whether to apologise to him, to say she had misunderstood. But she couldn't bear to make herself appear foolish. She wished she could re-read his letters, share them with him and ask him about his words. Where were his letters? There was a heart-stopping moment as she realised she had no idea. Had Louisa packed them in the bag? If not, then they were still tucked in a drawer in the bedroom in Mount Street. Would her father find them? If he did, was there anything in them to suggest they were travelling to Ramsgate? She didn't think so, but she wasn't sure. Her face was hot with shame at the thought she might have been instrumental in setting her father on their trail.

Daniel glanced at her. 'Isabel, you look rather warm. One more rest stop, and then not long after that we will arrive in Ramsgate. I would open the window, but the dust will be as bad as the heat.'

He was so kind and patient, Isabel thought, and immediately burst into tears.

'Whatever is the matter?' Daniel was all concern. He felt around in his waistcoat pocket and found a handkerchief, which he passed to Isabel. Then he sat beside her, patting her hand, which only made her cry all the harder.

'I ... I ... thought,' she managed to stammer, then stopped. 'I thought ...' she took a deep breath '... that you might, I mean that we might ...' She stopped again. Could she actually say what she meant and risk total humiliation? Daniel was waiting, a puzzled frown creasing his brow. He held her hand now, but like a brother, she thought. Had she been wrong to imagine from his letters that she meant something more to him?

She tried again. 'Do you remember, you asked me to send you a lock of my hair?'

Daniel nodded. 'I do.' He patted his pocket. 'And here it is, safe in my watch case.'

'And did you express a certain – tenderness towards me, in your letters?'

Daniel nodded again.

'And now you have helped me to escape from marriage to Lord Marchant – but why?' He didn't reply at once so she continued, 'I thought perhaps you meant to marry me, but throughout this journey you have done nothing to make me think that was the case. Indeed, we have travelled as the brother and sister you would have others believe we are.'

Daniel's face cleared. 'I see,' he said. 'I should have explained – I am so sorry.'

Isabel's heart sank. He was going to let her down – gently, she was sure, but he was about to tell her that marriage wasn't his intention.

'My aim was to reach Ramsgate, where we can lodge with Mrs Tremaine, who can vouch that we are above reproach. Then I was going to write to your father, to apologise for spiriting you away to prevent you making a marriage you didn't want, and to request his permission to take you for my bride. You would write to him too, to beg his forgiveness, and assure him of my excellent prospects.' Daniel made a wry face. 'If, indeed, I still have excellent prospects.

240

I dare say my father will have a thing or two to say to me, too. Now, have I set your mind at rest? I realise I am in the habit of making and executing decisions without seeking the opinion of others. It is what my father has trained me to do.'

Isabel felt foolish, but she was also doubtful. Money had been involved in the transaction between her father and Lord Marchant. Was Daniel aware of this? Would her father refuse to countenance his request?

Seeing she was calmer, Daniel returned to his seat opposite her. The coachman pulled in at another inn, but Isabel refused to alight. Her face would be blotchy from weeping, she knew, and her dress even more creased. She was not in a fit state to be seen.

They made only a short stop – Daniel went in search of cooling drinks and, although Isabel longed to step out of the carriage, she made do with fully opening the windows instead. Then they were on the way again, Daniel promising that they would be in Ramsgate within the hour.

Dusk had fallen by the time the carriage rolled down the hill towards the Tremaines' house. Isabel's heart leaped at the familiar sight of the white columns around the door as the coach drew up outside. She smoothed her dress as best she could, and tucked loose strands of hair behind her ears. The coachman was holding the carriage door for her, so she stepped out, shivering in the unexpected cool breeze that came off the sea. Daniel waited for her at the top of the white marble steps and she hurried to follow him into the hallway, where she barely had a moment to glance around and remember it from the night of the ball, before a maid bade them follow her along a corridor. They were going in the direction of the library, she realised, and then the maid was ushering them in. Mrs Tremaine stood before the fireplace, unsmiling.

Isabel's own smile of greeting faded from her lips. Their intended hostess didn't look at all happy to see them. Daniel began to speak, but Mrs Tremaine waved a hand impatiently at him. 'I have your letter, Daniel. I'm afraid I wouldn't have expected this behaviour

241

from either of you. You have put yourselves – and, may I say, me – in a very difficult position.' She gave each of them in turn a look that quelled any thoughts of responding.

'Isabel, your foolish, headstrong behaviour has not only sullied your reputation but displeased your father and an influential man, Lord Marchant, who is no doubt at this very moment considering what a lucky escape he had. I was made aware of your romantic nature in the discussions we had in this very room, but you appear to have forgotten the advice I gave you.'

Daniel shot a curious glance at Isabel, who remembered Mrs Tremaine's words only too well. 'By all means have a dalliance with Daniel, but do not lose your heart to him. Sir Charles has plans for him.'

Mrs Tremaine had turned her attention to Daniel now. 'You made your intentions clear in your letter, but I'm sorry to tell you your reasoning was flawed. You may have intended to arrive here with Isabel's honour intact and untainted by any whiff of scandal. Your wish to write to her father and request her hand in marriage is honourable. But you should have done that before carrying her off in your carriage, not after. You might have been lucky enough to escape censure after spending a day travelling together, alone in your carriage, although I am doubtful. You have not a chance of doing so after spending a night in the same inn.'

Isabel and Daniel began to protest at the same time, but Mrs Tremaine held up her hand once more. 'I have not finished. It matters not at all whether you slept in separate beds. The gossip is no doubt halfway round London by now, and let me tell you it won't be kind. You have no alternative but to follow the advice – nay, the instruction – that I am about to give you.'

She stopped again and walked over to the window, now a dark rectangle in the room. Isabel was burning with embarrassment from the scolding they had been given, as hot as if the fire was lit in the grate. Daniel appeared hardly less uncomfortable. They were for all the world like a couple of small children caught behaving badly.

242

Mrs Tremaine turned back to them. 'You must leave tomorrow for Gretna Green. I'm told it will be a journey of four days from here.'

Isabel, aghast, could scarcely believe her ears. Four days in a carriage! She felt she had barely survived the journey they had just completed. She swayed a little and Daniel reached out and caught her arm to steady her.

Mrs Tremaine regarded her with a steady gaze. 'I can't pretend it will be easy, Isabel. I imagine your father will send after you both, determined to stop it. Although I'm sure he must realise that there is no chance of you making a match with Lord Marchant, or with anyone of substance, after this.'

Daniel winced at Mrs Tremaine's words and Isabel bowed her head.

'If he comes to Ramsgate first in search of you, I will do my best to persuade him it is best to let you both marry. If I fail, I will do my best to detain him as long as possible. I fear, though, that his anger over what happened with your mother, Isabel, will make him determined to find you and take you back to Marston. If he does, you will be destined to live out the rest of your days there, unwed.'

She turned to Daniel. 'Do not think you have escaped my anger, Daniel. I have known you a long time, and your father even longer, and I fear he will be most unhappy at the turn of events. I know he had great plans for you, including a most advantageous marriage. But he is a pragmatic man and he will swallow his disappointment in the face of the inevitable. I will write to him and suggest the solution that has occurred to me. If he agrees, either he or I will send a letter to Gretna Green, to await you there.

'You must eat, bathe and sleep, and be ready to depart again before dawn. I will leave instructions with the boy to get you to the stage coach at five in the morning. Now I will say goodnight, for I will not see you in the morning, or see you again until you can stand before me as man and wife.'

Mrs Tremaine swept from the room, leaving in her wake a

chastened Daniel and Isabel, still smarting from their scolding. The maid came back in and, without a word, they followed her to the dining room where a light supper was laid out for them. Neither spoke as they picked at their food, appetite diminished by the prospect of what lay ahead. Then they were conducted to their separate rooms, where Isabel found the maid had unpacked her bag. The wedding dress, very creased, had been placed in the clothes press, along with the Indian muslin, while a nightgown lay on her bed, and her hairbrush and comb sat on her dressing table. Louisa had done well, an exhausted Isabel thought, as she let down her hair before splashing her face with the water the maid had left there.

For the first time, a niggle of doubt seized her. Mrs Tremaine's assessment of their actions troubled her. Had she done the right thing in spurning Lord Marchant? Would she regret her decision for the rest of her life?

THOMAS

PART THREE

AUGUST 1823 — MAY 1824

Chapter Fourteen

If the mill had not been so busy while Isabel was away, Thomas would have been thoroughly miserable. As it was, they worked from dawn until dusk and Thomas, so tired he could barely eat the dinner Mrs Hopkins had prepared, fell into bed each night and straight into a deep and dreamless sleep. Three weeks passed in this way, with only Sundays taken as a rest day. Despite his weariness, Thomas was grateful for the walk to church along lanes still lined with froths of cow parsley and dotted with red campion and lilac field scabious, the three Hopkins children laughing and skipping at his side.

It was in church that Isabel's absence struck home. The Cavendish pew stood empty and Thomas, instead of contemplating the back of Isabel's head throughout the sermon, turned instead to daydreams of what she might be doing, and when she might return. The miller was expecting Mr Cavendish back after a month, and with each weekly visit to the church, Thomas felt he was marking time, drawing closer to the moment he would see Isabel again.

There was no chance to indulge these thoughts on the walk home, or during the dinner that followed, but Thomas always looked forward to the evening. After the vegetable patch had been watered and the younger children were in bed, Mr Hopkins sat outside and smoked his pipe, while Thomas took a seat beside him and kept him quiet company. During the month of August, his thoughts at this time always returned to Isabel. He ran over in his mind each time he had seen her since her return from Ramsgate, what she had been wearing and what she had said. Although he tried to bend his thoughts to his wishes, he had to face the unhappy fact that Isabel cared not one jot for him. He had allowed himself to be used as a messenger boy, simply to feel that he had an important part to play in her life. He had been foolish and naive. When she came back, he vowed things would be different. He hoped it wasn't too late to try to win her affections.

'Is all well?' The miller was looking at Thomas, who realised he was frowning, with pursed lips.

'I'm just a bit tired,' Thomas said hastily, blushing at the lie.

'Aye, well, the busiest weeks should be over,' the miller said. 'We'll be back to milling grain from people's stores in the next week or two. And Mr Cavendish should return any day now. I'll be glad to see him, even though his estate has mostly run itself while he's been away.'

Thomas's heart began to beat faster at the thought of Isabel's return but he knew better than to mention her name to the miller.

'Well, lad, I'm going to turn in. An early start again tomorrow.' The miller yawned and stood up.

'I won't be long,' Thomas said. He wanted to make the most of a few moments alone with his thoughts. He tipped his head back to gaze up at the star-filled sky. Was Isabel watching the sky in London, too, thinking of her home in Marston? He hoped so. He hoped she had found a moment to think of him, too.

The miller's forecast of a quieter time ahead was premature. The harvest had been particularly good that year, and the sacks of grain just kept coming. Thomas lost track of the days that week, each one so much like another. Hard at work on the millstone floor, the noise of the machinery and the great stones grinding the corn drowned out everything else. He was focused – he knew the dangers of allowing his mind to wander there – and gave a great start when he felt a hand on his shoulder. The miller stood behind him, a frown on his face.

'Come down when you can, Thomas. I want to talk to you.'

Thomas, puzzled, did as he was asked. He found the miller outside in the yard, a letter in his hand.

'It's from Mr Cavendish,' the miller said, without preamble. 'Says he won't be back when planned. The wedding didn't happen and Isabel's run off, he doesn't know where. I always said she was a headstrong girl.' He shook his head.

'Wedding?' Thomas asked. Had Mr Cavendish gone to London to take a new bride, then? He thought him rather old but supposed there was no reason why not. And why had Isabel run off? Did she dislike her stepmother-to-be?

'Isabel's wedding. To some lord or other. Cavendish arranged it apparently. But that's neither here nor there. It means we have to manage a bit longer with you doing most of the work here, while I'm still needed over at Marston Grange. It couldn't have happened at a worse time of the year.' The miller frowned and stared at the letter, as if hoping to discover something he had missed in the words on the page.

Thomas sat down suddenly on the bench.

'There,' the miller said. 'I knew it. You look done in. I'm going to write back to Cavendish and tell him I'm needed here at the mill. He'll have to leave his lands to manage themselves until he gets back.'

He went into the mill to rummage through his desk, in search of paper and ink. Thomas sat and stared at the ground, trying to make sense of the miller's words. Isabel had gone to London to be married. Was it to the man she had been writing to? Someone she must have met in Ramsgate, he realised now. But why had she run off? What had gone wrong? His legs felt like lead and he couldn't raise the energy to stand up and return to his work, so he sat on in the sunshine, waiting for the miller to come back.

Then a thought struck him, which forced him to his feet. The miller had said that Mr Cavendish had arranged the failed wedding with the lord, so it was unlikely to be the same person to whom Isabel had sent her secret letter. Could he be of assistance to Mr Cavendish? Was Ramsgate the key to it all? Could he offer to find Isabel and bring her back?

He hurried into the mill, to tell Mr Hopkins his plan before he sealed the letter. It was the miller's turn to be confused.

'What's this?' he asked. 'Isabel was writing to someone she had met. But who? And how do you know?'

Shamefaced, Thomas admitted that he had helped her.

The miller bit his lip and glanced at his letter, unfinished, on the desk. 'We will go and speak to Mrs Hopkins about this,' he said. 'She'll know what to do, for I declare I don't.'

The miller's wife, taken aback at having her daily routine disturbed, grumbled that there would be no dinner on the table that night if they didn't let her get on. But she sent the children out in the yard to play, took off her apron and sat down at the kitchen table to listen to what her husband and Thomas had to say.

When they had finished, she clasped her hands in front of her on the scoured wooden surface and stayed silent for a good minute or two. Thomas shifted his feet impatiently, already planning what he must stuff into a bag to take with him on his journey to Ramsgate.

'Do nothing,' she pronounced finally. She turned to Mr Hopkins. 'Don't send a letter. There's no point in angering Mr Cavendish, not when he's no doubt beside himself already over that girl's behaviour. You've said yourself that his lands don't need your full attention. Well, let it continue that way until he gets back. If there's a problem, step in. Otherwise, let the mill be your priority.'

She turned to Thomas. 'I'm surprised at you. Agreeing to pass letters for that —' she pulled herself up '— for Miss Isabel. If she wants to get herself into trouble, then so be it, but why should she drag you into it, too? Forget these romantic notions of finding her. Even if you did, would she thank you for it? She's made her choice, chosen her path. Let her get on with it. You can't say we didn't

250

warn you, Thomas, not to get entangled with her. And now look at what's happened. If Mr Cavendish finds out you've played any part in this, well . . .' She let her words hang in the air, while the miller pondered them and Thomas blushed and glared.

'Thank you, my dear.' Mr Hopkins was smiling. 'I knew I could rely on you to get to the heart of the matter. Come now, Thomas, back to work. We'll leave Mrs Hopkins to get on. That fowl I see on the side won't get into the oven by itself.'

Looking pleased with himself, he led the way out into the sunshine. After a moment's hesitation, Thomas followed. He wasn't entirely convinced by Mrs Hopkins's words. What if he was able to find Isabel, and persuade her to come home and be reconciled with her father? Mr Cavendish would be grateful to him and perhaps Isabel would see Thomas in a new light. If he was going to put his plan into action, though, it was clear he would have to leave in secret, at dead of night.

CHAPTER FIFTEEN

As it turned out, it was quite a day for news to make its way to the mill in Marston. No sooner had Thomas climbed back up the stairs, ready to set the millstones in motion again, than he heard a wagon draw to a halt outside. Peering out of the tiny, web-festooned window, he saw Nathaniel leaning down from his seat to talk to Mr Hopkins. They glanced up at the mill and Thomas felt a stab of anxiety. He knew from the serious nods as they said their goodbyes, and the way the miller glanced up again at the window, that there was bad news.

He descended the stairs again, without restarting the machinery.

'Nathaniel has just brought word from Castle Bay,' the miller said. 'I'm sorry, Thomas, but your mother has been taken ill. In fact, it sounds as though she has been ill for a while. She was too unwell to write, but someone in the house felt it necessary to get word to you. You must go to her.'

Thomas swallowed hard. The plans he was making to seek out Isabel evaporated in the face of this news. He must be a dutiful son and go to see what he could do for his mother. Perhaps, he allowed himself to think, her illness had been exaggerated, and once he had reassured himself, he would be able to journey on to Ramsgate. In any case, if Bartholomew Banks was still about, it would be unwise to spend much time in Castle Bay.

'I'll take you myself this afternoon,' the miller decided. 'I have flour to deliver out that way, so it's no trouble to take the cart on to Castle Bay. I'll go and tell Mrs Hopkins now. Perhaps she can find something suitable in the larder to tempt an invalid.'

He hurried away before Thomas could utter a word. Not for the first time, he was struck by the thoughtfulness of his employer and his wife, and felt shamed by it. He went slowly to his room and collected a few things together, then returned to the yard to help the miller load the cart. Mrs Hopkins insisted they eat something before they left, but Thomas had no appetite. She took away his plate without a word and wrapped bread and cheese in a cloth napkin.

'Take this,' she said. 'You might find there's no food in the house when you arrive. And this is for your mother.' She held out a wicker basket, which Thomas could see she had packed with jars of chutneys and preserves, the end of a ham, bread, and vegetables from the garden.

'It's too much,' Thomas protested.

'Nonsense.' Mrs Hopkins was brisk. 'I only wish I'd been able to make some broth. More suited to illness than anything in there.' She sighed.

The children, who seemed aware that something important was happening, stood solemnly by. Thomas remembered the money he had hidden under his mattress and excused himself to run back to his room. He would need it to help his mother, or to finance his trip to Ramsgate. Back in the kitchen, he pressed coins into the hands of Ruth, Benjamin and Anthony.

It was Mrs Hopkins's turn to protest, but Thomas wouldn't hear of it.

'Just a small thank-you,' he said. 'For this,' he held up the basket, 'and everything.'

On impulse, he hugged Mrs Hopkins and each of the children in turn, which made Benjamin squirm and Anthony giggle. He thought Ruth and Mrs Hopkins might cry, so he hurried to join Mr Hopkins on the cart, first stowing the basket and his bag among the sacks of flour.

The first part of the journey proceeded in silence, Thomas and the miller both wrapped up in their thoughts. Thomas hopped down to help with the delivery of the flour at the first farm, then broke the silence as they set off again. 'This has come at a bad time. I'm sorry,' he said.

'Now, don't you worry about that. Taking care of your mother is more important than milling a bit more grain.' They rolled on a little further and the miller spoke again. 'It's helped put things in perspective, what with the letter this morning, and the news about your mother. There's no need to be running ourselves ragged now – there's more than enough flour been milled over the last few weeks. I dare say Cavendish will be back in a week or two – I'll go over to talk to his men later. Don't think about anything other than what you need to do to get your mother well again.'

Thomas was grateful for the miller's reassurance, but his thoughts were in turmoil. They swung between the news of Isabel's disappearance, worry over what might be wrong with his mother, and anxiety at the prospect of bumping into Bartholomew Banks. As they drew closer to Castle Bay, making deliveries along the way, Thomas felt very conspicuous sitting up beside the miller. But they attracted no notice. Thomas had forgotten how much busier Castle Bay was than Marston. A cart out making deliveries was of little interest to anyone.

Thomas directed the miller to Beach Street, then asked to be put down near the Fountain Inn. 'Prospect Street is too narrow for the cart,' he explained. He was glad of it – he didn't want the miller to see how humble his home was, and feared it would have fallen further into disrepair while he was away.

'On you go, then,' said the miller, as Thomas retrieved his bag and the basket.

'I'll write to tell you how she does,' Thomas said.

'Aye, do that. But there's no rush.' The miller nodded, then shook the reins and the cart moved off, leaving Thomas to walk slowly up the street to his front door. He opened it without knocking, then stood in the narrow hallway, listening. The house was silent, which he hoped meant all the lodgers were out. He went through to the kitchen, reeling back at the unpleasant aroma that greeted him there. Dirty dishes were piled on the surfaces and flies buzzed at the windows. He had been going to set the basket down on the table but changed his mind at the sight of the sticky and encrusted surface and took it upstairs with him instead.

He knocked at his mother's door and waited. When he didn't hear a response, he pushed the door open and went in. At first, he wondered whether she was there. The air in the room was stale, the curtains tightly closed, and he couldn't make out anyone in the bed. Then, as his eyes grew accustomed to the gloom, he saw a shape barely raising the bedclothes. His mother had referred to aches and pains in her letter – he had expected to see her confined to a chair, but what was this? He hurried over to the bed, setting the basket down on the floor beside it, and gently eased the covers away from her face. He had to stifle a cry at the sight that greeted him – if he had not known this to be his mother's room he would have thought the figure in the bed was a stranger, for he barely recognised her.

Chapter Sixteen

It soon became apparent that when Mrs Marsh had written to her son a month or so earlier, she had represented her situation as rather better than it was. Thomas discovered the truth of it from a man he found in the foetid kitchen later that day. He was small in stature, in his late thirties at a guess and, to Thomas's mind, rather weaselly in appearance. He hadn't been disposed to think kindly of him, being very upset by the state in which he'd found his mother and half inclined to blame the man for it.

'Ah, so you're the son,' the man said, introducing himself as Ernest. He soon put Thomas right as to the state of affairs, informing him of the vanishing lodgers. Mrs Marsh's illness had prevented her from working at first, but the money from the lodgers had kept her provided for. One by one, though, they had vanished, some of them no doubt still owing money.

'It went from bad to worse after your father left,' Ernest said, missing Thomas's gasp and continuing, 'not that they paid much heed to him.'

'My father has gone?' Thomas remembered thinking his mother hadn't mentioned him in her letter, but then neither had he enquired after him. It was something he had been long out of the habit of doing, having so little respect for the man. He hadn't even registered Samuel's absence that day, since he was used to him spending long hours away from home.

'You didn't know?' Ernest seemed mildly surprised. 'When was it now? February, maybe.'

'What happened?' Thomas asked, trying to come to terms with this new information.

'He didn't come back one evening. From the inn,' Ernest added, although it hardly needed saying. 'Your ma thought he'd fallen in the sea and drowned. She didn't find out until a week or so after that he'd taken up with some woman in town who liked gin as much as he liked ale. Your ma took to her bed after that.'

Thomas didn't know what to say. Had his mother known all this when she wrote to him? There wasn't a hint of it in her letter.

'So is she ill?' Thomas asked. He'd spent the afternoon sitting beside her bed, asking questions she didn't answer and watching the slow rise and fall of her breath in a body so changed, so devoid of flesh, that he'd wanted to weep, but restrained himself, fearful she might be aware of his distress.

Ernest frowned. 'Not ill exactly. I'd say she starved herself into this state. And then her aches and pains got bad again and made it hard for her to move. I had to beg her to let me get in touch with you.'

'Thank you,' Thomas said. It barely seemed adequate. He was filled with reproach. How could he have let this happen? How could he have neglected his mother for so long? She must have been determined to keep him unaware that his father had left, so that he didn't return to Castle Bay and run the risk of Bartholomew Banks seeing him. He knew it had suited him to stay out of touch. It had allowed him to fill his thoughts with Isabel. He winced. Just a few hours earlier, he had been wondering how quickly he could be done with seeing his mother so that he could move on to Ramsgate to seek out news of Isabel, then turn himself into some sort of hero in the eyes of Mr Cavendish.

He shook his head, hoping to rid himself of thoughts of his own folly. Then he stared around at the mess in the kitchen where they stood. Was Ernest responsible for this? He owed him a debt of gratitude for alerting him to the state of things, but had he contributed to this squalor?

'I know what you're thinking,' Ernest said, 'and I am partly to blame. But none of the others ever cleared up after themselves. They jeered at me for suggesting it and I got tired of doing it all.' He gazed around as though seeing the room for the first time. 'I'll help you clean up,' he offered.

Thomas bit back the suggestion that Ernest might like to do it himself, and nodded. Ernest had been kind. There was no point in angering him. If he was still paying rent, there was no doubt the money would be useful. Thomas could see himself having to stay there for some time to nurse his mother back to health, and his savings wouldn't last long.

Two hours later, the kitchen was as he remembered it when his aunt Meg had still lived with them. Clean and fresh, the table scrubbed, pots and jars neatly ordered on the dresser, china stacked in the cupboard or displayed on the shelves. Thomas remembered the basket sent by the miller's wife and went to fetch it from his mother's bedroom. She was sleeping, just as she had been when he had left her. The sight of her filled him with anxiety. He remembered Mrs Hopkins's mention of broth, and wondered where he might buy some.

Back in the kitchen he set down the basket and insisted Ernest shared food with him.

'None of this is suitable for my mother,' he lamented, as he laid out the ham and pickles, along with the bread and cheese from the napkin. 'She's so weak. I think broth might be the only thing she can manage, but I can't make it and don't know where to buy it.'

'I've been giving her weak tea with a bit of bread dipped in to soften it,' Ernest said. 'I never thought of broth.'

Thomas almost wanted to laugh at how helpless they both were, but it was hardly a laughing matter. 'Then I will give her weak tea tonight,' he said, slightly cheered by having a plan.

'Ask at the Fountain,' Ernest said, as he cut himself a slice of ham. 'Your mother told me they know your family there. The landlady is friendly enough. She'll supply you with broth, I'm sure.'

Thomas was warming to Ernest, despite his unprepossessing appearance. He knew he must be grateful for his efforts on Mrs Marsh's behalf, while Thomas had remained in ignorance of her condition. They ate a companionable supper, Ernest telling Thomas of his work at the new brewery in Hawksdown. He asked whether Thomas wished to know how to find his father but Thomas refused as politely as he could. The thought of what Samuel had done filled him with rage. It would be a long time before he felt able to speak to him again, if ever.

By the end of the evening, his mother had taken a few spoonfuls of weak tea and a mouthful or two of soaked bread. She didn't appear to recognise Thomas, which was a great worry to him, but he told himself she would be better once she had taken something more sustaining and begun to rebuild her strength. He made up a bed for himself in a room at the top of the house that had once belonged to his aunt Meg and, as he drifted into sleep, he reflected that he was beginning to settle back into the idea of being in Castle Bay once more. The mill, his home until a few hours previously, now felt like a distant dream.

Chapter Seventeen

The next morning, Thomas went to his mother as soon as he was awake, and found her just as unresponsive as she had been the day before. She was existing in a twilight world, neither awake nor asleep. She still didn't appear to recognise him and, with a stab of worry, he wondered whether she ever would. She shifted a little on her pillows and muttered something, and as he went closer to try to catch her words, he realised she had soiled the bed in the night.

He started back in revulsion. What should he do? He almost called for Ernest to help him, then stopped himself. Ernest had probably already left for work, and it was hardly something he could expect a lodger to deal with. Someone must have been doing it, though, he thought, as he rolled up his sleeves and went in search of clean linen. He set water to heat on the kitchen range, then sat down and buried his head in his hands. Was this to be his life from now on?

He allowed himself a few minutes of self-pity, then set about preparing to clean both his mother and the bed. He took a basin of warm water up to the room, along with some rags he found in a cupboard. Then, thankful now that his mother didn't recognise him, he raised her gently in the bed, stripping away the soiled night clothes and linen and bundling them onto the floor. He washed her as well as he could, eyes half averted, then dressed her in a clean nightshift and lifted her from one side of the bed to the other as he made it up around her.

Back in the kitchen, the dirty linen soaking in a bucket, he made her a cup of weak tea and soaked some bread, then burst into tears. Lifting his mother had brought home to him just how frail she had become. He must find a way to put some flesh on her bones as quickly as possible. He resolved to go to the Fountain Inn as soon as he had finished.

As before, he managed to get a few spoonfuls of tea past his mother's lips, before she sank back on the pillows and turned away from him. He went down to the kitchen, but had no appetite for breakfast. Restless, he decided to go to the inn at once.

He hadn't much frequented the inns of the town when he lived there, his father enjoying them quite enough for both of them, but he remembered Mrs Dunn had been the landlady when his aunt Meg had worked there. He had carried messages to the inn on Meg's behalf on occasion, and Mrs Dunn had sometimes sent food to the house, although he couldn't remember why.

As he pushed open the door of the Fountain, he wondered whether she would still be there. The wood-panelled interior, with its low ceiling and small windows, was gloomy after the bright morning outside and Thomas had to stand for a moment to allow his eyes to adjust. Smells from the previous night mingled in the air: wood smoke from the fireplace along with pipe smoke, stale beer, and the leftover fug of a crush of bodies.

'We're not serving yet.'

Thomas turned at the voice. A woman stood behind the bar, yawning, wearing a wrapper, her hair in rags. He stared at her, trying to work out if she could be Mrs Dunn, ten years older than when he'd last seen her.

'Come back in an hour – we'll have cleaned up by then.' She turned and made for the staircase leading upstairs.

'Mrs Dunn?' Thomas asked, still unsure.

'Depends who's asking.' The woman turned back to him. 'If you're from the revenue, the answer's no.' She sounded stern, but Thomas thought he caught the hint of a smile. He was quite sure he bore no resemblance to a revenue man.

'I'm Thomas Marsh. I live in Prospect Street. If you are Mrs Dunn, you might remember my aunt Meg?'

'Well, let me see now.' Mrs Dunn moved closer, behind the bar. 'Little Thomas Marsh. I wouldn't have recognised you. Are you still up to no good?'

'No,' Thomas protested. He remembered only too well being endlessly scolded for running wild about the town, helping himself to an apple here, a bread roll there – items from shops he swore would never be missed. But that had been a long time ago. 'I went to the Charity School. Then to the boatyard and now I work at a mill in Marston. Or, rather, I did, until yesterday.' He stopped, remembering why he had come.

'Well, good to see you again, Thomas, but I must get on.' Mrs Dunn turned to leave the bar.

'It's my mother,' Thomas blurted out. 'She's very ill. I think she might—' He stopped, unable to continue. 'She isn't eating. Ernest, the lodger, suggested you might be able to help. With some broth?'

'He did, did he?' Mrs Dunn pretended irritation, but Thomas could see by her expression she was concerned. 'I've known your family a long while – your grandfather was a good friend of mine.'

Thomas could barely remember his grandfather, who had died when he was five, but he nodded and didn't say anything.

Mrs Dunn reached a decision. 'Go home, Thomas. I'll come along to the house in an hour or so.'

She was fully awake now, Thomas could see, so he thanked her and hurried back, anxious in case his mother should have taken a turn for the worse while he was out. He found her in exactly the same position as he had left her, her breathing as shallow as it had been the day before. He went down to the kitchen to deal with the washing before Mrs Dunn arrived. Despite his best efforts, it was barely in a fit state to hang on the line in the yard. He was trying not to feel overwhelmed by the task when he heard a knock at the front door and Mrs Dunn's voice in the hall. 'Thomas?' she called.

'Here, in the kitchen.'

She came in, dressed in a print blouse and linen skirt, bearing a basket which she placed on the table. 'Where's your mother?' she asked. 'Then I'll see what can be done to help her.'

Thomas took her up to the bedroom, where she shooed him away. 'I'll be down shortly,' she said. 'You can make me some coffee.'

The smell of the coffee, while it was brewing, reminded Thomas he hadn't had breakfast and he was examining the contents of the larder when Mrs Dunn reappeared. He poured her coffee and she sat down, indicating to him to do the same. Then she pulled a napkin from the basket and opened it to reveal two bread rolls. 'Breakfast,' she said. 'Help yourself. I can't get on with the day until I've had something to eat.'

Thomas fetched plates and some of Mrs Hopkins's preserves, glad to have something suitable to share with Mrs Dunn. She didn't speak again until she had eaten the roll, picking up every crumb with her fingers, and drunk her coffee.

'I'll send some beef broth over at midday,' she said. 'You're to warm a little at a time and give her a few spoonfuls every couple of hours. After a day, increase the quantity. I've brought some cordial.' She pulled a bottle from the basket. 'I want you to give her some, diluted with water, three times a day. It's home-made, plenty of fruit and sweetness. My mother always gave it to me when I was sick.'

'Do you think she needs the physician?' Thomas had been worrying about this, and was glad for the chance to ask Mrs Dunn's opinion.

She shook her head. 'She's not ill, as such. No fever. Just very weak. She needs nursing back to health.' Mrs Dunn stood up and made ready to go. 'She had a reason for what she has done to herself,' she observed. 'Your duty is to give her a reason to change her mind.'

She was halfway down the hallway, Thomas following to see her out, when she turned. 'I dare say you could do with some help in the house for a week or so. A girl to do the laundry and sit with your mother when you need to go out.'

Thomas blushed at the thought of his feeble attempts to wash the bed linen. Mrs Dunn's keen eyes must have spotted it hanging in the yard.

'I'll send someone round later,' she said, before Thomas could reply. He watched her bustle down Prospect Street, towards Beach Street and the Fountain Inn. He had good reason to be grateful to Ernest and his suggestion, he reflected. And to his grandfather. Whatever his relationship with Mrs Dunn, their friendship was still holding strong down the years.

CHAPTER EIGHTEEN

Mrs Dunn was as good as her word and sent a young girl called Nell to the house at midday, bearing a pot of broth. 'Mrs Dunn says I'm to help,' she said.

Thomas was doubtful. She was young and small, slight with it. Could she really be of use to him?

Nell, however, stepped past him, bearing the broth into the kitchen. She found a pot to use for heating a small amount, and a china bowl to serve it in, then put the remainder in the larder.

'Shall I take it up?' she asked, when it was warmed.

Thomas, who had been standing by, bemused by the ease with which she moved around the kitchen, shook his head. He took the bowl up to his mother, and felt encouraged that she finished it all: three large spoonfuls, taken in small sips.

Returning the bowl to the kitchen he found Nell had boiled water and set to with the half-dry bed linen, having found a washboard and a block of soap somewhere in the house. Feeling in the way, he returned to his mother and, mindful of Mrs Dunn's words, sat and talked to her, expecting no response but hoping he would reach her somehow. He didn't know what to talk to her about, considering topics such as his own childhood and his schooldays before discarding them. There were painful memories among them for his mother, he felt sure, subjects better avoided. Instead, he talked to her about the mill, the Hopkins family and the work he did there.

He was just describing the pies that Mrs Hopkins made, hoping that might awaken some answering response, when Nell knocked lightly and stuck her head round the door. 'I'm going now, but I'll come back this evening and again in the morning.' She smiled and withdrew before Thomas could ask her anything further. Did she work at the inn? And how much should he pay her?

He noticed his mother was fast asleep, so stood up and stretched. Should he wake her when it was time to give her more broth? It seemed a shame to do so, but if she was to build her strength he supposed he must.

Down in the kitchen, he saw the laundry outside, looking much cleaner than it had done earlier. He peeked underneath a checked cloth laid over a dish beside the range and discovered a pie, waiting to be cooked. Had Nell brought it with her? He didn't think so – she had needed both hands for the pot of broth. Perhaps it had been sent from the inn. Then he recognised the floral design around the edge of the pie dish – it was one his grandmother had used for baking. Had Nell made it, as well as doing the laundry?

Over the next few days, as the household settled into a new routine, Thomas discovered that his first impression of Nell as a little slip of a thing couldn't have been more wrong. She had more strength in her slim arms than he would have thought possible, helping him to turn his mother in the mornings, and whisking away soiled linen without a word. She also took over washing his mother, making it plain she thought it was an unsuitable job for Thomas. He was embarrassed to let her, but also mortified at the thought of continuing to do it himself.

In the end, it was easier to confine himself to the things he felt he could do for his mother. He fed the broth to her as instructed by Mrs Dunn, delighted when she finished up every drop and cast down when she turned away from him. He went out to the shops and bought food for the larder, which Nell turned into pies and stews. However, Thomas considered his main task to be solving whatever it was that had made his mother seemingly shut down her mind. That proved much harder to deal with than any of the practical issues in the house. After a week, she was still as blank as ever, showing no sign that she recognised Thomas and spending much of each day asleep or dozing.

Thomas confided his despair to Mrs Dunn, when she called in one day to see how things were. He was quite sure that Nell gave her regular reports, but he supposed she wanted to see for herself.

'She's looking better,' Mrs Dunn said approvingly, after she'd been upstairs. 'She's got more flesh on her bones and some colour in her cheeks.'

'She has?' Thomas, who saw his mother every day, had been hard pressed to notice any change.

'Definitely.' Mrs Dunn nodded. 'I think it's time to move on to more solid food – stews, perhaps. And to get her out of that bed for a little time each day. Put a comfortable chair by the bedroom window, open it a little so that she can hear the sea and feel the breeze.'

She registered Thomas's expression. 'Do you have a suitable chair?'

Thomas thought. The front parlour had been a shop when he was a boy, and they had used the kitchen as a sitting room, although there had been little sitting in such a busy household, other than at mealtimes. The front room had been turned over to lodgers since then, and any chairs in the house were of the straight-backed, uncomfortable kind.

'I'll send one over,' she said. 'And I think you should encourage her to use a chamber pot.'

Thomas couldn't look at her. Nell had no doubt made her aware of the challenge they faced each morning.

'I'm not getting through to her,' he blurted out. 'I talk to her for hours each day but she isn't responding.'

'What sort of things do you say to her?' Mrs Dunn asked.

When Thomas explained that he spoke mainly about the mill, and Marston and anything he could think of that wouldn't raise unpleasant memories, Mrs Dunn shook her head.

'Talk to her about your childhood. Something she can remember, not tales of a place she has never visited. It doesn't matter if there are upsetting memories – it might just open the door to something, make her take notice and remember who you are.'

Thomas felt foolish. It seemed he had been doing entirely the wrong thing.

'You're doing a good job, Thomas,' Mrs Dunn reassured him. 'She was probably too weak to hear much of what you've been saying to her. But now – now, I feel sure you will find she is on the mend.'

She left, taking the empty broth pot with her, and Thomas went back upstairs to contemplate his situation. 'Well, Ma,' he said, 'looks like I'm going to be here for a while. I'd better write to the miller and let him know he must find a new boy to help him.'

As he spoke the words, Thomas was struck by a sense of finality. A door had closed on one part of his life, and another would now open. He would miss his life at the mill, and the kindness of the miller and his wife. He hoped Mr Hopkins wouldn't be angry when he received the letter. Making sure his mother recovered would have to be his priority, and he feared it would be a long, slow process. He would need to find work in Castle Bay once she was a little better, for the money he had brought with him would last only a matter of months. There was another problem to solve, too. Thomas hadn't been out a great deal in the town since his return, and Bartholomew Banks and his threat to have him killed had barely crossed his mind. But if he was to stay here for any length of time, it was important to face up to it and find a way to deal with it.

CHAPTER NINETEEN

Mrs Dunn had spoken wisely, Thomas discovered. He began to talk to his mother about his childhood, the days when they had all lived there together: Aunt Meg, his grandmother, his mother and father.

'Do you remember those clothes you bought for me to wear to the Charity School? You were determined to buy something I could grow into, but I reckon they'd still fit me now. I was only eight, and the trousers had to be held up with string, and the jacket sleeves rolled up. The trouser bottoms were rolled up too, but by the time I reached school in the morning, they were back to their normal length.'

Thomas chuckled. 'I think they were still too big when I was twelve and had to leave to work in the boatyard.' He stopped then, and cast a glance at his mother. She showed no sign of having heard him. He sighed. Leaving school to go to the boatyard wasn't a particularly happy memory for him. He decided to try again.

'Aunt Meg used to make biscuits for the shop every morning and she always gave me one for breakfast, and one or two to take to school.' Thomas smiled. It had been a wise move on his aunt's part. It had made him popular very quickly. There had been an older girl, he remembered. What was her name? Catherine. She had taken him under her wing and been like a big sister to him. Where was she now? Perhaps she was married and living in the town. He would ask Ernest or Mrs Dunn whether they had come across her.

Aunt Meg had been more like a big sister, too, than an aunt. There was no need to ask where she was now – buried in the chalk quarry at the back of Hawksdown Castle by all accounts, on the instruction of Bartholomew Banks. Thomas set his face in anger. That man had threatened to drive the family from the town if they spoke out against him. He'd never faced justice.

His mother stirred, pulling him back to the moment. Such dark thoughts – he could never share them with her. Mrs Dunn's advice was proving hard to put into practice. He remembered what she had said, though, about trying his mother with different foods.

'I'll be back in a moment, Ma,' he said. 'We're going to try something new to eat today.'

Down in the kitchen, he took the remains of last night's stew from the larder and heated a little on the stove. The aroma made his mouth water and he remembered he hadn't eaten more than a piece of bread so far that day. He hesitated, then tipped the contents of the dish into the pot. Nell would be there again in a while. She would make them something else to eat that night.

He took two bowls of stew up to his mother's bedroom, then lifted her to lean against her pillows. He dipped a piece of bread in the stew and held it to her lips.

'Try a little, Ma,' he urged. He thought he would have to put it down and reach for the spoon, as usual, but to his amazement, she opened her lips slightly and took a small bite.

'A bit more, Ma?' He dipped the bread again.

By the time she had finished the bowlful, helped along by the spoon, Thomas's own food had grown cold. But he didn't mind – he felt hopeful that this might prove a turning point. True, her eyes had remained closed throughout, and she seemed to slip into a doze as soon as she had finished, but still . . .

He took the bowls down to the kitchen and found Nell there.

'Nell, your stew is miraculous.' He could have danced her around the kitchen, he was so happy. 'Ma's just eaten a bowlful, and some bread.'

Nell beamed. 'Shall I make some more? Or would you like something different tonight?'

Thomas considered.

'I was going to make a pie.' Nell indicated the rabbit laid out on the kitchen table. 'But I could make stew with it instead.'

'I love rabbit stew!' Thomas exclaimed. 'Can you make dumplings, too?'

Nell nodded.

Thomas restrained an urge to hug her, and confined himself to saying, 'Thank you,' several times over. Then he asked what she needed to stock the larder, and went out to the shops, feeling blessed by the help that had come his way since he returned to Castle Bay.

He was walking back along Lower Street, enjoying the feel of the sun on his face, when he heard the brisk clip-clop of hoofs and a rumble that suggested a carriage of some size was approaching. He half turned. The horses were abreast of him and he could see the crest painted on the door. It was the crest of the Lord Warden, Bartholomew Banks's father, and this was the family carriage.

Thomas stepped back involuntarily, causing a collision with the person walking behind him, who dropped her basket. Onions and potatoes rolled into the roadway. The owner of the basket flung an angry glance at him as she dropped to her knees in the dust and began to gather up the vegetables.

'I'm so sorry. Let me help.' Thomas cast a quick glance after the coach, still rolling along Lower Street, before stooping to gather up errant onions from the gutter. 'There,' he presented them to her.

As he did so, he recognised Catherine, from the Charity School, who had come into his thoughts just that morning. She recognised him, too, he could tell, although her brows were knitted together in a frown, suggesting she'd forgotten his name.

'It's Thomas. Thomas Marsh,' he said. 'We were at school together.'

'So we were,' Catherine said, brushing dust from her skirt. 'I haven't seen you for a while. Have you been away?'

'I've been working in Marston, at the mill there. My mother's not well so I've come back to care for her.'

They stood looking at each other. Thomas wasn't sure what to say next. He should ask her about herself, and what she was doing now, he supposed. Instead, he blurted out, 'Was that Bartholomew Banks in the coach that just went by?'

Catherine appeared surprised by the question. 'Bartholomew Banks? I shouldn't think so. He's been banished by his father – told to stay away from the town.'

Thomas couldn't prevent a smile spreading from ear to ear. His mother had mentioned rumours of such a thing in her letter to him. The relief in knowing it to be true was immense.

'It was lovely to see you again,' he said, unable to wipe the smile from his face. 'I'd better be getting back to my mother.'

He hurried off, clutching his shopping. He didn't look back, but feared that if he had, Catherine would have been standing, watching him, a bewildered expression on her face.

CHAPTER TWENTY

Mrs Dunn kept her promise to send over a chair. A cart arrived the next day and two men offloaded an upholstered armchair, then stood and scratched their heads when they saw the narrowness of the doorway at number 5 Prospect Street. They tried the chair on its side, tilted at an angle, then tilted the other way. With much cursing, they managed to push it into the hallway until it became so firmly wedged that Thomas feared it would have to remain there for ever.

He retreated to the kitchen then, not wishing to stand over them. He supposed they would have to push it back out into the street somehow but, to his surprise, within five minutes he heard them clumping up the narrow staircase. There was more cursing as they negotiated the narrow turn in the stairs. Then Thomas had to hurry after them so they didn't burst into his mother's bedroom and startle her.

Mrs Dunn must have apprised them of the situation, though, for they entered very quietly and respectfully, and set the chair down in the window without being asked. Thomas was fearful that the upholstery would have been ripped by the difficulties of delivery, but it appeared intact. Had it come from Mrs Dunn's own sitting room? If that was the case, he feared it might be impossible to return it to her. It had got into the house, though, so it must be possible to get it out.

Thomas quickly followed the men down the stairs, calling them both into the kitchen. He supposed Mrs Dunn must have paid them but he felt he owed them a tip, at least. He pulled two bottles of beer from the larder – they were Ernest's, brought home from the brewery, but since he was benefiting from Nell's cooking in the evening, Thomas didn't think he would mind.

As he handed them over, it occurred to him that, since they probably worked for Mrs Dunn at the Fountain, ale would be easy enough to come by. They examined the labels, though, and seemed impressed, nodding and smiling.

'I've been wanting to try this,' the older of the two said. He gazed speculatively at the other man, who, Thomas now saw, was more of a boy. 'Reckon I'll have yours, too.'

'No, here, take another couple.' Thomas thrust two more bottles into their hands. 'Thirsty work today. Thank you.'

'You're welcome,' the man said. 'You take good care of your ma, now. Hope we see her out and about before too long.'

Thomas saw them back to their cart, wondering how they knew his mother. He supposed it was foolish to think the name of Marsh didn't still carry a certain notoriety in the town, after what had happened to Aunt Meg. And, more recently, there would have been gossip about his father and the woman he had run off with. His cheeks burned with anger at the thought.

He shook his head and climbed the stairs. It was a lovely day, and although Prospect Street was narrow, his mother's bedroom window caught a sliver of sun over the rooftops for much of the afternoon. He opened the window a crack, then went over to the bed.

'Ma, I'm going to get you up today and sit you by the window. It will do you good to feel the sun on your face.'

He was lifting her gently as he spoke. Despite Mrs Dunn's assurance that Mrs Marsh was looking better, he was taken aback yet again by just how frail she was, how fragile she felt in his arms. He had to bite his lip to prevent tears starting to his eyes. He deposited her gently in the chair, then worried she wasn't comfortable as she slipped sideways. With the help of pillows, he managed to

274

support her, then noticed she was shivering. He thought about closing the window, but the scent of the sea breeze and the cries of the gulls reminded him of Mrs Dunn's advice to let his mother hear sounds from outside. He fetched the quilt from the bed and draped it over her.

'I'm going to bring you some stew, Ma. You sit here for a bit.'

Thomas was getting used to uttering what he had at first thought of as pointless inanities. Her lack of response had silenced him at first, but he accepted it now. He feared he might begin to talk to himself at other times, though, and chuckled as he warmed a portion of stew, earning himself a look from Nell, recently arrived.

'The chair has been delivered,' he said. 'And I've moved the cabinet with the chamber pot closer to the bed. I hope it will make things easier.'

Nell, who had been there first thing as usual to deal with the sheets, nodded and Thomas hurried back to his mother, eager to avoid any further discussion of the matter. He carried a wooden chair over to sit beside her and was surprised and delighted to see her eyes were open.

'Ma!' he exclaimed. 'You're awake.'

She closed her eyes immediately. Thomas felt shut out. Was that the intention? She hadn't acknowledged him since he'd been there. Was she angry with him? Did she blame him for not coming sooner, for not visiting her all the while he was in Marston?

There was nothing to be gained by thinking that way so he devoted the next twenty minutes to encouraging her to eat the stew, wiping the bowl clean with the bread, and telling her, 'Ma, you'll be back on your feet in no time. You tell me what you'd like to eat and I'll get Nell to make it for you.'

As he got to his feet, he could have sworn she nodded slightly. His heart was filled with delight and he bent forward and kissed the top of her head.

'I think she's getting better, I really do,' he said to Nell, as he returned the empty bowl to the kitchen.

'It won't be long, I'm sure,' she said, busy chopping onions and carrots. Thomas didn't know whether she really meant it, or was just trying to reassure him. And yet, as the weeks passed, Eliza's health did improve. She ate a little more week by week, and Thomas noticed she was less easy to lift into the chair, or onto the chamber pot. He helped Nell with that part of their daily routine, then quickly absented himself from the room.

He had written to Mr Hopkins and received a letter in return, expressing regret, but not surprise, that he wouldn't be returning.

Mrs Hopkins and I had hoped that your mother would recover swiftly but we fully understand that your duty is to her. You must stay and look after her and do not think about us, except to promise to come and visit as soon as you can be spared. We want to hear all about your mother's recovery and your new life in Castle Bay. I will look for another boy to help but I feel quite sure I won't find anyone like you, Thomas. Your position here will always be open for you if you ever want to return.

Thomas had been upset by the letter. It reminded him forcefully of how alone he was now, despite all the help he had been given. It wasn't the same as feeling part of the Hopkins family. He would visit them, he thought, as soon as he felt able to leave his mother. And he would start to look for work locally, now that she was growing stronger. Perhaps Nell could be persuaded to stay on for a bit, to keep her company during the day. Thomas was not only conscious of the dwindling of the savings he had brought with him, but he missed the routine of work. Everyone had told him his duty was to see his mother get well, and now that she was on the mend, he must seek employment. He was flattered by the miller's words but working at the mill again was out of the question. He must find something closer to home.

CHAPTER TWENTY-ONE

There was a chill in the air now when Thomas got up in the mornings. Moisture coated the outside of the windowpanes and it took him a few moments to prepare to leave the warmth of his bed to wash and dress, then descend to check on his mother.

After eight weeks, she was now awake when he went in, turning her head and greeting him when he came into the bedroom. It had happened only recently, and when she had first responded to him, it had been a great weight off Thomas's mind. He had feared that either she would never progress beyond the semi-comatose state in which she spent most of her days, or that she was choosing to be like that in anger at his neglect of her.

She had first recognised him a fortnight earlier. She had been sitting in her chair by the window and he had been sitting beside her, talking of times past.

'Do you remember the time I got into trouble in that shop in Lower Street? I suppose I was about seven years old. You went to see them, took a look around and said the place was such a mess you couldn't see how anyone could be sure anything was missing. I'd picked up an apple – I said it had fallen on the floor, but it hadn't. I was always trying to see what I could get away with in there. It was usually Aunt Meg who had to get me out of trouble but for some reason that time it was you. They let me off and you said you hoped they'd stop picking on me in the future. You gave me such a clip round the ear when you got me home.'

Thomas couldn't help laughing at the memory. He'd been a

naughty little urchin, until Aunt Meg had found him a place at the Charity School. After that, he'd wanted to please her by staying out of trouble. And, in any case, he enjoyed school. When she was taken from them in such a terrible way, he knew he had to be good because everyone else in the house was so unhappy.

'Thomas, is that you?'

He realised with a start that his mother had spoken to him. She was looking at him – actually focused, rather than with her normal glazed expression.

'Ma! Yes, it's me. I came home to look after you.'

'Where's your father?' Eliza surveyed the room as though expecting to see him there.

Thomas's heart sank. She had forgotten. She would need to relearn what her husband had done. He feared it would be too much for her.

'He's not here, Ma,' he said. 'I'm here to look after you now. I was working at the mill, do you remember? You wrote to me there. I wish you'd told me you weren't well.'

She had, in a way, he supposed. She'd spoken about aches and pains, but said she was much improved. It had suited him to believe it.

'Samuel's gone, hasn't he?' She appeared to have remembered, which was a relief, Thomas supposed.

'Yes, Ma. I'm sorry.'

'It's for the best.' She had turned away from him and was looking out of the window.

'Have I been ill for long?'

Her voice was croaky, Thomas noticed, no doubt from lack of use. 'Yes, Ma, quite a long time. It's the end of September now.'

She was quiet then, thinking. It must be a shock to discover you had missed so many weeks of your life, Thomas thought.

He told her how Ernest, the lodger, had sent word to him and how kind Mrs Dunn had been, finding Nell to help them. 'Mrs Dunn even sent you her own chair,' Thomas said, patting the arm of it.

'Goodness.' Eliza's voice was faint and she sounded a little over-whelmed. She'd fallen asleep shortly after, but each day she had been awake a little longer and spoken a little more. Thomas had begun to help her down to the kitchen in the afternoons, where she liked to sit and talk to Nell.

He felt a little in the way, so he would go to the shops or for a walk around town. There was no longer a reason to delay in finding work, as long as he could persuade Nell to stay on until his mother was fully better.

He mentioned his plan to Ernest that night.

'I'm sure there are jobs at the brewery,' Ernest said. 'We're so busy. Do you want me to ask?'

Thomas deliberated. Ernest had told him about his work in the brew house – the smell of the hops that turned your stomach after a while, how hard it was to stir the ale in the great vats, the heat in the building. Did he really want such work? Would it be better to go back to the boatyard and ask there? Then he remembered how poorly they had treated him. There were seven flour mills in and around the town. It might make more sense to ask there, now that he had experience.

He made a start on that the next day, walking to the nearest one on a hill just west of the edge of town. His enquiry about work was greeted with 'Nay, lad, we're all right.'

Thomas tried to explain about his experience but his words elicited a polite but firm shake of the head. He tried Oakley's mill near Sandown Castle the following day, with the same response. Two more mills that were the closest to Castle Bay also professed themselves happy with the workers they had. After that Thomas gave up – the walk to the other mills was just too far to undertake each day. He would have to think again.

Ernest came home that evening to find Thomas despondent.

'No luck at the mills,' he said, in answer to the lodger's query. 'Since the soldiers left the barracks, there's not much call in Castle Bay for anything, it seems.'

'Except ale,' Ernest said. 'There's still plenty of inns in the town, and more than enough sailors intent on drinking them dry.'

It was true enough, Thomas thought. On any given night, a great number of ships would be at anchor in the Downs, the calm stretch of water inside the sandbank that stretched across the bay. Small boats ferried the sailors to shore, so that they could entertain themselves at the inns and brothels that lined the seafront.

'Why don't you try the brewery tomorrow?' Ernest suggested. 'At least walk out to it and have a look. There's no shortage of work – there's talk of extending to meet demand.'

As Thomas hesitated, he added, 'There's all sorts of jobs to be had – cask washing, bottling, turning the barley in the malt house or the hops in the oast. Looking after the horses, making the deliveries . . .'

Thomas hadn't heard a single thing described that appealed to him, or for which he felt he had the skills. Yet it was the income that mattered. He reached a decision. 'I'll go there tomorrow morning,' he said.

Ernest turned his attention to the herrings Nell had fried for them before she left. 'You'll be surprised,' he said confidently. 'You'll have been by it before and not given it much of a thought, but it's like a little town in there.'

Thomas, sceptical, devoted himself to mopping up the oil from the herrings with a piece of bread. He didn't relish taking on a new job, but his duty with regard to his mother was almost done. Now, earning money had to take precedence.

CHAPTER TWENTY-TWO

The next morning, Thomas spruced himself up as best he could, which was difficult as he had packed in haste and brought only his work clothes from the mill. His shirt was fraying at the neck and his trousers wearing thin, but at least Nell had kept everything clean. He walked out along the Dover turnpike, leaving Castle Bay behind as the road climbed towards Hawkshill. The brewery lay behind iron gates: an imposing three-storey building with a tall chimney and a collection of sheds and low buildings around it. An archway led through to a central courtyard, busy with men moving purposefully about the place, while carts rumbled through, some empty, others laden with casks that Thomas supposed were destined for the inns of Castle Bay.

Unsure of where to go, he stood and looked about. The main building seemed the most likely and he set off, dodging a man rolling barrels across the archway, and almost missing a staircase with a sign saying 'Office' and an arrow pointing upwards. As Thomas climbed the wooden stairs, he took in the view across the courtyard and reflected that Ernest was quite right – the brewery was indeed like a small town.

The office wasn't large, just big enough for the three or four desks occupied by men who all seemed immersed in the piles of paperwork stacked before them. Thomas waited, but no one paid him any attention.

'Excuse me,' he said.

The man nearest him reluctantly raised his head.

'I wondered whether there is any work at the brewery,' Thomas said.

'Plenty going on here, as you can see,' the man said, preparing to return to his papers.

'I'm looking for a job,' Thomas said.

'You're in the wrong place,' said the man. 'Back down the stairs, across the courtyard, far corner.'

Thomas wanted to ask what he should look for, or who he should ask, but the man had returned to his paperwork.

He went back down the stairs and set off across the yard, feeling discomfited.

'Thomas,' a voice called, and there was Ernest.

'Ernest! I'm glad to see you,' Thomas said. 'I'm a bit lost. Where should I go?'

Ernest led him to an unmarked door in the corner of the courtyard.

'This is Thomas Marsh, looking for work,' he said, to a man standing just inside. He turned to Thomas. 'I've got to get on. Good luck. Tell me all about it tonight.' Then he was gone, leaving Thomas nervously twisting his cap in his hands.

'Right, tell me what you know about brewing.' The man was standing behind a tall desk, where he was busy spiking pieces of paper handed to him by men arriving there at regular intervals.

'Nothing,' Thomas said, 'apart from the drinking of ale, I suppose.' He barely spent any time in inns, since it was ale that had brought misfortune on his family, but he felt that information was better kept to himself.

'Have you grown hops or barley, or handled them? Can you manage a wagon? Harness up a team of horses?' The man was firing questions at Thomas as he impaled more paper on the spike, every so often handing out a token instead.

'No,' Thomas confessed. 'I was working in a mill – a flour mill – most recently. And before that a boatyard.'

'Hmm. Why did you leave? Or were you let go?' The man stopped what he was doing to turn a piercing gaze on Thomas.

'No,' Thomas protested. 'My mother was taken ill, so I had to leave the mill and return to look after her.' He paused. 'I left the boatyard for family reasons, too.' It wasn't strictly accurate, but he didn't want to share the truth of it.

'We've unskilled jobs going,' the man said. 'In the malt house. You might be able to move on from there, if you show promise.'

Thomas's heart sank. The malt house was where Ernest worked. He was a good man, a kind man, and there'd be some advantage to working alongside him, but the unskilled jobs were the hardest and paid the most basic wage.

'I have schooling,' he said. 'I went to the Charity School in Castle Bay. I can read, write, do arithmetic.'

The man, dealing with a sudden flurry of papers, appeared not to hear him. Thomas was about to add, 'But I'd be happy to take anything you have,' when the man turned to him.

'Why didn't you say so in the first place?' he asked. 'Wait over there until I've dealt with this, and then we'll have a talk.'

Thomas went to stand against the wall and watched, trying to make sense of the comings and goings. By the time the man, who introduced himself as Jonas, called him over, he had worked out that laden and unladen wagons were leaving and returning to the yard. The papers, he thought, were receipts to show goods had been delivered and accounted for, while the tokens were to record goods leaving the yard.

The room he was waiting in felt less like an office than part of a bigger building, such as a barn. It was at least two storeys in height – he could see all the way up to the beams and roof trusses – and was partitioned by wooden planking from whatever lay next door.

'Right,' Jonas said, once the last wagon had been dealt with. 'I'm in need of an assistant. There's all this to be recorded in a ledger each day,' he pulled the papers off the spike, 'and supplies to be ordered and cleared with that lot upstairs.' He jerked his thumb in the direction of the office Thomas had first visited. 'Then the malt house and bottling room need inspecting twice a day and the stables at least once. Any complaints and requests from anywhere in the brewery have to be entered in this ledger,' he pulled one up from under the desk, 'and any requests from the tied ale houses, wanting changes to their orders, have to be entered here.' He pulled up another ledger and laid it on top of the other.

'I expect you're wondering what I'll be doing in the meantime.' Jonas smiled grimly. 'Well, Mr Cooper, the brewery owner, is set to expand the premises and he's put me in charge of overseeing the work.'

Thomas, having no understanding of the brewery processes, felt a little daunted by Jonas's description of what he was expecting of him, but he tried not to show it. 'Perhaps if you could show me around, I'd get a better grasp of how it all works,' he ventured. 'But the job sounds perfect,' he added hastily, in case he'd sounded as though he wasn't keen. 'I'm sure I can be a help to you. I learn quickly.' He racked his brains for what else to say to encourage Jonas to employ him.

'Good, good.' Jonas strode towards the wooden partition and opened a door, barely distinguishable from the rest of the planks. 'Follow me.'

There followed a tour of the site at dizzying speed, from the stables to the malt house, the cart shed and the oast house, the cask and keg store and the bottling room, where a young boy sat pasting labels onto bottles before they were set into wooden crates and sent off to be filled.

'Those are the offices up there.' Jonas pointed to the room Thomas had first visited. 'You'll go up there to say I've taken you on, and you collect your wages there every Saturday. Now, any questions or shall we get to work?'

Thomas hesitated. It seemed almost rude to query it, but he needed to know. 'You said I'd be paid each Saturday – but not how much?'

Jonas smiled. 'And you are right to ask.' He quoted a figure that was half as much again as Thomas had earned at the mill. 'How does that sound?' he asked.

It sounded very good, Thomas thought, but he didn't wish to appear too eager. 'Thank you.' He nodded, trying not to let a grin spread across his face.

'Then you are on a week's trial, starting now, if you're willing?'

Thomas bit his lip. He'd mentioned to Nell that he would be gone for the morning, but not for the day. Jonas didn't look as though he expected Thomas to demur, though, so he could only agree and hope that she would have the good sense to make sure his mother had eaten and was comfortable before she left for her work at the Fountain.

CHAPTER TWENTY-THREE

More than once during the course of that week, Thomas had reason to wonder whether he would be let go before the week was out. He'd listened and watched during Jonas's lightning tour of the brewery on that first morning, but found himself confounded on several occasions. Learning his way about the rambling site took time. Then there was the task of understanding the hierarchy among the different workers, let alone fathoming all the different procedures in which they were involved.

He forgot to record an urgent need for copper strips, required in the cooperage where the casks and barrels were made and mended. Jonas shouted at him when he discovered they were down to the last handful, and told him he would have to go to the ironworks in Coach House Alley, a little backstreet in Castle Bay that he had never known existed, before work on Thursday morning. He mistook a regular worker for the foreman in the malt house and asked his opinion several times, until Ernest put him right that evening.

'Don't worry,' he said, when Thomas clapped a hand to his head in mortification. 'No one has taken offence. Just apologise next time you see them both.'

They both waved away his apology, but he wasn't convinced of the foreman's sincerity and found himself grovelling the next time he had dealings with him.

He had to stand in for Jonas, spiking papers and handing out tokens one morning, which he'd found surprisingly straightforward.

At least he was in one place for an hour or so, instead of rushing from one part of the brewery to another.

When Saturday noon came, the men made their way to the office to collect their wages. Even that was done in a prescribed fashion – alphabetical order to avoid whole areas leaving their posts at the same time. Jonas was on hand to tell Thomas it was his turn. 'Marsh,' he said. 'Should be around twelve thirty for you.'

'And next week?' Thomas asked. 'Will you have me back?' Part of him wouldn't mind if the answer was 'No', he thought. He'd found the week exhausting and didn't feel he'd got to grips with the work.

Jonas regarded him for what felt like a very long time, then punched his arm. 'Of course,' he said. 'Mind you, you've a lot to learn. But so far . . .' He nodded solemnly.

Worrying about Eliza had added to Thomas's difficulties during that week. Needlessly, in fact: with Nell on hand for several hours each day to take care of the basic needs of the household, Mrs Marsh had quickly moved on from her invalid status and begun to do small jobs in the kitchen and elsewhere. She barely sat in the chair at her bedroom window any more and Thomas felt easier about leaving her for such long stretches of time.

One evening, during his second week of work at the brewery, he found himself alone with his mother at the kitchen table. Ernest, unusually, had announced he would be out for an hour or two. Thomas suspected he had arranged to meet a woman who worked in the bakery they passed every morning on the way to the brewery. Ernest always made a point of stopping to buy himself a roll to eat, even though Thomas told him he'd save money if he ate his breakfast at home. It was only when he realised Ernest left the shop pink-cheeked and smiling after his purchase that he began to think there might be more than food involved in his daily transaction. The woman wasn't in the first flush of youth, but neither was Ernest. Thomas hoped for a happy outcome for them both.

Nell had fried some sprats and left them for him, and he was just cleaning his plate with bread, when his mother said, 'I need to talk to you.'

Thomas's contentment was replaced at once by a stab of worry. 'What about?' he asked warily. 'Is something wrong?'

He searched his mind to discover what could be amiss, but found no answers.

'I need to explain to you why I was so ill,' Eliza said.

'Not at all,' Thomas said, hoping he sounded firm. 'The main thing is that you are well now.' He put his hand over hers on the table and gave her what he hoped was a reassuring smile. In all honesty, he didn't want to hear what she had to say. He feared that he was somehow at fault – that leaving Castle Bay in the way he had, with barely an hour's notice, then neither returning for months nor even thinking to make contact had precipitated her decline.

'It's important,' Eliza said, undeterred. 'I don't want you to worry about me when you're at work. I'm not going to slide back into that same state.'

'I know, I know,' Thomas said. He didn't wish to be reminded of how he'd found her on his return to the town, and he certainly didn't want her to ask anything about those early days. He didn't think he could bear her to know how he had had to deal with every aspect of her care until Nell arrived.

'It was your father, you see.' Eliza was talking almost to herself. 'When he upped and left, after all we'd been through, after everything I'd put up with, hoping for better times, well, I couldn't bear it. What a fool I'd been. And he left me with nothing. I've never really worked – only to help your aunt Meg with the shop. The lodgers had mostly gone – I could barely clean the place, what with the pain I was in, and they didn't like that. I didn't know how I was going to manage. It seemed easier just to give up.'

Although his mother sought to pin the blame on Samuel, her husband, every word she uttered pierced Thomas to the heart. If he had stayed in touch with her, he would have known how she

288

suffered. She could have disguised it in her letters, he supposed, but he should at least have visited her. Yet he had destroyed that possibility by foolishly threatening Bartholomew Banks. Although she was blaming his father, Thomas felt he alone was responsible. He had known how feckless his father was – he should never have stayed away without a word for so long. Yet, he knew, he had been relieved, and even happy, to do so. With the miller and his wife, he had seen another way of living – as a proper family. He had enjoyed it – so much, in fact, that he had put all thoughts of his own family out of his head.

'I'm back now, Ma,' Thomas said. 'I won't be going away again – ever.'

His mother squeezed his hand. 'We've had more than our share of bad luck in this house, Thomas. Your grandfather and Meg, both dead before their time. And Meg's baby.' She bit her lip. 'As for your father – well, you are nothing like him and for that I will always be grateful.'

She announced then that she was tired, and said goodnight, leaving Thomas to sit in the fading light, the candles unlit. He supposed it had been hard for her to revisit upsetting thoughts, and she had no doubt been brooding on it during the day. His path was mapped out for him now, though. He would make it up to his mother for the neglect she had suffered, both at his father's hands, and his own.

He owed the miller another letter, too, he thought, to let him know he was settled in work and that his mother was much improved in health. The sound of Ernest returning home distracted him from the intention. It would have to wait for another night: there was sport to be had in finding out what Ernest had been up to that evening.

CHAPTER TWENTY-FOUR

Thomas found the work at the brewery a good deal harder than his days at the mill. He arrived home exhausted and fit for nothing other than his dinner and bed. Winter was closing in and each day began in darkness, and finished the same way, and the weather – wind, rain and cold, sometimes all three – made the journey to and from the brewery increasingly unpleasant. He never complained to his mother, though he began to think that his wages, which had seemed generous at the start, were barely compensation for the hardness of each day.

Ernest didn't remain as their lodger beyond Christmas. His romance with the widow who ran the bakery progressed at a great rate. Despite their apparent mismatch – he was small, with a pointed face and a pinched appearance; she was large and jolly and rather older than him – they were extremely happy to have found each other and were married between Christmas and New Year. Thomas, his mother and the bride's young son were the only guests at the wedding, although many of Ernest's fellow workers joined them in the inn next to the brewery, where beer was available at a special price, to help them celebrate afterwards.

After the wedding, Ernest moved in with his new wife above the bakery. Thomas envied him the brevity of his walk to work – snow arrived in January to make his own journey even more of a trial. He made a few tentative attempts to find more lodgers for the house in Prospect Street, but Castle Bay was still in decline following the departure of the soldiers from the barracks at the end of the

French wars. It will be better in spring, Thomas told himself, only too happy to postpone solving the problem.

Spring was also earmarked for a visit to the miller and his family. Thomas had written to tell them of the improvement in his mother's health, and of his own fortunes in terms of finding employment at the brewery. The miller had replied, mourning the loss of Thomas – the boy who had first taken his place had proved lazy and had to be let go. The newest employee was eager but none too bright, it seemed.

I have to watch him all the time. But I hope, in time, he will learn.

Mrs Hopkins has asked me in the strongest terms to press an invitation on you to visit. She very much hopes you will bring your mother too, in the spring, when the weather is better. Please do look into how it might be managed. If we can enlist Nathaniel's help, do let us know.

I will get no peace until I have your word that you will come, so I hope you will send me some dates by return.

Your very good friend,

Adam Hopkins

At first, Thomas thought he must find a way to politely decline the invitation. Sunday was, in any case, his only full day off, and since the Hopkins family went to church, it would be difficult to manage. Thomas's own churchgoing had lapsed since he had been in Castle Bay, but his mother had begun to suggest they should attend St George's, as they had in the past.

He thought perhaps he could go to the mill on his own, walking over on a Sunday morning and finding some means of returning later that day. Then, as he pondered it some more, he decided he would like his mother to meet the family who had been so kind to him. It was another decision he would be happy to delay until spring, but he knew Mrs Hopkins wouldn't let it rest.

Every time Thomas wrote to the miller, he hesitated at the last line – should he add 'By the way, have you had any news of Isabel?' He never did, though. With each answer that came, he hoped Mr Hopkins might include a reference to where she was and how she did, but he waited in vain.

It was that, as much as anything, that helped to spur Thomas into a decision. It was May before he did so, excusing the delay by telling himself he needed to be sure his mother was well enough. In fact, she was now as well as she had been when Thomas left Castle Bay under threat from Bartholomew Banks. A letter having been despatched a few days earlier, and a reply received telling of Mrs Hopkins's great excitement at the expected visit, Thomas set about finding the means to get there. In the end, it was Eliza who found a way. She was telling Nell how curious she was to meet the family Thomas had lived with for twelve months.

'If only we can find a way to manage it.' She sighed. 'We must travel on a Sunday after church and return the same day. I don't know who would be prepared to help us on their day of rest.'

'I could ask my grandfather,' Nell offered. 'He has a cart and I think he would be happy to escape our house. He always complains about how crowded we are when everyone is at home. He usually takes himself off somewhere.'

Eliza made polite noises of refusal, thinking it a great impos-ition, but Nell clearly paid no attention, for the following evening, not long after Thomas had returned from work, there was a knock at the door. He glanced at his mother, who shook her head to signify she wasn't expecting anyone. Thomas went to the door and opened it to find a man he didn't recognise standing in the street.

'You must be Thomas,' the man said. 'Our Nell has told us a lot about you.'

Thomas, bemused, didn't know how to reply.

'She tells me you need to get to Marston on a Sunday. And back again. I'd be happy to help.'

'I'm sorry,' Thomas said, 'but who are you?'

The man didn't appear at all put out. 'Walter Carey,' Nell's grandfather. I have a cart and I'm more than happy to take you visiting – just say the word.'

Thomas, gradually catching up with the situation, responded much as Eliza had done. 'That's most kind of you, but on a Sunday it would be an imposition.'

'You'd be doing me a favour,' Walter said, breaking into a smile. 'Nell's the eldest of five – there's no rest to be had in that house on a Sunday afternoon.'

Thomas invited him in but Walter refused and so, following further discussion, it was agreed he would call for them that Sunday. Eliza was delighted that their outing could go ahead and promised to thank Nell the following day. Privately, she believed the girl's willingness to help might have something to do with her interest in Thomas. She knew Nell thought she had hidden it well, but the number of times she managed to introduce Thomas into the conversation during the day had given her away. Her son was oblivious, she was quite sure. Nell was a lovely girl, capable too – it would be a delight to have her as part of the family. But Eliza sensed that Thomas's heart was elsewhere. She hoped the visit to the miller's family might offer some clues as to where that might be.

CHAPTER TWENTY-FIVE

Walter arrived shortly after Thomas and his mother had returned from church on Sunday. Thankfully, the weather promised to be fine, with a clear blue sky and just a gentle breeze. Eliza settled herself on the front seat of the cart next to Walter, and Thomas perched on a pile of empty sacks in the back. He wondered idly what they had contained, but as the sun warmed them they released a smell of vegetables – carrots, he thought. He supposed Walter must do some work for a local farmer.

The cart rolled past the brewery and Thomas, with his elevated view, caught a first glimpse over the high garden wall of the house opposite where the brewery owner, Mr Cooper, lived with his family. It was larger than he'd imagined – much larger – with a sweep of lawn at the front. He was about to lean forward to point it out to his mother, when he saw she was listening closely to what Walter had to say. She was nodding every now and then, her Sunday-best bonnet giving her a dignified air.

Thomas leaned back against the side of the cart and watched her. She seemed so much better now: the sun and the excitement of the outing had brought a flush of colour to her cheeks. Walter turned off the turnpike and the cart bounced along the lane between fields, following the route that Thomas felt sure he had taken when he had fled Castle Bay. He thought back to that time, and all that had followed. It was inevitable his thoughts turned to Isabel and his first sighting of her. Where was she now? Had she been persuaded into marrying the man her father had intended for her? Or – the thought struck him with a jolt – had she returned to Marston? Was she even now at home in the Grange? It was something he hadn't considered before and it occupied his thoughts for much of the journey.

It was only when his mother turned her head and asked him, in some excitement, 'Is this the place?' that he realised they had arrived in Marston.

'Yes,' he answered hastily, then gave Walter directions to reach the mill. The cart rumbled past Marston Grange and Thomas craned his head to peer over the wall. The donkey wheel was empty and he thought the house appeared unoccupied, too. All his wild imaginings of seeing Isabel by chance, and what they might say to each other, crumbled into dust.

There was little time to dwell on it for now the cart was approaching the mill and Thomas spotted Benjamin, holding Anthony firmly by the arm, waiting at the gate. They vanished and Thomas thought they must have run inside to tell their parents that the visitors were here. Sure enough, as Walter reined in the horse at the gate, Mr and Mrs Hopkins hurried out, both wreathed in smiles.

'Thomas!' Mrs Hopkins exclaimed. 'I do declare you've grown. And this must be your mother.'

Walter had jumped down and was helping Eliza descend. The effort of managing the step, her dress and bonnet had increased the flush on her cheeks, Thomas noticed. He jumped down and the children gathered around, Benjamin and Anthony jumping up and down in excitement.

'Come in, come in,' Mrs Hopkins urged, ushering Mrs Marsh through the gate. Thomas stopped and turned back to Walter, now climbing back onto his seat.

'Would you like to join us?' he asked, uncertain whether that would be acceptable to Mr and Mrs Hopkins.

'Bless you, no,' Walter said comfortably. 'I'll take myself off. I have a friend to call in on. I'll come back for you in three hours. Don't worry if you're not ready. I'm happy to sit here and wait.'

With that he shook the reins and moved off, and Thomas quickly followed the others into the house, hoping his mother hadn't been overwhelmed by all the attention. He found her sitting at the table, being waited on with great solicitude by Mr Hopkins, while his wife busied herself at the range.

'Come and sit down, Thomas,' she said, over her shoulder. 'We want to hear all about your new position. But not until I've got the food on the table – you must be hungry after your journey.'

Thomas suspected that, in fact, the Hopkins family had had to wait for their lunch beyond their usual hour, but no one seemed put out. Benjamin was pulling at his hand, wanting to show him how well the vegetable patch was doing this year, while Anthony had climbed up and perched on his knee.

'We'll go out after we've had our dinner,' Thomas promised Benjamin, wondering whether he should move Anthony so he could help Mrs Hopkins. But she had enlisted Ruth, who was busy taking the warmed plates around the table, glancing shyly at Mrs Marsh as she did so. Thomas saw his mother give her a speculative glance, before turning back to the miller.

Then Mrs Hopkins was telling her husband to carve the meat or everything would be cold, at which he jumped up and went to fetch the knife. Thomas lifted Anthony off his knee and set him beside him, and Mrs Hopkins went around the table serving everyone with potatoes, carrots and leeks.

'All grown here in the garden,' Mr Hopkins said proudly. Thomas noticed the joint of meat was a particularly fine one – no doubt in honour of their visit – and tears pricked his eyes. They were such good, kind people, he thought, and felt immediately sorry that he hadn't been able to come back and work for Mr Hopkins.

'Will the new boy be joining us?' he asked.

'He's gone visiting today,' the miller said. 'His mother lives in the next village.'

Thomas wondered whether, in fact, he'd been told to stay away, but wasted no more time in thinking about it, for the jug of gravy had reached him and the aroma of his dinner couldn't be resisted a moment longer.

'I expect you're wondering about Isabel,' the miller said, when the plates had been emptied, to be replaced by dishes of apple pie. Thomas was so full, he was struggling to finish his slice but was determined to try, since Mrs Hopkins had put so much effort into entertaining them.

The miller's words induced an immediate wave of anxiety in Thomas's breast, which increased when he saw his mother throw a sharp glance in his direction.

'Yes, she ran off, didn't she?' He hoped he sounded unconcerned, as though he'd given it no thought until now. 'What happened to her?'

Chapter Twenty-Six

'Why don't you take Thomas outside and Benjamin can show him the vegetable patch?' Mrs Hopkins appeared keen to divert her husband.

'I can have a talk with Mrs Marsh,' she added. 'I want to hear all about Thomas as a boy.'

As Thomas rose to follow Mr Hopkins he heard his mother say, 'You must call me Eliza.' She was enjoying her day, he thought, smiling. Then impatience overtook him. What was the news of Isabel? He hadn't thought a great deal about her recently, but now that he was back in Marston, the memories flooded back.

He bided his time, though, paying close attention to Benjamin, who was telling him with great pride about the line of vegetables he had planted.

'These are growing beautifully,' he said, admiring the feathery tops of the carrots. 'Would you like to work as a gardener one day? Or will you run the mill with your father?'

'He's doing well with his schooling,' Mr Hopkins said proudly. 'Mrs Hopkins predicts great things for him.'

Benjamin had wandered off to fill his watering can so Thomas sat on the bench beside the miller.

'So, tell me the news about Isabel,' he said, wondering why Mrs Hopkins had been keen to change the subject.

'She's married now – Mrs Daniel Coates. Lives up near the Scottish borders with her husband.'

Coates – the name jolted Thomas. He felt sure it was the one on the front of the letter Isabel had written, the one he had enclosed in his mother's letter for her to send on.

'Got married at Gretna Green, by all accounts. Mr Cavendish was most put out until he realised the wealth of the family. Then he came round pretty quickly.' Mr Hopkins chuckled. 'Mind you, they're living in the back of beyond, in a tumbledown old place, it seems. Her father went up to see them and it took him four days there and four days back.'

'Goodness,' Thomas said, having no idea what else to say to such news. He watched Benjamin carefully watering his runner beans. He was struggling a bit with the heavy watering can but the determined jut of his chin told Thomas he would refuse offers of help.

'Aye, Cavendish was most put out at having to pay back all the money to the man he had arranged for Isabel to wed. Seems she didn't like his choice.' The miller laughed again. 'Always did have a mind of her own, that girl. You did well not to get involved with her.'

They contemplated Benjamin at work. Thomas was wondering whether it was time to leave – much as he had enjoyed the Hopkins family's company, he wanted time alone to digest this news.

The miller spoke up again. 'Have you found a sweetheart in Castle Bay yet?'

Thomas blushed under the miller's frank gaze. He brushed away the query. 'I've been too busy, what with Ma being sick and then taking on work at the brewery.'

'A young man like you needs to get himself settled,' the miller said. 'There must be girls aplenty in Castle Bay, but choose carefully. And don't forget our Ruth.'

Thomas smiled politely. She was far too young, he thought, and in his mind she would always be the little girl he had helped with her letters and arithmetic. The rumble of a cart's wheels in the lane outside saved him from answering.

'That must be Walter,' he said, leaping to his feet. 'I must go and tell Ma to make ready. And thank Mrs Hopkins for her hospitality.'

'You make sure you come back with your ma before the summer is out,' the miller said. 'We've enjoyed having you, and I know Mrs Hopkins will say the same.'

Back in the house, Ruth was despatched to tell Walter they would be with him in five minutes and to offer refreshments.

'He's had his dinner,' she came back to say, just as Mrs Marsh was getting to her feet and promising that they would return as soon as they could.

'Perhaps you could come to us,' she said, looking doubtful.

'No, no,' Mrs Hopkins said. 'There's far too many of us – it would be too great an imposition. You must come here again. It's a day out for you and it's been lovely to meet you. And to see Thomas and hear his news, of course.'

Walter helped Eliza up into the cart and Thomas settled himself in the back. He summoned up a big smile to bid farewell to the Hopkins family, waving at the children until a bend in the lane took them out of sight. Then he settled back with a sigh. He intended to devote the journey home to thinking over the news about Isabel.

His mother turned around in her seat. 'Who is Isabel?' she asked. Walter glanced back, too.

'She lived in the biggest house in Marston,' Thomas said. 'I used to deliver bread there. She was my age.' He was keen to discourage further questions.

'And?' his mother prompted. 'You said she ran away. What happened to her?'

'She got married,' Thomas said shortly. 'She lives up near Scotland now.'

His mother nodded, gave him a long look, then turned back to talk to Walter. Thomas heard her ask him how he had spent the hours since he had left them at the mill, then stopped listening. He had plenty on his mind to keep him occupied. He had wanted to know what had happened to Isabel and now that he did, it had put him in an ill humour. Earlier, he had been wondering whether she might have returned to Marston and, if so, would he catch a glimpse of her. He now knew that Isabel was out of his reach and he was unlikely ever to see her again. He would have to learn to live with that knowledge.

He would be done with notions of marriage, he decided. He had shown himself to be a poor judge of character – how could he trust himself not to make the same mistake again? He would turn his face away from such things and concentrate on bettering himself at the brewery. By doing that, he would make sure his mother could live more comfortably from now on.

As he climbed down from the cart outside the house in Prospect Street, Mrs Marsh thanked Walter for his help. 'It was extremely kind of you to give up your Sunday for us,' she said.

Thomas nodded and echoed her words.

'It was my pleasure,' Walter said. 'I would be more than happy to take you again, whenever you wish.'

He shook the reins and the horse set off as Thomas opened the door of the house. His mother waited and waved as Walter turned the corner, before joining him at the door. He couldn't help but notice the sparkle in her eyes. What had he missed on the way home while he was lost in his thoughts?

ISABEL

PART THREE

MAY 1824

CHAPTER FORTY-TWO

On the same day that Thomas and his mother were visiting the miller and his family, more than three hundred miles away, close to the Scottish borders, Isabel was out walking, marvelling as she so often did at the circumstances in which she found herself.

After dutifully attending the small church in the village, she had returned home to Broomfield House, always referred to by the Coates family as 'The Castle' – a jest, but not without some substance. It was – or had once been – an imposing stone building, with a turret at one corner, set on a hillside looking out towards the estuary. Perhaps it had originally been built to send a warning signal to possible invaders from over the border, signifying a stronghold belonging to a person of substance, an ancestor of Daniel's grandmother. Now, after years of neglect, it had fallen into disrepair and only a small part of it was habitable. This didn't include the turret, sadly, which Isabel coveted for herself, having a fancy to shut herself away up there to read, daydream and gaze out at the view. She would need to pinch herself regularly as a reminder that everything spread out below her was hers. Well, it belonged to Daniel, too, of course.

But the turret steps had crumbled away in places and Daniel had forbidden her to climb them.

'I don't want to return from my travels to find Mrs Musgrave waiting, grave-faced, to tell me that you have met with an accident while playing at being a princess locked in a tower.'

They had both laughed but Isabel reflected that Daniel knew

her only too well. She had already decided that the turret would be the perfect place to wear her wedding dress again, which, although pale blue, reminded her in some ways of the white lace gown that had belonged to her mother. That gown had been left behind at Marston Grange, but she hadn't shaken off her fanciful desires, as her aunt Sophia would no doubt have called them. She had already decided that she would ask Daniel whether repairing the turret staircase could be one of the first tasks to be undertaken, once they had some funds to do so.

Daniel was away now, travelling with his father, and Isabel had eaten a Sunday dinner prepared by Mrs Musgrave, before taking to the hills on her favourite walk. The hillside fell away, clothed in greenery and dotted with one or two cottages, before the land levelled out as it approached the great sweep of the Solway Firth, sparkling blue under the summer sky. In the distance, over the water, she caught glimpses of rolling uplands and at least one high peak. A slab of granite, laid flat among the bracken, afforded a good place to stop, think and take in the view. She rested there, considering the events of the last few months.

They had departed from Mrs Tremaine's house in Ramsgate, early on the morning following their arrival from London. The maid had repacked Isabel's bag and a young male servant had carried it down to the harbour, where they were to board the stage coach. Mrs Tremaine had appeared briefly in Isabel's bedroom before she left, still dressed in her nightclothes and looking weary.

'I am sure you think me harsh, my dear,' she said to Isabel, without preamble, 'but you have chosen a difficult path, one with which I am not unfamiliar. I have been thinking on it much of the night. Go well, the pair of you, and God speed.'

Isabel was momentarily cheered. After the scolding they had received the previous evening, she hadn't expected to see Mrs Tremaine that day. Although grateful for her words, Isabel was reminded once more of how her father would view their escapade.

She and Daniel had few words to say to each other as the boy conducted them through the streets of Ramsgate, chilly in the grey early morning.

Daniel went to enquire about their journey while Isabel waited beside their bags, keeping her eyes cast down to avoid curious glances from any of the other waiting passengers. Would they maintain the pretence of being a brother and sister travelling together? That might prove hard in the confines of a coach, where they would be unable to escape persistent questions.

Daniel returned, with news of a stage coach departing for Canterbury in the next half an hour.

'We will take that, then one onwards from there.' He hesitated. 'It will take us back towards London, I'm afraid, but we have no choice.'

Isabel exclaimed in horror. Were they to repeat the journey they had made yesterday? Apart from that being a most unwelcome thought, surely it raised the risk of running into her father.

'We cross the Thames before we reach the city,' Daniel assured her. 'We find a ferryman at Gravesend who will take us across to Tilbury. And then we travel north.'

'What will we say to our fellow passengers?' Isabel said in a low voice, looking around. 'I fear pretending to be brother and sister will be too easily disproved and raise suspicions.'

'You are right.' Daniel thought for a moment. 'You will be my distant cousin and I am entrusted with conveying you to stay with a maiden aunt whom you have never met, but needs your help. I will then be continuing my journey to join my father on business. I hope that will put paid to further prying.'

Isabel was unconvinced but forced to agree. In the end, they didn't arouse as much curiosity as she had feared. After initial introductions, other travellers mostly dozed or conversed among themselves. Daniel and Isabel faced each other for hour after hour, with little they could say since any intimate conversation would unmask them.

Four days of travelling from early morning to early evening, jolting over rutted roads, while sitting on uncomfortable seats and squashed against strangers, took its toll on the pair. By the time they arrived in Gretna Green, in a carriage hired from the last coaching inn in Carlisle, at a fee that an angry Daniel declared to be outrageous, neither was filled with delight at the prospect of marrying. They had barely discussed it, even when stopping at coaching inns along the route, so exhausted by their travels that words were hard to come by.

Isabel knew she must raise the question, before it was too late. So, once ensconced in the final carriage, she asked, 'Daniel, do you still wish to marry? We haven't talked of it and yet here we are.'

Daniel didn't reply at once and her heart sank.

'I have to confess that I would have preferred to do this under different circumstances,' Daniel said. Then he smiled at her. 'But marry we must. And I have a letter here, waiting for me at the inn, from my father.' He took it from his pocket. 'He says ...' Daniel's face clouded momentarily as he scanned the words '... that we are to live very close to here, in the family property near Carlisle. It will be our home.'

He smiled at Isabel again and she smiled back. But she feared that Daniel, as an honourable young man, was doing what he knew to be right, rather than what he wanted to do. Their approaching nuptials now had the air of a business transaction.

It was late afternoon by the time they arrived in the village, and Isabel was anxious. Would they be able to marry that day? If not, and they had to wait until the next, would her father catch up with them and prevent it?

As it turned out, it was easy enough to arrange, provided you had money. The chaise took them to the blacksmith's forge, the driver assuring them this was the right place. Daniel went in and exchanged a few words, then the blacksmith's boy was despatched to find the priest. Isabel later discovered he had no claim to that name, being simply a neighbour of the blacksmith who was regularly called upon to conduct the hand-fasting ceremony, all that was required under Scottish law.

She had felt foolish asking whether there was somewhere she might change into her wedding gown. The blacksmith's wife had kindly allowed her to do so in their cottage, adjacent to the forge. She had scrambled into it in some haste, aware of children peeping around the bedroom door.

Once inside the forge, she was struck by how ridiculous she must look. A dress that would have suited a church in a London square was completely out of place in the simple surroundings of the forge, warmed by the fire glowing in the other room. Isabel took in the whitewashed walls, the beams and planks of the ceiling, and the scrubbed floorboards, the blacksmith's priest waiting with the blacksmith and his wife to act as witnesses.

It was over in minutes, leaving Isabel weak with relief but unsure how her new husband felt, although he embraced her with enough passion to reassure her. Even now, though, she wondered whether they would live to regret their decision.

CHAPTER FORTY-THREE

Isabel sat on the hillside, watching great shadows fall across the land stretched out below, as clouds chased each other across the sun. She was happy here, living a somewhat solitary life with just the housekeeper, Mrs Musgrave, for company when Daniel was away. And she was very happy when he returned and they could spend several days together. She thought Daniel was content, too, although she wondered whether he missed his family and London. His father hadn't visited them yet, even though, to her great surprise, her own father had.

Mr Cavendish had arrived shortly after they had received a letter announcing his intention to visit. It was a month after their wedding and Isabel was both defiant and anxious. She was glad that Daniel was at home, for she wasn't sure she could have entertained him on her own.

At dinner on the first day, her father had wasted no time in berating them for the trouble they had caused him. 'Lord Marchant was not easy to placate.' Isabel's father glared at her. 'He felt he had been made to look foolish, and blamed me for your behaviour. Then he went around town declaring he had had a lucky escape.'

Isabel, with pink cheeks, exclaimed, 'Such impertinence!' earning an amused look from Daniel.

'He demanded the return of his engagement ring, which caused some difficulty as all your things had been packed up and sent back to Marston Grange. And, of course, repayment of the money he had loaned me.'

Isabel bit her lip. 'I'm sorry, Father.' She had barely given Lord Marchant a second thought. Now she could see the consequences of her impulsiveness.

Mr Cavendish leaned back in his chair and took in his surroundings. The dining hall was large, if rather shabby, and they were seated at one end of the long table, close to one of the two fireplaces. Isabel hadn't yet been able to fathom Daniel's relationship to the figures in each of the many portraits hung on the walls, even though she had asked him several times.

'I gather this is just one of your family homes?' her father asked Daniel abruptly.

'Yes, sir. The others are all in the south, beyond London.'

'And what does your father think of all this, eh?' Mr Cavendish demanded. 'Did he approve of you running off?'

Daniel didn't seem put out by her father's rudeness, Isabel thought, with some amazement. He regarded Mr Cavendish calmly, then replied, 'He was displeased that I hadn't taken him into my confidence, and he didn't approve of the manner in which we wed. But he didn't delay in offering us this house as our own, and settling a sum on us.'

Isabel was surprised. Daniel had mentioned nothing of his father's displeasure, or of any allowance. It hadn't occurred to her to ask how their expenses were met. She had assumed Daniel earned the money from his work assisting Sir Charles.

'Hmm.' Mr Cavendish looked from one to the other, nodding slightly. Then his grim expression lifted a little. 'You will have a hard time of it, managing my daughter, Mr Coates. She matches a strong will with very little sense. I wish you joy.'

Then, apparently considering he had done his duty and delivered a suitable wedding blessing, he poured himself another glass of wine and turned his attention to the dinner Mrs Musgrave had set on the table.

No more was said about the circumstances of their wedding, and the following morning, Isabel was pleased to see her father and

311

Daniel out walking in the grounds after breakfast. Later that day, they went out on horseback. Dinner that evening was dominated by the sort of conversation Isabel had been forced to endure with her father when she lived in Marston: complaints about the cost of hiring labour, and the vagaries of the climate. Daniel appeared to enjoy the chance of having such a discussion and Isabel began to fear she would be forced to have similar evenings from now on. Daniel, though, sought to reassure her once they were alone in their bedroom.

'It makes your father happy,' he said. 'And I confess I know little enough about managing the land so it doesn't hurt me to indulge him. I'm quite sure we will find better things to talk about when left to ourselves.' He pulled her to him and began to kiss her so that she forgot all about the trials and tribulations of managing an estate.

Mr Cavendish stayed for nearly a week before saying he must get back to his own lands.

'It's the devil of a journey,' he grumbled, as he made ready to depart. 'You must come and visit me before the year is out. Unless, of course, something should happen to make travelling unwise.' He gave Isabel a meaningful look and she blushed to the roots of her hair.

'By the way, I have given your new address to your mother,' he said, as he climbed into the chaise taking him to Carlisle. Then he slammed the door and was on his way, leaving Isabel open-mouthed.

'Your father likes to surprise, doesn't he?' Daniel remarked, as the chaise drew away. Then he embraced her. 'It passed off tolerably well, I think. You need not see him again for some time, unless you wish it. Now, I must make ready for my next trip. My father will meet me in Nottingham in three days' time.'

Daniel had been away several times since then and he was due back late that afternoon. Isabel had news for him. Her mother had written, from France, and asked whether she might visit the following year.

The Duke plans to attend to some business and I will accompany him. It will be the first time I have been in England since I left it, all those years ago. How sad I am to have been estranged from you all this time, my dear Isabella. I hope there will be some way to make it up to you.

Isabel wasn't sure how to interpret her mother's words. How could she make it up to her only child for abandoning her? Yet she had a special reason for wishing to see her, and next summer would be a good time. She hoped Daniel would agree, and that he would also be excited to hear her second piece of news. Summer would bring a new addition to their family, too – their first child. Perhaps Sir Charles would then be persuaded to put aside his displeasure over the wedding and to make a visit.

The clouds had gathered and the air was cooling rapidly. Isabel stood up and stretched, then picked her way carefully down the hillside. Broomfield House was visible through the trees, the turret always the first thing to draw her eyes. They should entertain visitors before the baby came, but who? She couldn't imagine Aunt Sophia and her cousins, Rebecca and Amelia, here. She would, though, have liked to see Mrs Tremaine again. She would ask Daniel whether they might invite her. She wanted Broomfield House to be a place their friends looked forward to coming to, not least because she had no intention of ever leaving it again.

THOMAS

PART FOUR

OCTOBER 1824 — JULY 1825

CHAPTER TWENTY-SEVEN

Visits to the mill became a monthly event for Thomas and his mother, quite often instigated by Mrs Marsh, at least until the autumnal weather put a stop to them. They made Thomas happy in many ways: it was a welcome escape from the pressures of his work at the brewery; he enjoyed seeing the Hopkins family; and he took pleasure in his mother's friendship with the miller and his wife.

He did sometimes wonder, however, whether she was keen to pursue the meetings as an excuse to ask Walter to take them there in his cart. She seemed to enjoy the journeys quite as much as the Sunday dinners, while Thomas, jolting around in the back, was less enthused.

When it became apparent that an outing at the end of October would probably be their final one of the year, Eliza was downcast. 'I look forward to the next one from the minute we return home from the last,' she said one evening as they sat together.

'Why don't you invite Walter here one Sunday instead, to thank him for taking us to Marston?' Thomas suggested.

Even by candlelight, he could see his mother had turned quite pink.

'Do you think we should?' she asked. 'I mean, would it be improper?'

Thomas laughed. 'I hardly think so.' If she was thinking about Samuel finding out, it didn't matter what he thought, surely. 'After all, I'll be here, Ma.'

And so it became quite usual for Walter to escape his

overcrowded house on a Sunday to eat with Thomas and his mother. Occasionally, Nell came too, and when she did, she insisted on cooking, which meant they dined better than when it was left up to Eliza. Thomas found he enjoyed these dinners almost as much as when they went to the mill. It was a long time since the house had echoed to the sound of chatter and laughter. He had come to realise, though, that it was folly to stay there. The house was too big for him and his mother. They would never open the front parlour as a shop again and he didn't want to entertain the idea of taking lodgers. He knew they must find somewhere else to live, but kept putting off the decision, knowing it would upset Eliza. She had lived there for nearly twenty years, ever since she had married Samuel.

Christmas came and went, with Walter coming for his Christmas dinner and Nell calling in later in the afternoon with a plum pudding she had made for them all. The Hopkinses had sent over a basket of provisions as a gift – a cured ham, pickles, chutneys and a rabbit pie, which Thomas and his mother sampled on Christmas Eve. Looking around the table on Christmas Day, he marvelled at how his life had changed since his days at the mill. He felt much older, and so much more responsible, yet not quite settled, despite the happiness around the table that day. He put it down to his unease about how much longer they could stay in their home, and thought no more of it.

In the New Year, a solution to his worries about the house in Prospect Street presented itself. Jonas took him aside at the brewery one day and said Thomas was in line for being made a manager.

'Really?' Thomas was astonished. He still spent most days thinking he was getting everything wrong, and daily expected to hear he was to be dismissed. Was this Jonas's idea of a joke?

'You're not perfect, granted,' Jonas continued, 'but you're doing a lot better than most of the workers here. You've got a good head on your shoulders and a sense of responsibility. You'll go far.'

Thomas, amazed, could only stare at him.

'And the best bit . . .' Jonas paused for dramatic effect '. . . the job comes with a house. One of the new ones built on the land behind the brewery. So you can be nice and close to work if they call you out at night.' He chuckled.

Thomas struggled to take in the news. The brewery had been getting busier week by week, and Mr Cooper had decided to build some homes for his workers on site, or as close to it as possible. He declared himself unhappy with the conditions in Castle Bay, 'Half the houses are falling down and the other half are infested with vermin. I want my workers to arrive at the brewery clean and well cared-for. They can't do that if they are living in those circumstances.'

Cynical words had been spoken by the workers, claiming that he was planning to extend what was already a very long day, using the excuse of housing them close by. But Thomas had thought this was likely due to jealousy of those who might be allocated a house. He never thought that he would be one of the lucky ones.

By the end of that week, he had had his new duties explained to him, and been taken to see the house by one of the busy clerks in the upstairs office. He seemed happy to escape his desk for half an hour, and proved quite illuminating as he talked to Thomas on the way to the site.

'They must be keen to keep you here,' he commented, as he opened the door. 'There's not many been offered these.'

It was in a row of six cottages, all the same, with another six cottages set at right angles to them. Thomas stepped inside, the smell of newly whitewashed walls hitting him at once. It was a two-up, two-down, with steep wooden stairs leading up from the sitting room. There was a little lean-to kitchen at the back, and a privy in the yard.

At first, it was a shock after the size of the Prospect Street house, but as he looked around he could see how it might work: a bedroom each for him and his mother, a cosy room at the front with a fireplace and another at the back, where they could eat. It wouldn't matter so much that the kitchen was small. It would be an easy place to care for – they wouldn't need the added expense of Nell.

He felt a pang – she had become part of their family and would be sad not to come and spend time with his mother nearly every day. But it would solve the problem that he had been putting off dealing with: Prospect Street was too big and the rent was too high for them now.

'I'll take it,' he said. 'But I should discuss it with my mother first.'

The clerk seemed mildly surprised. 'I don't think anyone has turned down a property yet. It's quite a privilege, you know.'

'I know, I know,' Thomas said hastily. 'It's just that my mother has lived in our house for a long time and she might find it hard to leave. But I'm sure she will see that this place is a huge improvement.'

He surveyed the sitting room again, nodding in what he hoped was an enthusiastic fashion. It would suit him perfectly, but as for Eliza, he wasn't so sure.

Chapter Twenty-Eight

When he got home that evening, Thomas wasted no time in telling his mother what had happened. She had been happy when she heard he was to be promoted, although rather vague in her understanding of what his new role entailed. He had kept the possibility of a new home secret, not wishing to unsettle her until he knew more about it.

As he had expected, she had been rather quiet when he told her about the cottage.

'It's very close to the brewery, and just built, on the orders of Mr Cooper, the brewery owner. There are six in a row, just two up and two down, but with a kitchen and a yard with a privy. It's a lot smaller than this place, of course, but it will be much easier to manage.'

Thomas waited, but Eliza didn't say anything. 'And the rent will be better. It will come straight out of my pay each week and, as a worker, I pay less than we would if we tried to rent somewhere else nearby.'

She still hadn't replied and he found it hard to read her expression. 'We'll have to take in lodgers again if we stay here,' he offered.

Despite his misgivings about the brewery cottage, he was already thinking about the advantage of being so close to his work, and the amount of time he would save on walking each day. It was a particularly welcome prospect, especially in winter.

'I'll have to speak to Walter,' Eliza said at last.

'Walter?' Thomas gazed at her, puzzled. Whatever could she mean? What did Walter have to do with it?

'You see ...' to Thomas's surprise, his mother's cheeks were bright red and she appeared to be groping for words '... you see, we've become fond of each other.'

Thomas stared, uncomprehending. His mother and Walter? They were both so old – well, his mother was about forty-five, but Walter was a grandfather. He was grey and grizzled, although he supposed he might be only ten years older than Eliza. Even so ...

'Walter thought we might rent a little place together.' His mother, obviously struggling to deliver this startling news, threw him a look of appeal.

'But ... but ...' Thomas, attempting to marshal his thoughts, could only come up with '... but you're married.'

His mother was affronted. 'And what heed did my husband pay to that when he moved in with his trollop?' she demanded, with some asperity.

Thomas tried to defend himself. 'People will talk,' he said. 'I'm only thinking of you.'

The look Eliza gave him made him wish the words unsaid. Then she relented. 'You are right. We both know it. Walter thought we might take a place where no one knows too much about us. Around Marston, perhaps. He has friends there.'

She watched him, waiting for his response.

'Ma, I'm very happy for you. It just came as a shock. I had no idea ...' He'd been blind, he supposed. He'd realised they were friends, but he'd never considered that anything more than that was involved.

'It's time you found someone for yourself, Thomas. You've taken good care of me since you came back. Now I'm about to be happy and settled, but what about you? You'll have a cottage all to yourself, just perfect for settling down and starting a family. You should find yourself a nice girl.'

It was Thomas's turn to colour. 'I haven't time for any of that. Work keeps me busy enough.'

'You'll be lonely,' his mother remarked. 'There's many a girl out there who'd be keen to have you, I'll be bound. A nice-looking young man like you, with a good job and a tied cottage.' She threw him a shrewd glance. 'You can't spend your life moping after that girl Isabel.'

Thomas felt as though his face was on fire. 'I'm not,' he protested. 'I'm happy just as I am.' He got to his feet and took his plate over to the sink, keen to put an end to the conversation.

'You'll need someone to cook for you and clean up after you, if you're so busy. I'll ask Nell tomorrow whether she might walk over to Hawksdown two or three times a week.'

Thomas frowned. He had thought to dispense with Nell's services, but if his mother wasn't coming to the cottage with him, he would need help. He could shift for himself, he supposed, but he'd grown used to a hot meal on the table when he got home. How would he manage that, and work as well?

His head was aching so he excused himself and went to bed. The house would need to be cleared out. Mrs Dunn had lent them her chair when his mother was ill; he hadn't got around to returning it. And this bedroom, which had once been his aunt Meg's, still held items belonging to her, untouched since she had vanished. He had hoped that sleep would blot out his thoughts but, despite his weariness, he tossed and turned until the early hours, attempting to come to terms with his mother's surprising announcement and the enforced change of his plans.

Mrs Marsh, no doubt relieved at confessing her and Walter's intentions, didn't waste any time in putting them into action. Walter took her out in his cart each day over the following week; at the end of it, she announced that they had taken a cottage not far from Marston, in the village where Walter's friend lived. Thomas suspected the plan had been made a little while before, and his mother had just been waiting for the right time to tell him.

'But how will you live?' he asked. 'I can help a little towards the rent but . . .' He trailed off, thinking that wouldn't leave him with a great deal if he settled an allowance on his mother.

'There's no need,' his mother said. 'Walter has enough money put by for us to manage on. And he can still get work with his cart if we need more.'

Privately, Thomas thought it would be a good idea if he saved a little money each week for them, just in case. He feared his mother was being unrealistic, and might need to call on him for funds in the future. He had reconciled himself to her plan to live with Walter, though. His father had made her unhappy for many years: she deserved a chance of happiness now.

CHAPTER TWENTY-NINE

One day as Thomas was walking home from work, mulling over what still needed to be done to clear out Prospect Street, he heard a voice calling his name. He spun around to find Catherine, his fellow Charity School pupil, hurrying to catch him up. He hadn't seen her since he had bumped into her several months previously, and it took him a moment or two to work out who she was.

'Goodness, you walk fast,' she remarked, breathless. 'I saw you some way back and I've been trying to catch you up ever since. I haven't seen you in a long time. Is your mother well now?'

Thomas couldn't remember having mentioned his mother, but said, 'Yes, thank you, quite well. She's moving ...' He stopped, collecting himself. He'd almost said something about Walter, then realised he would be revealing a secret he was trying to keep. Best not to start gossip, he thought, quickly adding, 'I'm working at the brewery now and I've just been given a tied cottage.'

'Ah, the brewery.' Catherine wrinkled her nose. 'I dare say you're used to the smell. It hangs over us for days on end when the wind is in the wrong direction.'

'You must live around here, then,' Thomas said, looking around. They had left Hawksdown behind and the outskirts of Castle Bay lay ahead. The only houses in evidence were rather too grand to be Catherine's home, he thought.

'Yes, just here,' she said, pointing to a terrace of fine houses overlooking the sea. Seeing Thomas's expression, she laughed. 'I live up in the attic and work mainly below stairs – I'm a cook for the family.'

Thomas was taken aback. He had assumed she would be married with a family of her own. He regarded her anew, taking in her glossy brown hair and brown eyes, now fixed on him with amusement.

'You thought I'd be married by now, didn't you, Thomas Marsh? My mother despairs of me. But I had no wish to marry a man in Castle Bay with no prospects – fishermen scratching a living, or smugglers risking their lives for rum and tobacco. So I decided to look after myself first and worry about the rest of it all in good time.'

'How did you become a cook?' Thomas ventured, finding himself eager to detain her longer.

Catherine shrugged. 'My mother cooked for the schoolmaster and I watched and helped from an early age. It seemed a natural thing to do.'

Thomas remembered her mother now. A small, neat lady, whereas Catherine was tall – possibly taller than he was. Mrs Morgan was widowed, but her work as housekeeper for the schoolmaster had come with two rooms at the top of his house, and a place for her daughter at the Charity School.

'Well, I'd better be getting on,' Catherine said. 'I had to deliver a cake to the Coopers, but I'll be expected back.'

'Mr Cooper? The brewery owner?' Thomas asked.

'Mrs Cooper,' Catherine corrected him. 'It's Mr Cooper's birthday and she wished to know where she could buy a particular cake she was served by my mistress. I had baked it, so she asked me if I would make one for them.'

'Goodness.' Thomas was impressed. He had never spoken to Mr Cooper, or set foot inside his grand house opposite the brewery.

They had reached Catherine's workplace now, and she stopped at the top of the basement steps. 'I'm glad I saw you today, Thomas. I hope our paths cross again soon.' She gave him a smile, then hurried down the steps, leaving him standing, before he turned and set off towards home.

Soon, quite forgetting his recent protestations to his mother that he was happy alone, Thomas found himself slowing his pace each time he passed the row of houses on the Strand, hoping to catch sight of Catherine, perhaps in the basement kitchen. He would be moving into the brewery cottage any day now, and would no longer have to walk this way so often. How could he see her? And once he did, could he make sure he saw her again? He would need to find out when she had time off, then ask her to walk out with him. Would she accept? She had said she hoped to see him soon, so perhaps she would.

Thomas had been living in his cottage for two weeks before he chanced upon Catherine again. He had been asked to make sure that a delivery of ale had been sent to Mr Cooper's kitchens, the wrong ale having been delivered previously.

Jonas said, 'It shouldn't be up to you, Thomas, but I've two men off sick and I don't trust the stand-in to have got it right. He muddled all the orders yesterday, and I don't want to hear that Mr Cooper has the wrong ale again.'

Thomas was curious to see the Coopers' house, Clayton Hall, even if he was only going to get as far as the kitchens, so he agreed readily enough. He circled the sweep of gravel that led up to the building and went to the back, where he found the steps down to the basement. A tantalising aroma of roasting meat drifted up from the open door, making his stomach rumble. He went down the stairs and stuck his head through the doorway.

'Hello!' he called. The room appeared to be empty, so he stepped inside.

A woman came through from another room at the back of the kitchen, with a jug she was carrying carefully, as though it was full. After the brightness outside, Thomas struggled to adjust his eyes to the gloom of the basement, but he saw her blue dress with a white apron over the top, and the white cap concealing her hair, before he realised it was Catherine. She started when she saw him, causing what he took to be cream to slop over the side of the jug.

'I'm sorry,' Thomas said. 'I didn't mean to startle you.'

He stared at her, forgetting his errand. 'I didn't expect to see you here.'

'I work here now.' Catherine set the jug on the scrubbed pine kitchen table and wiped her hands on her apron. 'The cake I made for the Coopers was such a success that they begged my mistress to let me come and be their baker. And here I am.' Her smile told Thomas she was happy with her situation. 'But what are you doing here?' she asked him.

Thomas collected himself and relayed the query about the ale. Having satisfied himself that the kegs were the correct ones, he left Catherine, now stirring something in a pot on the range. It was only as he crossed back to the brewery that he realised he had failed to ask when he might see her again.

CHAPTER THIRTY

Although he had never previously had reason to visit Mr Cooper's property, Thomas now found himself wondering several times a day what excuse he could manufacture to take him back across the road. Nothing plausible presented itself. A day or two later, it occurred to Thomas that since Catherine had lived in at her last job she undoubtedly lived in there, too. He found himself loitering by the gates of the brewery, bidding goodnight to the men as they went home, all the time glancing over at Clayton Hall to see whether he could catch sight of Catherine, perhaps at an upstairs window.

The evenings he had spent quietly enough at home were now filled with imaginings of how he might approach Catherine, and what he might say when he did. Nell appeared one evening, flustered because she was late delivering a pie she had baked for him, and found him gazing pensively at the fire.

'Is something the matter, Thomas?' she asked, concerned. 'I trust your mother is well?'

When he nodded, she pressed on. 'Look, I've brought your favourite, rabbit pie.'

'Just put it in the larder,' Thomas said. 'I'm not really hungry.'

'Are you ill?' Nell had never known Thomas not to have an appetite.

He shook his head. Then a thought struck him. Perhaps Nell could advise him about approaching Catherine.

'I'd like to ask you something,' Thomas said.

Nell stood very still, waiting.

'How would I go about asking someone – a lady – to keep me company?'

Nell was quiet for some moments before replying. 'There's a May fair on the mill field next weekend. You could ask her if she will be there and whether you might meet.' She hesitated, doubtful. 'Although really she should be accompanied by at least one other lady.'

'Would I write her a note, do you think?' Thomas, not being aware of the fair, had perked up at Nell's words.

Nell seemed puzzled. 'I suppose you could. But why not just ask her whether she intends to go?'

'It's not that easy,' Thomas said. 'But thank you, Nell. You have been very helpful. I think I will have some of the pie now.'

He went into the kitchen, oblivious to the expression on Nell's face. She stood looking after him for a few moments before she let herself out.

At the end of the following day Thomas, feeling much lighter of heart, went across the road to Clayton Hall, skirting to the back of the house as before. He clutched a note in his hand, intending to post it through the kitchen door, but came face to face with Catherine as he descended the basement stairs.

'Thomas,' she said, 'have you come to take away the kegs?'

'No, no, one of the men will do that.' He was indignant that she should think it his job, although perhaps she was teasing. 'I came to leave this for you.'

He held the note out to her and she took it, a smile playing on her lips.

'Why don't you tell me what's inside?' she asked. 'Since we're both here.'

Thomas, crimson with embarrassment, said, 'I – er – wondered whether you were going to the May fair up at the mill field on Saturday afternoon?'

'I hadn't thought to,' Catherine said. 'Do you think I should?'

Then she burst into laughter at the sight of Thomas's face. 'Would you like to ask me?' she said. 'If so, I will see you there, at three o'clock.'

She gave the note back to him, then turned and went into the kitchen, leaving Thomas feeling foolish and happy at the same time.

The fair was crowded by the time Thomas arrived there on Saturday afternoon, and he was seized with worry that he wouldn't find Catherine. But within five minutes he had spotted her. She was wearing a blue and white striped dress and a hat decorated with artificial flowers, and standing in front of a shooting range quite close to the entrance, intent on watching the men compete.

'Do you fancy your chances?' he said in her ear. He felt quite bold now she had agreed to meet him.

'They make it look easy,' she said, turning to him with a smile. 'But I suspect them of being farmers who have had plenty of practice taking pot shots at rabbits and crows. I fear I would waste my money.'

'I've never fired a gun,' Thomas confessed. Keen to move on, he suggested they take a turn around the field where the fair was being held, to see what was happening.

Neighbouring stallholders were competing to call out their wares as Thomas and Catherine went by. Sweetmeats and fudge were piled high on one table, glasses of lemonade being sold at the next, while Cooper's Brewery was doing a roaring trade from a tent set up next to the pen where a cattle show was attracting a lot of attention. It was a warm afternoon, so Thomas bought a glass of ale for himself and a lemonade for Catherine. Then they stood and watched a fire-eater perform, until they were approached by a man walking around with a monkey dressed in a blue jacket sitting on his shoulder. He was keen that Catherine should hold the creature, saying, 'His jacket matches your dress, miss,' but Catherine shook her head and made a face.

331

'He looks too sad,' she declared, as they walked on. 'By the way, we are being watched.' She gripped Thomas's arm as he stopped and began to turn around. 'Don't look. By a young girl who also has a sad face. Although I think it is a cross face when she looks at me.'

Thomas was filled with curiosity. 'But I must see,' he protested, trying to wriggle from her grip.

'You can look now. She has her back to us,' Catherine said. 'The one with the auburn hair, in the green dress.'

'Oh, that's just Nell,' Thomas said, recognising her at once. 'She helped me with my mother when she was ill, and she cooks food for me and brings it over. She's part of the family. Her grandfather and my mother are ...' he stopped himself '... are good friends,' he finished.

'I rather think Nell is sweet on you,' Catherine said.

'No!' Thomas exclaimed. 'You're wrong. She's just a child.'

'I think not,' Catherine said. 'She looks sixteen or seventeen to me. Quite old enough to have formed an attachment, Thomas Marsh.'

She gave him a playful shove but Thomas was standing stock still, filled with a painful realisation. Nell must have thought he was going to ask her to accompany him to the fair. And now he had not only upset her, without intending to, but he must look on her in quite a different way in the future. A little bit of his joy drained out of the day.

CHAPTER THIRTY-ONE

Thomas did his best to be attentive to Catherine as they wandered around the rest of the fair. He bought her fudge and sugary biscuits, then the aroma of pigs roasting on a spit made them both so hungry that they each had slices tucked into rolls, grease dripping down their fingers as they sat on the grass to eat.

Thomas ate quickly, wiping his fingers clean on the grass as best he could, then watching the crowd go by as he waited for Catherine to finish. He was looking for Nell, he knew. Whatever must she think of him? Had he missed the signs? He had always considered her a very competent servant who was also extremely kind to his mother. He hadn't even thought of her as a sister, he realised with some dismay. Would he need to rethink their relationship now he had realised she must have feelings for him? At the very least, he would have to apologise for making her believe he was going to ask her to the fair. He comforted himself by thinking Catherine was surely mistaken. In his mind Nell was no more than thirteen or fourteen – perhaps she just had a childish infatuation with him.

Thomas turned his head to find Catherine had finished her roll and was watching him.

'What shall we do now?' he asked, scrambling to his feet and holding out a hand to pull Catherine up. He was determined not to let his confusion over Nell spoil the day. 'What about a ride on the carousel?'

It had been mentioned on the posters for the fair and Thomas was keen to discover what it was. There was one area of the field they hadn't yet explored and, as they approached, over the heads of the crowd they could see brightly painted wooden poles, joined together at the top and rotating at speed. The screams of the carousel riders had drawn quite a crowd of spectators. Thomas and Catherine had to push their way through to the front, where they saw the poles supported a circular contraption, rather like a giant horizontal cartwheel. A variety of seats were attached to it, some in the form of animals such as a cockerel, a sheep and a horse, while another resembled a coach carriage, a crudely painted crest on the door. Thomas saw a donkey was harnessed to the inside of the carousel and was responsible for its motion, being driven to trot in small circles by a man wielding a large stick.

The beast came to a halt and stood, head drooping and flanks heaving, while a man wearing a grubby white shirt and workman's trousers rushed around helping the ladies to dismount onto a little step. The men were considered able to jump to the ground.

Once the carousel was empty, the man fixed his eyes on the crowd. 'Roll up, roll up, and take your seats on the world's first donkey-driven carousel. You'll be giddy with excitement as you whirl around.'

He turned his attention to Thomas and Catherine. 'Sir, madam. Are you ready to take the ride? You won't regret it.'

Catherine turned to Thomas, eyes sparkling. 'Shall we? I can't imagine what it must feel like.'

Thomas hesitated. 'You aren't worried it's – indecorous?'

Catherine was incredulous. 'No! I can hold my skirts down. Are you worried, Thomas? Are you – scared?'

'No!' Thomas protested. The truth was, the sight of the donkey reminded him of the donkey wheel in Marston, which in turn reminded him of Isabel. He was seized by a kind of melancholy, which he preferred to ascribe to his concern over the poor beast in front of him, rather than the muddle in his brain that seemed to be forming over Nell, Catherine and now Isabel.

I must have drunk too much ale, he thought, allowing himself to be coerced into climbing onto the carousel and parting with far more coins than he considered it to be worth.

They started slowly, causing Thomas to feel even more cheated, but a protracted application of the stick to the donkey's rump made it pick up its pace. The wheel rotated faster, and the fair became something of a blur as they flew round so that Thomas was no longer sitting upright but leaning into the centre. He found he couldn't right himself and he gripped the arms of the seat as hard as he could, thinking how foolish he must look.

Catherine, seated on the cockerel behind him, was shrieking and Thomas feared she was terrified, too, but when he managed to turn his head to look, she was calling out in exhilaration. Then he had to screw up his eyes – the movement was making him feel nauseous. It was only as he sensed a slowing of the rotation that he could bear to open them again.

His legs were shaking as they came to a stop. He feared they would give way and he would fall to the ground when forced to jump down, but the man took one look at his face and placed the step at his feet.

'Gets some people like that, it does,' he remarked, helping him down.

Catherine was already standing to the side, cheeks flushed and hair in disarray, a broad smile on her face. Then she took in Thomas's expression. 'Goodness, you're as white as a sheet,' she said, in some alarm. She took his arm and pulled him through the crowd.

'Sit down here,' she said, once they had reached a patch of grass at the edge of the fair. 'I'll fetch you something to drink.'

Thomas tried to protest that he didn't need anything, but she had vanished into the crowd. He sat quietly and wondered whether he might be sick. He took a few deep breaths and began to feel better, a feeling immediately replaced by a sense of shame. What must Catherine think of him?

At that moment, he saw Nell, still among the group of friends she had been with earlier. She saw him, too, and he thought she

335

was about to come over, but her friends pulled her onwards. She glanced back over her shoulder and their eyes met, just as Catherine arrived at his side.

'Here, drink this,' she said. 'Brandy. Should put you right.'

Thomas tipped his head back and drank it in one, feeling a fiery warmth in his throat, which began to spread through his body. 'Thank you,' he said. 'I feel better now. I'm sorry. I don't like heights. I should have said.'

Catherine was amused. 'Hardly a height. I expect it was the going around in circles that upset you. It's not something we do every day, after all.'

'Not unless you're a donkey,' Thomas muttered.

After that, they took a desultory look around the rest of the fair, but Thomas's heart wasn't in it. His head ached and he longed to go home, sit in the cool of his house and think about why he had felt so unnerved by it all. Yet he also knew he might not get another chance to spend time with Catherine, for he feared she must think him very odd.

'Well, Thomas,' she said, after half an hour, 'I must leave now, for my half-day is over and I'm expected back in the kitchen.'

With some relief, Thomas escorted her out of the fair and back the short way along the road to the gate of Clayton Hall.

'Thank you,' Catherine said, with a smile, before she turned to enter the garden. 'I've had a lovely afternoon. I hope you are none the worse for wear after the carousel ride.'

Thomas managed a weak smile, then remembered his manners. 'Thank you for coming with me,' he said. 'I enjoyed it too.' He wished he could have managed something better than that, but it was all his scrambled brain would allow. He stood for a moment, watching her skirt the drive, before he crossed the road to walk back to his brewery cottage. Had she had a lovely afternoon? He wasn't convinced. He didn't think he had made a very good impression. As he opened the door of the cottage he had a sudden vision of Nell waiting there for him, as she so often was on a workday, with a delicious dish of food and a few words for him. Easy words, because they knew each other well, Thomas realised. There was no unease between them, but would there be in the future?

He sat down in the chair by the empty grate and buried his head in his hands. He had no idea what to think, and longed for someone he could talk to.

CHAPTER THIRTY-TWO

Thomas attended church on Sunday morning, hoping that the service might bring some clarity to his troubled mind. But, despite his best efforts, his thoughts wandered and he had no idea of the content of the sermon by the time he stumbled outside into the spring sunshine. He had reached a decision, though. He would visit his mother and Walter in their new home the following week. He hadn't been to see them yet, and he told himself he needed reassurance that his mother was well set up. He also hoped to take the opportunity to ask her advice about his dilemma, having failed to reach any sensible conclusion himself.

He liked both Catherine and Nell, he decided. Catherine made him awkward and tongue-tied, but caused his heart to beat faster. Would he ever feel as comfortable with her as he did with Nell, who was sweet and kind and surely everything he could want? Yet she didn't stir him in the same way that Catherine did. And the fact that his mother was living with Nell's grandfather was a little awkward. Yet was there a possibility that Catherine reminded him of Isabel? She had a similar assurance and confidence and made him feel wrong-footed. It wasn't something he wanted to face up to: thinking back to his feelings for Isabel brought a certainty that he had poor judgement.

He was restless when he returned home from church and, once he had made himself something to eat, he fell to wondering what Catherine and Nell might be doing. Catherine would be involved in making the dinner for the Coopers, he supposed. He doubted she would have time to give him a thought. Nell's household was a busy one, according to Walter. She, too, would be preparing food or looking after younger brothers or sisters. He hoped she hadn't been distressed to see him with Catherine. He would have to speak to her about it, although he quailed at the thought.

The promising weather of the morning had given way to dark clouds and heavy showers, so Thomas decided he should make the effort to unpack the boxes from Prospect Street, delivered to him by Walter and his cart. The furniture was all in place, but Eliza had sent three boxes, along with a note that said they contained items that might be useful around the place, as well as a few things she hadn't had time to sort through.

> They're mostly from your bedroom and must have once belonged to your aunt Meg. I didn't like to throw them out, and I doubt there's anything of value, but you never know.

Thomas suspected his mother had found it too upsetting to go through them, given the tragic loss of her sister-in-law. He didn't relish the idea, either, having been very fond of his aunt. The first boxes he opened, though, contained a miscellany of items – a quantity of kitchen pots, a clock and a few pictures, which he welcomed to brighten the plain walls.

The third and smallest box held folded papers and a few books, as well as two small decorated wooden boxes that Thomas remembered from the shelves in his bedroom. They had contained little of importance – a shell or two, some scraps of cloth, items that had once meant something to Meg but had lost their significance over time. The papers turned out to be plain, which puzzled Thomas until he remembered the paper used to wrap goods in the old baker's shop in Prospect Street. He supposed Meg had used them to wrap her smuggled goods.

This idea was reinforced by the book he picked up next. It was an accounts book, listing in meticulous handwriting the prices she

339

had paid for goods, and the prices she had sold them for. At least, he had assumed it to be accounts but, as he flicked through, he found it interspersed with entries where she had recorded events, her thoughts and worries. He had begun to read it with some fascination until he realised she was writing about Bartholomew Banks. He was seized with such anger that he flung the book across the room. He couldn't bear to read about the feelings she had had for the man who was suspected – but never accused – of having arranged her murder.

He sat for a while, with no appetite to carry on sorting through the box. He bundled everything back in, intending to burn the book and the papers when he next lit the fire, then took the box upstairs and shoved it under his bed, pushing it out of sight. He didn't want to be reminded every time he set foot in the room.

Back downstairs again, he saw that a watery sun had replaced the rain. On impulse, he put on a jacket and stepped outside. He would take a walk to clear his head, he decided. He purposefully chose a route away from Clayton Hall, but on returning home, more at peace with himself than he had been all day after striding across Hawkshill and glimpsing the sea, his steps drew him to the front of the brewery. He loitered for a moment, looking over at Mr Cooper's house as if the solid brickwork and blank windows might reveal something to him. Then, resolute, he turned on his heel and made his way home.

Thomas looked forward to the distraction of work the next day, but was taken aback when no sooner had he set foot in the malt house than there were whistles and calls of 'So who's your lady-friend, Thomas?' The teasing was friendly enough, and the comments on Catherine nothing but complimentary, if coarser than Thomas would have liked. He should have expected it, he supposed. He had seen a few of the brewery workers at the fair – it would have been odd if he hadn't: such an event drew working people from miles around, intent on enjoyment.

He heard tales of the brawl that had developed later that

evening, and saw evidence in the black eyes sported by one or two of the men. He was glad he and Catherine had left by then, and was seized with worry that Nell might have stayed and been caught up in the trouble.

With a growing sense of unease, Thomas realised the men assumed Catherine was his betrothed. Something Nell had said about whoever he invited needing to be in the company of at least one other lady gave him pause for thought. Catherine would have known this, surely. Had he been naive? Had she agreed to go with him to the fair, knowing how it would look and intending to trap him?

He was assailed by doubt once more. He knew now that Isabel had been devious and scheming. Did Catherine have a similar nature? Nell, he felt sure, did not. More than ever, he wished his mother close at hand, so that he might ask her advice that very evening. Instead, he must endure nearly a week of anxiety before the opportunity would present itself.

CHAPTER THIRTY-THREE

By the time Sunday came, Thomas had exhausted himself trying to unravel the problem that he believed he had. He had written to Eliza to say he would visit, and she had made a prompt reply, saying Walter would come for him and return him home. Thomas's heart sank – they might do well enough on the journey out, but not on the return journey, after the conversation about his granddaughter.

Nell had been to his cottage to deliver food, as usual, but she hadn't lingered. By the time he came in from work he found a dish awaiting him, but no other sign of her presence. He was both relieved and unsettled, although as the week passed the feeling that he must explain himself to her began to dwindle.

Sunday dawned fair, after several days of showery rain, which had brought forth the blossom on the hawthorn hedges that they drove past in Walter's cart. Walter had plenty to talk about as the cart rolled along – how they had settled into their cottage, the vegetable garden he had established, Eliza's work at the poorhouse in Marston. The latter surprised Thomas, but Walter said she enjoyed it.

'It's just a small place, all women. They mainly weave and sew. Eliza helps out in the kitchens or does whatever else needs doing. The bit of money she earns comes in useful.'

Thomas remembered the place from delivering bread there in his days at the mill. He couldn't remember ever having seen any of the inhabitants. They rattled past the mill on the way to Walter

342

and Eliza's cottage and Thomas realised he should have written to the miller, too, and suggested calling in on them. All was quiet, the sweeps motionless, the family no doubt eating their Sunday lunch after their walk to church. At the thought of food, Thomas's stomach began to rumble and he was glad the noise of the cart disguised it.

They came to a halt outside a flat-fronted cottage opening directly onto the road, at the end of a small row of identical dwellings, each with a window beside the front door and another window upstairs.

'Let yourself in,' Walter said, 'and I'll take the cart round the back.'

Thomas did as he was told, calling, 'Ma,' as he did so. He didn't want to startle Eliza, but she had been alerted by the noise of the cart and came through from the kitchen, wiping her hands on her apron.

'Thomas!' she said. 'You've made good time. The fowl's roasting and the vegetables are in the pot. Let me get you a glass of ale and I'll show you the place – not that it will take long.'

The cottage was not dissimilar to Thomas's, although on a smaller scale with just one bedroom upstairs – but the main difference was the garden. Where Thomas had a yard, here the garden stretched a good hundred feet down to the field edge and, since they were at the end of the terrace, there was room for the cart beside the cottage and a stable for the horse at the back, along with Walter's vegetable patch. It took up a good part of the garden, Walter pointing out with pride the quantity of things he was growing.

'There's potatoes and carrots, runner beans over here, salads in this patch and here are the fruit bushes.' Walter was walking Thomas along the path as he spoke. 'Gooseberries, blackcurrants, redcurrants. I've put in a pear and there's already an old apple tree here, but I'm not sure how much fruit it will bear.'

'Goodness!' Thomas was impressed. 'I didn't know you were a gardener. But what will you do with all the produce? There's too much for you and Ma, surely?'

'I haven't had a garden before,' Walter said, 'but I always thought I'd enjoy the growing of things, and I do. As for the produce, I've a mind to sell it by the road, or mebbe take a stall at a market. Eliza is going to bottle the fruit, or jam it. We've plenty to keep us busy, that's for sure.' Walter chuckled. 'I'm building a hen house down the end. We fancy keeping a few hens, too.'

Eliza called them in to eat, and the topic of the garden and their plans for it kept them occupied throughout the meal. Thomas was full of compliments about how busy they had been since they moved, and how well they looked.

It was true, they did, he thought. His mother had never lived in the country before but she seemed to have embraced her new life. The pair of them knew all their neighbours, and Eliza said she had often chatted with the miller and his wife on her way to and from the poorhouse. Thomas felt a pang for a life he had lost. His days were now spent in the confines of the brewery, where he no longer noticed the overpowering smell of the hops brewing and was unaware of the noise and clatter as bottles were filled, crates and kegs were loaded onto carts and men shouted to make themselves heard above it all. The peace of the countryside, with birdsong filling the background, struck him forcefully.

All too soon, their dinner being over, Eliza was clearing the plates from the table. Thomas would have liked to sit on to enjoy the feeling of drowsiness brought on by a full stomach and a second glass of ale.

'There's one or two jobs I'd like to do in the garden.' Walter, standing by the back door, turned his statement into a question for Eliza.

'Go on with you, then,' she said. 'Put your hat on to keep the sun off your head. I want to catch up with Thomas.'

Thomas got to his feet, to help with the washing-up, but Eliza waved him away. 'Sit down, I can do this,' she said. 'I dare say you could do with a rest after a week in the brewery,'

Thomas flopped back into the nearest chair, glad to do as she asked but also mindful that, with Walter in the garden, now was the time to have a conversation about his dilemma.

After some general talk about the brewery, which he wasn't sure Eliza was really listening to, he broached the subject that had brought him to see his mother.

'Ma, I need your advice.'

Thomas had never asked his mother for advice before, and she seemed surprised. She didn't speak, but wiped the last dish, stacked it on the dresser to put away, and shook out the linen tea towel.

'It's about ... well, you see, I think it's time ...' Now that the moment had come, Thomas couldn't think how to begin.

Eliza sat at the table and waited. Thomas glanced out of the window. Walter was busy digging in the vegetable patch. He must seize the moment and say his piece.

'Ma, I think the time has come to marry. But I don't know who to choose.'

CHAPTER THIRTY-FOUR

As the cart rattled back towards Hawksdown, the sun sinking low on the horizon as afternoon gave way to evening, Walter and Thomas were much quieter than they had been on the journey out. Walter was tired from exerting himself in the sunshine after his dinner, and had received a scolding from Eliza, who instructed him to have a lie-down before he took Thomas home.

Thomas was glad that Walter had not been party to any of the discussion between him and his mother. Would she talk it over with him once Walter was home again with the cart? Not immediately, Thomas decided, but he felt sure she would. He could tell she and Walter were very close.

Eliza hadn't seemed surprised that Thomas was thinking of marriage, or that he had a choice.

'A good-looking young man like you,' she said, 'with prospects. I've said before there must be a few young ladies in Hawksdown and Castle Bay with their eye on you.'

It was Thomas's turn to be surprised. If there were, he certainly hadn't noticed. But, then, he spent all his hours at the brewery and rarely went anywhere in his free time. It was an intriguing thought, but he had enough of a dilemma to contend with as it was.

'I've met someone – or, rather, met her again after many years. Catherine Morgan was at the Charity School at the same time as me. She works as a pastry cook for the Coopers, the family that own the brewery.'

He waited to see whether his mother was impressed but she, in turn, was waiting for him to go on.

'I went with her to the May fair on the mill field. She's unusual and interesting and I think she likes me.' Thomas was seized with doubt as he said this. Did Catherine like him? Or did she think him a fool?

'But I didn't realise Nell liked me, too. I spoke to her about how I could ask someone to go to the fair with me, and I didn't realise until later that she thought I was trying to ask her.' Thomas blushed in mortification at the hurt he had inflicted. 'She saw me at the fair with Catherine. I think she was upset. Then I got to thinking about how kind Nell is, and how easy to get on with, because I've known her for so long. But she's part of the family and I don't know if I could think of her in any other way.'

Thomas was in an agony of embarrassment by the time he finished. He glanced outside again, and was relieved to see Walter still in the vegetable patch, although he had stopped and taken off his hat to wipe sweat from his brow. He glanced at his mother to gauge her expression.

'Nell's a lovely girl,' his mother said. 'I've thought for a while she was sweet on you. She'd make a good wife and mother. She's capable and loyal, and if she's anything like her grandfather, faithful and constant too.'

Eliza was smiling as she spoke. Thomas began to wish he had put the case for Catherine more fervently.

'On the other hand, it sounds as though you are captivated by Catherine. I'm sorry not to have met her, for I can't form a judgement. In the end, only you can decide, Thomas. You must follow your heart, but don't forget that love alone is not enough. You have many years ahead of you and a lot of life to live. Someone who will be a companion and a support is just as important.'

'I fear it is odd that Nell is Walter's granddaughter. With you and Walter together . . .' Thomas tailed off.

347

His mother shrugged. 'That's neither here nor there. Only you can make this decision. I think, though, you already have.'

Thomas wasn't sure he had, but Walter came in at that moment, in search of a cooling drink, and Eliza persuaded him to stay indoors. There had been no further opportunity to talk privately so, as they drew closer to Hawksdown, Thomas could only review Eliza's words and make of them what he could.

She believed he had chosen Catherine, he decided. Was it just the belief he had upset Nell and his anxiety over addressing this with her that had made him think she had a part to play in his story? Once he began to think of it like this, he felt a sense of relief. He must deal with that problem, then carry on as before, as if he had never known that Nell had any interest in him. It wasn't his fault if she had grown to like him. He had been unaware of it and never encouraged it.

By the time Walter dropped him at the brewery, Thomas's spirits had lifted. He glanced over at Clayton House, hoping to see Catherine at an upstairs attic window, then shook Walter's hand heartily, wished him luck with his vegetable patch and promised to visit again before too long.

Thomas sat in his chair as the evening drew on and contemplated his revelation. Catherine was mysterious and challenging – he never knew quite where he was with her, and he felt sure he would never be bored. She was tall and striking in appearance – the men at the brewery had commented on it – whereas Nell was slight and petite, with the palest of skin and more than a hint of auburn in her hair. They could hardly have been more different. Thomas told himself that he and Catherine would make a good couple – if she would have him, of course. He allowed himself to consider Isabel and was pleased to find, at last, that his heart was free. She meant nothing to him.

Now that he had reached a decision, he was impatient. He longed to see Catherine again, to apologise for being out of sorts at the fair and to beg for another chance to spend time with her. What if she thought him hopeless for being so unsettled by the ride on the carousel? Thomas's hope of a peaceful night, now that he had reached a decision, was dashed by this new worry. He tossed and turned through the night and yawned his way through work the following day, earning a reproof from Jonas.

'It seems to me you've been enjoying yourself too much with that young woman I've been hearing about,' he said.

'Not at all,' Thomas protested. He was too weary to explain, longing for it to be time to go home so he could get a good night's sleep.

When he walked through his door that night, no other thought was in his head. He was startled, then, by a voice from his kitchen.

'Hello,' Nell said. 'I've brought you a rabbit pie. My father was lucky with his snares again.'

She beamed at him and Thomas blushed to the roots of his hair. She couldn't know of the discussion he had had with his mother the day before, but he felt guilty, as though news of it must already have reached her ears.

'Thank you,' he said, then couldn't think of anything else to say.

'I saw you at the fair the other week,' Nell said, her back to him as she picked up her basket. 'Did you enjoy it?'

She turned to him. Thomas tried to read her expression. Was she asking him about Catherine? This was the moment to apologise if he had misled her. 'I did, thank you. Although not the carousel.' He made a face.

Nell gave a faint smile. 'I saw you there. You seemed most unwell.'

She edged past Thomas, who was still struggling to find the words he surely needed to say.

'Goodbye,' she said at the door, and then she was gone.

Thomas hung his head and sighed. Perhaps what he had wanted to say was best left unsaid. Nell seemed to have understood the situation. He sniffed the aroma of the freshly baked pie and realised how hungry he was. Taking a plate from the dresser, he cut himself a large slice and settled down to eat. He was filled with relief at how well his encounter with Nell had gone. He needn't have worried at all.

CHAPTER THIRTY-FIVE

On a hot day in July, Thomas stood at the altar of St Mary's Church in Hawksdown. He was grateful for the cool interior, but even so he tugged at the high collar of his shirt, feeling half strangled by his cravat.

He was still bemused as to how he had arrived at this day. Everything had happened very swiftly. He'd sent a note to Catherine, saying he very much wanted to see her but was at a loss as to what to suggest. Would she have some free time to walk out on a Saturday afternoon? When a knock came at the door one evening a few days later, he was startled, then anxious in case, for some reason, it was Nell. He opened the door to find a figure standing there, carrying a basket. It took him a few moments to realise it was Catherine, not Nell.

'Are you going to invite me in?' she asked impatiently. 'I assume you don't want your neighbours to see a young woman on your doorstep at this hour.'

It was about eight o'clock and not yet dark; Thomas peered anxiously over Catherine's shoulder to see whether anyone had observed her, then stood back so she could enter. He couldn't imagine what she was doing there.

'I brought this so it would look as though I was delivering something to you,' Catherine said, raising the basket. She laughed. 'Although I'm afraid it's empty.'

She gazed around the room. 'You've done well for yourself, Thomas.'

Without being asked, she went through to the back room, then peered into the kitchen. Thomas was glad he had cleared up after eating his dinner.

'Very nice indeed,' she said. Then she indicated the staircase. 'You have two bedrooms upstairs?'

Surely she wasn't going to ask to see them, Thomas thought in alarm. To his relief, she seated herself in the chair by the grate, leaving him standing.

'Too big for just one person, wouldn't you say?' She gave him a very direct look, which made him blush at once. Was this a hint to him? That she had come to visit under a pretext, invited herself in and was commenting about his accommodation made Thomas feel it very likely, but he was nervous. What if he made a fool of himself?

'Oh, for heaven's sake!' Catherine was impatient. 'Are you going to ask me?'

Thomas, hesitant, asked, 'Will you walk out with me one Saturday?'

'Thomas, we have known each other since childhood. We were good friends, were we not? We are well enough matched, don't you think? Shall we dispense with the walking out?' She gave him another direct look.

Thomas tried to speak, but couldn't form the words.

'We could marry in a few weeks' time, once the banns are read. I will speak to the minister at St Mary's on Sunday if you are in agreement.'

Thomas had a sudden memory of Catherine at school, where he had followed her around adoringly. Two years older than him, she had seemed very self-assured. Nothing had changed, he saw, and he started to laugh.

Catherine was taken aback. 'You don't wish it?'

Thomas hastened to reassure her. 'I do. I'm just surprised. And pleased,' he added hurriedly, seeing her brows draw together in a frown. 'I couldn't be sure you liked me.'

Catherine shook her head impatiently. 'Thomas Marsh, what are we to do with you?'

Then she took up her basket and went to the door. 'So, since you are happy with the plan, I will see you in church on Sunday.'

That night Thomas's dreams were haunted by Isabel, who was waiting in the yard of Marston Grange for him. But when she spoke, her voice was Catherine's.

'We are to marry, you and I, and about time too.' Even though her words were the ones he had once longed to hear, he was so disturbed to hear Isabel speak with Catherine's voice that he was filled with horror. 'Thank goodness one of us knows how to make a decision.'

He struggled to leave the yard to return to the mill, finding his legs turned to lead, and he stumbled into the wheel beside the donkey instead. Unbalanced by the motion, he fell onto all fours beside the surprised beast and had to scrabble along, as the donkey continued to pace, whickering in unease.

Thomas woke, sweating, in a tangle of bedclothes. He lay still, heart thumping, and thought things over. What had precipitated such a nightmare? Then he rose from his bed and found paper, ink and a quill. In the early light of dawn, he scratched a few lines on the paper, addressed it to Catherine, then climbed shivering back beneath the covers to wait out the night.

Nell, at his side, gave him a look and he snapped back to the present at once. They had reached an important part of the service and Thomas wouldn't forgive himself if he stumbled over his words. He gave her a sideways glance to reassure himself that she was really there, standing with him. She was wearing what he supposed must be her Sunday best, for he had never seen it before: a dress in the palest shade of blue, and she held a posy of white flowers. She seemed calm and serene, but Thomas saw her cheeks were slightly flushed and the flowers trembled a little. He was overwhelmed – by the gravity of the moment, by Nell's simple beauty, and by gratitude for his good fortune.

His terrible nightmare after what had amounted to Catherine's proposal had given him a flash of clarity and forced him to consider that he might be about to make a terrible mistake. Was she really the right woman for him? She was undoubtedly attractive but how would Thomas's life be in the future with such a strong character at his side? He remembered his mother's words, how she had spoken glowingly of Nell's qualities, how 'love alone was not enough'. He'd been impatient, wanting her to endorse Catherine, whom she'd never met, as the perfect bride. Pondering the import of his dream, he'd had the sense that it was trying to tell him something: that Catherine was too much like Isabel, and their life together wouldn't be happy. Although it took all his courage, he'd forced himself to write to Catherine there and then, and tell her he couldn't go through with the marriage after all. He'd delivered the letter the next day to Clayton Hall on his way to the brewery.

Thomas must have answered the minister automatically, for he had no recollection of his words as Nell took his arm and they walked back down the aisle together, smiling at everyone they passed. He found the congratulations overwhelming and dipped his head, feeling shy, but Nell positively glowed. His mother was weeping, he saw, while Walter beamed fit to split his face in two. As they gathered in a crowd at the doorway of the church, his mother whispered in his ear, 'I'm glad of your choice. I feel sure it was the right one.'

Then he was drawn away by Jonas, intent on wishing him the best, before they were carried along in a small crowd to the inn, where Mr and Mrs Cooper were waiting to say a few words.

'Thomas Marsh is one of our most valued employees, a most sensible, trustworthy and conscientious man,' Mr Cooper said, in his carrying voice. 'We hope he will be very happy with his lovely bride – Thomas tells me she is a most excellent cook, and what more could any man wish for?'

There was general laughter. Then Mr Cooper declared the celebration under way by raising a glass of ale to the happy couple. The next few hours flew by, with much laughter and ribbing, a great quantity of ale drunk, and general enjoyment of the roast pig provided by the brewery owner. By the time Thomas stumbled home with his new bride, his head was in a whirl, not only from the quantity of ale he had drunk, but from the amount of conversations started, and never finished.

He did remember Mr Cooper taking him aside and saying how sorry they were to have lost Catherine from their employment. Thomas flushed scarlet as he remembered Catherine's understandable reaction to his letter, telling her he had made a mistake and could no longer marry her. She had left the Coopers' employment that very day, but not before seeking out Thomas at his work and telling him in no uncertain terms, and in front of his work mates, exactly what she thought of him. It had taken him a few days to summon up the courage to speak to Nell, fearful of her reaction. She had said simply, 'Yes,' through tears and tremulous smiles, and he'd felt an easiness all at once. He had done the right thing.

Thomas's wedding night ended as so many similar nights throughout the land ended: he was fast asleep and snoring, fully clothed, before his bride climbed into bed. He was full of remorse the next morning, and barely able to move his sore head. Nell shook her head in mock anger, then shushed him and snuggled into his embrace. Thomas felt himself a very lucky man. Their marriage would prosper, he felt sure. A new chapter was about to open in both their lives. He had grown up, at last.

EPILOGUE
1837

The carriage moved briskly through the landscape. Time had changed it – had the houses along Beach Street always been so shabby? And the castle – the trees and bushes around the edge of the moat were all overgrown. Isabel supposed that as the soldiers garrisoned in the area had long departed it had fallen into disuse. As the carriage clattered out of town and pulled up the hill to Hawksdown, she could see that the brewery there had grown in size. Perhaps the need for ale was even greater in hard times, she thought wryly.

She experienced a pang of longing to be back at Broomfield House with her three boys. She was happy there and so were they, running wild in the fields and woods. At least, they had been, but now even her baby had been sent away to school. When they returned in the summer, they were a little stiff and formal with her and she despaired of what had been lost. But by the time the holidays were drawing to an end they had returned to their once wild ways and she rejoiced.

She knew their neighbours thought her eccentric and pitied her husband, muttering among themselves that it was hardly surprising he was away so much on business. This was no longer for King George IV, and not even for the King, since William IV had dispensed with many of his predecessor's advisers. Nonetheless, Daniel and his father, both with much experience in negotiations, had found new roles for themselves. And Isabel felt confident they would do so again, if changing circumstances demanded it.

Isabel wondered, but not too hard, whether Daniel had something other than this business to keep him in London. Since he seemed happy to be with her and his boys, and reluctant to leave once he was at home, she concluded that she wasn't in the same position as Mrs Tremaine or her aunt Sophia and hoped she would never discover anything to make her doubt that.

She would have liked a daughter to complete her family, but reasoned that since it was not to be, it was for the best. A girl had to face too many restrictions in her life, while a boy might live as he pleased – provided he had the means to do so, of course. And they did have some level of wealth. Sir Charles Coates might be an infrequent visitor to their home, but there seemed to be no shortage of money to keep the family, if not to save Broomfield House, which had fallen even further into disrepair.

As the carriage drew closer to Marston, Isabel thought back to her life there, without any great affection. She had only visited once since she left and she had found the journey then, as now, a trying one. She had once hoped that Broomfield House would be a destination for visitors, but the journey from London proved too lengthy for any to make more than once, and the house too draughty at any time other than summer, when there were other demands on people of fashion and consequence.

Her mother, grown stout and no longer recognisable as the subject of the elegant portrait hanging in Marston Grange, had visited Isabel in the first year of her marriage. She paid scant attention to her newborn grandson and exclaimed a great deal over the poor condition of the property, and the lack of servants, without offering any insight into how that might be addressed. Isabel had found herself unable to reconcile herself with her childhood abandonment by her mother. She had been glad to wave off the departing carriage, having found the duke quite insufferable, too.

A month after their wedding, her father had made the journey up north to visit the newly-weds. She had seen him only once since then, in twelve years, but now she had had word that he was ailing. At one time she had considered sending for him to live out his days in the Castle, as she referred to Broomfield House, but dismissed the notion. She told herself he had duties binding him to Marston Grange, and thought of it no more. Now the carriage drew closer, rattling past the mill. Isabel paid it no heed. Neither did her thoughts drift to the miller's boy, whose appearances in the yard at Marston Grange she had once eagerly awaited, although not for the reasons he had hoped.

As they turned through the gates of Marston Grange and the now stooped figure of Cook emerged to greet her, Isabel rallied herself. Cook had been a devoted servant at the Grange since Isabel was a child, and she owed her a debt of gratitude, even though she had barely thought of her since her marriage. She embraced her, the one person who had consistently shown her kindness throughout her childhood, and was shocked by her frailty. Cook had borne the burden of looking after her father over the last few weeks and Isabel felt guilty for her neglect. Nevertheless, she already knew that as soon as she had established how her father was faring, she would start to calculate how soon she could return home to the Castle. She supposed she had become quite the recluse, and she wouldn't have it any other way.

Thomas, meanwhile, also had three children, two girls and a boy, now thankfully all settled in a larger house on the brewery land. As the brewery continued to expand, he had risen to general manager. He was surely the most prosperous member of the Marsh family, for none of them had previously done so well. Thomas continued to work long hours at the brewery and was grateful for the delicious dinners that their own cook now provided each evening, under the close supervision of Nell. On a Sunday, they sometimes entertained friends and family – Mr and Mrs Hopkins and their now-grown children were visitors. Ruth, the eldest, was married to the mill boy who had finally replaced Thomas. They were well suited and most content, Thomas observed, remembering the miller's past cajoling to consider her as his future wife. The miller was his usual jovial self, but Thomas noticed that his movements were slower and he usually fell into a doze as soon as they had eaten. Mrs Hopkins seemed little changed – she delighted in Thomas and Nell's children and always arrived bearing gifts of food: chutneys and preserves or one of her famous pies.

Eliza had lived very happily with Walter in their country cottage, until a particularly cold winter had seen her felled by a chesty cough she proved unable to shake off. Thomas had been deeply saddened by her loss, and struck with guilt that he had seen so little of her since his marriage. Walter had brought her over when each of the children was born but after that they had declined most invitations to join Thomas's family on a Sunday. Their own cottage was too small to entertain in return and Thomas thought that perhaps the children were too boisterous, making it tiring for them. Nell reassured him that they were too caught up in each other's company, and Walter in his garden, to feel the need to visit. They were content as they were, in her opinion.

Thomas had barely seen Catherine since his marriage to Nell, and he was glad. He feared he had mishandled the whole episode and regretted it, but comforted himself with the knowledge that she had married the new boatbuilder's son not long after his own marriage. Since there would always be a need for boats in Castle Bay, he felt sure that they would be prosperous enough and therefore undoubtedly happy. The last he had heard, a few years ago now, the marriage had produced no children and Thomas wondered whether she minded. Would she have been a good mother? He supposed she would, although a part of him was unsure.

Thomas always looked forward to seeing his children when he got home from work. One of them would be watching out for him and they would cluster around the door as he opened it, vying to share with him a bit of news from their day.

'The cat has had kittens – can we keep them?'

'I have finished my sampler – can I show it to you?'

'I can count now,' followed by a haphazard route to arrive at ten from one.

Thomas was proud that they shared confidences with him as he tucked them up in bed in turn, having told them stories of his day at work, which he heavily embellished with non-factual occurrences. They came to him, too, for comfort when they feared themselves in trouble with their mother.

There was precious little time to spend alone with Nell once the eldest was asleep. Thomas yawned as she stitched placidly by the window to catch the last of the evening light, before they made their way up to bed hand in hand.

After many years, he had believed himself free of all thoughts of Isabel and so it proved, until that very day, crossing the road from his house to walk to the brewery, he had to stand aside to wait for a carriage to pass. He glanced idly at the occupant and his heart leaped in his chest, then began to beat furiously. He was sure it was Isabel, lost in thought and looking to neither right nor left. She showed no sign of having seen him. What was she doing in the area? He gazed after the departing carriage, his mind in turmoil. He was unsettled for the rest of the day, dreaming up schemes to visit the miller and discover whether Isabel had truly returned. Then, back in his house that evening, surrounded by his family, calmness and reason returned. What need did he have of the uncertain agitation in his breast that seeing Isabel had reawakened? He had moved on, and so had his life.

At the age of thirty, Thomas had every reason to look forward to the future. Why, only that week he had heard talk of the railway coming to Castle Bay, which was forecast to bring untold prosperity to the town. He found it hard to imagine, but, as with all things, he would wait and see. Letting life take its course had proved a good strategy in his life. Although he had never had any reason to regret one very important decision he had made – the choice of his wife.

ACKNOWLEDGEMENTS

As ever, thanks are due to my agent, Kiran Kataria, for her clear-sighted vision, calming words and unwavering support. I'm always uplifted by the enthusiastic appreciation of my writing by Eleanor Russell, my editor at Piatkus, ably backed up by her team. And without the sharp eyes of Hazel Orme, my copy-editor, my grammatical stumbles would be exposed for all to see.

Thank you to the brilliant volunteers at Drapers Windmill in Margate, who showed me around the mill from top to bottom and took the time to answer my many questions. I couldn't have envisaged the passages about Thomas at the mill in Marston without their help.

The book, started during lockdown, was finished during a long period of uncertain health and I'm indebted to my family for their support and assistance during this difficult time, as well as friends and neighbours who stepped in to make soup, shop for me, drive me to appointments, send me treats and generally keep up my spirits. So, in no particular order, here's to my family and their partners as well as Helen, Ginny and Joe, Elizabeth, Brenda, Sandy and Dennis, Jo and Adam, Flora and James, Jaine, Lorraine, Vicky, Marlene, Niamh, Yvonne and Merv (the shed . . .) as well as Liz, Claire, Pam, Kate, Mitch, Sally, Cheryl and anyone else I've missed. I've been so moved by all the love – and the flowers.